G000126543

THE EDITOR

SIMON HALL

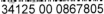

Print ISBN 978-1-912986-62-0

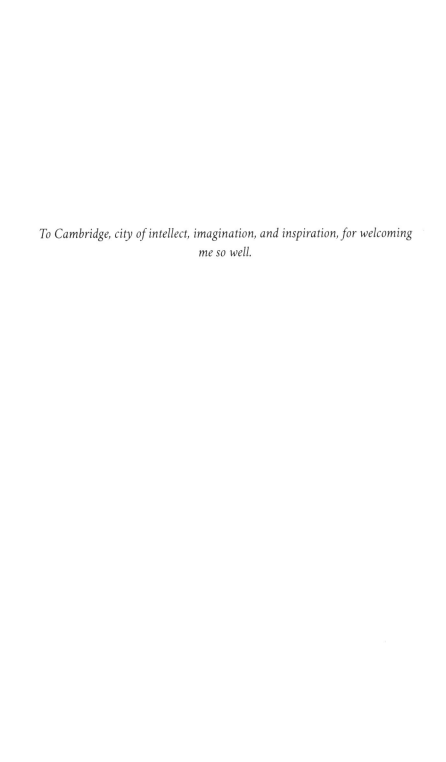

To Cambridge, city of intellect, imagination, and inspiration, for welcoming me so well.

Have you lost hope in life?
Wondering what's the use of going on?
Struggling to see the point in living?
Would you like to restore your sense of hope?*
The Falcon Labs, Chesterton Road, ten o'clock, Monday morning.
Very limited places.
*This is in no way a religious, cult or political movement, a con or moneymaking scheme, it involves nothing criminal,
there's no obligation for anything, and nothing being sold.**
**Apart from hope.

He hadn't been nervous for a long time because he hadn't cared for a long time, because a day hadn't really mattered for a long time.

Until this day. The day. Today.

Winter had finally taken the hint and released her icicle grip. The seasons were shifting at last, however reluctantly it felt, and the golden light was coloured with hope.

Lifeblood and heartbeat of this historic English city, the river was waking from its long hibernation. The waters flowed faster, clearer with new energy as spring reached out a warming embrace. The sluggishness of the dark months was fading and smiles were returning to the world.

So, would anyone come?

His walk, this watcher, already barely an amble, slowed further as a couple of joggers panted their way past, a dog trotting obediently alongside. The countdown was running ever louder; *tick, tock, tick, tock* in his mind. The time had reached twenty to ten.

In the whispering refuge of a canopy of shade, his fingers found the comfort of the waving leaves, and admired the sculpture of the willowy shapes, their smoothness. Away from the cares of now, he let himself slip, focused instead on the dew scent of the morning and contented muttering of the ducks. The shy rising of the brave new sun, all the beauty and joy of this tiny corner of the world.

Five to ten, that was when he'd leave the river. Climb the steps, cross the old stone bridge, turn the corner, and see.

The dog, an aged collie, was back. Bearded and grinning, the universal friend, sniffing through the trees, then at his legs.

'Jake!' one of the joggers called from beyond the willowy divide. 'Heel! Come back here.'

But the dog stayed and enjoyed a good and shameless scratch, as dogs did. Then settled on the dry earth, contented and impervious to mere human interruptions.

'I said heel! Where are you? Jake!' A woman's flustered face appeared between the flowing leaves. 'What're you doing, making me run even further? Have you found another bloody... oh!'

'Good morning.'

'Oh, um, morning.'

'Welcome to the inaugural meeting of the Hiding from Monday Club.'

'I'm sorry?'

'He's a lovely dog.'

'Sometimes, maybe. Can I have him, do you think?'

But Jake, looking back and forth between the strange humans, one flushed and fidgeting, the other so calm and assured, was going nowhere.

'Maybe it's my aftershave. I wondered why it was going cheap.' He rubbed at the dog's ears and was rewarded with a contented sigh. 'Or perhaps he just needs a rest.'

'I know how he feels.' The woman was fumbling for a lead when the leaves parted again and another face appeared, younger and not quite so reddened.

'Susan, what're you...? Oh. Sorry. Am I interrupting?'

The watcher smiled. 'We were just getting to know each other.'

'So I see.' She matched his smile and raised it. 'You are a one, Sooz. Shall I leave you to it?'

Susan didn't argue, just continued to stare at this man. 'Come on, Jake, you've got chaperoning to do, you lucky fella,' the fascination of a presence said, giving him a playful push. The weather-beaten old collie whined but skipped off, the two women following amidst mumbled goodbyes.

He watched them go because he knew what was coming, and waved when Susan glanced back. Then he retreated into the leaves once more and breathed in the dappled light, flickering with the playful breeze. The movement tightened the thread of a scar which bisected his neck, a legacy of the old life.

He'd woken early from what was barely a sleep, and wondered how to pass the hours until ten. He couldn't go to the labs. He'd just spend the whole time staring out of the window.

Waiting, hoping, watching. Hoping, waiting, wondering.

Because now, after the advert, he wasn't just a watcher anymore.

The hollow bang of wood on wood called him back to the world. A bulky figure, dressed in a hoodie, emerged from a hatch on a faded barge tied up by the bank. It stood, staring at the water flowing past, as if it were a siren, tempting him with its call.

The watcher knew that look. Had seen it on his own face in the reflections of a river not so far away from this peaceful place, and not so long ago.

More movement. A hand, a fumble, a curse, a coin emerged from a pocket and spun a silver trail through the warming air. Whatever the result was, heads or tails, it was far from clear whether it was welcome.

The figure huffed and shrugged, then turned and strode along the path towards the steps. The steps that led to the road, the bridge, and the labs.

'You okay?' the watcher asked.

'Sorry, mate, in a rush.' There was muscle in the bulk, a beard under the hood, and dark but shrewd eyes. The man checked his watch; expensive, a contrast to his clothes, and that stale unwashed odour. 'Gotta be somewhere.'

'Anywhere good?'

'Dunno.' A snort. 'Maybe.'

'What would "good" be?'

The figure hesitated, unable to shrug off the unusual, very un-English, persistence. Or perhaps his inability to ignore this curious, intriguing presence. 'I suppose… understanding. Even sharing, maybe.'

'Hope?'

Another pause, before, 'Right. You saw it too, eh?'

So maybe one person, at least, would be there. And he only needed three. Or perhaps just two would be enough.

But then another doubt came calling, as they did, unexpected and unwelcome, as they were. What if more than three answered the call? What if he had to turn someone down? Maybe more than one? Maybe two or three? Or seven or eight?

He'd tried to pitch the advert about right. To tempt a handful of the hopeful, no more. To say what he needed to say, and add a little fun, a forgotten taste of pleasure in life, but without sounding crazy.

Or not too crazy, anyway.

Although, maybe that stuff about crime and cults was over the top. Even here, this city where eccentricity came as standard. Maybe it'd just put anyone off.

He was about to start climbing the steps when a young woman pushed past, half at a jog, determinedly lost in her headphones, didn't even mutter an apology. She skipped up the last steps and broke into a run, following a map on her phone.

The words, 'Can't fucking believe I'm fucking doing this shit,' were just audible over the traffic.

She was very young, but as he knew well – what difference did that ever make?

So, maybe two then.

Just an ordinary man gazing down at the river, enjoying the view, as so many thousands had over the centuries of this thoughtful city. The drivers, the cyclists, the pedestrians passing by, all failed to notice how they were drawn to notice.

And how this man stayed a little longer than most. How he found pleasure, fascination even, in the colourful softness of a young lichen.

He was somewhere else, the watcher, a place only footsteps away. His niche for this moment of life, anyway. The four begrudging desks in the half-shadowed alcove at the far end of the former storeroom.

And the faces that would join him there.

Or the spaces, the blanks, the nothings and no-ones which would remain with him.

The street was busy for a Monday. Maybe emergency shoppers who'd run out of milk. Perhaps workers late for the office after the excesses of the weekend. Maybe a store was doing some desperate promotion, flailing for survival, one of the signature signs of these changing times.

There'd been a queue around the block last week when that toyshop closed, another victim of the stampede for the promised land of online. They'd stood at the windows of the lab, watching the bonanza of the going-out-in-glory sale. Decades of proud history at an end, talking about this never-resting world.

'When're you going to launch?' one of the younger men, a programmer with a barcode of a tattoo, had asked.

'Next week,' he'd replied without thinking, the words a surprise.

But they stayed with him, those words. Kept muttering in his mind. Refused to quieten until he gave in, phoned the newspaper and finally bought the advert.

And now the time was two minutes to ten.

Just one more pause, one brief hesitation. One glance up at the perfect sky, one very long breath, one more dance in the arms of life, and then the moment. Forcing his legs to stride around the corner, confident and strong.

Albeit, as he would admit in the weeks ahead, with eyes firmly closed.

Until they were forced open. By the noise, the hubbub, loud even above the relentless traffic of this intersection corner of Cambridge.

The unmistakeable sound of a mass of people. A dense block of humanity surrounding the glass doors of the labs. Politely jostling to shift a way forward in that very English manner, inching and edging, pressing in and pushing on.

Layer after ramshackle layer, circle upon random circle. A great wedge of a crowd filling the pavement and spilling out into the road, but always filtering towards the waiting doors.

3

Life has her smiles and frowns, sometimes plays, sometimes snatches her ball away. And occasionally she stages a mugging. Like now, right now, albeit with an unlikely assailant.

Swift was lurking inside the doors as he often did when waiting to ambush a wayward tenant. But today he was radiating even more sniffy disapproval than usual.

'I take it they're here for you.'

'Isn't it wonderful?'

'No. It is not. Far from it. I saw the advert. What was that nonsense about cults?'

'A little joke.'

Swift blinked hard at the unaccustomed concept. 'Anyway, you might have said.'

'I didn't know if anyone would turn up. And I didn't want to bother you for nothing. I know how busy you are. How important your work is.'

The appeal to the vanity, usually a reliable ally in any battle, almost helped scale the walls of Swift's displeasure. 'Anyway, what're you going to do with them? I can't have them disrupting business.'

The manager of the labs, Aaron Swift, was young but old, and looked to have been designed by an aircraft engineer. Everything about him was angular.

Relatively new to the bank, the labs' landlords, propelled at altitude by an accelerated career scheme, Swift glowed with a zeal for commerce that had been seared into him at business school. He had never been a fan of the latest occupant of the labs, wasn't alone in that, and wasn't shy of making his feelings clear.

The newcomer of a business was hardly mainstream, dead cert of a home run, easy to understand, and slam dunk moneymaking. It had got through the labs' board on a six-to-five vote, with Swift determinedly bearing the standard of opposition.

'We're a tech operation,' he had complained. 'Tangible, profitable tech.'

'And we're also a broad church,' one of the older, port and cigars executives had said, arm around shoulder in that bankers' club way. 'It's good to have some creatives around. They add… um, something.'

Swift had taken that minor reproach as a black mark on the otherwise impeccable ledger of his career, and never forgotten it. For the whole of the last week, he'd flayed the word mercilessly.

In his vocabulary, creative was on the same thesaurus page as murder, atheism, voting Labour, the financial crash, cannibalism, speeding drivers in residential areas, auditors, failing to wear a tie, and making a loss.

Maybe it was his upbringing. It usually was.

'You're a creative,' he sniffed. 'So create a way to deal with them.' And then, because Swift knew it would irritate, added, 'Edward.'

'Ed is fine.'

'Ed the Editor, eh? At least it's some form of branding, I suppose. Ed the Ed of our creative… thing.'

He hadn't needed a name for quite a while, not when he was only a watcher, but Ed felt as good as any for his return to the world. He seemed to recall once having a friend called Ed. So, if he was going to be an editor, he would be Ed the editor. But if Swift found that as near to funny as he found anything, it may not have been such a wise choice.

Swift was still talking, apparently. 'So, when's the first edition of your… thing coming out?'

'The newswire.'

'Yes, that. The newswire thing. When's it coming out?'

'Soon.'

'How soon?'

'Quite soon.' And because Ed could poke a stick of his own, added, 'When the ethereal inspiration that is the flow of the muses blesses us with an alignment of the creative stars.'

Swift blinked again. 'Could you manage very soon? We do have quite a demand for places in the lab, you know. It is supposed to be an accelerator. Not a…' he hunted for the words, 'parking lot.'

'I'll do some accelerating as soon as I can get on with recruiting my team. How does that sound?'

The hovering manager almost got the hint. He twitched a cheek like a turbine blade towards the doors, and the mass of faces. 'So, what are you going to do with them?'

Them. Swift probably meant people. Fellow human beings.

Them. Those faces out there. Some pressed against the glass like children at the sweet shop. Wondering. Waiting. Maybe daring to hope.

Them.

And this face in here; sniffy, snotty and sneery. Peering and patronising. Aloft and aloof.

Some days, that grand resolution to hold on to pleasure in the small things took more effort than others. Ed focused on a spider's web, the morning light settling into the fragile canvas of its gossamer art.

'You remember the interview you had for the bank?' he said. 'When there was probably a board of, I'd guess twelve, to appoint you to such an important position?'

Swift looked pleased to offer a correction. 'Thirteen, actually.'

'How appropriate. Anyway, this is going to be the other way round. A board consisting of just me, and all of them in the hot seat. Or seats, in fact.'

Ushered gently and kindly, the crowd trooped up the stairs. They were watched by curious workers from the other nascent businesses as they gradually settled in the conference room. Quite a few had to stand around the walls, arms folded, others sat on the floor at the front. It was like an overcrowded assembly from school days.

'Thanks for coming, and welcome along,' Ed said, because he thought he should say something, but had little idea what.

It was interesting how many of the crowd were trying to not be there. Each was on their own. Not engaging, not even acknowledging those around. Quite a few were wearing hats or caps, and some had their hoods up. Plenty more were almost obscured by large sunglasses, despite the dim cool of the room.

They were about half and half, men and women, and a range of ages; from perhaps early twenties to well into the retirement zone. From all sorts of backgrounds too, which was also interesting. And there certainly were a lot of them.

Twice Ed had tried to count, but given up. He wondered if, when he fell, he would have felt so despairing had he known how many were down there waiting. Alongside him in the solitary confinement of the endless darkness. Wounded and hopeless, however invisibly.

They were quiet, remarkably so for such a large group. They were watchful and waiting. But there was fight in them, this crowd.

He could see it in the stances, the expressions. They may have feared to say it, might hardly have dared to think it, but they wanted to hope again. Because, despite everything, they were enduringly human.

And he had space for only three. Not to mention a duty, an obligation, a heartfelt promise in fact. Not to hamper the journey back to the light for all those touching others who had faced their own awful truth and made that seminal decision.

She was here, the young woman who had pushed past on the embankment. Headphones still on, hiding in her music, face pinched so hard it must have hurt. He was here too, the man in the hoodie who had looked into the waters of the river and been saved by the fifty-fifty, heads or tails toss of a coin.

And so many others. So very many others. With every eye upon him.

Staring in silence at the half-lit figure in the shadow-filled room. With faded walls, threadbare carpet, and a lingering scent of dust and mustiness.

'We only have three rules,' Ed told them. 'One is that what goes on in here stays in here. We don't talk about who we've met, or what we've done with anyone outside this room. Or the magic doesn't work. Deal?'

They nodded and muttered, because what choice did they have? They'd come this far, and it was far too far to turn back.

'Two is that we start getting to know each other. So introduce yourself to the people around you. Take a few minutes, there's no rush. I know it's difficult, but it helps not to have to face what we face alone, believe me.'

And because they were staring, just staring, uncertain and agonisingly unsure, Ed shook hands with the man from the boat. And told him it was good to see him again, that he was brave and right to be here, and hoped coming along would help. And around them others started to talk too, and then others, more and more, until the room was filled with voices.

But this wasn't normal, ordinary, standard conversation, like the background talk in countless cafés and bars. And it took Ed a couple of minutes to work out why.

It was the chatter of people who hadn't chattered for far too long.

'And three, number three,' he called eventually, wondering where all this was coming from. 'Rule three is that you swap contact details with at least two people you've met here today. Share your struggles. Help each other along.'

This time, wonder of wonders, the response was immediate. They did it, not questioning, never hesitating.

Which was good. Very good. Because it gave Ed a chance to wipe his glasses, which had somehow misted over.

. . .

It was extraordinary. Each and every one of them, this group of awkward strangers in this anonymous room. Talking, sharing.

Maybe feeling once more.

Almost each and every one, anyway. Apart from two. Hidden in the mass, but not quite part of the whole. Still standing apart. Those invisible walls continuing to divide them.

The two.

'Right, you're probably wanting to know what the advert was about, aren't you? Well… well…'

And so Ed, the Editor of the newswire to be, explained. About his own estrangement with hope, even if he glossed over the reasons why. About how he had started to recover with what he had discovered. How he had ultimately found hope again, and how they could too.

'The good news is, I'm not asking for anything from you, apart from giving it a try. This really isn't about joining a cult.' He paused, let the trickle of so very self-conscious laughter fade, then added, 'The bad news is that there are only places for three of you.'

That caused plenty of muttering, as Ed knew it would. 'So we've got to find a fair way of deciding who it will be. I'm going to write a question on the board, and you've got ten minutes and a hundred words to answer it.'

He'd expected some to walk out then. Maybe a few, perhaps even more. Because this was ridiculous, wasn't it? Insulting, even offensive. An impromptu exam in the wild pursuit of a maybe something.

But no-one got up. No-one stalked out. No-one even looked as though they were thinking about leaving.

Apart from the two. Who still weren't quite here, who remained a little detached from the crowd, who weren't believing the believing.

But even they weren't quite able to go.

Oh, hope, sweet hope, and her extraordinary power. Most potent of all life's heady wonders. However slim the chances of finding her again, no matter that the odds may feel stacked upon stacked against you, giving up was near impossible.

'Write your answer on a piece of paper, add your e-mail address, and I'll let you know by the end of today. Everyone will get a fair hearing and an answer, I promise you that. It's the least you deserve.'

And slowly, carefully, Ed wrote the question on the board.

What is the best thing about life?

He couldn't just let them go. Once, not so long ago, he'd thought his heart was gone. Turned to ash by the horrors he had seen, been a part of. But it had just been hiding, protecting itself, as hearts sometimes do.

It was in the way they'd walked into the conference room. So quietly and orderly, despite the alien ridiculousness of the moment he had created. It was in the way they'd found the courage to talk to the others around them. And it was in the way they'd gone about their writing; thinking intensely, scribbling, crossing out, amending words, and all so very carefully. Looks of furrowed concentration, because this mattered, how it mattered.

It mattered more perhaps than anything they had done for a long time, this randomly gathered group of strangers, united only in that irresistible hope of hope.

And when they had handed over the sheets of paper, carefully folded, e-mail addresses painstakingly added, it was in the vulnerability. As if they were handing over something of their souls.

Apart from the two.

No, of course he couldn't just let them go. Those two most of all. So Ed stood at the front of the room and wondered, once again, where the words were coming from.

'Only a few of you will join me after today. But for those who don't, remember this. Hope is the true immortal in life. It never leaves us and it never dies. Sometimes, hope's gentle voice might be drowned out by all the noise in our lives. But find a hidden corner, listen hard, and you will always hear the quiet song of hope.

'Believe me, I know. Because I'm one of you. I could be sitting amongst you now. I've walked the lonely path you walk. Like you, I've stood at the top of buildings, looked down and fantasised about the fall. I've lingered on bridges and wondered about the freedom of that dive into the river. I've sat in bars and gazed into the hypnotic colours of the rows of bottles. But through all of that, when I closed my eyes, if I took the time, if I listened and believed, I could still hear the gentle lullaby of hope.

'For those of you who don't come to join me after today, remember this. The song of hope guided you here, even if you didn't know it. That beautiful melody is within you and will carry you onwards, wherever you may go and whatever you might do. And now you have allies in that journey, allies who can become friends. Keep listening to that enchanting song, keep following its call, keep believing and keep hoping.'

Ed held their looks, all and everyone crowded into this small room. Each and every set of eyes, long and true, before pushing open the door. But it was quite a while before anyone got up to leave. And when they did, the first one, two, then three shook his hand. But following that it was a hug, and then another, and then hug after hug after hug.

Apart from the two.

He marched past, hoodie drawn tight, head down, beard bristling, without a word. Pushing and barging an angry escape.

She stopped, although only for a second. Just long enough to release an animal's glare and to hiss, 'You arsehole of a fucking disgusting charlatan.'

4

To release the breath it felt as if he had been holding inside for the last hour, following rule two of the *How to be English* handbook, Ed made himself a cup of tea. The mural of the great minds with its swirls of colour, watched over him. Ed wondered if Hawking, Eliot, Austen, Sanger, and Curie were looking a little less haughty than usual today.

He rattled some money in the tea fund tin, tipped a cup of water into the plants that stood by the sink, and smiled at the bud of a tiny flower emerging into the world. 'Welcome along, little one,' Ed whispered. 'You're just in time.'

'That was pretty cool,' a voice said from behind. It was Steve, the programmer with the barcode tattoo. 'Are you really gonna give all those people hope?'

'I hope so,' Ed replied, and the young man snickered before silently vanishing again, in that way he had.

Back at his desk, Ed spread out the sheets of paper and began to read. *What is the best thing about life?* as he'd improvised for the big ask.

It was quite a question. And there were quite some answers.

The dawns. Since it happened I hardly sleep, and I've seen every dawn for the past 563 days. Some creep up on you, just a slow shift in the colour of the sky. Others are set on fire by a mighty raging sun ambushing the earth. The kindness of the dawns of summer, the brittle dawns of winter. But every dawn, every day, each and every wonderful dawn, for the past 563 days.

The laughter of my sons – when I actually get to see them. The innocence, the wonder, the delight in the world. The purity of their eyes before this life pollutes them.

Walking. Always walking, never stopping. I walk because I know every mile I walk is another mile nearer to escaping my prison. I walk over hills and across fields, along roads and riverbanks, through trees and towns, cities and country-side. I walk, walk and walk some more, and every day I know the past falls a little further behind, and the future edges a little closer.

Making it to the end of the day, and still believing tomorrow will be better.

The eternal hope of redemption. The chance to make amends for the things you've done. And every day, trying to do something, anything, to achieve that.

Ed sighed and stared at that answer until the writing lost its form, blurred into ink patterns slowly swirling on a page.

Back in the kitchen, he ran himself a glass of water, then let the cascade spray over his hand, skin tingling with the coolness, droplets flashing tiny rainbows in the sunlight.

. . .

17

The sweet scent of the earth after rainfall. The melody of a waterfall. The icy thrill of waves lapping over your toes. A rainbow painting the heavens.

Love. The wonder of love. No, not really. I bet everyone says that. It's the kind of thing you're supposed to say, isn't it? But actually I'd say hope. Which is why me, and so many others, are here. I've never been able to quash this hope inside, no matter how much I try. And yes, okay, I admit – it's a hope for love. But who doesn't hope that?

The mask you pull on to disguise yourself. My wife doesn't know, my kids don't know, my friends don't know. No-one knows but me. And no-one will. Because I'll keep going, and one day I'll find hope again, the mask will burn in a fire of my mind, I'll dance on the flames, and all will be well.

I don't know, but it won't leave me alone.

The best thing about life is that it still hasn't let me go, despite me trying.

Every answer, every single one, had something new, something different. Something else to make his throat a little tighter and his vision a little more blurry. Perhaps leaving that other person behind, the watcher, wasn't so fearful after all.

But it was the answer which fate saved for last that left Ed staring into space, struggling to deal with the emotions tumbling inside; spinning Catherine wheels of feelings which he hadn't known for far too long.

The best thing about life is its power to transform in an instant. Like when you meet someone who changes your world. Someone to believe in again. Just like today. What you're doing is incredible, and I wish you the greatest success. I won't leave my e-mail address because you've already achieved what you wanted with me and someone else needs your help more, but I'll never forget you. Thank you.

It's a challenge to knock on the door in an open-plan office, but, in fairness to Swift, a pointed cough was nimble improvisation. Ed remembered his resolve and took at least a little pleasure in the angular manager's tie. It was decorated with hints of impressionist colour, the only concession to personality in the regimented greyness of business orthodoxy.

Maybe there was life in there somewhere. It did have a tendency to sprout in the most surprising places.

'Are you applying to join us too?' Ed asked, beckoning him to one of the three empty desks.

Swift looked puzzled before his humanity programme finished its run and concluded humour was being deployed. 'Ah, no. No, no. I just wanted to say…'

'Yes?'

The lord of all he surveyed, in this small kingdom at least, didn't sit down. Instead he hovered in an awkward fashion and shifted his weight from foot to foot. 'Well…'

The struggle with words was unusual. Swift normally had plenty to say, albeit, in truth, not much that was actually worth hearing.

'I just wanted to say that was, well… interesting.'

'Our visitors?'

'All of it. The whole thing. It was… yes, interesting.'

Ed was about to say thank you for the fulsome and moving compliment, when Swift went on. 'We've never had so many people come to the labs before. Not even when we held that flagship Negotiation, Sales and Persuasion seminar.'

Ed kept his face set and didn't reply. He thought it was for the best.

As for Swift, he was still bogged down in the battle of Speaky Mouth. He looked as though he was chewing the cud on a diet of thoughts.

'I ought to mention, I should tell you, well, I listened in. To what you said. In the conference room. I wasn't checking up on you,' he added a little too hastily. 'I was just… well, curious, frankly. I hope you don't mind.'

It was Ed's turn to struggle. Swift spending time on anything that didn't burnish the sacred bottom line was unprecedented.

'I sometimes think about hope too. Everyone does, I suppose. Life doesn't always turn out the way we expect, eh?' Swift fiddled hard with the thickness of his wedding band, then quickly went on, as if to hide the hint of vulnerability that was doubtless taboo in business school. 'Anyway, I took some photos. Of you talking to the crowd. I thought you might like to use them for a story. Or just a reminder of the start of your creative thing.' He hesitated, then added, 'Sorry, your newswire. The creative newswire thing.'

Swift scrolled through the pictures as if to help disguise his discomfort. They were surprisingly good. Apart from the one of Ed with his mouth wide open and eyes closed, but such was always the way with photos.

'Nice angles and composition,' Ed said. 'Thanks, I'd love them. If we need a photographer, we know where to come, eh?'

'Me?'

'Yes. You.'

'Me, good with, well, you know. That arty stuff. Really?'

'Yes.'

'Well. Well, well, well.'

A strange silence held this small L-shaped corner of the Falcon Labs as the two men looked at each other.

'Anyway,' Swift said at last, 'I'd better be getting back to work. But yes, your creative… sorry, newswire. It'll be… well, interesting to see how it develops.'

He should head for home, at least to the home of now, but there was something else that had to be dealt with first. Fair was a big word in life, but hope was bigger by far.

Particularly given what could result from getting this decision wrong.

The answers had been read and were in his rucksack. The rest of the day would be spent writing replies to all of the hopers who had come to the labs that morning. Ed thought he knew which three would join him, but he had to be sure.

Today, alone in the days he had been here, there was something different in the looks of the workers who watched him make for the stairs. For once, he sensed, they actually saw him. Looked at Ed as if he was a real person with a real plan; not just a dreamer, drifting airily on a whim.

The street was abuzz with the joy of sunshine and Ed paused, letting it fill him with the spirit of tomorrow, before setting off on his short journey. The blessing of the skies had done its benevolent work in drawing people to the river. They ambled in families, couples, and sets of friends; strolling, sitting and marvelling. Sweet summer was on the way, and the world was born anew.

This time there was no-one on the deck, no bulky figure staring into the water. But the barge was in just the same place as earlier, a trail of smoke drifting from its chimney, rising and paling, until becoming one with the vast sweep of the sky.

5

The omens weren't good, just as he had feared. Ed tried knocking, first on the hatch, then the windows, then the hatch again, with no response.

But he knew the man with the hoodie and shrewd eyes was in there. He'd seen the changing light within. Could sense from the sounds of the boat, the tiny shifts as it moved against the flow of the river.

Ed remembered the way the boatman had gazed into the water and flipped that coin. How he hadn't quite talked to the people around him at the labs, instead just nodded along. How he had walked out amongst a group, but still, somehow, alone; lonely in a crowd.

On the deck there were some sacks of logs, one mostly empty. Ed covered the chimney and stood, leaning against it, counting off the seconds. It wasn't long until the hatch flew open and a choking spluttering figure, still with its hood up, erupted from amidst a cloud of smoke.

'Abracadabra,' Ed said to himself.

'You bastard,' the man gasped, swinging a half-hearted and easily avoided fist, but fortunately unable to say or do much else.

'Steady. Didn't your mum teach you not to hit men with glasses?'

'What the hell do you think you're doing?'

'Saving you. Want to talk about it?'

But the boatman was struggling to make sense of anything, apart from expelling the smoke from his body in a salvo of wracking coughs.

'You're obviously not so keen to die then. Maybe it'd be worth remembering that. And don't march out on me again.'

'What the fuck? I should kick your arse.'

'I don't think you could kick a football, the state you're in. If we're going to be working together you don't have to hug me. But you might say thank you, at least.'

'What?' Another break for a coughing fit and dabbing at his weeping eyes. 'What the...?' More spluttering.

'Special delivery. I've brought you something precious. You can't see it, but that just makes you want it more. It's kind of magical that way. We talked about it earlier, remember?'

They sat on the deck to talk, Ed propped up against the side, his victim squatting on a log. It was useful, Ed reflected, that he still had the body which was trained into him in the old days. It was guaranteed to make any potential aggressor think twice, even one with the mass of this man.

'I'm not going until we have a chat,' Ed said, and, after a few minutes of ritual male staring each other out, the boatman accepted that.

'Five minutes then.'

'That'll be enough.'

'You're full of yourself, aren't you?'

'I've just learnt when to have hope.'

'And you're a cheeky sod.'

'On the subject of which, sit downwind from me, will you? You stink of smoke.'

His name was Mitchell. He was a scientist by education, he said. Didn't know what to do when he left university, but heard about a job as a Crime Scene Investigator.

'It looked interesting, so I applied. And it certainly was interesting. To start with anyway…'

His words tailed off and Mitchell's gaze merged into the sun blaze of the river. Body language was always such a giveaway, and he'd begun to hunch into himself as he told his tale.

'It got too much?' Ed prompted after a while.

'Kind of.'

There was a time for talk and a time for silence. Ed had learnt that long ago. Not to mention a time for watching a procession of swans glide an effortless course along the river.

'Yeah, kind of,' Mitchell repeated. 'But hey, why should I tell you about it, anyway? Why am I even talking to you?'

'Because I understand.'

The man looked about to argue, but then, with a sigh, pulled back his hood. Released from the shadows, Mitchell would have been a handsome man, but his looks were eclipsed by the past. That beard was, in fact, little more than overgrown stubble, and highlighted the gauntness of his face.

'Have we met before?' Ed asked. 'You look familiar, somehow.'

'Don't think so. I'm pretty sure I'd remember a cocksure arsehole like you.'

Mitchell nodded to himself and almost smiled. It was the first time an expression anywhere close to an appreciation of life had come near to forming. Which was a shame, Ed thought, because a smile would have suited him; chasing away the shadows and complementing the enduring brightness of those eyes.

'I guess I'd remember a miserable bastard like you too,' Ed said.

'You've got all the answers, haven't you?' Mitchell replied.

'A few. Maybe enough, for now at least. They took a bit of finding, mind.'

'Don't they always?'

This time, it was Ed's turn to nod.

Mitchell emitted another sigh, then got up and disappeared back into the depths of the barge. It was a homely old craft, rundown and weather beaten in a comfortable kind of way. And it smelt of damp wood, a legacy of the long winter months.

Ed tensed, half turned, wondered what Mitchell would bring back. But it turned out to be another essential of the male-bonding ritual, a couple of beers.

'I saw some horrible things,' Mitchell said. 'So many bodies. In such dreadful states. You wouldn't believe what people can do to each other. Where there's money, love, or pride involved.'

Ed nodded. 'Or religion. Or politics. Or power. With some crazy zealot of a lunatic determined to inflict their own particular vision of the latest fashion in genocide on the world.'

'Been there too, have you?'

'I didn't just get the T-shirt, I printed the thing.'

'Army?'

'Something like that. But you were talking about what you'd gone through...'

A hesitation, then, 'The last case was a kid. Just eleven years old. A girl. Sarah was her name. She was beaten to death in a cellar by a gang in a drugs feud. Some kind of kidnap and revenge thing against her uncle. And she was... well, you can guess what the scene was like. Eleven years old. El-ev-en. One day running around at school smiling, happy with her friends. The next...'

The brightness of the day dimmed as the scene darkened the air around them. Mitchell took a long swig of his beer. 'But do you know what did me? It wasn't what I felt. It was what I didn't feel. I was standing there, looking at this girl. This Sarah. You would hardly know she was once a person. But I didn't feel a thing. That's when I realised. It'd chipped away at me, bit by bit, what I'd seen. Day in day out, and I didn't feel a thing. Not even when faced with that. The worst of the worst. So I got out. Right that afternoon. I just left. I had to. And I ran.'

Mitchell rolled his neck and took another drink. 'Well, actually I chugged, I suppose. I came down to the river here, saw a barge for sale, bought it and set off. Just like that.'

.   .   .

They sat in silence, because what do you say after a story like that? Sunshine smiled all around, but here, on the corner of this old barge, there was only shadow. Ed was about to speak, when Mitchell went on, 'And I used to be… hell, I can't even remember what I used to be. Someone else, that's for sure. Happy, I suppose. You know that word? Happy? Enjoying life. Maybe even optimistic about the future. That person I was then, I'd like to meet him again. I'd so like to… I just want to…'

'Hope again?'

'You and your bloody hope. You're like a salesman.'

Ed smiled. 'When you're in love, you're in love. But wasn't it hope that got you along this morning? No matter how much you try to deny it?'

'You never stop dreaming, I suppose.'

'The boating around didn't work for you?'

Mitchell tapped an affectionate hand on the side of the barge. 'She tried to help me, my little ship here. Didn't complain as we chugged our way more or less anywhere. I've been to so many places now. But I can't remember any of them. Not one. And you know why? Because you can't run from yourself. It's always the same old reflection of me in the water. Every bloody day.'

'But you've never actually tried to…'

Mitchell snorted. 'I've never had the guts.'

'It's just that, is it?' Ed looked into the man's eyes and said nothing, because nothing needed to be said.

'How come you're so damn… I don't know, serene?' Mitchell went on. 'Calm? Composed? Or maybe just comfortable with yourself. That's why everyone was listening to you earlier, even when we were wondering what the hell we were doing. What sort of a nutter you were. Despite all that, we listened. Because you've got what we want.'

Ed pointed to the river. The swans were still going about their gracious procession, gliding through the silver film of the sunshine waters. Discarded leaves bobbed in their wake, and the air was tinted with the fresh scent of springtime.

'Breathe. I mean, really breathe. Right down deep into your lungs. Don't simply smell the air. Taste it. Feel it.'

'Are we doing therapy now?'

'You're already well into the course. So, breathe.'

Mitchell slowly shook his head, but did.

'Now close your eyes. And listen. To the breeze in the willows. The lapping of the river. The slow creaking of the barge.'

'That old motorbike as well?'

Ed smiled. 'Life never quite follows the script, does it? But give it a chance.' And when the gunning engine of the growling bike had conquered its corner and roared away, 'Try again.'

They sat in silence, for all the world two old friends sharing a memory.

'Now slip your hand into the water. Feel the river flowing through your fingers.'

This time, there was no argument. And, in perfect harmony, all the instruments of nature's magnificent orchestra played around them, lifting the emotions as only the music of life can.

'Finally, open your eyes again and look at the swans. That wonderful tapering of their beaks, not to mention the colour. The calm watchfulness in their eyes. The graphite patterns in the feathery layers of their wings. And here's the trick...'

'Yeah?'

'For all the contentment and ease, you know exactly what's going on beneath the surface.'

This time, Mitchell did laugh. It was unfamiliar and a little forced, more of a reluctant chuckle, but it would do for now.

So life went. A lost laugh can take a long time to recover.

'Are you going to reunite us then, hope and me?'

'If you're up for that. And if your answer was good enough.'

'How will you know which one's mine? I didn't put my name on it.'

'I'll know.'

Ed was getting up to leave when Mitchell asked, 'You've found hope again. That's obvious. So, what's in this for you?'

'Does there have to be something?'

'Isn't there always? Isn't that life?'

This time, it was Ed's turn to laugh. 'What's in this for me is a friend of hope. Maybe her best friend. One who walks hand in hand with her, and is just as mesmerising.'

6

The sun was dipping fast towards the horizon by the time he got home. Or, at least, the home of now.

Ed didn't head straight for number nine. He cycled a slow lap of the park first, making sure there was no indication that he was doing what he was doing. He whistled a tune, carefree as the breeze, stopped to check his tyres, picked free a stone, called out a couple of greetings, looked in at the shop and bought some milk.

But never a hint of searching for anything unusual; a new face, a different car, a twitch of movement in the trees.

The mobile home park was on the edge of Cambridge, and set into the nearest the area had to a valley. Which, in this notorious flatland, meant the slightest of amicable gradients. Still, it made the unaccustomed art of cycling easier.

The park was surrounded by young trees, the standard landscaping recourse of the uninspired developer. It gave out onto *a magnificent lake for all your nature and recreation needs*, according to the marketing. An overgrown and perfunctorily reclaimed gravel pit would have been a more honest description. But it was the thought that counted.

Number nine was one of the smaller homes (*ideal for the discerning single occupant*). It reminded Ed of American houses with its colours and design, if not scale. He checked it over under the guise of locking up his bike, and settled on the sofa, a pile of papers to his side. An emotional night beckoned.

It took long enough to sketch out the words he would write to everyone.

I can hardly thank you enough for joining me in the search for hope. I can honestly say that you've helped me along the path, and I wonder if the time we shared together, all of us, in that overcrowded conference room, has helped you too.

At the start of today, I had no idea how many people would respond to my advert. Like you, I have often felt lonely and very much alone in my struggles. Today, for the first time, I realised I was far from alone. And what an understanding that is.

I know how hard it was for you to come. How difficult to admit to yourself, let alone others, that you had lost hope.

As I stood before you today, I was touched, moved and humbled. But there was another emotion as well, one which I had never expected.

For the first time in I don't know how long, I was filled with optimism. So much hope. And at that moment, I realised something.

I never lost hope. I really didn't. Never.

Just as you haven't truly lost hope. Because hope is a foundation of what we are, a fundamental of what we do, a pillar of our humanity. It's written into every line of our DNA. We never truly lose hope.

We might think we do. But, in fact, we just lose sight of hope. Suffer a temporary blindness. Miss it in the storms that life sometimes directs our way. Storms we have all suffered.

I saw today, I knew, I was sure, that hope was with us all. And I believe you sensed it too.

I know you may struggle to be convinced of that. But look back... remember –

It was in the way you started talking to the other searchers around you. In an instant, shifting from strangers to... allies? Fellows united in a common cause. Friends in the making, even?

It was in the way you left the labs, so different from how you arrived. No longer alone, but talking to each other, listening, sharing, and understanding.

As you know, my experiment is very limited, and I only have space for three of you. It's been an agonising decision, who to choose. Every one of your answers has touched me in a different way.

I'm sorry to say I can't ask you to join me. Despite your incredible thoughts about...

His glasses had misted up again, and Ed had to get up from the sofa and run his face under the tap. These were the most difficult of all the words. The pipes clunked and sputtered, but it was curiously reassuring. A homely sound, the sort of noise he hadn't known for far too long.

The twins from number ten were making the most of the dying light, kicking a ball back and forth, careful to evade the flowerbeds. That was a red card offence in their house. Ed closed his eyes, rubbed at the scar on his neck, listened to the beat of the football, the contented shouts, and then returned to work.

Despite your incredible thoughts about...

The beauty of the dawns... I know that feeling so well. Many times I've woken with the new day, and it's given me strength.

The laughter of your sons... What a profound emotion. I could see their faces, and yours too. Never give up on being there, and always share the laughter of life with them.

Walking... It was one of the ways I began to find hope again. Exploring, observing, understanding, wherever I went. How often the simplest pleasures are the most powerful.

Making it to the end of the day... True to say, sometimes that can be the greatest of our achievements. For a while, it was for me. But then other feelings began to seep into my life, feelings of renaissance, as I know they will for you.

The hope of redemption... Is something I feel in the beat of my heart, every second, minute, and hour.

The scent of the earth after rainfall... One of the simplest but most uplifting feelings, the joyful sigh of the planet as it delights in the blessing of the heavens.

The purity of love... With its electrifying power to surprise us, lift us, exhilarate us, as breathless as a plunge into a lake on a summer's day.

The mask of the disguise you wear... I wore it for many months. But one day I found the strength to take the mask off and see the world again, in all its colour and glory. As will you.

The way life won't let you go... No matter how hard times can be, there's always a hand somewhere to guide you through the darkness. As I think we all felt today.

The transforming power of a single minute... What can I say? Except that, with your answer, you made me cry. You made me feel. You made me worthwhile.

And so many other answers, so many. Ed lost count of the number of times he had to stop typing to wipe his glasses, before he was ready to finish the replies.

I think, like me, you sensed something today. It was in all of us, between us, and everywhere around us, in the air, in our minds, and in our blood.

And it was hope. The beautiful enthralling angel of hope.

Quiet in the night, the clock ticked around, and it was time for the final three.

Darkness had surrounded the little mobile home, lights bright in the windows of its neighbours. Ed had no idea what the time was, but he didn't want to know.

He was focusing on a noise. It wasn't quite there, but then it was, teasing the edges of his senses. A movement, slow. A rustling, a pause, then again. Not a human sound.

But close by. Inside the lounge.

Ed scanned the room and broke into a smile. The noise was coming from the hibernation box.

'Welcome back, fella,' he told the box. 'You've chosen a strange time to rejoin the world. Why not get yourself a few more hours and we can sort you out in the morning?'

As if trained – something Ed quickly realised tortoises had no interest in – the rustling stopped. It would be a couple of days before

Tommy was ready to emerge. They were the archetypal not-morning creatures.

But that was fair enough. When you've been sleeping for months, it's bound to take a while to wake up.

On the scale of little things meaning a lot, Tommy was high up in the highest. Ed didn't know whether it was the touch of his shell, the wise prehistoric eyes, or the sedentary lifestyle, that he found most appealing. The tortoise was never anything other than grateful for a fresh head of lettuce, or any less than fascinated by the latest playground of a lounge he could slowly – very slowly – explore.

Tommy's painstaking progress, hauling his home within a home around a room was a wonderful antidote to so much of modern life. Ed sometimes thought every family should have a Tommy. He particularly admired the way the tortoise would find a couple of metres advance more than enough for one marathon effort, withdraw back into his shell and fall asleep for another indeterminate rest.

The timeless creature was a legacy of the home before last before last, a discovery in the back of an airing cupboard. Tommy was a low-maintenance friend of unknown age and limited horizons, but reliable, dependable, thought provoking and entertaining, just as friends should be.

His was the only light left in the park by the time Ed got to work on the final replies. Maybe he would ask them, the three, to come to the labs at ten o'clock the next day, rather than nine. He wondered if they were waiting, staring at their phones, laptops or tablets, waiting for a message. Or pretending not to care. Or just sleeping, perhaps dreaming about, maybe dreading, what the new day would bring.

The best thing about life is feelings. Even those – particularly those? – we fear.
You can't appreciate happiness without sadness. You can't value content-

ment without pain. You can't delight in the sunshine until you've been shackled down in the darkness.

And like so much else of life, you don't appreciate feeling until you've been numb.

Too many people see life as a chance to take. To grab, grab, and grab some more, enriching and embellishing their selfish selves.

But for me, the best thing about life is to give.

Because with that comes the unique reward of being wanted, needed, and worthwhile.

The true joy of life is relishing its beautiful gift, and being able to hand on that gift a little more beautiful still.

And then there was the final answer of the three, the most original of all. From a young woman, Ed thought, burning with an attitude that could set fire to the paper.

Fuck you. Fuck you and your stupid games. You think you're smart, but you don't know what smart means, you shitty charlatan of a total dickhead.

The best thing about life is truly being smart. But the problem is, that makes you a very fucking lonely individual.

7

Much in life might be predictable, but never people.

Ed did his best not to imagine the faces of the three silhouettes who would arrive – if they did – a big if – but human nature being what it is, he imagined anyway.

To distract himself, he tidied the office again, but there's only so much you can do with four empty desks. Instead he headed to the kitchen, gently picked up the pot with the flowering bulb, and placed the plant at the heart of the newsroom.

'Come join us on the journey,' he told the tiny foray of life. 'I get this feeling we'll be generating a lot of carbon dioxide, and you'll like that, eh?'

He was still bent over, staring at the tip of the bulb, when a voice said, 'Would I be interrupting if I said good morning?'

She was hovering at the edge of the office, not sure enough of herself to step inside. There was a vulnerability about her, as if she wanted to be a part of something, but had too many somethings turn her down.

'I don't think he'll mind. He's not feeling very talkative today.' They shook hands and the woman introduced herself as Florence.

'The early bird gets the desk of their choice,' Ed continued. 'Take your pick.'

She did, and chose the most discreet of the four, the corner of the corner. 'Is anyone else joining us?'

'One for definite. Or as definite as anything ever is in life. One I'm not sure about at all.'

'But you're ever hopeful, eh?'

Florence had been gifted with the grace of a smile which transformed her face. It chased away the hesitancy and replaced it with pure kindness. She unpacked her bag, took out an old laptop, a notepad, a pencil, and placed them carefully on the desk.

Many suits on the streets of life had seen better days, and hers was certainly one. But Florence must have been aware of that, perhaps ashamedly so, and she had eclipsed its faded wear with a colourful wrap.

The arrival of Mitchell, only a few seconds later, was a statement of compare and contrast. The sound of him jogging up the stairs, puffing in time, carried clearly across the labs. Ed introduced him to Florence and he sat down, still with that shadow of a beard, and, endearingly, hiding a little in his trademark hoodie.

Then, they waited. With cups of tea, of course. Trying not to look as though they were sizing each other up, this strange band of hopeful travellers.

They exchanged a little small talk. About the weather, the budding plant, the labs, the traffic, the weather again. Talking about everything and anything except what they wanted to be talking about, and should be talking about, in the very British way.

The time was ten past ten when Mitchell asked, 'When do we assume he, she, or whoever's not coming?'

'It's a she, I think,' Ed replied. 'And a young one at that. I'd say she's been fighting a battle with herself, which means she'll be here anytime now. Give it another five minutes.'

In fact, it took another four; all of even smaller talk, which can make four minutes seem a whole lot longer. The force of a woman marched straight into the room and dropped her bag on the sole remaining desk as if she had owned it since birth. She glared around at the eyes staring at her, stood there as defiant as a rock face and said, 'What?'

Her name was Olivia, she was in her mid-twenties, wearing armour made of denim, and there were demons dancing in the firestorms of her eyes.

'Don't know what the hell I'm doing here,' she said by way of a winning introduction to her new colleagues.

'Snap,' Mitchell muttered, 'but I know I could be doing a whole lot worse.'

'Yeah? Like what?'

'Like sitting alone at home, staring at my miserable reflection. Or sitting alone in a pub, staring at my miserable reflection, or standing alone beside a river, staring at my miserable reflection.'

Florence nodded with all the wisdom of the centuries and asked Olivia, 'Would you like a cup of–?'

'No,' she interrupted. And then, when the silence had gone on in that pointed way that silences sometimes can, added, 'Thanks anyway.'

'Would you like to sit down?' Ed asked.

Olivia stared at him, then the others, but sat. Eventually. And angrily. However it's possible to angrily sit down, she managed it.

'What's the point of all this, then?' she asked.

'Life?' Ed replied, making Florence turn away to hide a smile.

'This thing that you're doing. Our *salvation*.'

Mitchell snorted, but Ed said, 'Salvation is either with a well-known army down the road, or within yourself. But whichever you choose, I'm only your guide. Not your chauffeur.'

'I assume, given that you've decided to grace us with your presence here, you're up for that?' Mitchell added.

'I'm not doing anything else this morning. Apart from contemplating the utter pointlessness of existence.'

'Join the club. Gets tedious, doesn't it?'

Now Florence did smile. And she let the gentle warmth of the look soothe the room, to the extent that even Olivia, through her denim armour and shield of anger, seemed to feel it.

'Are you sure you don't fancy a cup of tea?' Florence asked. 'It might be the first small step on the road.'

'Is that to the Salvation Army, or the thing within you?' Mitchell said.

'Or maybe even hope,' Ed added.

Olivia gave them both a machine gun look. 'Go on, then. Since I'm here. Tea'd be good. Thanks.'

Swift wandered past with that look of wanting to linger, followed by Steve, the programmer. But both must have sensed the mood and didn't interrupt.

What, Ed wondered, would such wandering observers have made of the four unmatching figures in the twilight corner of the old loft space that made up these accelerator labs?

Bold visionaries? Or another forlorn business, staffed only by dreamers, fated to sink below the waters of life without so much as a ripple?

He wouldn't have blamed them. Seldom could a stranger bunch have been assembled. A student with an attitude problem, an out-of-work (again) lawyer with a heart that still wanted to hope, and a former crime scene investigator trying to thaw an existence that was trapped in permafrost.

And there was him. His vision and his promise, to them and himself.

And he was the assembler, the instigator, so it was down to him, the path ahead.

'Do you want another of my speeches, or shall we just get on with it?' Ed asked.

The looks on the faces were far more unanimous than any vote. And so, full of tingles and flutters, unsure all the way, this once a watcher got on with it.

8

Maybe it was something understood from school days, perhaps he simply needed to add a little authority. Or confidence, more likely. But Ed got up from his desk and stood by the whiteboard.

'This is how it goes,' he said, and began writing.

Or he would have. Except that, with all the anguish of a dying mouse, the marker pen managed an agonised squeal and gave up on the world.

'Nice omen,' Olivia muttered.

Florence slipped out of the room and returned bearing an array of colours.

'You've passed the initiative test,' Ed told her.

'Initiative isn't a problem. It's a few other things I'm short of.'

And so they returned to the banner under which they had first come together, however unknowingly.

What is the best thing about life?

'Thinking, feeling and writing, that's what the question was about,' Ed explained. 'Those three are the holy trinity. Our friends and guardians on our adventure together. They were my guides for the way back. Now they're yours too.'

To emphasise the point, Ed added the words to the very top of the board. And because the room was silent- even Olivia couldn't find a slingshot of a comment for once - he tried a little fancy scripting, all curls and whirls.

Thinking, feeling, writing

Then thought: Maybe that's too showbiz.

Thinking, feeling, writing

And that's probably too whacky with its 60's psychedelic feel.

`Thinking, feeling, writing`

Too upright, stark and scientific? Lacking in creativity?

Thinking, feeling, writing

No, too dark. Pressing like a kid with a point to prove. This whole thing was about finding the light again.

Ed was going to try another style when he realised the roomwas still silent. 'Are you all okay?'

'Kind of,' Mitchell replied.

Florence didn't say anything, but Olivia very much did. 'I'm so sorry to interrupt the calligraphy stream of consciousness show, but what the flying fuck are you talking about?'

The little plant was making bold progress, stretching out into the world, Ed noted. Bless the thing, its tender leaves and the pastel hint of colour in its bud.

It had a point, the small miracle of botany. There's a time to step out, stop stalling, quit tiptoeing, and get going.

His fingers found the coil of knotted skin. 'Do I have a scar?'

'You can hardly notice it,' Florence replied.

'It's okay. It's a reminder. Harry Potter style. Except real life, and very near real death for me. The damn thing even hurts sometimes when there's trouble around, just like in the books. A lifelong reminder. And I was just reminding myself.'

'Of what?' Mitchell asked.

'Memories. Only memories. So...'

Thinking, feeling, writing

'There was an explosion. A bomb. I nearly died. I was out for ages. Others, some were innocent bystanders, plenty were colleagues, some were friends, they did die. Just like that. Alive to dead in an instant. The weird thing was that this scar was the only injury I suffered. But it was enough. It cut through... well, lots of stuff. And when I came round...'

Ed paused, paced over to the window, let a long breath colour the glass with films of rainbows. 'I was lucky. That's what I found out when I came round. Really fortunate. The others I was with, they weren't so lucky. Nowhere close. Their families... they didn't have a lot to bury in some cases. That was what did it, I think. Not what happened to me. What happened to them. And others like them, lots of them. At least, I think there were lots. At different times. Over the years. I think they were years anyway. It's hard to be sure.'

The reluctant time traveller at the window kept his back turned to the watching eyes. Sometimes it was the only way.

'I was in hospital for ages. Don't get me wrong, I was really well cared for. They did everything they could for me and tried all they knew to reach me. But I don't think I ever really responded, or rested, or slept, like they told me. I just lay there, all the time, hoping the next day would be better. But every morning, it was another dark dawn. And through the day, all I did was stare out of the window – like I am now – like I sometimes still do – remembering and trying to... find some reason. Some explanation. Some sense. Some...'

It was Florence, dear kind Florence, who helped him along. 'Some hope?'

'Yes. That. That's it, exactly. Hope. Our old friend. That was when I lost it. Gone, just like that. And it took some finding again, I can tell you.'

Olivia asked, 'How long?'

'What's that thing people say about how long's a piece of string? This was more like a coil of rope. Maybe even a transatlantic cable. I didn't even think it had an end some days. I don't know how long it took. I had no sense of time. I guess you don't when you lose hope. It goes with the territory. I had no idea how to find it again. I didn't even believe it existed, sometimes. It sounded just like a word that meant nothing. Hope, hope, hope. Hope, hope, hope. Hope, hope, hope. But what I can tell you is the way I found to get back.'

Thinking, feeling, writing

'I started to think about people. Places. Ideas. Events. Happenings. Discoveries, understandings, innovations, actions, decisions, adventures, philosophies, passions, foods, drinks, arts, sciences, politics, economics, beliefs, disagreements, war and peace, harmony and discord, travel inside and outside yourself, life and death. Everything. The lot. All there is. And more besides. Every day. The whole bloody works.

'Then I started to feel my way through it. And I mean really feel. Put myself in the places of the people involved in everything I could ever think of. Plunge myself into the times, the views, the friends and enemies, the values. The hopes and fears. The wants and needs, the dreams and desires. The inspirations and the aspirations, the dreads and the dilemmas.

'And then I wrote about it. Everything. The whole damn lot. For what must have been months and months. Trying to understand every thought and feeling, all the motivations and the malice, the happiness and the horrors. Every dark corner of emotion I explored. And then I wandered. Watching people and trees and birds and rivers and skies and passing bicycles and planes and seasons, times and weathers, and plays and programmes, and foods and drinks, and scents and sensations, and crimes and passions, and instincts and calculations, successes and failures, rises and falls.

'And I wrote about everything I saw and thought about and knew and wondered about, deep and long, and tried to understand. And at some point, I don't know when, I started to feel again. It was just a tiny sense at first, somewhere on the fringes of my mind, but I knew it was there. So I kept wandering and watching, observing and thinking, and I could sense more and more feeling coming back. And then, one day, it was the summertime, like I suppose it always is, I sat watching the sunset. It was an amazing moment, the daylight shifting to darkness, minute by minute, in warmth and stillness, and the bravest stars starting to venture out, and the rustling of birds roosting in the trees, chirping away to each other, and that taste of the summer air, and I realised I was looking forward to tomorrow. For the first time in I don't know how long, I was actually looking forward to the future. And the next morning, the sunrise, it was even more beautiful than the sunset. For the first time in I don't know how long, the dawn wasn't dark anymore.'

Ed turned back to the group. He expected to find all eyes upon him, but no. Not a bit of it. Everyone was staring at the little plant.

He nodded, then finally, 'There was one more thing I noticed as I wandered. One very big shock of a thing. It was how many people had become like me. No matter what disguises they wore, how they tried to hide it, they looked like me, the way I was, and I could see it. So that's when I decided to do what I – what we – are doing. It was the right thing to do. It was the only thing I could do. Simple as that. To share the journey back.'

And so, for now at least, the story ended. Leaving a room filled only with silence.

More silence.

It had become one of the themes of the morning.

The good news was that no-one had walked out, at least not yet. Maybe they were too deeply sunk inside themselves. The bad news was that, if it was hard for them now, it was only going to get worse with what else he had to say.

And there was the promise. The writ that ran through this curious stream of life.

Ed cleaned his glasses. For some reason, they had grown misty again. 'Right, so the plan is…' he began, but was interrupted, so very gently, by a Florence smile. 'I suppose this is the Alcoholics Anonymous' moment.'

Every equal has its opposite, and Olivia scowled in a way that could intimidate a pack of wolves. 'WTF?'

'I'm Florence and I'm a… hope-aholic.'

'Hello Florence,' Mitchell replied.

'Hello Florence,' Ed added, while Olivia muttered something indecipherable; the only certainty being that the words were a long way from *Hello Florence*.

So Florence told her story. And here, in one amongst the billions of guests this beautiful planet had invited along for the ride, was a person-ification of the old saying: *Life's not fair*.

She'd grown up in Leicester, and despite these allegedly more civilised times, still met with regular abuse more befitting of the Dark Ages. 'But it was only a few idiots,' Florence said in her soothing, understanding way.

She trained as a lawyer and joined a good firm, but got fed up with the relentless worship at the altar of chargeable hours. 'It wasn't exactly what I went into law for.'

Then it was travelling, seeing a little of life. Hunting down long-ago genes that grew in the warmth of the Caribbean, before returning to teach English to overseas students. 'It was fun and I felt like I was making some sort of difference.'

But fate wielded the knife once more. Britain's retreat into the past and isolationism put paid to that, as it did so many nascent hopes.

A part-time position as a low-paid legal adviser to a small charity followed, along with the heartbreak of the end of a relationship. And with that way life can have when it's in a strop, cutbacks at the charity meant Florence *had to be let go*, as the cliché of euphemism put it.

'I was feeling sorry for myself,' she said, with charming understate-ment. 'And I needed the money. So I did what I swore I wouldn't and went back into full-time law.'

A couple of temporary jobs came and went, in conveyancing, ('And I thought I knew what boredom was'). Then wills and legacies, ('Not exactly an uplifting area'). Before – in a shock move for Florence's life – the sun broke through the clouds.

A new law firm had started up, with a focus on helping those who had been unfairly dismissed or wrongfully treated by companies, councils, or the government, but couldn't afford legal support. There was no shortage of customers, depressingly far from it, but there was a familiar problem.

'For all the good we were doing, it just didn't pay,' Florence said. 'And you know how it goes. To start with, you get understanding. From your landlord, and suppliers, and contractors, and anyone you work with. But reality is reality, business is business, and the goodwill quickly ran out.'

And so Florence, living day to day in a small rundown flat, had seen the advert and come along in the hope of a reunion with hope.

She had a range of smiles which would impress an actress, but this one was a squeeze on the heart; a look which summed up the punch, after kick, after slap and swipe, of a lifetime of spiteful unfairness.

After a pause, Ed thanked her and looked to Mitchell to tell his story. It was that kind of a morning. But before he could, Olivia interrupted, as jagged as broken glass.

'You want to talk about hopelessness? I'll tell you what fucking hopelessness is.'

In a city of dreams, this was a young woman who had never been a dreamer. Or so she said.

The scowl was gone, replaced instead by an intemperate ominous greyness, like the horizon serving notice of a coming storm. 'It's supposed to be hard to get into this university,' Olivia told them. 'Crap it is.'

None of the other three gathered around the table had ever been parents, and so forced to learn long and painful lessons in advanced tolerance. But now they were getting a crash course. And in fairness, they were learning fast. They'd already mastered the art of the knowing smile.

'It was a breeze, a piece of piss, an absolute bloody doddle. Getting in and getting on. But then, it always is for me.'

'Maybe that's your trouble?' Mitchell ventured. And sat back, waiting for the detonation, as did they all. But – surprise, surprise – it didn't come.

'Yeah. Maybe it is,' Olivia replied with a tone which, just for once, wasn't a challenge to a duel.

She was the top student at her school, and by an unprecedented margin. The *dear old parent universities*, as Olivia's teachers put it, were suggested, and of the twins she chose Cambridge. ('It was better at science, further away from home than the other place too, and you know what it's like when you're that age.')

Even if she wasn't so very far along from *that age* now, no-one mentioned it. Except, apart from more knowing smiles.

Olivia was warned that competition for such a hallowed scholarly establishment was fierce, and she had to work hard. But she won a place with all the effort of a summer breeze easing its way around the ancient cloisters.

'I couldn't see what all the fuss was about. Piece – of – piss.'

'Even the interview?' Ed asked. 'Didn't you find that scary?'

'Have you been through it?' Florence asked, picking up on the hint in his voice. 'Did you study here?'

'Olivia was telling us her story,' Ed replied, with an itch of his scar. 'The interviews can be notoriously tough, can't they?'

'Mine was more like a chat. I enjoyed it. It was the first time I'd ever talked to someone who knew a bit about science.'

A first-class honours degree in Natural Sciences was duly obtained, again apparently, with the input of minimal effort. That was followed by the decision to continue her studies for a doctorate. In computing.

'I like computers,' she explained. 'You know where you are with them.'

They might never have been parents, the trio watching and listening, but they knew when to keep quiet. No matter how much they might have liked to comment.

'You seem to have done okay in life,' Mitchell said, after a diplomatic while.

'Suppose so.'

'You're young. Smart.'

'Oh, yeah.'

'Healthy. All that stuff.'

'Yeah.'

'And the future's not looking so bad.'

Oh dear. And he'd been doing so well. But now, the calm was

banished and the storm swept in once more; all emanating from a slight young woman sitting at a desk in the corner of an ordinary office, in an instant glowing like embers, and filled with the rage of creation.

'What the fuck do you know about it?'

'All he was saying…' Florence tried, attempting to launch a lifeboat that was sunk before it had even set sail.

'What do you know about my future? How I feel about life? What's going on in my head? Why does everyone think they know more about my life than I do?'

'She was just saying…' Ed tried, but was also swatted mercilessly aside.

'You know what hopelessness is? You want to know? Hopelessness is being able to do everything without any fucking effort. None whatsoever. Zilch, zero, and zip. It's knowing the answer to every bloody question before it's even been asked. Before it's even been thought of, in fact. It's knowing the way without a map, knowing the person without meeting them, and knowing life without wanting anything to do with the fucking thing. That's what hopelessness is. Okay?'

And so ritual defiance followed the outburst, a true wall of a castle, impenetrable and imperturbable stare. But it was as brief as it was hollow, a citadel built of straw, ready to surrender to the slightest of knocks at the gates.

Which came with that she least expected, and to which she was most vulnerable. Not the countering anger Olivia was used to, the rush to dispute, debate, mock or cajole. But instead a quiet understanding from those who shared her suffering.

From Mitchell, in a voice dry with regret, 'It was a stupid thing to say. I'm sorry.'

And then it was gone again, this battering, crashing, incandescent anger, as Olivia laid her head on her arms and sobbed. Cascades of gagging, despairing tears.

They exchanged looks once more, the remaining three, but so very different from those which had gone before. Once more, without a word, a decision was made. And it was a surprise.

Tentatively at first, then more insistently, but so gently all the while, Mitchell reached out. First, with fingers on Olivia's forearm, then a hand on her shoulder, before finally lacing his arm around her.

Olivia didn't resist, not at all, as the kind touch eased away the remaining fragments of her will, and she dissolved into his arms.

Tea is the unofficial official panacea of the modern-day kingdom of England, and tea was their refuge now. Made by Ed, assisted by Florence, while Mitchell continued his unexpected pastoral duties.

Under cover of a boiling kettle, Steve did his materialising act, asking, 'What's going on in there?'

'Team building,' Ed replied.

'Don't sound like any team building I've ever done.'

'We couldn't find enough toilet rolls to turn into a scale model of the Eiffel Tower,' Florence said, her voice filled with painful memories of a solicitors' office. 'So we improvised.'

Back in the office, after a suitable interval, it was as though the outburst had never happened. Olivia and Mitchell were talking about quantum computing. Although it would be more accurate to say Olivia was talking, with enthusiasm, while Mitchell was listening, without.

Ed let them finish because this part he was dreading, and he wanted to make sure he got the words right. Or as right as they could possibly be, anyway. Because he doubted they were going to be welcome.

But before he could speak, fate decided to set the stage in an unhelpful way. Perhaps it had noticed the presence of Florence, and remembered its traditional way of treating her.

Swift had clearly been looking for an opportunity to check in on *the newswire thing*. The angular manager staged yet another awkward walk-about through the labs, stalking like a heron, all the while heading this way. But now he stopped, lingered and lurked, as was his trademark.

'I'm glad you're here,' Ed said, introducing him to the others and noting his stare at Florence. 'I was wondering if you could take a team photo for us. To mark the start of our adventure. Given your talent with a camera.'

Computations ran beneath Swift's lean features, but only briefly. 'I'm sorry. That just wouldn't be appropriate. I can't get too close to any of my... sorry, the bank's tenants. Just in case, you know.'

Ed knew, and very well. Plenty of companies had disappeared overnight, never to be seen again. 'No problem.'

'But on that subject, if I could just use this opportunity to remind you about our terms and conditions regarding tenure and payment of rent. They are, as you know, both strict and non-negotiable. As I have mentioned, we do have a waiting list for the labs. And as you were given a grace period by the bank...'

And then he was gone, leaving behind the words like a swarm of wasps. Swift headed for the sanctuary of his office, a gatehouse next to the entrance to the labs, moving fast and certainly not looking back.

'What a dick,' Olivia observed, with a graceful return to her normal state. 'A grade A-star cock and a half, if ever I saw one.'

'He's not all bad. Just a little confused,' Ed replied.

'Good front, wobbly insides, I'd say,' Mitchell added. 'Classic managerial type. Trying to live up to what's expected, struggling to do so.'

'I think you're going to get the character profiles for the newswire at this rate.'

'I did a bit of psychology as part of my degree. And got lots of practical experience in the police.'

'What did he mean about the rent?' asked Florence.

'That. Ah yes, that.'

The very different surroundings of the Internet and the towering University Library had been familiar haunts after the advert appeared in the paper. Ed had searched out just about everything he could find about starting a business, particularly in the media.

He'd also researched the art of being a news editor, holding newsroom meetings, media law, how to build a loyal audience. Story writing, pyramid structures, headlines and sub headings. Photos and videos, interviewing and quotes, the whole works.

One morning, as his mind wandered, a related article on the field of public relations had also caught his attention. Ed hadn't read much of it, didn't have the time, not to mention inclination, but the headline had stayed with him.

Good news in tranches, bad news all in one go.

'We do have one or two challenges to face,' Ed told them. 'The first of which is paying the rent.'

Another silence had fallen in the office. But this one felt denser than those before. Even the little plant seemed to have tucked in its leaves.

'How many others?' Olivia asked.

'One or two.'

'Just one or two?'

'Maybe a few more.'

'Like?'

Ed quickly explained his vision. That the newswire would be a broad canvas of breaking stories for an eager populace to hungrily consume. But also filled with features to tingle the feelings, editorials to stretch the mind, interviews to probe and explore, and essays to spread new thinking and deliver new understandings. How it would fascinate the community of this ancient city and spread its reach far and beyond, to every corner of the world. And how it would quietly help them, its creators, on their path.

Thinking, feeling, writing

'Can't quibble so far,' Mitchell said. 'But there's a but?'

'There's always a but. It's part of the thing called life. And in this case, in fairness, a few buts.'

'Which are?'

It was going to be impossible to say to their faces. When they had already ventured this far. When they had dared to hope for hope once more, when they had managed at least a little bonding, when they were such a fascinating band of travellers.

Ed grabbed a marker, turned to the board and began writing. He kept up a commentary as he did, trying not to think of the expressions forming behind his back.

'We think we're special – we are special – but we've got to remember, to the rest of the world, we're just like everyone else. We've got overheads, rent, and other bills, as every business has. We need to raise at least a few pounds to pay ourselves so we can survive. We've got no brand, no brand awareness, no reputation, and no base to build on, not yet anyway. We've got no readers. We've got no experience at this. We haven't got any stories, either. And on top of that, we've got no platform to put them on anyway.'

Still he didn't dare to turn around. Instead stood, pen in hand, at the board. Focused on the g of *writing* and admired the elegance of its arcs. But wondered if it should be a little more elaborate. Or maybe a little less so? Although, perhaps it was about right.

'Anything – else?' Olivia asked, each word as lethal as the double discharge of an assassin's gun.

'Since you mention it, we don't have a name yet either.'

It's quite a feat to fill a silence with contempt, but this slight pillar of compressed anger managed it. 'Christ. Jesus fucking H Christ. WTF? You twat. You fucking knob end. I mean, for fuck's sake. Now you tell us. After that advert. And bringing us in here, and putting us through your stupid tests, and leading us on, holding out this sacred journey to hope, like you're some kind of messiah. A fucking shit-arsed charlatan of a cock sucking fuck nut, more like.'

The g really was a tiny work of art. How many people ever appreciated the thought and feeling that went into such everyday details of life? The little things, it was always the little things.

But, for all its elegance, what the g couldn't do was quell the rage boiling away behind. It was still venting lava bombs, as erupting volcanoes did.

'What a fucker. A grandmaster dick weed squared. Talk about taking the piss. Adding insult to injury–'

'Olivia…' Mitchell tried to intervene.

'No,' Ed replied, still without turning. 'Let her speak.'

'Damn right, let her speak. 'Coz there's plenty to say, isn't there? About you raising our hopes so you can smash them down again. What do you think that'd do to us? Problem is, now the truth's being told, you know how fucking fragile we all are. Might as well tie the noose for us, eh? Or shove us in front of the train? What'd you do that for, eh? Make us hope again when you've got nothing to give. Jack shit and sod all. Nothing, not a fucking thing. Just your pompous wank-arsed puffed-up waffle words. Attention seeking, is it? Makes you feel good, does it? Gives you a cock on? Look at me, everyone, I've got the answer to all your problems. But it's just words, words, words, and a big *I'm the man* act. 'Coz when it's time to actually do something, you're nowhere, are you? WTF? You're not Mr Hope, like you make out. You're Mr Fucking Hopeless.'

Now Ed did spin around, propelled by a feeling he hadn't known for a long time. 'I won't lie to you. I won't ever lie to you. That's part of the deal. I didn't say it would be easy. Quite the opposite. And nor should it be easy. You don't learn a thing that way. The easy way is the one we've all thought about in our darkest moments, like you say. The easy way out. But we never took it, did we? So be honest and ask yourself – why is that? Why did you never make that final, fateful decision? Why did you respond to my ad? Why did you put yourself through my test? Why did you wait up all night to hear if you'd got in? Because I know you did. And why did you come along here, this morning, when you could've walked away?'

He stared at the faces, into their eyes, right into them. The iridescent tunnels to the core of the self, journeying inside them, this strange trio, each in turn. Heart to heart and soul to soul, willing them, wanting them to recognise, to understand. To feel that tiny flame that still flickered within, no matter how much they might try to snuff it out, hide it away, disown, deny and denounce it.

The moment, this moment, the critical moment, lingered until the light fluttered as a pigeon landed on the windowsill. Stared inside, its head askance, its expression surprised, interested, amused, perhaps bemused at the human zoo it had chanced upon. Its feathers ruffling in the spring breeze, its eyes mocking, superior, aloof, maybe even entertained.

And Ed could have laughed. For all the pressure of this melting pot moment, for all its intensity, all its tightrope, fulcrum, toss of a coin, yes or no importance, he could have kissed the quizzical grey crook of the bird's beak.

Joy and delight in the smallest of small things.

'So what do we have then?' Olivia asked, but this time holstering her voice and not using the words as weapons. 'Given your hell of a list of what we don't have. What do we actually have?'

It was a while before an answer came. And when it did, it was from Florence.

'We've got hope. Something to hang on to. To believe in. To try, at least. Haven't we, Mitch?'

'Yeah,' he replied. 'That we have... Flo.'

'Haven't we, Ed? We've got hope... again.'

Big moments in life rarely have the decency to announce themselves, Ed thought, but that wasn't a bad effort.

'And we've got each other,' Florence said.

'Hopefully,' Mitch added, with an impressively straight face.

'Oh, for fuck's sake,' Olivia replied, casting a glance towards the far end of the offices and the stairs. But it was just one look, only one. The thought came and went, and she stayed.

Flo produced one of her smiles. 'Let's start at the beginning then. It's time to name our new baby.'

'Mitchell?' Mitch suggested. 'That's a great name.'

'Maybe not for a newswire. Try again.'

'Something to do with us? Our mission? Like... The *News Posse*.'

'I like the posse idea,' Flo replied. 'The *Newshounds Posse*?'

'Maybe a bit too canine?' Ed said. 'The *News Hunters Posse*?'

With supreme self-restraint, Olivia had managed not to pass comment. But such control could only last so long. 'For Christ's sake!' she snapped. 'Given the state of us, the *Armpit Posse*, more like.'

'Guess that's anything posse ruled out then,' Ed said after a pause. 'The *Daily Hope*?'

'How about... The *Livewire*?' Flo tried.

'The *New Edition*?' Ed said.

'Wasn't that an eighties' pop group?' Mitch pointed out. 'Which makes me think of pink leg warmers and big hair. So maybe not so good.'

'In which case, how about the *First Edition*?'

'FFS,' Olivia replied. 'Give me strength. The *Last Edition*, more likely.'

Which, strangely, provoked no further debate, but instead left them all nodding.

I f any of the three standing on the pavement outside the Falcon Labs had looked around, they would have seen a face at a window, watching them. In the tradition of fathers throughout the years, Ed, his body trembling with competing feelings, was waving his charges on their way.

It was a risk, as it always was. But it had to be done, as it always did.

They chatted a little as they stood in the springtime brightness of this intersection corner of Cambridge, but only for a while. Then, at Florence's insistence, and albeit hesitantly on Olivia's part, they shared a group hug and began walking their separate ways.

In the absence of any better way of assigning them each a beat, as is the tradition with new recruits to the news trade, they had opted for the points of the compass. Mitch was heading east, a direction he had requested, if for reasons he wouldn't say. Flo was travelling south, and Olivia north.

Somehow, those last two felt strangely appropriate.

Ed himself would go west. That was his decision, and partly super-stition, born of the films he'd watched in his early years; the fate of the character who made their final journey in that ill-fated direction. If there was danger, in his self-appointed paternal way, he would face it himself.

In fairness, the only danger from the story he was planning was to his sanity, and it had been tested by many more-formidable dragons. Ed wasn't planning to travel far, not far at all. Just a few metres, and not even down the stairs.

The *Last Edition* needed some breathing space, and the price would be a fine spread of flattery. Not to mention a shameless breaching of the core ethics of the news trade.

But needs must, as Ed had said and heard so many times in his past. If never quite like this.

The default way to get around this ancient yet modern city was the bicycle, and Olivia was head down and pedalling fast on hers. Apart from being the quickest transport in yet another gridlocked community, it offered an additional advantage; one which she would happily admit to enjoying.

The smugness of immeasurable superiority in cruising past the lines of cars and irritated faces glowering from the windscreens.

She'd taken a few minutes to sort out that other matter, one of those on Ed's irritatingly long list. And it was just a few minutes, no matter how much he thought it would need otherwise. He'd been grateful in his intense composed way, and genuinely so; not like the narrow-eyed envy she was used to experiencing from all too many men. Which had made her feel, frankly, rather odd.

It was a perfect day for cycling; dry and not cold, but not hot, either. The exercise also helped to distract her mind from the ping-pong of its thoughts. Back and forth, from one extreme of emotion to another. Back and forth, back and forth, in a furious rally.

She was amidst the high-tech sheds and hangers of the Science Park almost before Olivia realised it, and had to brake hard to turn off the main road. But locking up the bike took a lot longer than usual, as she stared at the doors to the Barnfield Centre.

Open and closed, open and closed they slid, as visitors came and went, the smooth, silent movements matching the back and forth, back and forth in her mind.

Somewhere long ago, and to their amusement, they had been sent on an acting workshop. The young Mitch and his fellows had laughed as they walked into the seminar room. What the hell kind of use was this for what they would be doing?

Plenty, as it turned out. On numerous occasions, they'd had cause to thank the middle-aged paunchy and jowly actor, with the voice of a thousand cigarettes, for helping them to play out convincing parts.

With that in mind, Mitch headed for his destination following a longer and more dangerous route than was necessary. Dangerous for how he had to be that week, anyway.

The river was the river, just as it had been the previous day, when he stared into its waters. And Mitch was aware of it, on the periphery of his vision. Rowers rowing, ducks muttering, eddies swirling in the willow-shadowed waters.

He stopped to stare, as he knew he should. But it was just the river.

Nothing to gaze into and wonder. No hint of a dark presence, with a cowl and a scythe, waiting beneath the water. Just the river. Nothing more.

He walked along, a little further and a little slower than was necessary. Then turned in, towards the city, and started to whistle a tune.

Until he remembered. And the happy-go-lucky whistling faltered to become a more mournful song.

Unlike the other three, Florence had no idea where to go. Find a story, that was their task, nothing more and nothing less.

It sounded so simple.

Talk to people, that's what Ed had told them. Journalists say it's all about contacts. If you've got some – family, friends, colleagues, the woman who runs the paper shop, the landlord of the pub, anyone and everyone – use that and talk to them.

If you haven't, go and make some contacts. Talk to people, listen – really listen – and find some news. Because news is what we need.

Through streets she walked, as always surprised by the fast changing character of Cambridge. From a small run of shops to a long row of houses, a cemetery, a business park, narrow streets filled with chained-up bicycles. Wider roads full of traffic, more homes, a tiny church, an art gallery. The noisy discovery of a nursery school on one corner, the solemn quiet of an undertaker's opposite.

How life enjoyed her ironies.

A noticeboard called for her attention. The Renaissance for Beginners, Tai Chi for the Time Poor, Yoga and Aromatherapy to Lift the Work Place, The Secret Messages Your Cat is Sending.

Oh this city. Realm of brilliance and eccentricity.

And another poster. *This Lunchtime! The Alehouse Philosophers Debate the Benefits of Spectator Sport. All welcome.*

The event was being held a few minutes' walk away, in a pub on Millhouse Road. Of course it was. The legendary Millhouse Road.

Ed strode past Swift's office, observing without looking, just like in the days of the old life, before knocking. The manager was sitting at his desk, staring into space, fiddling with his wedding ring once more.

If there had been a bookie around, Ed could have won a few pounds, which would have come in useful right now. But he could imagine the look he would get for asking about the odds on – *the moment I knock, he'll call "hold on a minute", grab some papers, pretend to be engrossed in them, and keep me waiting for a while before he says "come in".*

Ed knocked, heard the expected words, waited for the anticipated period, and was invited into the mighty sanctum of supreme executive power.

'I've got a team together. We're looking at getting the first issue out in the next couple of days.'

A nod of the angular head. 'Very good.'

'All the necessary…' Ed hesitated, because language was important with Swift, and Business Speak wasn't his native tongue. 'The necessary infrastructure is being put into place.'

'Splendid.'

'And the finance, of course.'

Now there was kerosene in the aircraft's tanks. 'Excellent.'

'We're currently deciding which stories to feature in the first edition,' Ed went on, tactically deciding it wasn't the time to mention either the current tally of stories, or the newswire's name.

'Very good.'

'And I had a thought.'

'Which is?'

Ed gestured around, as though they were privileged to be witnessing the migration of millions of wildebeest across the plains of the Serengeti. 'The labs. This pounding heart of the local economy. The remarkable success they've enjoyed. Under your visionary stewardship.'

Close links to industry were a demand of her studies, which made the Science Park, and the café in particular, a familiar haunt. Usually, Olivia would be an in-and-out customer; grab a drink and go. But today, for the first time, she lingered.

Tables were dotted with twos and threes, the scent of fresh coffee lacing the light air. The self-conscious muted background chatter of the

British rumbled and buzzed. Olivia scanned around, perhaps half recognised a few faces, maybe not.

WTF? What was she doing?

A couple of young men were down to the dregs of their cups, so she chose them. A full coffee's worth of chat was an impossible fear.

'Can I join you?'

'Um, sure, yeah,' the broomstick-thin one replied, shuffling in his chair at what was quite possibly a unique request.

'We were going, but I guess we might stay a bit now,' his friend, chubbier and alarmingly albino like, added. His smile was almost as queasy as his chat up lines, Olivia thought, but managed not to say.

'What company are you with?'

'Starburst Marketing.'

Shit squared. Marketers. Olivia was plenty self-aware enough to know that if computer scientists thought another career was crap, it really was down there with the estate agents.

'Do you come here often?' Broomstick asked, matching his friend's charm and raising it.

"I'm never ever coming here again" suggested itself as the most appropriate response, but instead, Olivia willed herself to tell them about her need to find a news story.

'We're carrying out a really interesting new form of market research,' the wraith said, slurping the sludge of his coffee leftovers as though he was sucking the remaining life from a corpse.

'Yeah, you wouldn't believe the socio-economic sectoring potential of this one,' Broomstick added.

Olivia put on a forced smile, and began busily scratching herself. 'I'd love to hear more but I've just remembered, I've got an appointment at the clinic.'

Tucked in behind an occupational therapist and an African restaurant, often the way in this city, was the Triangle Café. It was a perfect geometric box of a building, not triangular in the slightest, but creative licence was also a civic obsession.

Even from outside, through the sun blaze and fogged windows, it was obvious the café was packed. Figures were standing, clustered at the back, each one of the tables full. And the time was still twenty minutes before the event was due to start.

'I'm really sorry,' the older, wrinkled and improvised bouncer told Mitch. 'If you haven't got a ticket, I can't let you in. We're already well over capacity.'

No Man Left Behind, the posters on the windows proclaimed. An opportunity to challenge the taboos on mental health and help save a man's life.

That it was already so full told its own story. Ed had been very right in one thing, at least. They, the staff of the *Last Edition* were far from alone in their suffering.

He'd almost come to such a meeting before. That was last year, in another place, after a particularly tough assignment. Another blood bath of human horror which was so hard to escape from. Mitch had walked past, back and forth, never quite finding the courage to actually go in. But this was a story, as important as any, and one which needed telling.

'I'm with the press,' Mitch told the guardian of the door, then heard himself add, 'Plus, I think I might want to speak.'

The colours and scents of a Lebanese food market had taken over Millhouse Road. University types pointed, shared anecdotes, and asked questions of patient and tolerant stallholders. Students and locals just ploughed on in and enjoyed. So it went.

Florence briefly considered it as a story, but only very briefly. World food on Millhouse Road was as unusual as the sun coming up in the morning, or another politician being caught up in a pants-down scandal.

The shops here were as if a mix of periods, places and needs had been shaken up and set down at random. An antique furniture store, a Polish food shop, a hairdresser, vintage fashion, a Turkish café, a mini supermarket, a pizza parlour, chocolatier, off licence, and, ubiquitous to Cambridge, bike repairs.

There were stories in each, but none that would intrigue a reader, not when they knew the setting was Millhouse Road. And there was a deadline to consider, the end of the day, so on Florence moved, through the swirls of the crowd.

The pub was rather too sticky floored and filled with overbearing TVs for her taste, always danger signs. And it was remarkably busy for this time of day. But here, on Millhouse Road, no-one stared and no-one cared about the new visitor.

The young languid barman was unsurprised at her request to sample some of the beers, and her choice of a half of light, hoppy ale. Florence would have preferred a pint, but already suspected the conclusion she would come to about the merits of a story on the Alehouse Philosophers. She'd recognised them as soon as she walked in.

A small group of men – and it was only men – was clustered in the far, darkened corner of the bar. The one currently speaking – and at some length – was sitting back, hands over his mound of a belly, and pontificating through a beard which would impress a pirate.

Despite the background noise, his drink-worn and self-important voice ensured the words carried. Which was to the obvious annoyance of a couple of lads in fluorescent jackets who were trying to watch a repeat of a football match from years ago.

'It is then, my contention, that the folly of the distraction of the fog of a major sporting event is easily transparent to we, the thinking classes, yet nonetheless a useful means of control of the mass of the populace by those vain enough to declare themselves the leaders of this nation, or alleged nation, as has often been my argument both to you, my friends, and to…'

Every one of the listening band could have been a clone of the speaker himself. And each was readying for a reply, no doubt of equal longevity and fascination.

Florence finished her half, allowed herself a forlorn smile, and slipped back out of the door.

The drumbeat of *WTF*? echoing ever louder in her mind, Olivia was standing around the corner from the Barnfield Centre, hiding from the marketers. Her bike, and the salvation of escape, was calling. But something, just something, was making her stay.

She thought of Ed, Mitch, and Florence, probably struggling to choose between the range of amazing stories that dozens of willing confessors were raining upon them. How Olivia had breezed into this city, this university, and never struggled with anything in life. Nothing, not once.

Well, perhaps one thing. If she was honest. And the trouble was that they were all around her and everywhere, swarms of them. And fuck it all, they also ran this damn planet, even if they should never be allowed anywhere near the controls.

A young couple was sitting on the grass, chatting, enjoying the unaccustomed warmth of the early days of the English year. They were animated, nodding, excited, entangled in smiles and happiness.

Olivia remembered some of the business talk she had heard in this place, and on the TV. 'Onto a winner, are you?' she asked, trying to sound natural.

'You bet,' the woman replied.

Both were fair haired in a strikingly artificial way, and muscled and toned fit to advertise swimwear. They were also tanned, in an utter mismatch with the season.

'So…?'

They exchanged glances. 'It's commercially sensitive, obviously,' the man said, with the hint of an Australian accent.

'But we reckon we've invented an intensive total workout gym session without the need to leave your desk,' she added. 'We'll get this lardy couch potato nation all fitted up, won't we, Mikey?'

'You betcha. And make a packet in the process.'

Holy shitting wombats. It was time to nod and move on, as, Olivia had quickly realised, it often was here. Towards the sanity of her bike, and the chance to *get the hell out of here.*

That was when she saw the burger van parked at the end of the street, and the gang of laughing men.

It still happened sometimes, in some places, even in this city so familiar with the footfall of a thousand nations. But even so, it was always a shock.

'Fucking black bastard.' It was a guy sprawled in a doorway, bedroll beside him, staring at Florence with bloodshot and bleary eyes, glaring through the sunshine. 'We'd have jobs and homes if it weren't for you.'

'I'm from Leicester,' Florence replied. 'Via Jamaica, if you want to go back to my grandparents.' She was about to walk on, but, with an afterthought, tipped some money into his hat.

'That won't make no difference to what I think about you,' he grunted.

She smiled. 'Won't make no difference to what I think about you either.'

Some days sunshine, others rain, but never in equal measure. This woman, try as she might to walk upright through life, had grown bowed with far more than her share of ill fortune. And fate hadn't given up on testing her yet.

With her first step into the light, Florence scored a direct hit on the landmine of a patch of chewing gum. It pulled as she walked, accompanying her tread with a mocking squelch.

The solicitors, her most recent hope, was just off Millhouse Road, and Florence avoided heading that way. A woman could have enough for a morning.

She made her way back through the food market, hardly seeing it. Not noticing the patter and the offers of free samples, the smells of herbs and frying, the chatter and the laughter. Just keeping on moving, keeping going, always keeping on moving.

Because to stop moving was to start thinking.

On she walked, almost to the end of the road, towards the historic centre of Cambridge, spires looming in the clearness of the sky. But then halted abruptly, mid motion, mid pavement.

If there wasn't a story here, there wasn't a story anywhere. Even in this city of the everyday extraordinary, Millhouse Road was renowned.

Around her was another pub, no more promising than the last, the modern cleanliness of a doctor's surgery, a comfortably disorganised wholefood store, and a laundrette.

Two women were inside, one listening, listening, listening, above the rumble of the machines, then comforting the other.

She was shaking her head, in tears, the hug not seeming to help, not at all. The distress was far too rigid and deep set to be soothed away. Through the glass, Florence caught her look, hesitated, and then walked in.

The group watched Olivia every step of the way as she approached, several murmuring in appreciation. There were five, all about her age, standing beside the van. Stubbly, streaked with sweat, and muscular in their T-shirts, fluorescent jackets and boots.

One was a little shorter than the rest, but with teeth that were ridiculously un-British. *He must*, Olivia computed, *have been working plenty of overtime to fix that smile.*

'All right, love.'

'Hello.'

If people in general were strange, the subset of men was by far the oddest. Standing and gawping might be acceptable in a zoo, but at a fellow human on a street corner?

'Can we help you?'

'I hope so.'

'How?'

'I need a story.'

The group exchanged looks, and Olivia realised they didn't understand. Perhaps these men weren't so different from computers after all. You had to make sure you programmed them correctly and then asked the right questions.

'I mean a story for a newspaper. An online paper. A newswire.'

'Oh right.' The leader produced a red-topped tabloid from a back pocket. 'Like in here?'

'Yes.' Olivia noticed the headline. *Screw You, Inspector Poo.* 'Well, similar.'

'What sort of story?'

'Something from around here. Something local. Just something you find fascinating, amazing, interesting, or inspirational.' The looks turned to puzzlement. 'Or really strange would do. As strange as you like.'

That was the breakthrough, Nobel Prize style. 'Oh yeah. Yeah, yeah, yeah.' Teethman nodded hard in time with his words. 'I've got a really bizarre story for you. We were just talking about it. It's my brother-in-law. And what he does at weekends.'

This produced a lot of laughter, which went on for a long time. And it was accompanied by cries of *Oh no, no way, seriously, get real, you can't tell her that, Rick.*

'Are you sure I want to know?' Olivia asked.

'It is bloody weird, just like you said. If you want a story, this is it.'

'Tell me then.'

Rick's lighthouse beam of a grin grew even brighter, a sure warning of rocks ahead. 'What's in it for me, love? A date?'

If Olivia paused before answering, it was only through disbelief. That she was faced with this again. Once more, how many times, yet again.

'What the fuck? Why's it always a date with you lot? Stupid, clumsy, hopeless, halfwit, deranged attempts at fake charm, crap chat, and pathetic doe eyes for bed? Do you know how bloody ridiculous you are? What dickheads you look. Men, for fuck's sake. You're just a bunch of utter twats.'

So much for the resolution of self-control. Maybe it was time to fail at something. It couldn't be so bad, surely? Everyone else did it.

Behind Olivia, her bike was calling again. Silently yelling *Let's get the hell out of here. And forget Ed, Florence and Mitch, salvation and hope, and all that Last Edition shit. You're caught up in a con, girl, let's get going.*

But the five mocking faces had vanished. Obliterated by the shock and awe barrage of her accidental attack.

'Christ,' Rick muttered. 'I reckon I want a date even more now.'

'All right then. Fair enough. I'll go out with you. If… if you can beat me at a challenge.'

Now there were *oohs* amongst the gang. But if there's one thing you can guarantee with a bunch of lads, no matter how advanced their programming, it's that they can't back down. Not in front of their mates. And certainly not in the face of a woman, even one like this, where backing down might be the wisest choice by far.

Rick nodded, albeit a little warily. 'All right then, yourself. Whatcha thinking?'

Olivia nodded to a tree, just behind the burger van. 'That branch. Pull-ups. Military style. Thirty seconds to see who can do the most.'

The man was at the window again.

If it had been the kind of area where people noticed, there would surely be a crowd looking up and staring. Perhaps pointing, maybe even concerned and trying to attract his attention, checking if he was okay.

Because there was something in the man's stare.

It wasn't the legendary thousand-yard look, but more distant even than that; way over the horizon and far, far beyond.

It was the look of a man who had once lost. And who was wondering, more and more, minute by minute, whether he was about to lose again.

It was the look of a man who had gambled with high stakes and even higher hopes. But now feared the gamble was a folly and those fledgling hopes would be crushed.

His look shifted fast with the beat of the passing footfall. From this road to that, the pavement opposite, the cycle lane adjacent. The bridge, the alley, the street, the road. Buses, cars, taxis, bicycles.

Always searching, but never finding.

Yet always hoping.

If it had been the kind of area where people noticed, they would have spotted the thin scar on the man's neck. And the way he kept rubbing at it, further inflaming the weal of raw skin with each passing moment.

But this wasn't the kind of area where people noticed. They scurried into shops and out of offices, jogged for their cars before predatory parking attendants could pounce. Skipped into meetings before the never-resting clock condemned them to lateness.

And the man at the first-floor window watched, and waited, rubbed at his scar, and wondered, and worried.

'They'll be back.'

Startled, Ed turned around to find Steve, the young programmer, hovering at the edge of the office.

'I heard them talking as they went out. They'll be back with something for you. They were well determined.'

'I hope you're right.'

'They owe you. Or they think so, anyhow. You chose pretty well, I reckon. They strike me as the sorts who'll want to pay you back. Did you manage to tickle old Sneery Swifty's belly?'

'How'd you know about that?'

'I like to keep an eye on what's going on. Or an ear. And it was the look on your face when you went to see him.'

'That bad, eh?'

'Worse.'

'I secured a fascinating in-depth interview with our glorious manager, if that's what you mean.'

Steve smiled. 'Insomnia, erectile dysfunction, and baldness.'

'What?'

'There's a fortune to be made for whoever comes up with a cure for any of them. And I reckon you might have insomnia cracked.'

Despite his tick-tock fret-filled mind, Ed smiled too. 'You should come join us. You could write a few jokes. Maybe do a cartoon.'

'Nah. I got programmes to write. That's my language. But since we're talking that way, a couple of things, business-wise…'

'Yes?'

'I do the marketing for us. You know what it's like, small start-up, everyone does a bit of everything. So I wanna place an ad. How much?'

Ed realised he hadn't thought about any of that. 'It depends on how big, how prominent, and how many editions you want it in for.'

'I want it in the lot. However many you do. Something tells me you lot are gonna make a right splash. I reckon I'll get a bargain if I buy up space in advance.'

Ed wrote a note on his pad, and tried not to notice it was the only entry under *Income*.

'I'll get back to you with our rates. What was the other thing?'

Steve's smile grew. 'That woman in the denim. What's her name? The one with the really cute scowl.'

'Cute scowl? You really should come work with us. You've got quite a way with words.'

'It is though, innit? Well cute.'

Ed was about to reply when heavy footsteps interrupted him. It was Mitch, breathing hard, and looking a mixture of shocked and spellbound.

It was difficult to get Steve out of the way, try as Ed might. The programmer insisted on lingering, and kept asking Mitch if he was okay. 'I mean, really okay?' he said, in a curious tone that made Ed look back and forth between the two men.

Eventually, in a distracted manner, Mitch replied, 'Okay, yeah, I'm all right, let it go.'

Steve finally ushered out, Ed and Mitch sat and talked. Or, to be accurate, Ed talked while Mitch stared into the shifting waters of the obligatory cup of tea.

'I guess you found something good? That's great. Take a minute, then tell me about it. There's no rush.'

And when it was clear there was no rush whatsoever, to the extent that no words were forthcoming, Ed tried, 'I got a good interview. Useful, anyway. And we've sold our first advert.'

Then, to help fill the continuing echoing silence, 'Have you heard from the others at all? Any idea where they went? What they were working on?'

Ed gave it another minute, then, 'Mitch, are you okay? What the hell happened? You look like you've seen a whole family of ghosts.'

And because nothing was getting through to the shrewd-eyed shadow-bearded shadow of a man sitting at the desk, Ed pushed the little plant towards Mitch. 'Talk to him then, if you can't talk to me. He's a great listener. I can vouch for that. Not judgmental at all. And he loves carbon dioxide.'

The movement caught Mitch's attention and slowly, as slowly as a lunar landing, he focused on the nascent bud. 'I did it.'

'Did you? Did it? Did what?'

'I found a story. A good one. Really important. For you. For me. For us.'

'Great. That doesn't sound like so much of a problem. So why're you…?'

'But I didn't just sit and report it. I got up. And I spoke out.'

Back they went to the words on the whiteboard; their guardians and guides on this quest for the land of hope.

Thinking, feeling, writing

'You've obviously been thinking about it on your way back here,' Ed said. 'And you've really felt it. So now write it.'

And because Mitch was still struggling, the two men sat side by side, like school teacher and pupil, and wrote the story together.

The room into which Mitch had walked was hot and crowded way above capacity. 'That was the first thing that got me,' he said. 'You wouldn't believe the range of men. There were youngsters, no older than students, right up to guys who must have retired years ago. They were black, white, Chinese, Japanese, Indian, from all over the place. And what really hit me, some of them, they looked like builders and workmen, and all the sorts you'd never think would struggle. Covered in tattoos, shaved heads, full of muscle, yet inside...'

'Openings are all important in writing,' Ed said. 'And I think you've already found yours. Or maybe it found you.'

Muscles and tattoos, old and young, black and white, and every shade in between – it's not what's on the outside, but the suffering within that brought this extraordinary group of men together.

'That okay?' Mitch asked.

    'More than okay. Much more.'

    'So, right, next...?'

    'Did you get any photos?' Ed asked.

    'Loads. And some of me speaking too. My friends took them.'

    'Friends?'

    'They are now.'

The event was called No Man Left Behind. *Why? Because, the statistics say, suicide is the biggest killer of men aged under forty-five.*

Men take their own lives because they suffer with depression and other mental health issues. But men being men, they don't – can't – or won't – talk about it. Instead, they find another way out. The only way they think they can.

The final way.

We heard from a student – Trev – just nineteen years old, he said, in a quiet and nervous voice. Doing well in his biochemistry degree. A handsome young man, in a nervous way. With so much to look forward to in life. But many mornings, Trev wakes up in tears and wonders how to end that life of so much promise.

"I just wish that I had never been born," he told us. "And I know how wrong that is. When I'm actually lucky because I've got so much. And do you know what? That makes it worse. I feel guilty about feeling shit when I've got no right to. Not when there are so many people who are much worse off in the world."

Joe, a father of two young girls, Bea and Bridget, talked about knowing what his suicide would do to them, not to mention his wife, Sandra. But he has never been able to talk to them, and still fantasises about filling his pockets with rocks and walking out into a lake.

"I just can't see any other way out of this. Every morning, on the way to work, I stop the car at the park, get out and stare at the lake. I hear my girls calling me, asking where I am, why I've abandoned them, and it stops me from walking down into the water. But their voices are getting quieter and quieter, and I don't know if I can live like this much longer."

Then there's Tim. Tall, well groomed, reeking of success. A professional in a bespoke suit and colourful silk tie, talking about the data company he founded, and the hundreds of people he employs. The expensive car he drives, the beautiful house he owns, and how he can have just about anything he wants. "But all I really want to do is end it all. End this endless suffering."

And here's the common theme. Every single one of the men who spoke out, you could see them in a café, or pub, at work, or walking down the street, and you'd never think they could be suffering with depression.

They hide their struggles behind a smile. By being a joker, or a hard worker, or a weightlifter or bodybuilder, a family man or a businessman. Anything and everything. Just anything to hide that endless pain inside.

'Bloody hell,' Ed whispered. 'I know I told you to really feel it, but…'

Mitch scanned back over what he'd written, and all in just a few minutes. 'I don't know where that came from.'

'It came from exactly where it should.'

The two looked at each other, in that way men sometimes do. 'I didn't know I could… I mean… thanks for helping me write it.'

'Do you know how much help I gave you?' Ed replied. 'A total of none whatsoever. All I gave you was permission to write it.'

Mitch breathed out hard and rubbed at his stubble. Something was still bothering him. It was in the way he was trying to look at Ed, but couldn't quite manage it.

And Ed, a skilled inquisitor from the experience of the old life, knew. 'Is there something you want to tell me?'

This time, Mitch did manage to look at him. 'Yes and no. But not here. And not now. Later. Hopefully.'

There was something in his words that made Ed look behind, check over his shoulder. 'Good or bad?'

'Not sure yet. Anyway, shouldn't we be getting back to this article? It's not quite done, is it? How do I finish it?'

Ed held their look so Mitch understood the moment wouldn't be forgotten, then said, 'How did you finish the meeting? I think there's one important detail missing, isn't there? Maybe it's time for another photo.'

And then came the hardest part of the article. In every single picture they scanned through, Mitch was standing at the head of the crowd, all the faces intent upon him. And each of those static snapshot images burned with the passion of a heart which had been silenced for too long.

I went to the meeting to report on it. Because I'd come to a similar gathering before – or tried to – as that time around I couldn't find the courage to join in.

I only meant to write about what happened. That would have been an achievement enough, to honour the courage of the men gathered around me. But in a moment like that, with such emotions running, I found myself on my feet and speaking out about my own suffering.

And I am glad, so very glad I did. Because I felt it, and all those around me felt it too.

This truly was a day when no man was left behind.

To reach out in the face of suffering is a human instinct, but more than that with this woman. It was written into her DNA, one of the drivers of her being. Which made it all the more puzzling why life insisted on treating her so unkindly.

The two women could have been sisters, with their blonde hair and generous proportions, but it turned out they were actually neighbours. Florence did what she always did in moments of high emotion, when the risks of becoming a vent for the anger were highest.

She sat down and radiated kindness in that remarkable way she had.

On this occasion it was on one of the hard plastic chairs by the line of tumble driers on the worn lino flooring. In previous incarnations, it had been across a desk, or on a comfy chair, cushioned by a soothing carpet and colourful pastel prints, next to a tearful miserable woebegotten wretch.

But the principle was the same. Whether it was her understanding smile, the openness of her arms, or the gentleness in her eyes, it was a universal language.

The comforter was Ellie, the comfortee Charl. And the reason for the contortions of distress was a surprise.

'He's gone. Gone,' were the words Charl kept sobbing, then whimpering into her friend's shoulder as she cried herself into exhaustion.

Which left Florence doubting her instincts. What story was there in yet another imploding relationship, sad though it might be for those involved? It was the standard currency of every café, coffee bar, pub, gossip corner of an office, or kitchen of a house. She herself would have enough such tear-soaked tales to fill the *Last Edition*, if that was what would fascinate the public.

It was only Ellie's intriguing reply that kept her faith and kept her sitting in the laundrette, waiting to find out what had happened.

'We'll get him back, love. We will. I'll go and get a nice bit of fish and we'll soon have him come running.'

It was the depletion of the impressive supply of tissues that gave Florence her opportunity. She offered one of her own, was duly thanked, and made the most of the opening to try to establish a rapport. 'Can I get you some water? Or some more tissues? Or some... fish?'

Ellie replied, 'Thanks, but–'

'Mackerel, he loves mackerel,' a breathless Charl interrupted. 'Have you got any?'

'No, not on me. Mackerel's not something I tend to carry around. But I can get some.'

'Would you? It's just I'm a bit short right now, and he loves it. It's the most likely thing to get him come running, my big fella, and I miss him. We all do. We so miss him!'

Florence and Ellie exchanged looks and an explanation followed. The *he* in question was Hector, and he was a twelve-year-old much-loved tortoiseshell tomcat.

Which left Florence doubting her instincts all over again. Except that, just for once, fate was on her side.

'They've got him,' Charl went on. 'I know they have. The same lot that grabbed all them others. And he's never coming back.'

Olivia would have thought it was a wind up. She certainly wouldn't have put it past her new gang of friends. But it was the photos which convinced her.

They stood in the shade of a tree, the six of them, next to the burger van, and she looked, then stared, then stared again. They just couldn't have been faked. No-one had that much imagination. Or weirdness. No-one, but no-one.

True to his word, Rick told her all about Tyson, his brother-in-law, and his legendary hobby. And when he, and his gang, saw her look, he took out his phone to prove it.

'I need to talk to him,' Olivia said.

'I dunno if he'll be up for talking. He's a bit shy about it.'

Olivia nodded. She often struggled with human emotions, but thought she could understand that.

'I need to talk to him anyway. Can you phone him please?'

'Are you for real?' Rick was sweating even more now, as if the torrents he'd shed during the pull-up challenge weren't enough.

'I need to talk to him and I don't have much time.'

Rick hummed and hawed, and twisted his boots in the dirt, even if the gang were egging him on to do it.

'I won our challenge,' Olivia pointed out.

'Yeah, but I didn't say nothing about actually talking to him.'

'That's a double negative.'

'What?'

Olivia quickly computed that emotion would be more effective than logic here. 'I didn't say nothing about putting the video of beating you at pull-ups all over social media neither.'

That prompted another *ooh* from the colourful assembly of fluorescent jackets.

'Bloody hell,' Rick muttered, finding the number in his phone. 'Are you really sure you don't want to go on a date?'

While they waited for Tyson to pick up, Rick added, 'How come you beat me, anyway? How can a cute little thing like you do so many pull-ups?'

'Is that your idea of charm?'

'It was only a question,' replied the crestfallen wreckage of a once-cocksure man.

'Iron woman races.'

'What, swimming for ages, then biking miles, then running a marathon? Really? I mean, really?'

'I only did a few. They were too easy,' Olivia replied, in a not very successful attempt to make Rick feel better about his abject humiliation.

It was just an ordinary living room, with one extraordinary feature. The portrait gallery of pictures of the cat which filled the coffee table.

Hector was well loved, well fed, and very well photographed. There he was, in a gilt frame, reposing quite regally on a lawn. Or, in smaller shots, contentedly asleep, tail dangling, on the back of the sofa. Or as a babe in arms, albeit a sizeable one.

And then there were the phases of Hector's life. From a kitten, playing with a shoe, to an adolescent, eyes gleaming with mischief, to a feline teenager, on the prowl for birds, mates, or enemies.

The pictures didn't just mark the life journey of the revered Hector. Many featured Madison, or Maddy. She was Charl's only child, now fourteen and hunkered up in a defensive ball, knees tight to chest, in the corner of the sofa.

'How're you feeling, love?' Charl asked her, as they walked into the room.

'How'd you bloody think?' was the response, the only one Maddy had so far managed. But, in fairness, it must have been difficult to talk with a face set with such resentment.

The teenager was excused with the explanation that she, of all the family, loved Hector the most. They had grown up together, played together, and now he was gone.

A poignant silence of deep respect followed that last statement.

Which, not for the first time, left Florence wondering exactly what she was doing there.

Especially given the strange dynamic running through the family. For all the upset in Maddy, there was a slyness too. Whenever Charl or Ellie was talking, Maddy would glance over out of the corner of her eyes. At those moments, Florence noticed, the anger in her face eased, as though she was acting the part of a misery-engulfed teenager, but couldn't quite embrace the role.

'You said some other cats had disappeared,' Florence tried, but was interrupted by Maddy springing up, muttering, 'Jesus,' and stalking out of the room.

'Four, that we know of,' Ellie replied, because Charl had slumped down on the sofa and looked incapable of speech. 'People're saying there's a cat snatcher on the loose.'

'And, um, any clues what might have happened to them?'

'There's load of theories. They're being taken for their fur. Or to be cut up to be made into weird foreign medicines. Or maybe someone's got a grudge against cats and is just taking them to torture and kill...'

Ellie's creative, if not sensitive, flow was stopped by a new burst of sobbing from Charl.

'Let's see if we can help get Hector back then,' Florence heard herself say. 'I might just have an idea.'

Tyson lived on the outskirts of Cambridge. Like so many, he had been priced out of the historic centre by the dizzying ascent of house prices into the unreachable stratosphere.

As she pedalled into the anonymity of the suburbs, Olivia noticed the rhythm of the bike was no longer a consistent *WTF?* And, at one point, she caught herself humming what she thought was a number one hit from her childhood days.

This was an area she didn't know. The houses were modern, iden-tikit, and as regimented as soldiers on parade. Brownfields and bulldozers were never far away, symbols of the insatiable growth of the city.

The area was so new that her phone said she was cycling in a field, and Olivia wasn't quite sure which house she was heading for. But as she turned into Rosehip Street, and pedalled slowly along, she knew the place immediately.

It was the house at the end of the cul de sac, the one with the electricity pylon looming like a mugger high above it.

With some smiles, warmth, making of tea and promises of help, Florence managed to get Charl and Maddy sitting together on the sofa and communicating. She pushed the table full of pictures of the much-lamented Hector aside. They weren't helping.

If anything, Florence was surprised by how quickly Maddy was persuaded out from her pit of misery. The conversation, kindness, and reassurances felt like a kind of ritual, something that was expected, but not really necessary.

After promises of being allowed on the school trip to Italy, along with a new pair of shoes for the summer, she uncurled herself and rejoined the world without too much protest. This was a teenager who was more like a twenty-something.

It was also interesting how little Maddy was like her mum. Once the scowl had been soothed away, a beautiful young woman broke through. She had the sort of eyes that, in the years ahead, would make men walk into lamp posts, and perhaps already did. They matched the liquid darkness of her hair and shade of her skin.

Florence already had a notebook bloated with information about the disappearance of Hector and the other cats. It made for quite a story. She hadn't been able to restrain her growing excitement and had sent Ed, and the others, a message to tell them.

Onto a great one. Really good story. Lots of emotion and mystery. Think it could make an excellent lead for the first edition.

Just as she expected, a message quickly came back from Ed.

Brilliant work. We've got other interesting stories, but no splash of a lead yet, and we really need one. Can't wait to see it.

One feature of the story kept coming to her, irresistible, no matter how much she might try to dampen it. All the vanished cats were known to prowl the Victorian cemetery behind Millhouse Road. One of the more extreme neighbours, the elderly and eccentrically dressed Mrs Eustace, had apparently claimed ghosts were responsible for the disappearances.

Florence could see the headline, bold and illuminated, in her imagination. It was clickbait from dreamland.

She was staying a little longer to see Chris, as even Maddy called her dad; another oddity in this offbeat family. He was a police officer, and on his way home from work. A quote from authority should round off the story nicely.

The way the women spoke about Chris was, however, a little unsettling. With Charl, there was a clinginess, almost desperation, the implication of trouble if Florence left without speaking to him. With Maddy there was a pronounced curl of the lip, which felt more than just teenage disdain for a crusty parent.

'Yeah, you've got to meet him,' she said. 'My brilliant dad.'

The sarcasm could have stripped the paint from the walls. Ellie muttered some disapproving noises, but they were half-hearted at best. And with both Maddy and Charl, at the mention of Chris, there were glances behind, as though they were being watched.

Then there was Charl's make-up. Far too heavy for an ordinary day. Applied not to enhance, Florence suspected, but to hide. If all families hid secrets, those that ran beneath the surface here felt particularly unpleasant.

She had also met Alan, the next-door neighbour who had lost his cat. He was a balding, nondescript man of standard build and height, wearing ordinary clothes. It was as though blending in was his only desire in life. A statistician in need of an average human would have loved him.

It took Ellie and Charl a while to coax Alan into the house. 'Chris isn't going to come home, is he?' the man kept asking.

It was only the intervention of Maddy which eventually swayed the argument. 'Please, we really need you. You wouldn't turn your back on us, would you?'

'Nice,' Florence breathed to herself, admiring the wiles of the old-before-her-time teenager. But the appeal worked, even if it prompted a curious look from Alan; a mix of knowing and fondness.

When Alan finally found the courage to step into the family home, he was rewarded with long hugs and shared consolations from Maddy and Charl. Maddy started crying at more talk of Hector, and grabbed Alan for comfort. With a fine flounce of teenage melodrama, she proclaimed, 'He's my only friend in the whole world.'

It was far from clear whether she was talking about Alan or Hector.

'Elsa, she's mine,' Alan said, passing over his phone. The screen was filled with a portrait of a predatory-looking ginger beast who exuded a bad attitude. 'She's always fighting,' he added, to explain the missing half an ear. 'But she's got a heart of gold.'

Florence didn't comment, instead restricted herself to an understanding smile.

Alan knew Hector well, along with most of the other cats who had disappeared, and was also familiar with a large part of the local dog population. 'I'm a pet groomer,' Alan explained. 'That and a poet. And yes, before you say it, I know that's a strange mix. Writing's my passion, but you can't make it pay. Hence the combination.'

He nodded to the pictures of Hector on the table. The gesture acted like a cue and set Maddy off into another cascade of tears.

More shared lamenting and consoling followed, which lasted for quite a while. Alan was about to leave, to work on a poem in memory of the missing cats, when the door flew open.

A large flushed man strode into the room. 'What the hell's going on?'

14

If Tyson had been named after the boxer, it could only have been with gleeful irony. He was reedy, pasty, and dressed in a shirt and trousers which both looked as though they'd been handed down from a much larger brother.

'I'm not talking to you,' was his welcoming opening gambit, as he stood defensively in his doorway.

'You are,' Olivia pointed out.

'Are you threatening me?'

'No. Just being factual. You are talking to me. I said hello, you said you're not talking to me. But that's a contradiction. You clearly are talking to me.'

Tyson's eyes narrowed. 'I meant on the record.'

'I don't want you on a record. I want you on the news.'

'Blimey, Rick said you were something.'

It was Olivia's turn to pause. 'Of course I'm something. You're something. We're all something. Everything's something. That's called existence.'

'Whatever, I'm not going on the news.'

Tyson shuffled backwards and looked about to close the door, so Olivia tried, 'Are you ashamed of your hobby? Rick said you loved it.'

'I do. It's just… mine. No-one else needs to know.'

'That's a shame.'

'Why?'

'I thought it was fascinating. So original.'

Tyson hovered in the doorway, balanced between suspicion and interest. 'Are you taking the piss?'

'Not at all. My hobby's computing. Look at how yours stacks up. You're outdoors all the time. You go to some beautiful places. It must be quite an adventure to get to some of them. You keep fit and you get a sense of fulfilment at the end of the day when you've collected more numbers. How many have you got?'

'You really want to know?'

'Yes.'

'Twenty-seven thousand.'

'Out of?'

'Eighty-eight.'

Olivia did a quick mental calculation. 'So you're thirty-point-seven per cent of the way there.'

'Something like that.'

'Precisely like that actually. Are you going to complete the set?'

Tyson nodded hard, with an unexpected steel of purpose. 'You bet I am. Every single one. Including them that some say are impossible. I've even applied for permission to get into nuclear power stations to…' He stopped himself. 'But like I said, I'm not talking to you. I'm not falling for one of your tricks, like no pull-up contest.'

'That's a double negative. Which makes a positive. I had to teach your brother-in-law about those too.'

'Jesus, you really are something. Anyway, whatever. Leave me alone. I don't want to talk to you. That's a single negative. Clear enough?'

Given Tyson's less-than-mighty frame, built from pipe cleaners and straw, more pull-ups seemed like an unfair challenge. But Olivia sensed there was a better way. The man with the strange hobby that was made for a compelling *Last Edition* feature, still couldn't quite close the door on her.

The small, stark white and very modern house had that feel of the single occupant. It was a little hollow, not quite filled with the people and possessions that made a home.

'I imagine you don't get to talk to many people about what you do?'

'So?'

'Wouldn't you like to? I can see how much you love your hobby. And maybe we could help with that?'

'Yeah? How?'

'I thought we might follow you in your quest. Immortalise it. Chart your progress towards the eighty-eight thousand.' And when Tyson didn't look convinced, she went on, 'You could make the hobby really popular. Help thousands of people get fit and have fun at the same time. Wouldn't you like some company on your adventures? You could be the leader of a whole new movement. A hero for our times.'

Tyson stared at her. 'You really for real?'

'See previous discussion. We're all something, and thus for real. Really. So how about it? Fame and fortune? You immortalised as a man of the moment. Recognition at last for the simple brilliance of your wonderful hobby.'

'Jesus, shit. You're not leaving until I talk to you, are you?'

Olivia didn't have to answer that. Just stood there, so slight in body, but utterly indomitable in her purpose. As so many had found before, there really was no answer to her.

The poor browbeaten and befuddled Tyson shook his head, pulled open the door and beckoned Olivia inside.

Yet again, life had turned on her. Once more and yet again. And just when it looked like she had a break, Florence reflected, as she stood outside the house. She should have known better than to think she might actually be winning for once.

'I told you before I don't want you in here, you pervy piece of shit,' the beast of a man yelled at Alan. He performed an impromptu holding up his hands and cowering dance, before slipping quickly away, rapidly followed by Ellie.

Maddy and Charl sat quietly on the sofa, eyes down, not daring to interrupt, their only comfort reaching out for each other's hands. 'What the hell's your story?' Chris barked at Florence. And despite her best soothing smile and calming voice, she too had been summarily ejected.

'We don't want any reporters, or news nonsense. I have enough of that shit in my bloody job. We'll sort out what's happened for ourselves, thank you. Now fuck off and don't come back.'

Charming, Florence thought, but didn't say. No wonder everyone who knew him seemed to be living in fear of the wrath of Chris.

And that was that. Defeat snatched from the jaws of victory. Again.

Yet again.

Just when she had been sure she had a story to lead the debut *Last Edition*. The first ever front page, found and written by her; a splash striking enough to draw in thousands, maybe tens of thousands of readers.

A story that would provide a memorable launch for the newswire and ensure its continued survival, growth, and success. One that would make Ed, Mitch and Olivia proud, and keep at bay those dark and dangerous thoughts Florence knew they all suffered. A glorious story to hold them together and keep them working as one for the months ahead.

Her strange new family, as Florence had quickly, if unspokenly, come to think of the others. Fellow sufferers in life, but also hopeless optimists, united in the endless pursuit of hope.

She let out a long sigh, glanced at the sky, shook her head and began walking slowly back to the office.

15

It might actually be happening. It could even become a reality. What felt so many times like a stupid dream, an impossible gamble, was forming right here in front of him.

The newswire was coming together, and much better than he had dared to hope.

That word again, Ed thought, from his station at the window, looking into the labs and out on the world. The word he loved and hated, admired and feared. The word which had tempted him out from the shadowlands of life. The word which had brought them all together, and which now had wrapped them up in its fickle embrace.

Something was wrong with Olivia. Or, perhaps, it would be more accurate to say that something had changed.

She sat at a computer, Mitch beside her, watching as she set out the newswire. But her face... her face for the world wasn't set quite so battle hard as usual. There was a crinkling at the corners of her mouth, which might just – just – have been the precursor to a smile.

And if Olivia smiled, Ed thought, *that would be a story in itself*.

'I still can't believe you got him to talk,' Mitch said. 'I don't think I'd want the world knowing about a hobby like that.'

'It was simple logic,' Olivia replied. 'I inputted what I thought he needed and kept refining it until the experiment worked. It was a kind of human equation.'

'Some might call it empathy,' Ed observed. And waited, waited, waited, but there was no snap of a rejoinder. Not even a fading of those crinkles around her mouth.

Joy in the little things. It was always the little things. He exchanged a look with the plant, imperceptibly yet busily growing on the table, and wondered if he saw a slight nod of agreement.

Not only had Olivia tracked down and brought home her story with all the persistence of a veteran hack, she had written it up in a few minutes, and written it well. And before she'd even left the labs, she had set up the hosting and all that technical, online, updating, interactive, easy to use but impossible to understand functionality stuff that was required for a newswire.

Now she was teaching them how to lay out the paper. Getting a little frustrated when Ed and Mitch took more than milliseconds to understand certain functions, but teaching them nonetheless.

Her story would take up the entire mid section, but with a big tease on the front page. Olivia had somehow managed to borrow dozens of photos from Tyson, and they were clamouring to be highlighted.

'A small one for the front, to whet the readers' appetite,' Ed said. 'Maybe that selfie he took under the pylon on top of the forest? Then the main splash inside.'

Is This the World's Strangest Hobby?

It caused some debate, that headline. But Ed, as editor, overruled the objection.

'I don't want Tyson to come out looking like a weirdo,' Olivia said. 'I promised he wouldn't.'

'Is that an option?' Mitch asked.

'We don't say he is strange,' Ed pointed out. 'We just... pose the question. And questions always make good headlines. It'll definitely get people reading, and that's what we need. Mitch?'

'I'm with you. Isn't that our job? Anticipating what people will ask?'

'You can deal with Tyson if he complains then,' Olivia said.

'You really are getting the hang of empathy,' Ed replied.

He'd given the three staff writers of the *Last Edition* a rundown of how journalists build stories. The importance of the opening line, a structure where the most interesting information comes first, and some zingy quotes to spice up the story. Ed still, however, expected to have to do a considerable amount of rewriting as they all learnt the trade together.

But no. Not a bit of it. Not with Mitch and Olivia carried along on currents of conviction like these.

Some collect stamps, others spot trains. But Tyson Barton is proud to enjoy what might be the strangest hobby of all.

'Great opening,' Ed said. 'It draws the reader right in. Now let's hit them with a photo.'

'They're worth ten thousand words in this case,' Olivia observed, quickly getting over her attack of empathy.

They chose a picture of Tyson standing underneath a pylon next to the River Thames, the cityscape of London grey and cluttered behind. He could have visited St Paul's, Buckingham Palace, so many museums, historic buildings, and art galleries, but no. In the heart of England's capital, this man had a very different mission.

Tyson collects the serial numbers of electricity pylons.
Yes, that's right. You did read correctly. He collects the serial numbers of

those gangly steel towers you see everywhere around you, but hardly ever notice.

It was time for another photo, this one of Tyson by a pylon next to a magnificent lake shining in the sun.

Each pylon has its own unique identifying number. And Tyson has set himself the mission of collecting every single one in the United Kingdom.

'It must be time for a quote or two,' Mitch said. 'Readers will be wanting confirmation that he's as weird as they're thinking.'

'I suppose it's important every workplace has someone in charge of the obvious,' Olivia replied, without even deigning to look at him.

'I know some people might find it strange,' Tyson told us. 'But look at the benefits. You get to travel to some amazing places. You get lots of exercise, and it's quite a challenge to track down some of the most out of the way pylons. And pylons really are beautiful if you take the time to get to know them.'

'Sorry, he's not as weird as I thought,' Mitch muttered. 'He's weirder.'

The next photo was another selfie, of Tyson under a pylon next to a busy motorway. For this caption, they added a rundown of the tools of his trade. A map, a camera, and the longest selfie stick money could buy.

Believe it or not, Tyson is far from alone. He's a member of the Pylon Appreci-ation Society. The club take photos of the pylons they've ticked off their lists and post them online.

. . .

'You write like Hemingway,' Ed observed. 'Short and sharp, and with a lovely sting of ironic humour.'

'I doubt Hemingway was ever moved to write about electricity pylons,' Mitch said.

'Shut up,' Olivia told him, then to Ed, 'Is that a compliment?'

'Very much so.'

It took a second to check for mockery, sarcasm, or some hidden jibe. But when the simple everyday reply came, it was straight and very human. 'Thank you.'

After a few more photos, they left the last words of the story to Tyson himself. It was, Olivia said, only right, and something she had promised she would include, the reason he had agreed to be interviewed.

'The only thing missing from my lovely hobby is someone to share it with. If any women out there fancy coming pylon spotting with me, they'd be very welcome.'

Mitch's story would be the second lead, a testament to its power and emotion. Ed's own write up of Swift and the labs would be safely buried somewhere towards the back, only to be found if a reader was having a seriously slow day.

Which wasn't to say Swift wouldn't hunt it out and gleefully forward it on to his bosses at the bank seconds after publication.

The Economic Engine of the Future

There are many like it. But none quite the same.

'Now who's the Hemingway?' Olivia asked, making Mitch grin.

'I thought it worked as an opener,' Ed replied, a question in his voice.

'It does,' replied the slight young woman in the denim jacket who had apparently become the style guide of the *Last Edition*.

In a quiet corner, on the edge of Cambridge, stands a nondescript building. Thousands pass by without ever suspecting what goes on there.

But within, buzz fine minds and entrepreneurial spirit, the next generation of business leaders for the nation.

Mitch said, 'Swift will be pinning copies on his bedroom ceiling and–'

'Enough,' Olivia interrupted. 'Decency. Humanity. Empathy. Please.'

Ed's report described some of the businesses based in the Falcon Labs, including quotes and a couple of pictures. He praised the great institution for not just backing tech companies, the norm in this city, but those with a creative bent too. Then, as he put it, came the moment they had all been waiting for.

And the driving force behind this quiet but impressive economic powerhouse? Step forward Aaron Swift.

The man himself stared out at them. Swift was doing his best to appear imperious, but it wasn't a look which suited him. The photo gave the impression that someone had farted badly in the near vicinity.

. . .

Don't be fooled by Mr Swift's youth. He was selected specially for this position as the bank invests such money, time, and hope in the labs.

Mitch laughed. 'Make that pinning copies to his bedroom walls as well.'

'I'm proud to lead such a wonderful team of new businesses,' Mr Swift told us. 'I know the future of the economy is safe in their hands.'

'If he gets knighted, we'll hold you responsible,' Olivia said.

'It's bought us a reprieve on the rent,' Ed replied. 'I think it's just about worth it.'

'Do you think we should mention we're part of the labs as well?' Mitch asked. 'Out of journalistic integrity.'

'Of course. In the smallest print we can find, right at the end.'

He was trying to be cool, a little detached, like a true editor. But inside, Ed was smiling, and couldn't stop glancing at the words on the board.

Thinking, feeling, writing

It was incredible that only a day earlier, an ordinary Monday, this crazy experiment had begun. By today, he had a team, and they had found their stories. Already, they had enough news for the debut *Last Edition* to be released tomorrow. If all went well, hopefully into the waiting arms of thousands of eager readers.

After Steve bought some advertising, a couple of other businesses in the labs had shown solidarity and done the same. All the contributors had been told as well. They would receive a link as soon as the newswire went live, and had promised to forward it on to everyone they knew.

Ed had used some of the money from the advertising to buy a few adverts of their own, to give the paper its best possible start. All around

Cambridge, from buses, to billboards, on the radio and in local newspapers, the word would spread.

Mitch had got in touch with everyone they, this small team, knew, and anyone in the labs who would play along. He'd sent out messages asking for support, and for the link to the paper to be forwarded on, and on and on.

As for Olivia, she had a social media bombardment all ready to go. Posts full of teases would fill the Internet like an electronic blizzard. She had also set up a countdown for the *Last Edition* website, running busily towards launch, and all helping to build anticipation and interest.

In a voice choked with feeling, Ed thanked them for their efforts. 'I think we're good to go,' he said with great British understatement.

He thought he could see it. He could certainly sense it. And he knew the others did too.

Thinking, feeling, writing

So they looked at each other. And although no-one said it, each knew what they were all thinking. Because every time the screensavers kicked in, they wouldn't hesitate to reach out and immediately restore the debut pages of the *Last Edition* to their desktops.

All that remained was the front page, waiting for Florence, and her grand splash of a story. Which would complete this inaugural edition and help it make the impact they would never have thought possible.

Which they sat, and talked about, and analysed, and talked about some more, and couldn't help anticipating.

Right up until the moment Florence returned.

16

Like a king in a turret of medieval times, the window really was a perfect vantage point.

To watch over the labs for any signs of a predatory fast-approaching Swift. To keep an eye on the *Last Edition* team, currently Mitch and Olivia, sitting together and debating the finer details of the layout of a page. And to watch the outside world of this late Tuesday afternoon.

Whether it was the mums and dads with their children newly out of school and full of energy – or resentment – as they were dragged around the shops. The older couple who must have been married for fifty years, but still toddled along, hand in hand.

Ed smiled. The little things. It was always the little things.

The queue of cars at the traffic lights; building and waning, building and waning in the rhythm of a modern city. The endangered species of the grocer, standing proud by the colour palette of his wares, welcoming each of his customers by name.

Or Florence, appearing around the corner and walking quickly into the labs.

Ed just had time to say, 'She's here,' before Florence reappeared on the street and walked away again, just as quickly.

'And something's wrong,' he added.

'What?' Mitch replied.

'Come on.'

Ed led the charge, the three of them jogging past the other desks and watching faces, tumbling down the stairs and out of the labs in pursuit.

They ran round the corner to find Florence ahead, standing on the old stone bridge, staring out at the river.

'Shit,' Mitch grunted, because he knew that look better than anyone. 'Not Florence. Shit, shit, shit.'

'Couldn't have put it better myself,' Ed replied. 'Gently now.'

'WTF?' Olivia whispered, almost to herself.

Carefully, quietly, step by step, they approached. But it would have made no difference if they'd sprinted and yelled.

Florence was a prisoner of her own misery. She had eyes only for the slow flowing waters and didn't even register the existence of her colleagues. Ed to her far side, Mitch to the near, Olivia behind her, gradually they encircled this lost woman and waited.

Still Florence stared, her unfocused gaze fixed upon a floating log winding its way with the current. It was almost under the water, like a drowning swimmer, mostly submerged, just hanging on to that last, desperate, fragile link to hope.

'It's not that bad,' Ed said eventually, because he couldn't think of anything else. Then added, 'Whatever it is.'

'Yeah,' Mitch added. 'We're here for you.'

Florence slowly shook her head. 'And that just makes it worse.'

Another moment's silence settled between them. Then Olivia, newcomer to this world of empathy, snapped, 'What the hell're you talking about?'

'She means let's go and have a chat,' Mitch said before the outburst could gather momentum.

He laced a gentle arm around Florence, but she might as well have been one of the carvings on the bridge. She resisted hard, with a strength born of despair. Her body was both immobile and cold, despite the easy warmth of this early spring day.

'Please,' Ed said, adding his own arm to the hopeless embrace, and trying not to recoil at the deathly rigidity he found. 'We can sort it out, whatever it is. We're a team.'

'You're a team,' Florence replied. 'I'm just… what I always am. A failure. A jinx. A liability. A Jonah. I should never have come along, never have inflicted myself on you. You were relying on me, and I–'

'Please,' Mitch interrupted, the pain of a fresh and unexpected wound in his voice. 'Don't say that. No-one thinks that.' He ignored Olivia, who let out a hiss and looked away. 'Whatever it is, at least give us a chance to sort it.'

But Ed noticed Mitch was looking beyond Florence and down at the river too. In just that way he had on Monday, when he stared into its depths and tossed his coin.

Back in the office, Florence sat at her desk and continued her gazing into space. One either side, as they had been on the bridge, Ed and Mitch gently teased the story out of her. Olivia stood by the whiteboard, arms folded tight, denim armour wrapped close around.

Florence wasn't crying, but the dam was close to breaking. Her eyes were inflamed and watery, and her dark skin was oiled with a layer of sweat. The tears were within and edging ever closer to the surface.

'I'm sorry,' she kept repeating. 'I know you were relying on me. I thought I had the story. And it was great. Just what we needed. I was so happy. For once, something had worked out for me. And then…'

That was the trigger. The sobs crashed through the thin defences of restraint and slid down her face. And Florence collapsed into herself, trembling wreckage of humanity spread across a desk.

Mitch cuddled, Ed provided tissues, then they reversed roles. Both whispered the best soothing lies they could manage.

It's okay, we weren't depending on you. We've got lots of other stories lined up. We can use another one for the front page. We can put off the launch if we need to. It'll all be fine.

But even to the two men, the words sounded pathetic. They had no other stories. The missing pets, however strange, would always attract the readers they needed in this cat-crazy society.

They couldn't put off the launch. They had marched the troops up to the top of the hill, and pinned their colours on a day and date. They would have no credibility, no backing, nothing if it didn't happen when they said it would, in just the way they had promised.

That was business. The way of the world.

And Florence knew it. Knew it all too well.

So nothing could make any inroads into the hopelessness of the woman strewn across the desk. And then there was Olivia, absorbing every sentence like she was gorging herself on gunpowder, and growing more dangerous with it.

First it was intakes of breath, edgier and edgier, then mutterings. Growing harsher as each new sob filled the room. Soon a little pacing started up, a couple of steps, back and forth, but ominous as the dull beat of thunder.

When Mitch tried, 'We'll get through it somehow. We'll work it out together,' Olivia's own fragile restraint, equal and opposite to that of Florence, exploded.

'Like fuck we will!' she yelled. 'I'm out of here, you bunch of losers.'

'Hey...' Mitch tried, but that was as far as he got. One word, a single breath, his attempt at calming smashed aside.

And anyway, he had no spirit for it. That look was back in his eyes, Ed could see, and the shadows of gauntness had returned to his face. His hood was already up around his neck, and Mitch was close to pulling it over his head once more. Hiding away in the safety of the thick drape, running for his barge and his love affair with that fatal temptress, the river.

'She says she should never have come,' Olivia went on, flinging an arm of contempt towards Florence, still prone on the desk. 'Bollocks to that. Bollocks to her, bollocks to all of you. It's me who should never have come.'

The tornado tilted and spun towards Ed, propped on the desk next to Florence, unable to do anything except listen and hurt.

'I should never have taken any notice of your crap, and your dreams, and your fantasies. Hot air and wank, that was all it was. Hot air and wank. Hope, I can offer you all hope. I can brighten your dark dawns. Follow me on the glorious path to hope, let me restore you, blah, blah, blah, like some fucking modern-day messiah. Yeah, right. We'd be better off following the yellow brick road. A charlatan, that's what you are. A charlatan and a fantasist.'

Mitch had no strength to intervene. Florence was lost, able only to quietly sob into the desk. And as for Ed, perhaps he didn't want to defend himself. His glasses were misting over again, although this time with the darkest of emotions. And he was wondering if what Olivia had to say – to yell, to be more accurate – could be true.

'Getting our hopes up like that. Giving us something to believe in. Then smashing them all down again. That's beyond cruel, that is. It's fucking sick, if you ask me.'

There was movement behind them, in the other world of the labs, wary but irresistible. People standing to watch, edging towards this corner, theatre of quite a drama, unprecedented in this quiet, orderly and efficient place.

'Look at her,' Olivia went on, gunning laser eyes over Florence. 'Look at all of you. Look at yourselves. What a bunch of fuckwits. Losers United, that's what you are. It's a bloody good game you talk. Get out there and find stories. Use your wits and charm. Be bold and persistent. Yeah, right. I found myself a story, didn't I? Had to go hunting for the fucking thing. It didn't come to me, did it? And even when I found it, I had to work for it.

'Do pull-ups against some sad twat who was only interested in getting into my knickers. Stand in front of his gang of wankers and face them down. Jesus! And then I had to persuade an even sadder twat to talk to me about his crappy freak show hobby. *Oh yes, I can see why you find electricity pylons so interesting.* Talk about talking shit! I'm surprised I didn't have mushrooms growing on me, I was so full of crap. But I did it, didn't I? Just like you asked. I brought the story back. And what does she do, the moment she hits a problem? Bends over, gives up, chucks it in and goes running home. For fuck's sake!'

The little things, this really was a moment that demanded comfort in the little things. The budding plant, sitting there on the table, was no help for once. It was directly in Olivia's firing line and had tucked in its leaves to shelter from the fusillade.

Thinking, feeling, writing

That would have to do. The artistry of the letters he had written on the whiteboard. It was hard to believe that was earlier that day. It felt so very much longer ago.

Olivia had listened to one thing, at least. She was certainly feeling.

'Do you know what really pisses me off?' she went on. 'I let myself start to believe. I actually let myself start to believe in you and your cock snot circus. For fuck's sake! What was I doing? I should've known better. All the bullshitters and the braggers and the bollocks merchants I've met in my life, and I actually fell for your crap. I could punch myself in the face for that.'

A small crowd had gathered at the doorway to the office. They were busily engaged in the traditional British ritual of exchanging looks but not saying anything.

There was a brief outbreak of silence in the theatre of battle, a precious respite while Olivia reloaded.

Mitch, a fist clenched, used the moment to lift his head from the desk and grunt, 'Enough.'

'No, it is not fucking enough. Nowhere close. I've hardly started yet.'

Mitch was on his feet, a raptor's look in the darkness of his eyes. He stalked towards Olivia, closing the space between them fast. 'Give Florence a break.'

'Yeah, right. Fuck that. Fuck all of you. Fuck off, you bunch of fucking losers. Who's giving me a break?'

'I will. Happily. What part do you want broken?'

'Mitch,' Ed warned, stepping towards him, remembering how the man had swung a fist at him on the barge.

'Stay out of this. It's time someone taught her some humanity.'

Olivia had angled herself side on, in a crouch, a classic defensive position. 'Like you're man enough for that.'

'You two, enough,' Ed said, positioning himself between them.

'Fuck off,' Mitch replied.

'Yeah, fuck off the both of you,' Olivia added.

They glared at each other from either side of Ed's substantial frame. The crowd at the door was silent, waiting to see what would happen. Even Florence had stopped crying and lifted her head. She was mouthing *No, no, no,* but couldn't find the spirit to make the words real.

Olivia was about to speak again, but was interrupted by a clipped, 'That will do.'

It was Swift, unlikeliest of saviours. He pushed his way into the room with surprising determination and stood, hands on hips, looking even more angular and disapproving than usual.

'Bollocks to you as well, mister fucking king fuckwit,' Olivia snapped, smiting away the manager's veneer of authority as if it were a mere fly. 'Uptight snooty effeminate twat.'

While Swift gaped and deflated, Olivia and Mitch continued their glaring. Ed kept them apart, and wondered what to do next. Seldom had the old saying about things not going according to plan rung more true. But help came from an unexpected source. It was a quiet but emotional voice which demanded attention like a cello striking up in the silence.

'You've made me sad.'

Steve, the programmer, sounded much worse than sad. It was a tearful heart-squeezing voice; as though he'd been abandoned by his family, friends, workmates, everyone in his street and the entirety of his city.

'I loved what you were doing. Those people you brought here. All of them came here hopeless, and went away with something to believe in. I saw it all. And I loved what you four were doing. With your writing and newswire thing.'

Steve was looking at all of them, but in particular Mitch. Who caught his eye in return and shook his head with what Ed thought was a message. But he had no time to pick up on the strange moment because Steve hadn't finished. And his words were having quite an impact.

'You touched me, you lot did. Right to the heart. That's why I put money into you. I thought you were great. Blooming brilliant and beautiful. Just the sort of thing we needed. That's here in the labs, and in life. And now...'

He didn't have to say another word. The staff of the *Last Edition* looked to each other, and then to themselves. It was all they needed to do.

When the population of the labs had drifted back to their own businesses, Ed did a quick round of visits to heal some wounds. But first, a trip to the toilets to splash some water on his face. His scar was throbbing, which was never a good sign, and his glasses were tinted with fog.

Following the principle of getting the worst of any ordeals out of the way first, next he made for Swift's office.

'I really should consider disciplinary action,' the manager huffed from behind his desk. 'I simply cannot have my authority challenged in such a manner.'

'Didn't you get it?' Ed asked, pulling his best puzzled expression.

'Get what?'

'Our little play.'

Swift frowned, skin wrinkling around his nose cone.

'It's one of the things we creatives do, as I'm sure you know,' Ed went on. 'We just love to role play. We had a newsroom meeting and it got a bit heated. So I stepped in and gave them all parts to play, to explore the range of our feelings and truly understand each other's motivations. Okay, it's a bit drama school and method acting, and the improvisation got a little out of hand. I will speak to them about that, of course. But overall, as a management and personal discovery tool, it worked really well. Didn't you think? I mean, no doubt you studied the technique at business school. It's all very modern, progressive, and popular. Just the sort of thing I imagine the bank is keen on.'

'Um, yes, of course,' Swift replied, after a calculating pause. 'Very effective indeed, I always find. But rein it in a little in future, will you?'

He tapped an angular finger on his far-too-tidy desk. 'By the way, how is the article on me – I'm sorry, I mean the labs – coming on?'

'You're not trying to interfere with our editorial independence, are you?'

More calculations followed, doubtless along the lines of how the bank would react to such a claim. 'Oh no. Of course not. Never. I believe most profoundly in a free press. One of the pillars of our great democracy, is it not?'

'It's okay. I was only joking.'

'Ah, I see.' Swift fiddled hard with his wedding ring again. This was even tougher to comprehend than role playing, emotions, and creatives.

'As for the article, it's looking great. I'm really pleased with it. I think you will be too. It's out tomorrow, as discussed.'

Next, Ed retrieved Florence's handwritten note from the *Last Edition* pigeonhole, but didn't open it. This wasn't a confessional, and some regrets should live forever in silence.

Then, Ed stopped at Steve's desk to thank him. 'I don't know what came over me,' the programmer said. 'I don't even chirp up much at our business meetings, let alone in a bear pit like that.'

'I'm very glad you did. It was a big moment. Without you, it might have gone a different way.'

'Always here to help, if you need me,' Steve replied in a way which felt strangely meaningful.

Back in the office, Ed found the team still silent, but at least sitting together. Which was a big improvement on earlier. Even the plant had opened its leaves again, bless it.

'Anything to say?' Ed asked from his customary station at the window.

There was some shrugging, but no words.

Olivia, from slouched down in her denim, managed, 'What's there to say? We're screwed. It's five o'clock. We've got no lead story and everything's set for the paper to come out tomorrow.'

When no-one disagreed, Ed said, 'What brought us together? That magical word?' And when there was still no reply, 'Say it. Come on. Don't be afraid of it. We were getting to like it, weren't we? What brought us together?'

'Hope,' Mitch relented.

'So, are you going to give up on hope so easily?'

Ed strode over to the whiteboard, making sure the words were above his shoulder.

Thinking, feeling, writing

'Did you really think it was going to be so easy? Do feelings only run one way? Is that your experience of life? Is it the way of the world? Do I need to keep asking rhetorical questions?'

The attempt at humour, however weak, produced a strange noise from Olivia. It was a kind of huff, mixed with a hiss.

But it wasn't a snarl, sneer, or another cannonball retort. Which Ed would take, for now.

The little things. It was always the little things.

'How did you feel last week? Before you saw my advert?'

'Shit,' Mitch offered.

'And the week before, and the week before that?'

'Even more shit.'

'And how did you feel yesterday morning? When you were on the way here, to find out what the advert was about? Florence?'

'Interested.'

'Just interested?'

'Maybe even excited.'

'And when you got my e-mails, saying you were in? Mitch?'

'Yeah, pretty good.'

'Flo?'

'Pleased.'

'Just pleased?'

'Okay, really excited.'

'Happy?'

Olivia said, 'Now you're pushing it.'

'Hopeful then?'

No-one disagreed, so Ed went on, 'And then when we all got together and went out hunting stories?'

'Your point being?' Olivia asked.

'That's the journey. That's life. That's the way it is with hope. It's not a smooth and easy stroll back into the world. Hell, it's not. My own journey... it was down into the canyons, up into the stratosphere. Down into the blackest pits of hell, up into the highest reaches of the heavens. And do you know what?'

'You love speechmaking?' Olivia said, which almost got a smile from Mitch. And Ed too, if he was honest.

'I love life. And the way it works. However hard it is. Whatever games it plays. However much it teases you. That's the way it is. Highs and lows. Smiles and frowns. Ups and downs. And I came to welcome the lows, because I knew the highs would follow. If I gave it time. And if – most importantly, if – I didn't give up.'

'Easy for you to say,' Olivia replied.

'No. No way. Not in the slightest. Not easy at all. I'm in this with you. I'm here with you. I'm journeying with you. Okay, I might have found hope again, but now I'm hunting a friend of hers. As I said to Mitch, maybe her best friend. Someone who walks hand in hand with her, and is just as mesmerising.'

Now, at least, there was interest. And maybe a little belief. Curious eyes. Engaged minds.

'Who?' Olivia asked. 'Or what? What are you hunting?'

'Later. I'll tell you at the end of this. When you've found hope again. And maybe I've found what I'm seeking. But let's get there first.'

'So, what're you saying?' Mitch asked. 'What can we do? Given we've got just hours until the paper is due to come out. And no lead story. No big splash to make the impact we need.'

Florence was fiddling with a pen, still not quite back with the world, so Ed asked her, 'How many cats disappeared?'

'Five that I heard of. Maybe more.'

'How many owners have we spoken to?'

'Two. The family I met and their neighbour.'

'So,' he turned to Olivia, 'You're the maths person. How many owners does that leave us still to work with?'

'Are you taking the piss?'

'I'm doing my thing, which – as you pointed out – is the speechmaking. You do yours.'

'I might need to check this, and I could do with a second opinion, but I'd say… one… two… um, hang on… three.'

'So, just because one guy tells us he doesn't want any publicity, what does that mean? It's only his view. What about the rest of his family? What about the others who've lost their cats? We've got three more owners to talk to, and a few hours to make the story work and get it ready for tomorrow. So come on, let's get going.'

But if Ed was hoping for a stampede towards the door, it failed to materialise. Florence was still looking shaky, Olivia at her favourite arms folded and militant station. Only Mitch was showing signs of life, and even that was an effort.

The shadows of the other way were stretching across the room. What it could – perhaps would – mean if these three were cast down again.

Not to mention himself.

'Come on, what are we waiting for?' Ed tried to rally them. 'The clock's against us and we need to start getting results. So this time, we don't go into battle alone. We take strength from each other. We're a team, remember? Mitch, you go with Florence. Olivia, you come with me.'

But still there was a notable lack of enthusiasm, and indeed movement. And this was the binary moment. It was a one or a zero, a yes or a no. So Ed lifted his voice and gave it his best Shakespeare: Branagh, Olivier and Gielgud, all in one.

'Are we going to give up? When we've come so far already? Stepped out of the shadows and stood together, ready to show the world what we can do. Faced down the darkness of the demons within. Begun our journey back to everything we want and all that we deserve. Stood tall and proud at last, no matter what the world has thrown at us. Or did I choose the wrong people? Should I have picked those others who came here, hoping for hope?'

It took several seconds, each and every one a long precarious twitch of the clock, but first Mitch, then Florence, and finally Olivia got slowly to their feet.

'One last chance, then,' Mitch said.

'One last chance,' Florence agreed.

Ed shepherded them from the office before any second thoughts could take hold. He tried not to look back and wonder how – perhaps if – they would return.

But at least they had a chance. The hope of hope was back. Life might just give them another ride after all.

Until, at the doorway, Olivia stopped and said, 'I've got a better idea. Why don't I go with Florence?'

17

Dusk suits Millhouse Road. It's the kind of place where ordinariness is frowned upon, mundanity marginalised. Patches of darkness mixed with splashes of light from the cafés, restaurants and bars, make for a layered, microcosm world of mystery and discovery.

They had marched along there, the standard bearers of the *Last Edition*, in two-by-two formation, not speaking the whole way. Ed tried to find out what Olivia was planning, but all she would say was, 'I'm on it, don't fuss.' And she and Florence had headed off into the twilight, Olivia very much in the lead, as purposeful as a torpedo cutting through the waves.

By a food stall, in its spill of light and plume of spices, Ed and Mitch stopped to work out their own plan. 'Did I get that right, the way I played it?' Ed asked. 'Back in the office?'

'You're not always as sure as you seem, are you?'

'Who is? I just felt trapped between the two extremes. With Florence so upset and Olivia so angry, I didn't know how to handle it.'

'Who would? Aren't emotions always the hardest?'

'Are you the one doing the rhetorical questions now?' Ed replied.

The two men almost exchanged half a smile. 'What's our plan then?'

'The guy who chased Florence out sounds like a bully. So let's go see what his neighbour says when he's not under the cosh.'

'And then the man himself?' Mitch asked, with a little too much enthusiasm. 'Now you're talking.'

'Depends on what we find.'

'What's Olivia up to, do you think?'

Ed thought for a second. 'You might as well try to predict next year's weather. And now I'm wondering whether it was right to let them go off together, with Florence so fragile and Olivia on a mission like that.'

'Do you think you could've stopped her?'

'Fair point.'

'I guess it's kill or cure.'

Ed nodded. 'Then let's hope for the latter.'

Not only had Olivia never had children, she had never even thought about having children, she realised. In fact, she had never even wondered what having children might be like.

Until now.

Florence was trailing a little behind, not quite keeping up, in a very sulky and childlike way. While it wasn't defiance, it wasn't exactly commitment either. More like a subtle rebellion of a very British type.

And it was, frankly, fucking annoying.

But, for once, Olivia said nothing. Didn't turn on the problem, confront it head on, with a snarl and a fiery look. Ways which, she had come to realise in the last two days, were her default mode, her go-to weapons of choice.

As they worked a way through the streams of people, heading home and heading out, she let the irritant run. Because another unexpected emotion was nagging away inside her. Ed had used the word, and – damn him, the perceptive, smart ass, cocksure piece of shit – he'd gone and got it absolutely right.

Empathy.

Not content with that unexpected new arrival, another emotion was surfacing too. At least, Olivia thought it was. It was hard to tell, to be honest, as it wasn't one she had much, if any, experience of.

Was it… could it be… guilt?

They reached the parade of shops which made up the heart of Millhouse Road. Olivia found a lee in the flow of people beside a postbox, and stopped, Florence just behind her. And there was a silence.

Florence had weaved her hands together in her lap and was looking at the pavement. Shit, it really was just like dealing with a chastened kid. For fuck's sake.

Olivia sighed. 'How are we going to find the other cats then?'

'The actual cats themselves?'

Another sigh, another caging of the temper. 'Okay, their owners. Or, if you really want to be that pedantic, probably their former owners, given that it's most likely the cats are dead.'

'I don't know.'

FFS. 'Then let's have a think.'

The ensuing silence, longer than the first, tested Olivia's patience even further. But it held.

Just.

'What shops – or stores – might cat owners – living near – this road – go to?'

'The vet's?'

Hell, it was hard not to sound patronising, but Olivia gave it a go. 'Good try, but the vet's is closed, so that's no use to us. Where else?'

'The pet shop?'

'Yes, that's possible, but one small problem. Have you seen a pet shop along here?'

This time there was no answer, just a slight shake of the head. And silence number three ensued.

.   .   .

Olivia let it run for a while, then snapped. 'For fuck's sake! I'm getting sick of this. Are you feeling sorry for yourself by any chance?'

And for the first time, there was an instant reaction and a return of life, full blooded and right back in her face.

'Brilliant. You got it. Well done. Frankly, yes I am. Or, if you want it in your terms, FFS! I fucking am. I try my best and nothing ever works. Okay? I give life everything I can and it always shits on me. I thought I had a break with you lot and the *Last Edition*, and that story I was chasing, and I screwed it. Just like I screw everything up. I made a big mistake. I started believing something might actually work out. Like that was ever going to happen. Not for me. Not for life's punch bag, poor old Florence, the woman everyone and everything likes to dump all their shit on. So yes, I am feeling sorry for myself. Well done, and thank you so much for pointing that out.'

There was defiance in that kind face, the hurt of decades, but painful frailty too. Florence's eyes were damp with tears, just like they had been on the bridge earlier, and her body was trembling.

Which left Olivia doing something she had never expected. Something alien and unknown.

Without thinking, or calculating, in a way that so wasn't her, she reached out and gave Florence a hug. Tentatively at first, but then with feeling; holding her and soothing away the hurt as best she could.

The world passed around them, no-one noticing the enormity of this small moment in the dark recess of a bright and busy street. On they hugged, on and on. Until Olivia gently freed herself and stood back. Facing Florence, although no longer with anger.

'There's something I want to say. Or maybe need to say would be more like it. I need to say sorry. I was wrong to go on at you like that. I shouldn't have done it. It's just that, well… I guess I'm not very good at emotions.'

Through the sheen of tears, Florence nodded, and found a smile. 'You can say that again. But maybe you're learning. Thank you. That means a lot.'

The two women looked at each other, then Florence found a tissue and began tidying her face.

When the patch up job was done, she said, 'By the way, I think we should go to the corner shop. Everyone runs out of food sometimes, don't they? I guess cat owners are just the same, and cats can really screech when they're hungry.'

Olivia gave her a look. 'Did you know all along that was what I was planning?'

'Do you know another thing about emotions and relationships?'

'Are we playing a questions game?'

'What do you think?'

Olivia almost smiled. 'Okay, you win. What's another thing about emotions and relationships?'

'It's good to know when not to answer a question.'

The café was conveniently across the road from their target. The windows were misty, and the gathering darkness helped to complete the disguise.

'Just like old times,' Ed said to himself, rubbing at his scar.

They'd chosen a table a little back from the window to make sure they weren't spotted. That was at Alan's insistence. He'd been so shocked to find them at his door that Ed feared he was going to faint. It was as though the secret police had come to arrest him for crimes against pet grooming.

But Ed could see his point. He and Mitch were plenty bulky enough to fill the doorway. And Mitch, with those eyes in blazing mode, must have looked like a demon calling in the dusk.

They'd explained what they wanted, leaving Alan breathless with the grip of a dilemma. He looked as though the two halves of his brain had divided into camps, and each was giving him passionate but contradictory advice.

Yes, of course he wanted to help them find his cat, not to mention next door's, and all the others which had disappeared. No-one who hadn't been through it could understand the misery of not knowing what happened to their beloved friend. And yes, he did have concerns about Chris. Plenty of them.

The mere mention of the name was enough for Alan to glance nervously towards next door, and urging them to keep their voices down. Yes, they could talk, he decided eventually, and after much persuasion. But no, it definitely couldn't be in his house.

That thought added to his distress as much as if an undertaker's van had turned up along with Ed and Mitch, ready to take him away. The thought of Chris knowing he was talking to them… Alan didn't want to think about it, let alone elaborate.

So they settled on the café, even if it was a little too close to home for Alan's comfort. But, as Mitch said, 'We'd like to keep an eye on this Chris.'

'He'll be out soon,' Alan replied. 'You can set your watch by him. Every night, about this time. You wait.'

Even in the clattering and homely safety of the café, sitting close around a small rickety table, Alan was nervous and fidgety. The strip of pale skin busily pushing its way through the hair on his head shone in the subdued light. But he was happy to talk about Elsa, albeit in a remorseful way.

'I really miss her,' he said, sharing a series of photos of his bare-knuckle boxer of a cat. 'She's more loving than she looks.'

'She'd have to be,' Mitch replied.

They borrowed some photos of the cat, and quotes from Alan, for the story. 'I thought Chris had scuppered that.'

'We have a quaint tradition in this country,' Ed replied, trying not to sound too pompous. 'The freedom of the press. No-one gags us. And especially not bullies.'

The words filled Alan with a little courage. He nodded approvingly as he sipped at his tea, a dishwater shade of Earl Grey. But then it was on to the more dangerous ground.

'Is this Chris as bad as we're getting the feeling?' Ed asked.

'Worse. Much worse.'

Alan was about to elaborate, but was halted by the sight of Maddy emerging from her door and heading out of the gate. It was a short and simple walk that she must have taken thousands of times before, but this felt somehow different from the norm.

She moved slowly, looking up and down the street the whole time, as though measuring how long it would take her to be out of sight from home. She was also wrapped up in a hat, coat and scarf, all of which looked far too warm for the mildness of the evening.

'What's that about?' Mitch asked.

'Trying to hide from the world. And making sure no-one's lurking there to grab her, I imagine,' Alan said quietly. 'With all she's going through, the poor girl's probably scared stiff of her own shadow.'

At her gate, Maddy paused, then walked fast along the street and turned into a side alley, out of their view.

'She's gone into the cemetery,' Alan said. 'It backs onto our houses. She walks around it quite a bit. I do as well. Lots of people do. It's the nearest bit of green space we have here. It's a good place for some peace, and she doesn't exactly get that at home.'

'Chris?' Ed asked.

'Chris,' came the confirmation in a voice that was a mixture of fear and loathing.

Alan scanned around the café, as if to be sure the man wasn't sneaking up on him. 'I hear noises,' he confided, leaning forward. 'Through the wall.'

'What sort of noises?'

'Shouting. Yelling. Screaming. Then worse. Much worse. Thudding. Crashing. Smashing. And crying.'

Mitch flexed his knuckles. 'You've called the police?'

'Oh yes. They've been round. But...'

'What?'

'He's one of them, isn't he? One of their own. You know how it goes. So nothing gets done. And it just goes on.'

'How long's it been happening?'

'Ages. Charl's always covered in bruises. She tries to plaster make-up over them, but everyone knows. And Maddy's always in tears. The poor girl. So young, so beautiful, so innocent… having to deal with that. It's outrageous.'

Tears were flowing and Alan made no attempt to hide them.

'Poor, poor Maddy. She deserves so much better. She's come round a few times asking for help. I've tried to think of things to make her life better. Cooked her some food, given her money, let her just sit and watch TV, or use the computer, anything so long as she's safe, away from her dad. But what else can I do? They're both lovely, Charl and Maddy. But the police don't want to know, and Chris is vicious. As for me… I'm not exactly a fighter.'

That was certainly true. Alan was having enough of a struggle holding his cup of tea steady.

He turned to look out at the street and flinched. As though a devil invoked by the mention of its name, the dreaded Chris was walking out of his door and striding off along the road.

'He's going to the pub. He does every night about this time.'

'If you're going to live a cliché, you might as well live it to the full,' Mitch noted.

It was only a couple of minutes after Chris had disappeared that Maddy returned home.

'Avoiding him, no doubt,' Alan said. 'And who could blame her? Chris is the sort of man who makes a place better by leaving it. But he'll be back just after closing time. And then I'll be woken by the shouts and screams. Again.' The misery of a man swirled his tea ruefully. 'I've tried ear plugs, and meditation music, but nothing shuts out that awful, awful sound.'

He looked about to elaborate, but Ed and Mitch were on their feet and heading for the door. 'Are you going to… do him in?' Alan asked.

'Not exactly,' Ed replied.

'Not yet, anyway,' Mitch added.

The flat was a time capsule of 1950s England, presided over by an anachronism of an owner. As *honoured guests*, nothing but the finest china would do, apparently. It was a little grimy, but, Florence mused, with the restoration of all her usual kindness, it was the thought that counted.

The living room tasted of dust and was cluttered with ornaments to the extent that sitting down anywhere was a risk. It wouldn't have been a surprise to find a decorative plate on the vintage sofa. She and Olivia lowered themselves carefully and listened.

Elizabeth fussed around them, talking intermittently about the weather and the loss of her beloved Regal George. The manager of the corner shop, the portly and excessively helpful Mr Askew, had directed them straight there. *I know the person, the very person to talk to. A true lady of this neighbourhood.* And Elizabeth had swept them from the doorstep and upstairs before they'd even had a chance to talk their way in.

'Anything if it might bring Regal George home,' she said in a clipped but sad tone. 'Simply anything.'

Florence and Olivia had to wait while Elizabeth changed her clothes and applied a little make-up in order to *receive them correctly*. They'd exchanged looks, sharply aware of the clock unwinding against them.

That small hiccup overcome, however, the story not only settled in their laps but purred happily in the process.

If the job of a journalist was to ask questions, they didn't perform brilliantly. Frankly, it was hard to insert a word into the endless flow. But if gathering information was the goal, they quickly became top scorers. And if people and pictures are the key to a story, then they were on the way to becoming champions.

Elizabeth was probably in her seventies, tall and properly upright, her hair tinted with purple. She and Regal George had been *happy together, just the two of them*, as she put it, for ten years. Their lives were domestic bliss until the terrible night the cat disappeared.

That stopped the monologue as surely as a guillotine falling. Elizabeth massaged her chest and just managed, 'I so miss him,' before diplomatically disappearing into the kitchen to make more tea.

Regal George eyed them from every wall. And he was a well-named creature. Apart from a splash of white, the cat was a block of the purest black, and in all the photographs, gazed magnificently down upon the camera as though it was one of his subjects.

'I fear I know what's happened to him,' Elizabeth said quietly, as she returned with a clinking tray filled with more refreshments. 'His fur. Look at it. That beautiful fur.'

Olivia and Florence duly did as they were asked and made the required approving noises.

'He's been taken to make a coat. I know he has. Poor Regal George, his life cruelly cut short in its prime for some selfish person's desire for a fashion accessory. Oh, poor, poor George.'

On the sofa, Olivia and Florence adopted understanding smiles. When words prove elusive, sometimes you just have to improvise.

'I miss his purring when we go to bed at night. His pretty yowling when it's time to get up in the morning. And his beautiful padding about the flat. I'm trying to keep a stiff upper lip, but it's hard. Oh, poor George.'

Elizabeth lapsed into a silence, the first the flat had known during Olivia and Florence's visit. The downcast queen of this small empire looked sufficiently upset to be contemplating suttee. If, that was, the remains of George could one day be returned to her.

Ever practical, Olivia asked, 'Can I take some photos of your pictures of George, please? For our article.'

'Anything. Anything if it might help to bring him home. Do you think there's a chance he might come back? I miss him quite dreadfully.'

Olivia was about to quote the harsh probabilities, but then remembered the strange new word she had got to know over the last two days. 'There's always hope,' she said, surprising herself with the feeling in her voice.

Elizabeth lived around the corner from Maddy, Charl, and the equally missing Hector, and knew the family. It was interesting that Elizabeth shared the apparently widespread opinion of the much-unloved Chris.

'I won't say too much about him, but he's a brute. An absolute brute of a man. And Maddy and Charl are both so pleasant. Maddy often comes round here and does a little cleaning for me. I don't really need anything done, but I find things, just to keep her here, and safe. A most charming young lady. She's like a daughter to me.' Elizabeth checked herself with a smile. 'Well, a granddaughter I suppose. Those poor girls, how they suffer with that awful man. I wouldn't be surprised if he had got rid of Hector just to spite them.'

The thought opened up a whole new window of misery for Elizabeth. 'What if that was the case?' she asked of no-one in particular. 'Might he have taken Regal George as well? Out of spite for... everyone. He is of that type.'

Olivia reassured her it seemed unlikely that was what had happened to the missing cats, although she would bear the thought in mind. But before the discussion could gain momentum, Florence intervened.

She had been busily writing down quotes – lots and lots of quotes – and said, 'What do you think should happen to whoever might have taken George, and the other cats?'

'Death!' Elizabeth declared, with all the certainty of her soul. 'I never understood why we abolished the death penalty in the first place. Here now, if ever there was one, is surely a case for bringing it back.'

Given what the mother and daughter went through, night after night, the appearance of two large men on the doorstep had to be handled carefully.

'Leave it to me,' Mitch said, easing Ed behind him. And when Maddy answered the door, he told her, with remarkable gentleness, 'We know how you're suffering. I'm former police myself. It's more common than you think. It can be dealt with, believe me. And we're here to help you.'

The girl looked him up and down, balanced between hope and suspicion. Like Florence before him, Ed noted the nascent beauty and the intelligence in Maddy's eyes. It hinted at the swift and shrewd calculations going on in her mind, which she had not yet learnt how to disguise.

'How?' she asked, like an adult speaking, never a fourteen-year-old. 'How can you help us?'

'No-one's listening to you, are they? No-one's believing you. No-one's wanting to get involved?' And when there was no answer, Mitch went on, 'We don't turn a blind eye to behaviour like that. You know it's wrong. We know it's wrong. So we'll help you sort it.'

With a tilt of the hips, Maddy angled herself in the doorway. She looked sidelong at Mitch in a manner few teenage girls would have been able to master. 'He's my dad.'

'And he can still be your dad. A proper dad. When he's learnt how a real dad behaves.'

In Mitch's shadow, Ed nodded to himself. The man in the hoodie was rediscovering that forgotten heart.

'You'd better talk to Mum,' Maddy said, as though remembering she was the junior partner in the relationship, officially at least.

'I think we'd better talk to both of you.'

They were escorted into the same living room where Florence had sat earlier. The pictures of Hector were still there on the coffee table.

Charl was sitting, watching television, which she didn't move to turn off. *And that*, Ed thought, *said so much in a single gesture* – or lack of it. The pride had been beaten out of her.

When Maddy introduced Mitch and Ed, Charl still didn't get up. Instead she said, 'You'd better get out. He'll kill you if he finds you here.' And when she saw Mitch's look, amended that to, 'He'll kill us then.'

'No, he won't. Those days are gone. I can promise you that.'

Ed added. 'He won't be back from the pub until after eleven. He'll be drunk and angry. The same as ever. Which means you'll get another beating. Just like always. Or…'

'Or what?'

'There is another way,' Mitch said. 'However impossible it seems. There is.'

Charl's look slipped back to the television. Against the façade of an ancient church, a couple were getting married in a haze of white dresses, smart suits and smiles.

How life enjoyed her ironies.

'We can't guarantee you a return to those honeymoon days,' Ed said, gently turning off the TV. 'But this can be dealt with quietly and effectively with no-one else knowing.'

'He's a good man, really.'

'They always are,' Mitch said. And let the words linger to make the weight of his meaning unmissable.

'Can you really help?' Maddy asked, sitting down beside her Mum and cuddling into her. The child had taken her over once more, as befitted the back and forth age of fourteen. 'It'd be, like, so amazing if you could. The best thing ever.'

'Yes. We can really help. And we will.'

'I don't want to lose my dad. But I don't want Mum to go on suffering, either. I want to do something.'

'You can. Let us help you.'

'How much'll it cost?'

'Nothing,' Ed said. 'Almost nothing. Just a photo, in fact.'

Sometimes you can tell the kind of people you're going to meet by the names they give their pets. And sometimes you can be very wrong in that assumption.

Florence expected Hannah and Izzy to be pompous, all too eager to show off their intellect and education. So it often went in Cambridge, home to some of the finest minds on the planet. But they turned out to be very straightforward, entertaining and likeable.

Elizabeth had directed them to this flat, just up the street from her own. Olivia, for all her knowledge of science, wasn't an all-rounder like her colleague. She hadn't reacted when the name of missing cat number five was passed on.

Florence smiled and recited, '"Macavity, Macavity, there's no-one like Macavity, There never was a cat of such deceitfulness and suavity. He always has an alibi, and one or two to spare: At whatever time the deed took place – MACAVITY WASN'T THERE!"'

'Did you write that?' Olivia asked, for once almost looking impressed.

'Not exactly. It was a fairly well-known writer called T. S. Eliot. The poem was a favourite of mine when I was a kid.'

Hannah and Izzy were the keepers of the mysterious Macavity. He was ginger, just as the story demanded, but slight and demure. Nothing like the sly bruiser of Eliot's imagination.

Izzy was an English teacher, but it was hard to imagine her keeping order in a class. She was diminutive and quiet, and almost as ginger as the cat she had named. Hannah was both louder and larger, with everything about her measured and exact.

She was, they discovered, an army officer. Which would explain the remarkably minimalist tidiness of the flat. Never had Florence seen a home so devoid of possessions. Even those that were permitted were regimented and orderly.

The décor left plenty to be desired too. The colour scheme might have worked in the mess, but not for a small second-floor flat.

Macavity had gone missing on the same night as most of the other cats. He patrolled the same grounds, often frequenting the cemetery. 'But don't start talking to me about that ghosts nonsense,' Hannah said.

With time against them, Florence and Olivia didn't stay long and didn't even sit down. Frankly, it wasn't the kind of place you would feel comfortable sitting in anyway. They explained their mission, hoped it might help restore Macavity to the couple, and secured some photos of the tom.

'He will come back, I know it,' Izzy said.

'I think we need to prepare ourselves for the worst,' Hannah replied. And Florence could all too easily imagine her giving a *casualty of war, gone-but-never-forgotten*-type speech when the two women were alone together.

'Do you know any of the other missing cats, or their owners, apart from Elizabeth and Regal George?' Olivia asked.

'Jones, he's owned by Ben and Vicky up the road. We often joke about Macavity being a literary cat, while Jones is a film star.'

'I'm sorry?'

'The Alien films,' Florence explained. 'Ripley's cat.'

Florence gave Olivia a look which suggested she shouldn't comment and perhaps upset the rapport. But she quickly realised that wasn't a risk. Olivia was too busy trying to find some logic in the way that people named their pets.

And failing. Badly.

Hannah nodded. 'They're out, Ben and Vicky.'

'You don't have a photo of Jones, I suppose?'

There followed some quick-fire exploring of the memory of her phone, and Izzy produced one. Jones was stretched out on a sofa, black and white, a little overfed, and as serene as a summer's day.

'We also know Hector. And Charl and Maddy,' Izzy went on.

There was an obvious name missing from the list, and Florence pointed it out. 'Chris as well?'

The silence that followed was one of those which, for an absence, reveals a great deal. It was Hannah who broke it, and with style. 'Wanker. Category one, grade-A, complete wanker.' Making Olivia nod in appreciation at the effortless machine gunning of abuse.

'Hey...' Izzy tried to intervene, but the military was on the march and not to be stopped.

'We, I, tried to help. I saw Charl and Maddy and said there were places they could go, things that could be done. They listened, or I thought they did, but they must have told Chris. The next thing I knew, he was round here. Talking crap, how I didn't understand what was really going on. Making threats. Like that sort do.'

Already impressively muscled, Hannah inflated further as she tensed with readiness for the fight. 'I told him it wasn't so smart threatening a British Army officer. He backed down double-quick time then, and we haven't seen him since. Typical fucking bully. Stand up to them and they wet themselves and go running. Funnily enough though, our car got vandalised the next night.'

'We don't know that was him,' Izzy said without any conviction.

'It was enough for me to put in some extra practice at work the next day.'

There was another silence, this time one of those where no-one wants to ask. Which, naturally, meant Olivia did. 'What were you practicing?'

Hannah smiled, but without a trace of warmth. 'Bayoneting.'

Downstairs in the street, safe from the thrust, turn, withdraw of any bayonets, Florence and Olivia found a quiet corner and took stock. They had everything needed for the report and the time was getting on for ten o'clock. All around them, darkness had settled in. It was time to head back to the office to write the lead story and compile the inaugural edition of the *Last Edition*.

They sent a message to Ed and Mitch to tell them, then started walking.

'We can make this work,' Olivia said. 'It's going to be okay. We're coming out tomorrow, as planned.'

And Florence, despite her sad experience of how life could always find a way to confound her, smiled. Optimism was always one of the toughest drugs to quit.

It took a couple of minutes for a reply to come through. And when it did, it made enough of an impact to leave the two women staring at the phone, their minds flying to Ed and Mitch and what they were doing.

Great work. Now get writing. We might be a couple of hours. And don't panic if we come back a little dishevelled.

He was a regular at the pub, that was for certain. In his mind, maybe the ruler of The Glorious Empire, as the place was named; ironically, given its modernity and shabbiness.

Chris was really living the cliché, indulging himself in all the irritating habits of the dedicated barfly. Never content to sit at a table in a corner talking quietly to his friends, he propped up the counter, holding forth to a small gang of equally tedious looking men.

And it was men. All men. Of course it was. Not just at the bar, but in the rest of the pub too.

Men in clusters watching the oversized TVs. Men in clusters drinking lager, only lager, and always lager. Men in clusters at the light show of a fruit machine. Men clustered outside in smoking huddles. This Tuesday night, the Empire was a throwback to a time long ago, but, despite this allegedly more civilised era, not yet extinct.

Chris didn't know them, the two men, covertly watching him. But given what was going to happen a little later, Ed and Mitch walked the occasional pass of the pub without venturing inside.

'Which is good with me,' Mitch said with feeling. 'The place would be better off being called Wankers' Bar.'

It was a kind spring night, one filled with T-shirts rather than coats.

Which was fortunate, because they had a couple of hours of waiting around to work through. Chris wasn't the type to leave before last orders.

'After a good ignorant discussion of politics, preferably as right wing as it comes. And football. And women, of course. Actually, "bloody women", no doubt.'

'I'm getting the feeling you don't care for Chris,' Ed replied. 'But seriously, one thought. We're way outside our brief here. We're only supposed to be producing a story for a newswire, remember? Not embarking on a crusade.'

'Could you let it go? Walk on by, knowing something like this was happening?'

Ed nodded. 'Pass up the opportunity to offer someone hope, you mean?'

'I wasn't going to mention that word. But it's true that you didn't do so well with your own retreat from life, did you?'

'Watcher to stakeholder again,' Ed replied quietly. 'It's not so easy to shut your eyes as you might think.'

It was only a five-minute walk back to Chris's house. Along the main road, left, and then left again. They passed the time walking the route and calculating the best place for what they were planning.

'Here,' Ed said, as they stood in a stretch of darkness between two streetlights. 'Those bushes me, that tree you, this spot. Pincer movement, surprise attack.'

'You've done this before, haven't you?'

'Once or twice.'

'That scar?'

'Another day. And another place for that. One battle at a time, soldier.'

Mitch chuckled. His eyes were the brightest Ed had seen, even through the darkness of the night.

'Keep it professional,' Ed warned. 'However much you might enjoy this. After the ambush, we haul our friend to the alley along the side of the church there for our chat.'

'Amen to that,' Mitch replied.

They returned to walking the street on the other side of the road from the Empire. Just two old friends, chatting away, heading back from veterans' five-a-side football maybe, or on the way to pick up their kids from a sports club. They did ordinary and unnoticeable well, this pair.

The night flowed around them. Groups of youngsters on the street corners, couples heading into and out of restaurants, bikes, cars and taxis speeding past. For all the high spirits, everything was genteel and restrained, as was the way with this city.

'I've got a question for you,' Ed said. 'Do you know Steve, the programmer?'

'IEvery pace we took was filled with dread. That each of us might be the one to glimpse the terrible unspeakable sight that would bring the search to an end.

But also, we hoped. That we might find a clue. A note maybe, perhaps a piece of clothing, anything that would lead us to Maddy and see her returned safe.

ed a couple of times. I like the guy. He seems to be on our side. But that's about it.'

They walked on, calm and slow. Letting the seconds tick by with the rhythm of their pacing.

'I've got a question for you. Is it going to work out, the newswire thing?' Mitch asked.

'I hope so.'

'You and that bloody word. I hope a lot of things. But will it? Really?'

'What do you think?'

'You've got one hell of a weird team together.'

Ed nodded. 'Present company included?'

'Me or you?'

'Both of us.'

'Can't argue with that.'

They dropped into a shop to get a bottle of water and a packet of biscuits. Back outside, Ed said, 'You know what? Yes, I think it will work. I've got faith in you all. And to be honest, I'm surprised by how much. But I guess we'll get a proper sense of it tomorrow when the first edition comes out.'

The time was nearly eleven o'clock. The Empire was almost empty, had run its time, as empires do. Only Chris and a couple of drinking buddies remained at the bar. The others who had emerged were all a little unsteady and concentrating hard on the challenging art of walking in a straight line.

'Perfect,' Ed said. 'Let's get into position.'

Along the street, Chris stumbled, heading right into the trap. He was whistling loudly, despite the hour, the darkened houses clustered around, and practicing his shadow boxing.

Through the bushes, Ed watched his approach. He tried to focus on the graceful shapes of the leaves, how the streetlights flickered through the cloak they cast around him. Memories whispered from the darker corners of his mind, thoughts of the other life, but he shushed them away.

Even so, Ed noticed he had reverted to the clinical, detached mode that had been trained into him. Yes, he was prepared for the fight. But in a calm, dispassionate and professional way.

Opposite him, hidden in the depths of the tree, he could just make out the shape of Mitch. Poised, tensed, and ready, a furnace filled with the heat of an anger which was only just under control.

All was ready, all was set. But, as Ed knew too well was the way of these things, then came a complication.

The arrhythmic click of heels announced the arrival of a young woman. She was tall with flowing hair. Dressed only in tight jeans and a spangly top, and grabbing onto cars, then a wall, to try to stay upright.

Unfortunately, what she mistook for a wall turned out to be a gate. Which withdrew its support, swung silently away and left her sprawled gracelessly on the pavement, a mess of arms and legs.

And that, in turn, presented Ed with a dilemma, and just a couple of seconds in which to resolve it. Blow the ambush and reveal themselves to Chris. Or defy all his instincts and leave the young woman struggling on the ground, perhaps at the mercy of a man who may have little mercy flowing through his veins.

But before he could move, Chris was with her. Helping her up, sitting her on the wall, finding her bag, his words carrying easily through the night.

'No worries, love, it's easily done. I'm always falling over on the way home from a night out. Don't you worry, I'm a police officer and I'll make sure you get home okay. What's your name?'

From the safety of the bushes, tense and ready to intervene, Ed watched a flawless performance of professionalism and citizenship. Jackie, as was her name, was calmed down, reassured, and given space to compose herself.

'A good mate's on duty tonight,' Chris told her. 'She's a top cop and she'll look after you. We're not supposed to do this, but hey. What else is the job for?'

He made a call and within five minutes a police car drew up. The woman at the wheel got out, was introduced, and also made some soothing noises. Jackie, full of apologies and thanks, was gently helped in and waved off.

Through the leaves, Ed could see Mitch open his arms and pull a face. *What do we do now?* could have been written on his expression.

Chris watched the police car disappear around the corner before resuming his journey home. He was walking remarkably easily, unperturbed by the ballast of alcohol, the mark of the practiced drinker.

Alongside them he stepped, then walked on past, still whistling, oblivious to his fate, shadow boxing once more. Perhaps practicing the greeting he was preparing for Charl.

That hot poker of a thought spurred Ed to a decision and action. Springing out from the bush. An arm around Chris's mouth. A kick to the back of his knees to force him off balance.

He stank of drink, was quite a weight, heavy with muscle bulk and strong too, immediately struggling hard. But Ed was no novice at this. Knew exactly how to brace himself to stay in control and out of reach of Chris's flailing legs.

Mitch was quickly there to help, which left their victim facing a hopeless fight. Hoodie up over his head, he grabbed Chris's throat in a bruising grip and together they forced him soundlessly into the interrogation cell of the alley by the church.

Mitch was in Chris's face, right in it. Grip even tighter, constricting his throat, the brutal message very clear. Hoodie pulled so close that all Chris would be able to see was darkness where there should be the humanity of a face.

If he was attempting to impersonate death himself in full vengeful flow, Mitch was doing a highly effective job.

But only for an instant did Chris get to see that black void of inhuman nothingness. Before his own face was thrust into the smooth unyielding stone of the wall. Pushed so close, so hard, that it was a struggle to breathe. While Ed kicked the man to his knees, he and Mitch each grabbed a flailing arm and yanked them behind his back.

'Fuckers, wankers,' Chris managed to gasp.

'How'd you know our names?' Mitch replied.

'I'll have you for this.'

'Yeah, right.'

'I'm a cop.'

'We know,' Mitch grunted. 'And we're your personal professional standards department.'

Chris tried to struggle, even if he knew it was hopeless. All Mitch and Ed had to do was twist his arms to inflict more pain and subdue any resistance. The man tried to let out a yell, but it was strangled in his throat as his face was squashed harder into the wall.

'No noise,' Ed said, as quiet and calm as if he was out for a Sunday stroll. 'It's a broken arm for every attempt to yell out, or escape.'

'And when we run out of arms, we'll find something else,' Mitch went on. 'Your neck's my current favourite.'

'Behave yourself, answer the questions nicely, and you'll be let go.'

'Maybe,' Mitch added.

They hadn't scripted any of this. *But*, Ed thought, *they were doing as effective a job as any he'd known in his previous life*. Mitch was a natural. And Chris certainly seemed to understand their meaning. He didn't move or try to speak.

'We represent an organisation dedicated to making the world a better place,' Mitch went on, producing a quizzical look from Ed. 'And you have come to our attention as a person who is not in harmony with our glorious vision of a happier future. Far from it.'

'What the…' Chris tried, but was silenced by another shove into the wall.

Mitch let the moment run, then, 'Here's how it goes. And it's so simple even a dick like you can understand. You stop beating up that poor wife of yours. You apologise to her. And to your daughter, while you're at it. You explain what a pathetic inadequate arsehole you are. How you only hit out because you're a hopeless apology for any semblance of a human being. At that point, you might add you think it could be down to you having a very small cock. You solemnly promise never to do any hitting or mistreating of your family anymore. And you reform yourself and stick to your word. Or we come visit you again, and next time, we're not so touchy feely, gentle, kind, and forgiving.'

'We also have a word with your employer,' Ed added, thinking he should contribute something, however impressively Mitch was doing. 'And before you think you've got that covered, don't kid yourself. We have ways of making sure some very high up people know exactly what kind of a person you are.'

'Got all that?' Mitch said. 'We know it's a lot for a brain like yours to take in. But we require an acknowledgement and agreement before we can let you go – intact.'

Chris didn't reply immediately. But it was remarkable how effectively another twist of his arms helped the man find his voice. 'Okay, okay.'

'Just okay?'

'I promise, yeah.'

'Scouts' honour?'

'What the fuck?'

'Filth ball's honour, then.'

'Just promise you're never going to hit your wife again,' Ed intervened, before Mitch could get carried away.

'Yeah, I can do that. No problem at all. Because there's something you need to hear. Now I know what this is about.'

'Don't bother,' Mitch said. 'We don't negotiate.'

'You need to hear this. You're being taken for suckers.'

There was something in Chris's voice that made Ed frown. 'We don't negotiate, but we do listen. You've got thirty seconds.'

They eased the pressure so Chris could lift his face a little from the wall. 'But one false move…' Mitch warned.

'I only want to talk,' the man replied. And so he did. For longer than the thirty seconds he had been allowed, given the strangeness of his story.

The relationship with Charl had been in trouble for a couple of years, Chris said. She had an affair, he claimed, and with a cop, a man who had once been a friend.

'We just about got over that. Me and Charl, I mean. For the sake of Maddy. Or we tried to. Mick, the cop, we had it out. In the car park behind the nick. It's the cop way. And it wasn't pretty.'

The tone of Chris's voice told them exactly what had happened, and who came out worst.

'Things were okay at home for a while after that. Then she started getting on my case again, Charl did. Told me there was another guy she liked. That she was thinking about going off with him. Fucking taunting me, she was. Even then I wanted us to stay together, for Maddy at least. But Charl wanted an open marriage, to agree to that. And there was no way I was having it. Her coming home, reeking of another bloke. Fuck that.'

Mitch let out a hiss. 'You expect us to believe all this? We've seen the bruises you beat into your wife.'

'You believe what you like. But let me finish first.'

Ed nodded to Mitch and they let Chris go on, albeit face to face with the wall, his arms still held tight.

'She kept goading me, going on at me. Even when we had to go out together, put on the happy families face, she'd whisper about some man there she wanted to shag. And at home, it was even worse. I tried to keep it out of sight of Maddy, although it was obvious she knew something was wrong. But she was driving me nuts, Charl was. That was when I started going down the Empire every night. I had to. I couldn't stay in the house with her.'

'And the bruises?' Ed asked quietly. 'And the noises from the house? All the neighbours know.'

'She waits for me to come in. Then starts going on at me again. When I refuse to kick off, she chucks things at me and attacks me. Most of those bruises she's done herself when she goes mental. It's true, I put a few there. But that was only trying to restrain her. You should see her when she goes off on one. She's fucking crazy.'

'Very interesting, but we've heard a different story. Very different.'

And if Ed expected an angry response from Chris, it didn't come. He snorted then breathed out hard. 'Let me guess. That fucking Alan's been bleating on at you. But there's something you should know about him. He puts on a nice face, doesn't he? Kind, quiet, trying to be helpful, a good neighbour, good citizen. All that shit. But it's pure bollocks. The guy's a kiddy fiddler. Why'd you think he's set himself up as a pet groomer? That's his idea of a joke. It's kids he wants to groom. There've been a couple of complaints about him. Nothing ever stuck, of course. It never does with that sort, they're too cunning. But he's on our watch list.

'Young girls, he likes. Girls about Maddy's age in fact, and a bit younger too. You've seen Maddy. You've seen what she's like. She's got boys around her like flies round shit. She's too damn pretty and smart for her own good, and she knows it. But she doesn't know how to handle it. Not yet. She's only fourteen, for fuck's sake. Alan loves that. The way the bastard stares at her... Jesus.

'He's cosying up to Charl, giving her his fake sympathy and horror, trying to get to Maddy that way. I've done my best to talk to her, banned her from going round to his house, banned him from coming round to ours, but no-one listens to me. Everyone's got me down as the villain and Alan's the good guy. Just like you two. You swallowed it as well, didn't you? And I'm the only sane one at the party. For fuck's sake. You couldn't make it up.'

Behind Chris's back, Mitch and Ed exchanged looks.

'Have you got any evidence for all this?' Ed asked.

'Course I fucking haven't. They're too smart for me, Charl and that pervert. They're both champion liars with smiley faces. They're a damn good pair. Jesus, even Maddy's got the manipulation thing going. She twists Alan and Charl round her fingers whenever she wants. It must be a bloody genetic thing. Straight off her mum.

'I know you don't believe me. But it's the truth. Why'd you think the cops haven't done anything? It's not because I'm one of them and we're all mates. Those days are long gone, shame to say. We might actually get some fucking criminals off the streets if they weren't. It's because they know what's really going on. Nothing's been done because it's all true.

Whatever you think, whatever you've heard, what I've just told you, that's the way it really is.'

There was another pause, long and loud in the quiet of the night. The church loomed behind them, the thrust of its spire a dark sword in the starry sky.

'All right,' Ed said at last. 'We've heard what you say. We'll have a look and we'll get to the truth, whatever it is. You're free to go home now. You walk away and you don't look back, got that? We'll be watching you. Just like we will when you get home. And if there's any hint you are hitting Charl…'

He let the words linger in the still air as they walked Chris back along the alley to the road. Ed and Mitch kept hold of his arms, just in case. But perhaps they were being a little less sure, less forceful.

The two men gave Chris a shove and watched him walk away, slow and thoughtful, and not once looking back.

Serial Cat Snatcher on the Loose?

It caused quite a debate, that headline.

'The question mark doesn't look good,' Mitch said. 'Shouldn't we be saying something we know for a fact for the lead story of our first edition?'

'It does draw your attention, though,' Florence said.

'It just looks like clickbait to me,' Olivia added. 'Designed to get people reading.'

'Precisely,' Ed replied. 'At this stage, when we're launching and need maximum impact, we'll do what it takes to get noticed.'

The day had turned to Wednesday, and the time was almost one o'clock in the morning. The quartet was clustered around Ed's laptop. All were upright and alert, with no hint of a yawn. They had gathered back in the office, in darkness and deserted, apart from their corner. Florence and Olivia wanted to know what the two vigilantes had been doing, but Ed insisted on getting the newswire together first.

'We need to put the paper to bed.' And when the words succeeded only in provoking blank looks, Ed explained. 'It's an old newspaper term. I found it in my research. I've been wanting to say it for ages.'

All that was missing was a lead story. And now they had it. Florence and Olivia had already written most of it, and written it well.

Five much-loved pet cats have disappeared from a small corner of Cambridge, prompting fears a serial cat snatcher is on the loose.

'That's great for an opening line, particularly the *much-loved* bit,' Ed said. 'It really makes the story ring with the emotion.'

Florence was far too modest to claim the credit. But she might as well have done so, given the blush that spread across her face.

She was smiling again, Ed noticed. Just shyly, with slight and fleeting looks, as was her way. And that indefinable warmth of her presence was back, charming the room. It had been a colder time with it missing. Florence without her warmth could have given rise to the old tales of shamen who stole souls, snatching away the very essence of a person.

Olivia had created a montage of pictures of Hector, Elsa, Regal George, Macavity and Jones, which would dominate much of the article. They stared out from the screen, some of the feline eyes watchful or serene, others aloof or belligerent. But every set lamented.

"I know it sounds daft, but the house isn't a home without Macavity," Izzy McCloud told us. "We just miss him so much and wonder all the time what's happened to him. We can't stop hoping he'll come home."

The story went on to detail when and where the cats went missing. But the majority was taken up with more quotes from their owners, along with their photos.

'That just felt kind of right,' Florence said.

'Spot on,' Ed replied. 'Follow your instincts and go for the feelings over the facts every time. Think back on the most powerful memories in your life. What is it you remember? Maybe a couple of facts, yes, but much more in the way of feelings. You've done a brilliant job on the story. Great work.'

Florence blushed all over again and was saved from her usual recourse into self-effacing modesty by a high five from Olivia. With a few more clicks and whirls at the laptop, Olivia playing the keyboard like a virtuoso, the *Last Edition* was ready to go.

'Hit that button and we publish,' she said, standing back and offering the laptop to Ed.

'You do it,' he replied. 'You put it all together.'

Olivia reached out a hand, but then said, 'I think it should be Florence. For getting the story in the end. And doing it so bloody well.'

'Mitch should do it,' she replied. 'That *No Man Left Behind* report was so beautiful.'

'Ed should do it,' he said in turn. 'For bringing us all together.'

And so there was a silence as the other three stared at Ed. 'We'll worry about that in a minute,' he said. 'But first, because we've always agreed on honesty here, we'd better talk about what Mitch and I were told earlier. So we're clear what we may be getting into.'

The labs felt hollow at that lost time of night, with just this small far corner occupied. A tang of mustiness lingered in the air, as if the dust was finally resting after the continual disturbances of the business of the day.

As though preparing for a board meeting, aware there were serious discussions ahead, the four settled in their seats. Ed and Mitch outlined what Chris had told them and waited for the reaction.

It was quick to come and, unsurprisingly, from Olivia. With a face as hard as flint, she said, 'Pure bullshit is what that is. The usual pathetic excuses from a turd of a guy who gets a hard-on from beating up women.'

'That's certainly one way to look at it,' Ed replied.

'The right way, you mean.'

'I know you think I can be on the soft side, so...'

Ed looked to Mitch, who picked up with, 'I was all out to give the guy a good kicking. No messing about, it was what he deserved. But... but...'

'Yeah?'

'He might be a great actor. He might have spun this story to his mates, the cops. He might even have spun it to himself. But I have to say, he did sound pretty convincing.'

Olivia shook her head. 'You're shitting me. His sort always sound convincing. That's how they get away with it so much. Let me guess, did you get the immortal words – *he's a good man really*. Now where have I heard that before?'

'That's all fair enough,' Ed replied. 'But he did make us listen when we didn't expect to. And he helped that young woman who fell over, drunk. That wasn't a performance. He had no idea he was being watched. He was a model of gallantry.'

Olivia let out a hiss. 'His sort always are. Until the door's locked behind him. He's probably kicking the shit out of Charl right now.'

'He isn't,' Mitch replied.

'You reckon?'

'I know. Did you think we'd leave it to chance? We followed him back to his house. He went in really quietly and sat in the lounge, drinking a cup of tea. As far as we could tell, he just sat there, sipping and thinking. Then he made himself a bed on the sofa, settled down and turned off the light.'

'That was probably just for show. In case you were still watching him. He might be an arsehole, but he's not stupid. What about Charl and Maddy? Their story about what he's like?'

'They were convincing too,' Mitch replied.

'I know who I believe.'

'Florence?' Ed said. 'You probably talked to them the most.'

She thought for a moment, as she did. 'I believed them. And when I saw Chris, he was angry, really mad, and I did get the sense he could be violent.'

'And Alan? He seemed plausible to us.'

'To me too. Like a decent man and a good neighbour.'

'But,' Mitch said. 'The number of paedophile cases I worked on where everyone said *he seemed such a nice man.*'

Olivia stood up, stretched, and pulled her denim jacket closer. It was growing cold in the labs.

'I don't want to sound heartless,' said the young woman who had only recently discovered the sacred organ. 'But to be frank, what's all that to do with us anyway? We're trying to put a paper out. Our story is about missing cats. And the paper is supposed to be out now. Right now.'

'True,' Ed replied. 'It's just…'

'What?'

'We should know what we're getting into when we publish the story. If it takes off like we hope, it's only going to bring more attention to Charl, Maddy, Chris and Alan. That'll put more pressure on them, which might trigger more trouble – whoever's really responsible, and whatever's really going on.'

Florence nodded. 'I feel that too.'

'None of which is going to be an issue in the slightest if we don't get the paper out,' Olivia replied, with her usual logic. 'As you said before we set out tonight – no launch as planned, no future.'

'Can't argue with that,' Mitch said. 'We need to get the thing out there. That's what tonight was supposed to be about. And we've done what we set out to do.'

They looked at each other, all nodding in time. 'So, who hits the button?' Olivia asked.

Ed stood up too. 'We all do.'

And so the four staff of the *Last Edition* clustered around Ed's laptop. They linked hands, and pressed their fingers together. Ed took a second to indulge himself in his resolution. He felt the warmth, the smoothness, the firmness, the insecurity and the determination in the touches.

Thinking, feeling, writing

Just one more second, one more, and together they hit the button.

Ed sent them all home for the night to try to get some sleep. Even if he suspected it was pointless, because he knew how they were feeling.

He was trained and experienced in controlling it. But even so, the excitement was pumping through his body, the blood pounding fast in his veins. He tried to cycle slowly, breathe deeply, to calm himself. Enjoy the rare peace of this sleeping city. But it was impossible to quieten the thoughts yelling and chasing each other around his mind.

This crazy, stupid, ridiculous idea, launched with a bizarre advert in a newspaper, might just be in danger of actually working.

Ed had told the rest of the team to stay off their phones, computers, social media, anything online. To focus on getting some rest. They would only really find out in the morning what impact the edition had made.

And if – if – it had done well, if – if – it had been shared, commented on, quoted, noticed, spread across the net, then they would need to capitalise on their momentum. Get out there, find more stories, burnish their reputation, build their brand.

If it worked. If, if, if.

Ed cycled without noticing the journey, through the massed darkness of the city, only the occasional car for company. Past colleges, schools, houses and shops, not one registering in his spin of thoughts.

Back at the mobile home park, he did his usual check around, but found nothing of concern.

And inside there was a welcome awaiting, a small dome of a shape in the middle of the carpet.

'Tommy, good morning,' Ed told the tortoise. 'You do keep some strange hours. But then, I suppose, so do I. Maybe that's why we get on, eh?'

Those dark prehistoric eyes looked back up at him in their unblinking way. So Ed got Tommy a fresh head of lettuce and left him slowly and contentedly chewing. At this time of night – or morning – a low-maintenance undemanding, non-judgmental friend was just what a man needed.

In the bedroom, Ed turned off the light, waited for a couple of minutes, then got up and, crouching, peered through the curtain. It was habit, instinct, something he should leave behind, forget about. But Ed knew he would have no chance of ever resting without going through the ritual.

He couldn't be certain. Not with the spread of darkness outside and the jumpiness of his eyes. But Ed thought he saw a shift of movement in the shadows, perhaps a hint of the paleness of a face slipping back into cover. And, as if an omen, the scar on his neck began its low ominous throbbing.

Ed watched for another twenty minutes, but saw nothing and so returned to bed, well aware that he had no chance of sleeping.

Every set of eyes was on Ed as he walked into the labs for the second time that Wednesday morning, albeit at a more civilised hour than earlier. And the reception he found was unexpected, but encouraging.

First one woman, then another, then a huddle of men started to clap. And within seconds, the whole converted storeroom was resonating with applause, perhaps in a way it never had before. Certainly not in the reign of Swift anyway.

For once, not quite sure what to do, Ed stopped. He even checked over his shoulder to make sure the clapping was for him. Which prompted laughter and even more enthusiastic appreciation.

'I'd better, um, go see the team,' he managed above the noise, and made his way to the far corner.

They would all be there, he knew. Gathered around a laptop, pointing to the statistics of how many times the *Last Edition* had been shared, or which story was the most popular. They would have spent much of the night doing what he had told them not to, but which he himself had also been doing. Endlessly checking to see what impact the paper was making.

But at their corner, Ed stopped and wondered if he was in the right place, or whether the tiredness had prompted a hallucination.

The room had been transformed. No longer a drab and functional office, around the walls were banners, sparkling with their congratulations. Balloons swayed in currents of warm air. Even the little plant had been graced with a necklace of tinsel.

On the table, on top of a bistro-style tablecloth, was a spread of a breakfast; from pains au chocolat, to avocados, cereals, and even bacon butties, blessing the office with their delicious scents. To complete the spread was a colourful line of jugs of virgin cocktails.

And on the wall, to the legend *Thinking, feeling, writing* had been added a large tick, carefully shaped, and in gold.

The leaden fugue of tiredness, even that urge to keep looking out of the window to check for watching eyes, evaporated. The disbelief went with it and the emotion flooded in.

'We did it,' Mitch said quietly, standing above the spread, Florence and Olivia either side. 'You did it. And we wanted to say thank you.'

He might have had more to add, could even have rehearsed an impressive and moving monologue. But if so, it was forever lost to posterity as Mitch didn't have a chance of finishing his speech.

With a noise utterly unlike her, something more befitting of a child unwrapping the Christmas present of her dreams, Olivia pounced on Ed and gave him a gripping hug.

It took a while until he was released, but even so, the respite was brief. Because Florence then repeated the process. And when she had finished, Mitch offered a far more restrained and manly shake of the hand. But his eyes were sore and his voice was hoarse, and neither just with tiredness, as he said, 'Congratulations. And thank you. Thank you so much.'

Olivia had appointed herself Minister for Statistics, which frankly was never going to provoke an argument. Dressed as ever in her denim, she took them through the impact the *Last Edition* had made.

'It started slowly, as you'd expect from publishing at that time of day, and given that we had no loyal audience eagerly waiting. But then…'

They were sat around her laptop, looking at a graph. It started with the sort of hills you got to know well in Cambridge; those that were barely deserving of the word. But after a few hours the gradient gradually shifted and quickly moved on to ascents that looked like a mountaineer's dream.

'About six o'clock was the key time. I'm guessing that's when a lot of people woke up. The first thing they do is check to see what's been going on overnight. It's human nature, apparently.' Olivia looked a little puzzled at that concept, but then continued. 'Those that we'd primed were curious to see what we'd been up to. And then…'

Sometimes, the rest of the team had quickly realised, you had to translate Olivia speak. Like now, when she started talking about exponential growth theory, and with considerable enthusiasm.

'Break it down, nice and simple for those of us who aren't so mathematically minded,' Mitch said.

Olivia sighed, but it was a mark of her mood that the reply was tolerant. 'The bigger something gets, the bigger it grows.'

'Like a sci-fi monster?'

Florence giggled and Ed couldn't help smiling as well, a grin which only grew bigger with Olivia's scowl. 'FFS. Trust you to put it that way. But okay then, if you must.'

The upshot was that, whether by luck or judgment, they'd pitched the *Last Edition* just right. The stories were not only interesting enough for people to want to read, but also – critically – to share. And share, and share, and then share again. And keep on sharing. On and on. Way beyond Cambridge, across the nation, and apparently, edging a way around the world.

'Basically, we've gone viral,' Olivia concluded.

'Wasn't that easier to say?' Mitch asked.

'Not really, no. It lacked… rigour.'

A chortle from the doorway interrupted them. Steve, the programmer, was gazing at Olivia in a way a film star in a love scene might adopt.

'Can we help you?' she asked.

'Just wanted to add my congratulations. You've smashed it. And we've already had enquiries about work because of the ad we placed.'

'Thank you.'

The pair looked at each other in that way young people did. And then Olivia, proud master of any given situation, broke the stare and instead set her eyes on the ground. She might even have let free the flicker of a smile.

'See you later then,' Steve said.

And Olivia looked back up and replied, simply, 'Yes.'

It took a few seconds for composure to return, before the lecture could resume. That this thoughtful and historic city had an internationally famous name had helped the *Last Edition's* assault on the Internet. But the stories had been extraordinarily well received too.

'The missing cats is the most read,' Olivia told them.

'As you'd expect for the lead story,' Ed said. 'Well done, Florence.'

'It was a team effort,' she replied quickly. But for once, briefly closed her eyes and basked a little in the praise. And, perhaps, the achievement.

'Next comes Tyson, the pylons man.'

'Well done, Olivia,' Ed said. 'And as for Tyson, there's got to be a follow-up in how he's coping with fame.'

'If he's still talking to us.'

'He should be. This weekend, I bet he'll be leading teams of hundreds on his pylon hunts.'

'The most commented on story is *No Man Left Behind*. There are some really touching words about it being such an important issue, and congratulating us for talking about it.'

'And well done, Mitch,' Ed added. 'Campaigning journalism at its finest.'

'Some things just have to be said,' he replied. 'Or written.'

'The least read – but still with some pretty hefty numbers – is the lab profile and Swift's interview.'

'It was a necessary evil. We got our breathing space. And look what we've done with it.'

But on this occasion no-one joined in the mutual appreciation, the beautiful song of the morning. Because, one by one, they had sensed a new presence in the room.

It was fortunate they were grouped together around the computer and talking quietly. For, like a creature of legend, the very uttering of the name had the power to conjure up the beast itself.

A polite but pointed cough from the doorway announced the arrival of Aaron Swift.

Whatever the inhabitants of the labs said about Swift – and there was a lot – you knew where you were with him. The nose cone was either up, or down. And today, it was in the stratosphere.

'I won't interrupt you for long because I know what newsrooms are like,' Swift said, even if he didn't have a clue. 'It's always busy, busy, busy in the creative world, eh?'

'Very much so,' Ed replied when it became clear no-one else was going to. And because a little flattery never hurt, he added, 'But not as much as with big business. Or senior management.'

Swift had never been good with irony. 'I have to say, I can't deny it. But be that as it may, I wanted to offer you my congratulations. That round of applause you received earlier. It was most untoward for a working environment, but on this occasion, I would say justified.' Swift looked surprised with himself and rapidly continued, 'Although let's not make a habit of it, of course.'

'Of course.'

'Anyway, the bank has been on. Yes, the bank…'

Ed was tempted to ask whether the whole bank had been on. And how it was possible for a bank to be on, assuming Swift meant some form of communication, and on what anyway?

'An early call from the bank. It's unprecedented. Unless it's a critical market matter, of course. A crash, or suspension of trading, or the like.'

The staff of the *Last Edition* waited patiently for the point, and, in fairness, Swift seemed to realise he was struggling to make it. Perhaps the trial of delivering unadulterated praise was proving too much.

'Anyway, the bank is very pleased. With your creative newswire, the impact it has had, and the feature you wrote on the labs. As you know, your tenure here was not without controversy. I am, however, delighted that our bold, innovative and risk-taking vision to engage with the creative sector has been fully justified.'

At this point, Ed tried hard not to react to Swift's miracle conversion to the cause of the *Last Edition*. But fortunately the man himself didn't notice the flinch and shudder.

'Yes, indeed so,' Swift went on. 'Well done us. Well done you. Well done all of us. We look forward to more issues to come.'

Olivia had been keeping an eye on the statistics during the regal visit of Swift, and not too subtly. She shared the news that the missing cats story had begun to feature in the mainstream media.

'They're all running it,' she said. 'Broadsheets and tabloids, and even the BBC.'

After a couple of minutes admiring the splash of their story across the net, Mitch said, 'I suppose we need to think about what we do next.'

'That's simple, isn't it?' Florence replied. 'Find more stories. Build on what we've already achieved.'

'Fuck!' Olivia exclaimed. 'Sorry, I was just looking through our mailbox. Didn't have a chance with tracking everything else that's going on.'

The inbox boasted its usual share of miracle cures for obesity, hair loss, and offers to turn a man into a bedroom marvel. But more interestingly, there was a series of enquiries from companies about advertising rates with the *Last Edition*.

'Bloody hell, I think we might just have a future,' Mitch said.

'Shit, there are even people applying for jobs with us,' Olivia added.

'This is getting silly,' Ed replied. 'The day's going too well. Something has to go wrong.'

'Don't say that,' Florence replied, her voice full of vulnerability. Which prompted Ed to apologise, and he gave her a quick hug.

'Oh,' Olivia said, as she clicked further through the overgrowth of the inbox. And quiet though the word was, it made them all stop and listen. Because this was the sort of *oh* you just didn't expect to hear from her.

Within the last hour, an anonymous e-mail had arrived, the address of the sender carefully disguised. But that hardly mattered, because they knew very well who it was from.

You two fuckers. I know it was you. I know who you are and where to find you. Next time it'll be me doing the ambushing. You'd better watch your backs.

'Shit,' Ed said.

'More importantly, if he knows who we are,' Mitch went on, 'I can only think of one way he found out. Which means… oh, no.'

'Charl,' Florence whispered. 'Oh God. Maddy.'

Ed grabbed his phone and rang Alan. Then quickly put it down again. And for once, this master of composure was shaken as he struggled to form the words.

'He was about to phone us, Alan was. Oh fuck, oh shit. Charl's just been rushed to hospital in an ambulance. Apparently she's taken a real beating.'

I t would have been comical, ridiculous, what they were doing, if it weren't such a bitter moment. But no-one was laughing and no-one would be, not for a long time.

Not after that phone call.

Any lingering tiredness had fled under the assault of the adrenaline coursing through their bodies. The four staff of the *Last Edition* were heading for Millhouse Road on bicycles. Standing outside the labs, ordinary life flowing around, they'd briefly debated what to do. But only briefly.

'We've got to get there. Right now. To help Charl. And maybe Maddy too,' Olivia said.

'And sort out Chris,' Mitch added with the voice of a hitman.

Bikes were by far the fastest way to get around Cambridge, its few arteries clogged by the endless stodge of cars. Olivia had parked her bike outside. She made for it and pointed to the cycle sharing station on the opposite side of the road. A smart line of brightly liveried bicycles waiting for a customer.

'Fuck that,' Mitch spat. 'I'll run. I'm going to kill him. It'll be a good warm up.'

'We'll kill him,' Olivia replied, matching his anger with a fearful cold fire. 'I want to look into his eyes as the wanker breathes his last. With my foot on his throat ideally. But this is the quickest way. Before he gets arrested and we can't get near him.'

Florence watched the exchange, silent, but with eyes sore in the brightness of the morning sun. 'Did we make this happen?' she asked eventually, and so hesitantly. 'Charl, poor Charl... just for our story. Was it because of us?'

'Because of Ed and me, more likely,' Mitch replied. 'And our little chat with him.'

'We don't know that,' Ed said.

But no-one replied. No-one could.

The other three looked to Ed. Just a minute ago, so elated with what the *Last Edition* had achieved. In the heavens, in control of the world. And now feeling...

There was only one word. And it was hopeless.

Yes, hopeless. The absolute reverse of their sacred word, their beacon and their guide. The worst of the worst, the depths of his personal pit. Utterly, miserably hopeless.

Where once there had been sweet hope welling within, and so much of it that Ed had shared it around. Like some Father Christmas figure bringing everyone the very gift they had yearned for. He had showered hope upon these chosen three alongside him, and the scores who had come here to the labs only two days earlier.

But now the revered word was gone again. Vanished in an instant. Worse, had turned traitor. Betrayed him, betrayed them all; twisted a rusty knife into their stomachs. Let the hope gush out. And leave behind a frozen void, where something so glorious had once flourished.

Still the three were looking at him. Like those others had, one day, many years ago, in the depths of the old life. And his scar, that weal of a near death memory, was throbbing hard.

'Bikes it is. Let's get going. We've got work to do,' Ed said as calmly as he could.

Seldom could a stranger gang have ridden together under the banner of justice. How they must have looked. And look people did as the amateur cyclists wobbled their way past. But the quartet never noticed and even less cared.

Instead, they rode on, on and on. Trying to shout a conversation above the noise of the city, whilst dodging pedestrians, cars and other bikes.

Olivia led the way, yelling instructions over her shoulder. *Mind the pram... next left, then sharp right straight after... watch out for the pothole... get a move on, will you!*

Mitch, Florence and Ed were every bit as out of breath as Olivia wasn't. But the anger drove them onwards. Pedals turning, wheels spinning, as if powered by an engine of rage. Through flashes of sunlight and patches of shade on another warm early spring day.

One more corner, one more road, and they reached Suffolk Street. Olivia put on an extra spurt and they caught up, then pulled up outside the house where Charl, Maddy and Chris lived.

Police tape was fluttering in a perimeter around the garden and an officer stood sentry duty outside.

Alan was watching from his garden, holding onto a gatepost to try to keep himself steady. He wasn't an average-looking man today, but one who had been tarred and feathered with trauma. He was trembling, lips trying to form words, but even so could hardly speak. He kept glancing back at his door, as if wanting to run inside and lock himself away, safe from this fearful world into which he had been pitched.

'I saw it. Right there, right in front of me. It was horrible, just horrible,' he stammered.

The first he knew of trouble was a siren wailing along the street.

Neighbours looked out, as they did, Alan amongst them. To see the ambulance pull up.

'I knew then. I knew. I don't know how, but I just knew. Oh God help me.'

Alan thudded down onto the wall, head sagging between his knees. Florence hesitated, perhaps remembering what Chris had said about this man. That within the fragile exterior lurked a paedophile. But then she sat alongside and laced an arm around him.

Ed saw the others thinking just the same as himself. Chris's talk of Charl injuring herself and blaming it on him, this concerned neighbour actually being a predator upon children. Lies, all lies, the gushing falsities of a desperate man in fear of a righteous beating. The way Chris had treated Charl on his return home, when their protective eyes were no longer watching, surely told them that.

All of which left Ed, Mitch and Olivia continuing to glare at the house next door. As if the power of their loathing might force Chris to emerge and face his nemesis.

'He's not there,' Alan said, sensing the venom. 'He was arrested. He's gone to the police station.'

'Shame,' Mitch breathed. 'But there'll be another time.'

The force of his words seemed to infuse some spirit back into Alan, and he managed to tell them the rest of what had happened. Two paramedics had run into the house. There was a delay, punctuated only by figures shifting to and fro past the windows. Their movements were fast and urgent, Alan said. And then the stretcher had emerged.

'Charl was on it. I knew it was her. You could see her hair dangling down. She had one of those mask things over her face. And a drip above her. And she was… she was…'

It took a few seconds for the final words to emerge from Alan's breathless mouth. And when they did, they were quiet, but so very loud for that.

'She was completely still. Not moving at all. Not in the slightest. She looked absolutely lifeless.'

It was a long time before anyone spoke. And when they did, it was Mitch, and what he said was simple, but summed up exactly what they were feeling.

'Fuck.'

The unspoken fears which had accompanied them throughout the ride gathered their forces. Alan stared down at one of his well-tended flowerbeds and its budding shoots of life. The others kept their gaze on the house opposite, maybe in disbelief, or the hope that this was not the vicious reality they had come to know.

'What do we do?' Olivia said, eventually.

'Two strands to the plan,' Ed replied, when it became clear no-one else was going to speak. 'One, get the story written and…'

'Fuck that,' Mitch said. 'He was warned. With his e-mail to us and this, it's a declaration of bloody war. And I'm up for that. So who cares about a story now?'

'We do. Because that's the business we're in and it's what we're going to use. I said strand one, remember? Which fits in with strand two. And that's sorting out Chris. A story which makes it clear he's been arrested following a vicious beating for his wife is a good start.'

'We don't know for sure it was him that did it,' Florence pointed out.

'We don't have to. We won't say it was. We just state the facts. Charl badly beaten, husband arrested. The readers can decide for themselves what happened.'

'Start a propaganda war if we haven't got anything else for now,' Olivia said. 'Smart.'

'Smear his name across the net,' Mitch added. 'Far and wide, for everyone to see. That works for me. As a starter, anyway.'

'So let's split up again. Two teams to work the area and see what we can find out. Mitch, you and me…'

But then came an interruption and from a surprise source. 'No,' Florence said. 'Not this time. That didn't work so well before, did it? I'm with Mitch this time. Ed, it's you and Olivia.'

Florence folded her arms and stared at them with a look that said there was going to be no debate.

Anyway, even if anyone had tried, this fast-turning early spring morning was about to shift its stride and move even quicker. From Millhouse Road came the wailing of another siren, a sound which had become the backdrop to the day.

A police van appeared around the corner, slewed to a halt, and disgorged a tumble of cops from within. Instinctively, Ed grabbed his phone and took some photos.

One of the officers, a young man with an ill-fitting helmet and a flush of unprofessional excitement strode over. He was carrying a handful of sheets of paper and thrust one out.

'Have you seen her? Have you seen this girl? Has anyone seen this girl?'

They didn't need to look at the face which stared out at them. Sometimes, in the endless whirlpools of the worst of days of life, you just know. When you've suffered enough of the world's ways and understand all too well how a moment can take you from bad to worse, and then, on a whim, deteriorate.

But look they did. Perhaps to torment themselves just a little further. Because, maybe secretly, they thought they deserved it.

Ed, Mitch, Florence, Olivia and Alan all looked into those beautiful old-before-their-time, yet still vulnerable, eyes.

'Oh God, oh no, I don't believe this,' Alan muttered. 'No, no, no, please, no.' His eyes flicked back to the house and Alan lurched to his feet, tried to make for the door. But Ed reached out and stopped him.

'You're in shock. Stay with us. We'll look after you.'

The man was so weak he could hardly move. But Ed eased his trembling body gently back down to the security of the wall.

And so they watched in silence as the hunt got underway. Left and right, up and down, and all sides around, police officers jogged and strode. Knocking on doors, talking to people as they stared in their knots and groups. Stopping cars, pedestrians and cyclists, spreading the urgency of their message across this unremarkable street.

All held out identical sheets of paper. All asking the same question as the young policeman standing, waiting and expectant, in this garden.

'Have you seen her? Come on, this is important! Maybe life and death. Have you seen her? Her name's Maddy. And she's disappeared.'

Some say it's long extinct. Gone the same way as the dodo, woolly mammoth, black rhinoceros and the quagga. But no, it's alive and well, if endangered, often in hiding, and sometimes needing the right encouragement to emerge.

And now was the time, and this the place.

Within ten minutes of the police arriving, spreading word of Maddy's disappearance, search parties were forming. Along the road, they gathered around officers, eyes bright with urgency, faces set with determination, listening hard. Men and women, old and young, newcomers to Millhouse Road alongside residents who could remember when life was different and this kind of thing didn't happen.

Amidst the worry, the fear, and the intensity of the hunt, were quietly whispered words of pride. Talk of a community spirit that endured here in this modern but ancient city, even in these fast-changing times.

Everyone had a photo, those teenage eyes looking out, as though asking for help, silently pleading to be saved. And from the garden, in the early spring sunshine, Ed, Florence, Olivia, Mitch and Alan watched the acceleration of this tumultuous day, and made some equally fast decisions.

'We need to find Maddy, and we need a story,' Ed said. 'So…'

But before he could continue, Olivia interrupted, 'We can do both. Me and you, write this up and get it out, right now.'

It was what he was going to say, but reassuring to hear someone else say it. So Ed nodded, hopped up on the wall and took more photos of the search parties organising themselves. It was quite a sight.

'What about us?' Mitch asked.

'You and Florence join a search party. We can use some of that as an *inside the hunt for Maddy* type follow-up story. But also…'

'We tap into the police and local people to try to get more info,' Florence said, apparently feeling it was her turn to take the lead. 'About Chris's arrest, and whatever else we can.'

In the intensity of the moment, they had almost forgotten the existence of the woe begotten Alan. He was still propped up like a pile of human refuse on the garden wall.

'I can't believe this is happening,' he whispered, as they looked to him.

'Do you want to come with us?' Ed asked.

He might have challenged Alan to a duel to the death, such was the reaction. 'No,' he replied quickly. 'I think I'm going to have a lie down.'

'Do you mind if we sit in your house to write the story?'

And if Alan was alarmed before, now he looked as if Death himself had materialised at the gate and was pointing a bony finger his way. 'No, no, I can't let you do that, I'm sorry. I, um, I've got a particularly sensitive cat in there who desperately needs grooming. It's a rush job. Some kind of show. Yes, that's right. The owners are coming later, she's already taken long enough to calm down, and she doesn't like strangers. She'll get all upset again if anyone else comes in. I'm sorry, really sorry.'

Before anyone could argue with the miserable and unconvincing ramble, Alan lurched up from the wall and into his house. As the door closed, they heard a loud miaow, followed by another, and his thin and nervous voice attempting to comfort the hypersensitive feline hiding within.

Being first with the news has been a totem for journalists throughout the ages. But it's become even more important in the online era, when the fastest updates for a hungrily waiting public can attract swathes of new subscribers.

A story on this scale would soon bring a scrum of reporters. So Mitch and Florence went to find a search party, and Ed and Olivia got to work with what they knew.

'The good news is that the paper's still going strong,' Olivia said. 'We've got thousands of followers already. And we're still being shared around the world, although not at the same pace as before.'

'Wait until we break this story,' Ed replied. And he dictated while Olivia typed, suggested edits, and composed the page.

'First we need a breaking news banner.' Fingers flying, Olivia clicked, clicked, whizzed and whirled, and there it was, appearing at the top of the screen. A ticker bearing the words which had been sacred to hacks since the dawn of the industry.

'Next, the headline,' she said.

'Missing girl prompts massive search?'

'Not dramatic enough. Search parties scrambled in hunt for missing girl?'

Ed nodded. 'Much better. Go with it. And plaster a big photo of Maddy right underneath. I'll get the intro sorted.'

It took a few seconds and the striding past of one of the search parties for Ed to find the right words.

'A full-scale police search has been launched after the disappearance of a vulnerable teenage girl,' he dictated.

'Vulnerable?'

'Her mum's been beaten senseless and her dad's under arrest. I'd say that qualifies as vulnerable.'

'Fair enough.' Olivia rapidly typed the words, then added, 'Great opening.'

'Thousands of local people have turned out to help the police in their hunt.'

'Thousands?'

'Pure journalese. One or two become scores. Ten or twenty become hundreds. Two or three hundred becomes thousands. Et cetera.'

Ed was about to dictate more words, but Olivia was into her stride and leading the field. 'We've got to put in the basics. Maddy's name, where she disappeared from and when, and that the police are asking everyone to look out for her.'

Following that, it was a photo of the search parties and a couple of quotes from local people. The usual kind of thing that any reporter would have heard so many times over a career.

Oh, it's shocking. Who'd have thought this sort of thing would happen around here?

'Now, let's get him,' Olivia said with a cold relish. 'It's time for Chris's starring role.'

'Maddy's disappearance follows her mother, Charl, being taken to hospital this morning in an ambulance. She had suffered serious injuries.'

'Add *in her own home*,' Olivia said. 'To really skewer the bastard. And then the coup de grâce.'

Her husband, and Maddy's father, Chris, was arrested following Charl being injured, and is currently in police custody.

'Can I add that he's a wife beating piece of shit with bad breath and a tiny cock?' Olivia asked, as they reviewed the story.

'Tempting, but no,' Ed replied. 'Now, it's time for something else I've been wanting to say since we set up the *Last Edition*. Another little nugget of media history. Publish and be damned!'

More and more people were turning out to join the search parties as word spread of Maddy's disappearance. Olivia spotted Hannah and Izzy heading along the road, Elizabeth just behind. She called out to them and the trio stopped briefly by one of the gardens.

'Not working today?' Ed began, hardly believing the hoary old words had tumbled from his mouth. It was a gambit of British conversation second only to lamenting the weather.

'We both called to say we wouldn't be in, not until Maddy's found,' Hannah replied. 'Some things are more important than work, even in the army. On the subject of which...'

She pointed to the house next door and its police guard. Olivia explained what had happened, and Hannah replied with a burst of invective that made even Ed blink.

'Wish I'd brought my fucking bayonet,' she concluded, puffing out her substantial frame as if she were on parade.

'I wish you had too,' Olivia replied, apparently pleased to have found a comrade with a similarly robust outlook on life.

'I wholeheartedly agree,' Elizabeth joined in. 'Or perhaps a carving knife, in my case.'

It was hard to imagine such an elegant older woman, wearing a cardigan and walking boots, heading out from her flat armed and dangerous. But given the look on her face, not perhaps impossible.

'That poor kid,' Hannah went on. 'I bet she's run away. She was cut up enough about her cat disappearing. She really loved Hector. Put that alongside everything that's going on at home, then Mum gets another beating and she's off. I don't blame her. Wish we'd have done more to help her.'

'We should have done,' Elizabeth added. 'Regardless of the consequences. Or the threats from that foul man. If something's happened to
Maddy, I shall never forgive myself.'

Izzy broke her usual silence. 'You wouldn't believe how many children grow up in homes like Maddy's. They don't stand a chance in life
if that's what they know from the start.'

The four shared a suitably reflective silence until Hannah said, 'We
won't get anything done by standing here talking. Action's what we
need. We can deal with Chris when he's released. But for now, let's
focus on finding Maddy.'

And with that, she strode off up the street as though it was a parade
ground, self-declared leader of this curious trio. Izzy followed, her
ginger hair trailing in the morning breeze, and Elizabeth kept up the
pace alongside, her shrewd old eyes casting around for any hint of the
missing teenager.

There are words in the modern world which have forged a demonic
alliance, in being magical to both marketing departments and young
people alike.

Even the older generations have come to understand the concept,
given that the pair of words has grown so critical in contemporary life.
And now, with a reverence hitherto unknown for her, Olivia got to use
them.

'We're trending.'

In the shade of a well-trimmed fir tree, she showed Ed a screen
packed with graphs and statistics, and traced a loving finger across
them. Ed watched and listened, then politely coughed. Olivia got the
point and was kind enough to offer an interpretation.

'We're being shared everywhere. By thousands of people. Tens of
thousands, actually. And we're getting loads of comments. Everyone's
saying to everyone else that they need to look out for Maddy. People

are posting that they're heading here from all over the place to join the search. London, Lincoln, Birmingham, Bristol, bloody hell, even Newcastle. There are well-wishers from all over the world saying they hope she's found safe. And all through us. Our site. Us. The *Last Edition*. Basically, we've set the net on fire. Wow.'

In a rare moment of letting down her guard, Olivia held out a hand and Ed, being Ed, joined her in a high five.

'We've got thousands more followers,' Olivia went on, and played her way through a chorus of clicks. 'Our inbox is busting with people wanting to know more about us. There are loads of job applications. Lots more requests to advertise in the paper. Even journalists wanting to do stories on us.'

Ed sat down on the wall where Alan had propped himself up and let the sunshine soothe his face.

'All that on the back of a missing girl,' he said quietly. 'This wasn't how I wanted it to be.'

Olivia sat alongside him. Across the street, a dozen men and women were following a police officer, heading for the cemetery. All were carrying photos of Maddy.

'It's how it is,' Olivia said. 'All we can do is deal with it. And maybe our story can help find her.'

'Maybe.'

'What's bothering you?'

'I'm not sure. Just, something. An itch in a corner of my mind. Something doesn't feel quite right.'

'Like what?'

'What indeed? That's the question.'

Ed noticed his scar was throbbing again. He looked up and down the street, but no-one was watching, no-one paying him and Olivia any attention. The centre of all thoughts was a girl who wasn't there, luminous by her absence.

'Let's get going then. We're ahead on this story. We need to stay there. Mitch and Flo are with the search parties. We can…'

'What?'

Ed paused while the idea took shape. 'There's one angle on Maddy's disappearance we haven't covered yet. Given what's happened, we probably won't be welcome, to say the least. But what the hell. Let's try it anyway.'

Even the most sunshine of days can be tainted with darkness. It was there, a permanent shadow on the edge of their vision, always lingering, continually threatening, waiting to be discovered.

Flo and Mitch felt that, and keenly. As did, judging by their silence, the other three in the group. All were in a line following the portly Sergeant Bradley through the renaissance of greenery that marks the coming of the springtime.

A few metres into Millhouse Road Cemetery, he stopped to give them a briefing. It was exacting and direct, and the tones were clipped, a giveaway of bygone days of military service. Even if the man's girth may have expanded considerably since those halcyon times.

As far as possible, they should walk alongside each other, close enough to be able to see into all the undergrowth. An arm's length apart was ideal. At the sight of anything suspicious, they should call out, but not approach what they had found, and absolutely not disturb it.

Everyone knew exactly what they were looking for, the darkness in their minds, even if no-one would ever say.

There were a thousand hiding places here, perhaps many more. Thick and gnarled trees dating back almost two hundred years spread their boughs wide. Overgrowth gathered around them, brambles and grass cosying up to create dense thickets. Graves upon graves, some 1960s new, some Victorian old, marked the progress of the years across this sacred pasture in the heart of Cambridge.

In the centre was the old rundown mausoleum, grey and mildewed where once there was proud white stone. It was an obvious place for a runaway girl to hide, and police officers were already searching there.

The sun glinted from puddles and shone from headstones, both upright and drunken with the passing of time. Muddy paths wound their way around the edges of the cemetery, and one or two thinner and far less trodden, dared to wander within.

But the mass of this panorama of urban greenery was untouched and unexplored. Whatever the irony, it was an ideal place to hide an unspeakable secret. Particularly one created in a neighbouring road. The cemetery backed onto Suffolk Street.

They hadn't declared themselves as journalists. 'I don't actually feel like one,' Mitch had said in a hurried conversation as they found a party to join. 'Just someone doing what any good citizen would.'

'Let's hope we don't find... please don't let us be the ones to find...' Florence replied, but was unable to finish the sentence.

From anyone else, it would have sounded ridiculous, the tremble in her voice. When the odds against it happening were surely so very steep. But for this fated woman, if there were to be a discovery of that which they most feared, it would surely fall to her.

And that, Mitch knew, from looking at her, sensing her dread, would be the worst. The very worst she could ever know in a lifetime of ill treatment from the gods. The blow from which there was no return.

He reached out and put a hand on her shoulder. But even Florence, kindest of the kind, rosiest of the optimists, couldn't find a smile. All she could do was let his fingers slip through hers in a brief touch.

Bradley spread the group out to the side of a thin track. Another party was beginning its solemn work on the opposite side of the cemetery, a third from their flank. A pincer movement across the land.

Mitch manoeuvred himself to take up station at the far end of the line, and made sure to keep Florence beside him. If there was to be a discovery, he was determined it would fall to him.

Not her. Please not her.

Two men, briefly introduced as Arthur and Josh, and a woman, Lesley, made up the rest of the line. Both the men were older and carrying sticks, Arthur dressed in a mac and wellington boots, despite the warmth of the day. Josh wore a jumper, trainers and oversized sunglasses. Lesley was tall and sported a baseball cap which cast a band of shadow across her face.

No-one had attempted the usual pleasantries. Meaningless words about being delighted to meet you, or so-very-British comments about the weather. It wasn't that kind of a day.

They paced slowly, step by careful step, subconsciously in time. Eyes flicking back and forth, ranging across the undergrowth. With a mindset like this, it was painstaking work.

Each and everything looked suspicious. From a tump of earth to a flash of litter flapping in the warm breeze. Everything required a second look, a poke and a prod, wary and hesitant, just to be sure.

It took long enough to cover a few metres of ground. The overgrowth was so thick in places that the searching was physical and ponderous. Mitch felt a sweat spreading across his back. The day was growing warmer and they stopped in the shade of an aged yew. Arthur brought out a bottle of water and shared it around.

'How're you doing?' Mitch asked him.

'I'm feeling grim, frankly,' he replied in a well-polished voice. 'There are many things I would rather be doing today. Many, many things. But sometimes you have to do what you have to do.'

'And pray to God we don't find anything,' Lesley added.

Mitch nodded but didn't reply. He could hardly take a note of their words, so he repeated them in his head, tried to imprint them on his mind, ready for the article they would write later.

'How're you doing, sergeant?' Florence asked, playing her part.

'What's the old saying?' Bradley replied, all flushed and puffed out.

'A policeman's lot is not a happy one. I can certainly vouch for that. Some days it's downright traumatic, I can tell you.'

In Mitch's mind, the article was coming together. There was just one vital element missing, and if there was a moment to deal with that, it was now.

'I guess we should put this on social media, to make sure everyone's keeping watch for Maddy,' he said. 'Do you mind if I go ahead and get a couple of photos when we go back to searching?'

'That's a little unseemly, isn't it?' Arthur replied, his taciturn peer nodding agreement.

'It's just the modern world,' Florence said, in a way which could soothe a coming storm. 'And anything we can do which might help, I think we should. Don't you?'

It was hard to argue with Florence, her calm and her logic, and no-one raised any more objections. So Mitch strode on and took some shots of the mausoleum, with police all around it. Then, through the trees, the line of his fellow searchers, step by step going about their dismal work.

It was only a five-minute walk to the police station, and like a child, Olivia spent the whole time asking questions.

'What're you going to do? What're you planning? What're you up to now? How's this going to help? How're we going to get that fucker Chris? What'd you mean when you said something wasn't quite right? When're we going to get another story sorted?'

To give himself a moment to think, Ed asked her how the story on the hunt for Maddy was doing. It involved a screen and plenty of numbers, which was guaranteed to keep Olivia quiet for a while, by her standards at least.

The upshot of the flurry of a briefing that followed was that the article was doing very well indeed. It had racked up countless more shares, generated pages of debate, and attracted thousands more followers for the *Last Edition*.

'But so what?' Olivia concluded. 'Yeah, okay, we're doing great online and all that. But what about our real-world shit?'

Ed was so surprised he would have stopped if their mission hadn't been urgent. As it was, he faltered, then kept going, although he did almost collide with a postbox.

'I thought you preferred online life to the real world?'

'I used to. Sure. But now…'

The subsequent plunge into another deep swimming pool of thought gave Ed a little more respite to think. Which was just as well. Because he was far from sure about what he was doing.

'You don't have to come with me for this, you know,' he said. 'In fact, given what I'm thinking I'm going to have to do, you might not want to.'

Olivia didn't need to reply, but instead produced one of her looks. It wasn't quite a battalion of tanks, but it certainly wasn't to be messed with. And on they marched. Ahead was the flat and open expanse of grassy nothingness that was Parker's Piece, laughingly referred to as a park in this charitable city.

They crossed the Eastern Road and were almost at the police station. And because Olivia's edginess might well be needed, Ed said, 'Look at the park. What do you think of it?'

'What kind of question is that?'

'Just tell me. What do you reckon to the park?'

'In what way?'

'What it brings to Cambridge.'

Olivia contemplated for a moment. 'It's shit. It's not a park. It's just a field. A bit of flat green land. There's nothing to the bloody thing. It's like someone thought they'd create a park, then got a better offer.' Warming to her theme, she added, 'A few pasty trees, no hedges, no flowerbeds, no, I don't know, rockeries, swings, slides, roundabouts, water feature things. It's crap. Just a bit of flat land, like someone's forgotten about it, or is embarrassed by it.'

'Would a pair of kittens happily playing together all tangled up in some royal-blue ribbon annoy you?'

'Maybe not annoy. Just… irritate.'

With that, they walked up the grimy steps into the police station.

More searchers were joining the hunt, parties spreading out across the cemetery. The work was being coordinated from a pair of trestle tables hastily set up beside the mausoleum. So far, no hint of Maddy had been found.

Most of the land was being covered. It wouldn't be long before these few acres of urban greenery returned to their usual peace. Lesley kept getting ahead of the rest of the line and was told to calm down by Bradley.

'Sorry,' she said. 'I just worry that she's lying here somewhere, unconscious and hurt, and we need to find her before…'

They moved on, searching more quickly. All around, other parties were doing the same. The momentum of the hunt was growing.

Other journalists had arrived. A woman with a microphone was interviewing a couple of bystanders. In the far corner of the cemetery, a TV crew filmed, a reporter standing alongside, writing in a notebook.

'We should get going and get this article written,' Mitch said.

'She's not here, thank God,' Florence replied. 'How're you feeling?'

'What'd you mean?'

'Honestly?'

'Yes.'

'You were beating yourself up enough thinking you were responsible for what happened to Charl. Which you weren't, by the way. But if we'd have found Maddy…'

Some words didn't need saying. And Mitch certainly didn't need to hear them. He didn't reply, just kept on pacing, set strong and determined, eyes flicking back and forth, searching the overgrowth.

'Shit! I mean, um, I say. Oh, gosh. Here. Here!' It was Arthur from the far end of the line. Immediately they stopped and gathered around. Glancing to each other at first, but eventually having to look at what he had found.

A shallow barrow of dark earth had been dug in the greenness of the cemetery. 'Shit,' Arthur said again. 'Was that me? Did I do that? I mean, did I find… oh dear, oh my.' Josh wrapped an arm around his shoulders to try to comfort him, and Lesley, in turn, rested an arm on Josh's.

Mitch felt Florence beside him, very close, her breathing shallow. Without thinking, he reached out and eased her into him.

Bradley squatted down to look. With a pen, doubtless in the way he'd watched superhero detectives on the television, the sergeant pushed aside some overgrown grass. Gently, with exaggerated care, blade by blade. Until Mitch said, 'I don't think so.'

'What?' Bradley replied.

'The size. It's far too small. Unless there's been dismembering, which doesn't really happen, despite what you see on the TV.'

'And what do you know about it?'

'I used to do this stuff. Scenes of crime. For years.'

Bradley rose back up and turned around. 'So how do you explain a freshly dug grave when we're looking for a missing girl?'

Mitch pointed to a small piece of wood, mostly hidden by the grass at the side of the barrow. Bradley peered over and read, 'RIP Freddie, finest of the Collie kind.'

Unusually in modern policing, with forces the whipping boys of austerity, the desk was staffed by a cop rather than a civilian.

'I need to see the superintendent,' Ed said.

The woman peered at him through the thick scuffed plastic of the security barrier. She was young, looked stark, without any make-up, but with an impeccable uniform. In a coldly efficient voice, she said, 'I'm afraid he's busy with the hunt for the missing girl.'

'That's what we're here about. We want to help.'

The permafrost thawed a little. 'If you've got something to pass on, you can tell me. If you want to join a search party…'

'This is important. I need to see the superintendent. Face to face.'

'As I said…'

It never took Olivia long to lose patience, and today's feat was a record breaker. 'It was a simple enough request. We need to see the superintendent.'

'And I'm telling you…'

It was Ed who completed the hat trick of interruptions, but gently. 'When you're looking for a missing child, the protocols tell you that every second is vital. As is, potentially, every piece of information. Particularly when it comes from a very significant source. And I've got something the Gold Commander needs to hear, and he needs to hear it in person from me, right now.'

The jargon of death and disaster made an impact, just as Ed knew it would. If there was one thing a police officer could never ignore, it was police speak. The woman muttered something but picked up the phone.

25

The superintendent's office was at the top of several long puffs of stairs, and certainly made a statement of pride in its inhabitant's work.

The walls were adorned with photographs. All were black and white, and – according to the labels – the product of a challenge to the local further education college. Whether deliberately or not, the first was a classic of a cliché; a young officer was helping an older lady across a busy road. She even carried a couple of bags of shopping.

Others showed determined officers patrolling at a football match. Or smiling outside the gates of a school, amongst parents and children so happy they looked as though they had been given a shot of something illicit. Or an intrepid officer on a motorbike, flashing past, the background an arty blur of speed.

Olivia let out a low growl and muttered something about Soviet propaganda posters. Ed gave her a look that he hoped she would understand, given the delicacy of their position. It was fortunate they were alone in the room.

It was several minutes before Superintendent Saxton strode in. He was a Viking of a man, in olden days far more suited to pillaging than upholding the law. Incongruously with his looks and physique, he wore a regulation police sweater, although it did strain hard with the challenge of holding in his chest.

A mind which is wandering elsewhere always betrays itself, and Saxton hesitated with a telltale half-second pause as he consciously shifted his thoughts. His body may have been in this room, but his brain was with the search for Maddy. Even before he said a word to them, Saxton glanced at his watch.

They shook hands and Saxton lowered himself behind a roadblock of a desk. Ed and Olivia sat facing him, side by side, on the sort of chairs that suggested they wouldn't be staying long. Following some very rapid preliminaries, Saxton said, in a voice that hinted at northern roots, 'I'd appreciate it if this was brief. You'll understand why.'

'Of course,' Ed replied.

'You're ex police? The desk said so.'

'Kind of.'

'Meaning?'

'I worked with the police. Amongst others.'

'Doing what?'

'What we were all trying to do. Help the good and beat the bad.'

Saxton shifted in his seat. 'I don't have much time.'

'We're very sorry to bother you,' Olivia said. 'But we thought we might be able to help in the hunt for Maddy.'

The superintendent peered at her and recalculated. Anyone who has reached the higher echelons of policing has gone through a long and intensive course in dealing with people. Which means they usually know the quickest route to getting what they want.

'Apologies. It's been a difficult morning. I'm a father myself. Twin girls, a little younger than Maddy. That makes this feel personal.'

'Understood and appreciated,' Ed said. 'As for my credentials, I worked on the shady side of law enforcement. Enough to know command structures for a critical incident all too well. And that this police station was built in the 1980s, at the height of paranoia about an uprising against the state. Which is why the windows are narrow. So they can't be easily smashed by a mob. And so, if the worst came to the very worst, marksmen could be positioned here to fire on a crowd. Will that do you for giving us a few minutes?'

Saxton nodded. 'Go ahead.'

Mitch and Flo established a camp in the corner of a backstreet and bohemian coffee shop, and began writing. The waiter, sporting a peacock shirt and explosion of hair, brought over their drinks and spotted what they were doing.

'You dudes work for that *Last Edition*?' he asked, as though the café had been transported back to the tail end of the 1960s. 'You've really blasted onto the scene.'

'Just putting together another story now,' Flo replied. 'On the hunt for Maddy.'

'Man, I hope she's okay. She used to come in here. With her mum. She, Maddy that is, was always really cool.'

The man lingered a little longer, in that way people do when they have something to say but want to be asked. So Flo, understanding as ever, did.

'There was something odd about her, though,' the waiter went on. 'I mean, really something, man. She was older than fourteen, if you know what I mean. She flirted with me, which was kind of embarrassing, but cute too. She sure's got guts. That chick is way ahead of her time, you know what I mean? And sometimes it felt like she was the one telling Mum what to do, not the other way round.'

'Like how?'

'Like Mum was really quiet one day. All withdrawn into herself, you know the kind of thing. An interior day. So Maddy made out the plan of what they were going to do. Get the shopping, sort out some school stuff for her, then go look at some clothes, with a trip to the cinema as a treat. Made sure to slip in an upgrade to her phone as well. She knew how to play the game, that girl. But she was cute with it. Really sweet. Just like a little girl sometimes.

Loved that cat of hers. Always showing me pictures of him, she was.'

'Do you want to be in the story?' Mitch asked.

'Cool, Daddy,' came the appreciative exclamation. 'But not saying that downer sort of stuff. The story's a bummer enough as it is. How about… Maddy is such a lovely girl. The whole community's in shock. Everyone who can is out hunting for her. We just want her back with us. And what's that thing they always say? Our thoughts are with her family at this difficult time.'

The waiter considered for a moment, as though surprised at his sudden elevation to community statesman. 'Actually, scrub that last bit. Zap it, like it was never there. Her dad's a no good dick and a half, ain't he? He came in here a couple of times to get them, face like a smacked arse, and they stopped talking pronto. They looked as though they were being taken off to be executed, man. Death row for them. Bummer.'

Flo and Mitch exchanged a look. 'Can we put that bit in?' he asked.

'No way, man. I want to keep my job. And my teeth. The guy's crazy. Mr Mental Macho Man. Charl was always wearing big shades and lots of make-up. And you know what that means.'

'Covering up bruises again,' Mitch replied, subconsciously clenching his fists. 'He's going to need some real big shades of his own by the time I've done with him. Enough to cover his whole scabby body.'

'That's the spirit, man. Don't let the fascists win. But I know they were thinking of ways to sort him themselves. To get shot of him, at least. Last week, I heard them talking about the two of them running away somewhere. And then Charl said it was impossible, but Maddy was the one saying she'd find a way somehow. Researched it all, she reckoned.' The waiter let out a whistle. 'That's one cool chick. Respect to her, and you. I hope you find her, man.'

'I think I know what might have caused Maddy to disappear,' Ed said. 'But before I tell you, we're going to have to come to an understanding.'

'Why don't you tell me, then we can talk about an understanding,' Saxton replied, his eyes full of Viking determination.

'Because that's not how negotiations work,' Olivia cut in. 'They're a trade. Not a donation. That's charity. Not business.'

'The disappearance of a fourteen-year-old girl isn't business.'

'Nor is justice,' Ed said. 'And we're on sensitive ground here, aren't we?'

'Meaning?'

'You've got one of your own in the cells. Who, I'm guessing, you had your concerns about before. But you didn't act on them. And now his daughter's missing. And his wife's in hospital. Which leaves you with a problem. A big problem.'

And when Saxton said nothing, just stared at them, Olivia added, 'You did say time was critical here, didn't you?'

The superintendent leaned forward across his mass of a desk. 'Maybe we should have this conversation in an interview room. With you two under caution.'

Despite the photos, the attempts to make the office a less oppressive place, it was still the heart of a busy police station. And so not somewhere for smiles. But Ed let one creep across his face anyway.

'I used to use that trick too. When I was in your position.'

'Which, if you analyse it, isn't so strong,' Olivia continued, because there was only ever going to be so long that she would keep mostly quiet. 'We're trying to help. You're stopping us doing so. Which is not smart.'

Ed added, 'Particularly not when we could establish a relationship which would work for both our benefit.'

'We're journalists, by the way,' Olivia added, because the double act was working well enough to keep Saxton guessing. 'The *Last Edition*. We're pretty new, but maybe you've heard of us. We've been leading the way with coverage of Maddy's disappearance. I could show you the stats, if you like? Hundreds of thousands of people are waiting to hear from us with an update. That's a voice direct to a concerned public. Potentially very useful, wouldn't you say? So perhaps we should talk about what we're going to tell them.'

'And what you're going to do about a certain police officer, currently sitting in your cells,' Ed concluded.

The café was filling up, but Mitch and Flo didn't notice. They didn't see the stream of customers shuffling in for takeaway coffees or sandwiches. Or the gossip corners growing around them, sharing their news over a drink and early lunch. They didn't feel the blaze of sunshine which fell across their small corner table. They didn't even register the heady smells of the drinks and frying bacon.

The article was all.

Flo made a couple of attempts to start it. Maybe it was the pressure, but the words weren't giving themselves up easily. Unusually hesitant at the keyboard, each stroke was an effort of thought. And, as is so often the way, the harder Florence tried, the more elusive inspiration became.

We gathered with a sense of duty and dread.

'No, that's way too much, terrible melodrama,' she said, and deleted it.

We came from across the city, called by the most fundamental human instinct – to help protect our children.

'I quite like that,' Mitch said. 'Apart from the hyphen.'

'It's awful. It's like the start of a low-budget film.'

'We're a low-budget paper. And very low budget reporters.'

Flo didn't laugh. 'We've got to get this sorted soon. To stay ahead of the game with the story. But we've got to get it right as well. It's too important not to.'

'Keep going. It'll come.'

'That's fine for you to say. It's not coming at the moment, and it needs to. Why don't you have a go?'

Mitch shifted his hoodie around his shoulders. 'You're the touchy feely one.'

'Yeah? After that article you wrote on *No Man Left Behind*? Who are you trying to kid?'

A nudge and a smile, albeit fleeting, from Florence was plenty enough to persuade Mitch to give it a try. But for a lack of anything much, a blank screen can be remarkably intimidating. Mitch stared at it, but the dull glow wasn't giving away a hint of how to write the article.

Quite the reverse. It was mocking him.

He pulled the hoodie over his head and stared into the darkness. Thought back to the days before the *Last Edition*. Tried to push aside those memories of why he was here. Instead, recalled staring into the depths of the slow river.

With a shudder, Mitch freed himself from that other world and began writing.

What else can you do when you hear about a missing girl, but try to help?

Saxton was still staring at them with those penetrating Viking eyes. And because the superintendent was right, because every second counted in the search for a missing person, Ed came to a decision.

It was something he had hoped he would be able to hold back, perhaps even indefinitely. But if there was one thing he had come to learn, it was that the bizarre pantomime of life never followed the script.

Thinking, feeling, writing

He took comfort in the blueness of the sky, away in the distance, framed by those narrow windows. Noted how similar the colour was to Saxton's eyes. Thought of Flo and Mitch, who doubtless would have secured the story Ed had requested, and would currently be writing it up.

And of Olivia, sitting next to him. Bristling to march into battle. But managing to restrain herself, because, in the last couple of days, she had come to understand there was always a better way than war.

They had travelled so far together, and so fast. They had found that sacred beautiful land again, the one they thought they had lost forever.

And Saxton really did have fantastic eyes.

The little things. It was always the little things.

'This scar,' Ed said, rubbing at his neck. 'I got it in the line of duty. Your duty and mine,' he told Saxton. 'We were up against a terrorist cell. They were making suicide vests for some spectacular attack, as they call it, and they were smart. Well organised. They got a sniff that we were onto them. We managed to get them all, apart from one. He grabbed a vest and ran for it. Right into the street. We were after him, but… shit. There were so many people all around us. We couldn't get a shot. He could have pulled the cord any time. We were trying to clear the area, but you know what it's like. So many people, things happening so fast. We didn't have a chance.

'I was right up on him. I could see him looking around. He knew he was done. That we were going to get him. There was no way he was going to surrender. You know how these people think. It's all martyrdom and virgins. He was looking for somewhere to take out as many people as possible. So I had an idea.

'There was a subway ahead. I knew a team was moving in from the other direction. I reckoned if we got him down there, we could take him out. It wasn't perfect, but it was the best we could do. The only plan we had. The only form of containment. So I tried to chase him that way. And it was working.

'The other team had managed to get the subway evacuated. I saw him head for it, because he knew. The bastards always know. They do their research well. Train and prepare like bloody professionals. A confined area amplifies the blast and causes the most carnage. The explosion, the nails, ball bearings, the shock waves... Jesus.'

Ed hesitated, because this was the part of the story which was hardest. He was aware of Saxton and Olivia staring at him. He was safe in this corner of a police station, high above an ancient and peaceful city. But all he could see was that urban Tuesday morning, all those months earlier, and the subway.

'I was still up with him. We were almost there. We hit this square, there were still loads of people around, and I feinted left. That kept him heading right and he went for it. He went into the subway. He knew I was right on him and he was looking for somewhere to do it. I could see him grabbing for the cord. But then he realised there was no-one in there.

'There were bags and newspapers and all that kind of stuff strewn around, in the panic where we'd got everyone out. But no people. No targets. There was just the team at the other end, and me behind him. We yelled at him to surrender, and he hesitated, just for a second. Right then, I thought we'd got him. I really thought so. I thought everything was going to be okay. Then he ran towards the other team. They started firing, but he got close enough. He was probably dying as he pulled the cord.'

Another hesitation. Then the light, the sound, they exploded once again, ripping through Ed's mind. As they did, night after night after night.

As they always would.

'I don't remember anything else, apart from coming round in hospital. I was lucky. The guy running towards the other team, that was what saved me.' Ed rubbed hard at his scar, felt it warming and throbbing as the worm of skin inflamed. 'I got this and a few other scrapes and burns. Plus a bit of emotional trauma. You know the sort of thing. The kind where every dawn is dark. They got... well, blown to bloody bits. My friends, my colleagues. Blown apart. As simple as that.'

And now, in this sunlit room, a silence detonated. Ed stared at the sky outside because he couldn't look at the two people watching him.

But they were looking at him. And how they were looking.

He felt a pressure, a warmth on his shoulder. Jumped a little with the touch. The link back to today, to here and now.

It was Olivia winding an arm around him. And her eyes, oh her eyes. They were diffuse, shining, full of tenderness, and perhaps – even – empathy.

'Is that what this is all about?' she whispered. 'What you said about you needing to find a friend of hope? Maybe her best friend.'

Ed didn't answer. Maybe he couldn't. Not here, not now. Not yet.

'Jesus,' Saxton said, quietly. 'Okay, deal done. We've reached an understanding. What was it you wanted to tell me?'

It took a moment for Ed to reply. To gather himself back in this office, to be sure he was here and safe, to free himself from the claws of the past.

'I might know what caused this, as I said,' Ed replied. 'Charl getting a beating, and Maddy disappearing. And I think it might have been me.'

26

The conversation began in that curious place known as *off the record*. Where nothing is reportable, unless an eyebrow is raised, or a head nodded at a certain point and in a certain way.

'What's your primary interest here?' Saxton asked. 'Just to check we're on the same page.'

Olivia said, as though she'd been asked the most stupid question of her life, 'Finding Maddy safe and well.'

'And maybe we can use our insights and the *Last Edition* to help,' Ed added more diplomatically.

'And after that?'

'Whatever comes next.'

Preliminary negotiations over, they discussed what might have happened to Maddy. And it was a mystery. Because, given all the police knew so far, she had simply disappeared.

There was no CCTV in Suffolk Street where the family lived, apart from one camera. It was trained on a garage and didn't help. But there were plenty on Millhouse Road, with its shops, restaurants and bars. And there were no sightings of her. Not a single one. Neither by cameras, nor people who knew Maddy.

'And there would have been, if she'd gone that way,' Saxton said.

'The family have lived in the area for years. Most people knew her. They would have said hello. Maybe intervened if she looked upset. At the very least, they would have remembered seeing her.'

Millhouse Road was the route Maddy always took to school. She was always on time and prepared for the day. The alarm had been raised when she hadn't turned up.

'That was completely out of character,' Saxton told them. 'It's a good school and they phoned home immediately. They got a paramedic, instead of Mum or Dad, so then got straight onto us. Hence the scramble.'

The cemetery backed onto the row of houses that included Maddy's, which was why the search had focused there. There was no gate leading from the family's garden to the cemetery, but the wall wasn't tall. The cemetery was the first thought about where she might have gone, perhaps to hide away from a world which was growing too vicious and distressing.

Or where she might have been taken.

'But there's been no sign of her,' Saxton said. 'Nothing in the cemetery itself. We've done house to house along the road. And in all the houses around the cemetery. No-one saw Maddy. No-one saw anything unusual. There were no reports of a girl being forced into a car. No talk of shouts or screams, or a row going on. No fights, no confrontations, no hint of an abduction. No nothing. Everything was quiet and normal. She just disappeared.'

'So what happened?' Olivia asked.

'The honest answer is that we simply don't know. But the theory we're working on is that Maddy has run away. Her mum's just got a beating. Dad's been arrested. Things have hardly been good at home and now they're infinitely worse. She's not thinking straight. She just wants to get away. Maybe she disguised herself somehow. She's smart enough, according to what we've been told. Put on shades and some of her mum's clothes, perhaps. And just slipped away.'

'To go where? To be with who?'

'That's exactly what we're trying to work out. But she's clearly vulnerable. There are more than a few people about who would be delighted to bump into a fourteen-year-old in need of comfort and help, sad to say. So I've called in every cop I can find to join the search. But so far… not a thing.'

Saxton leaned forward across his mass of a desk and said to Ed, 'So what did you do that might have caused this?'

'Talking in the terms of our understanding?'

'Is there any other way of getting to hear this?'

It was one of those questions which didn't need an answer. Ed blew out a long breath, adjusted his glasses, then told Saxton how he and Mitch had ambushed Chris.

Then came another pause in a morning which had been marked with them. Saxton stared across his desk at Ed and Olivia, and they stared right back.

The superintendent's Viking roots had previously been a matter of conjecture. But now the warrior coloured visibly with a lust for battle.

'What the fuck did you think you were doing?'

Unusually for Olivia, in the face of such a challenge, she stayed quiet. Which confirmed Ed's suspicion that the mission he and Mitch had undertaken was excessively macho. Fuelled by pride, more than logic. A lesson he thought he had learnt years ago.

And now they were paying the price. With Maddy missing. And currently… who knew where? With who knew what happening to her?

'Kidnapping a police officer,' Saxton went on, building the momentum of his charge. 'Threatening him. Coercing him. Humiliating him. And then thinking you'd been smart and tough enough to sort the problem out and letting him go home. When you knew what kind of man you were dealing with. Full of boiling rage, no doubt, even if he managed not to show it. And with one person to take it out on. I'm having second thoughts about this understanding. Not to mention your heroism in hunting down a terrorist. And even talking to you, come to that. You're a fucking idiot.'

Beside him, he felt Olivia bristle. It never took long with a temper like that. But he stretched out an arm to stop her from retaliating.

'You're right. I was stupid. We were stupid. We got way ahead of ourselves. Fell victim to the vigilante thing. No excuses, however much it might have been excusable. It was wrong and I'm sorry. I screwed up. It's as simple as that. But now I'd like a chance to put things right.'

Saxton deflated a little, with the scent of battle snatched away. 'I should arrest you for what you did,' he said eventually.

'Just like we should put out that the police knew one of their officers was a wife beater, but didn't do anything about it,' Olivia replied, because, inevitably, that volcanic spirit had forced its way to the surface. 'I can see the headline now. *Cop cover-up puts mother in hospital and daughter on the streets.* Imagine how that'd go down.'

Ed managed not to react. But it was a tough act to pull off. Olivia really was getting the hang of the news business impressively well. Not to mention life in general.

Saxton, however, did react, and with a resurrection of the force of his warmongering forebears. 'Are you threatening me?'

'No-one's threatening anyone,' Ed intervened quickly, before Olivia could confirm it. 'We have an understanding, remember?'

'Which I went into blind.'

'But not deaf,' Olivia shot back. 'You knew what you were doing.'

'And now I might be reconsidering. So you remember that. If it comes to a point when I have to arrest you…'

'Now who's threatening who?'

'I don't need to. It's Chris I'd worry about. He's not the forgiving type.'

Ed held up his hands to calm the warring parties. 'There's wrong on all sides here, which means we need to accept that and work together to put it right. Don't we?' But Olivia and Saxton continued the battle of the eyes, so he went on, 'We're wasting time arguing. Let's get back to our priority. Which is finding Maddy. Isn't it? Well?'

189

Ed waited, waited, waited, and eventually received huffs and breaths from the two eager combatants. Which might be far from a legally binding armistice, but would do for now.

'Any suggestions?' Saxton asked.

'Maddy knows about the *Last Edition*. And as you said, she's smart. She knows there'll be a big fuss about her disappearance, and what happened with her mum. She knows we're likely to be covering it. So we should put out a message designed to make her come home.'

'Or…' Olivia added, 'Worst case scenario, pressure whoever might have her, or have given her somewhere to stay, into giving her up.'

'Assuming she's still alive,' Saxton said. 'Or will be for much longer. The stats say if we don't find her fast, we don't find her at all. Not still with us, at least.'

A knock at the door and a hovering uniformed presence interrupted them. But Saxton waved the distraction away. 'What message were you thinking?'

'An interview with you. Making it clear Maddy's not in trouble. That you just need to make sure she's safe and well. But also…'

'You've got to make it clear her dad's out of the picture,' Olivia picked up, forging ahead as ever. 'Given that it's most likely she's run away because of him.'

'And what would help all that even more,' Ed continued, 'are a few words from her mum in the article. In fact, that's the most important thing of all.'

'How is she?' Olivia asked.

'She's conscious and she'll be okay,' Saxton replied. 'There are a couple of officers with her now. But…'

'Let me guess.' Olivia's words were dripping with bile. 'She doesn't want to make a complaint against her so-called husband?'

Saxton didn't need to answer, so Ed said, 'But she does want her daughter back.'

'She doesn't know Maddy's missing yet. They're telling her now.'

The agreement was holding, if rather unsteadily. Ed and Olivia had been instructed to wait, but not in the comfort of the superintendent's office. Instead, they sat in the far less hospitable surroundings of the reception area.

This was no place for soft-focus photographs of smiling police officers. It was one notch up from being a cell, with its colourless unyielding walls and thick plate glass. The people who came and went were either in tears or in bandages, and sometimes both.

Ed and Olivia sat side by side on a row of fitted plastic seats which had apparently been designed as an additional punishment for criminals, and waited for the call. To find out whether Saxton would grant them an interview, or offer a few official quotes.

But more importantly, whether Charl would be willing – and able – to talk to them.

They phoned Mitch but got Florence. He was too busy writing to be disturbed she said, a pronouncement which made Olivia roll her eyes.

Yes, they had the story. And yes, it would be ready for publication in the next few minutes.

'The shares, likes and follows are tapering off a bit,' Olivia said, doing her keyboard tapping techno whizz thing.

'Then get it out there ASAP,' Ed told Florence.

She also mentioned what the waiter had told them about Maddy. 'Which makes it look more likely she has run off somewhere,' Ed said to Olivia. 'She's not daft enough to be conned by someone who might want to take advantage of her. But she is driven enough to do her own thing.'

'But where? Where has she gone?'

'That's the question.'

Chris was still in the cells and had been interviewed. Saxton didn't need to go into what he had said because he had said nothing. He was a cop and knew the power of a no comment to every question. And if Charl refused to make a complaint, that meant Chris would soon walk free.

'But he won't be going home,' Saxton added. 'The house is a potential crime scene and we've got more work to do there.'

'I hope he won't be going back on duty?' Ed asked.

'I won't be able to stop him if there's no complaint or case against him. Not officially, at least.'

'Meaning?' Olivia asked, with one of her sniper-shot questions.

'I'll keep him close by my side. Doing some critically important admin.' For the first time, the superintendent almost smiled, but the look had a malicious edge. 'I've got a couple of projects that need urgent attention. The cycling in the wintertime health and safety liaison sub group could do with being re-energised. As could the multi-agency public spaces decriminalisation strategy committee. All that might give him time to reflect on the error of his ways.'

They did learn one piece of important news. When Ed raised the concern that Alan might have been a paedophile, according to Chris, at least.

'So, his house…'

'Give us a bloody break,' Saxton replied. 'We'd have been all over it, inside and out, looking for Maddy if he was. Checking all the family's neighbours was one of the first things we did, starting with next door, surprise, surprise. The man's got no criminal record, no complaints against him, and there's not even a hint that he's a paedophile. He's a good citizen of this proud nation, according to the record.'

Back in the charming surroundings of the reception area, a young woman walked unsteadily up to the police station's glass doors, then hesitated, lurched away and was violently sick.

'You take me to all the nicest places,' Olivia said. And when Ed didn't reply, they lapsed into a long reflective silence, waiting. Just waiting.

It took another ten minutes before Saxton himself emerged. 'You're not great, far from it. But you're the best I've got, for now anyway,' he told them. 'Let's get to the hospital. Charl's okay to give you a few minutes.'

27

E ddervale Hospital was on the edge of the city, not far from the mobile home park where Ed lived, and a town in itself. The campus was vast, filled with clusters of buildings, some rising into the sky like blocks of flats, others squat and somehow menacing.

Even on a sunshine day like this, the hospital felt dark. And that wasn't just because of the deep shadows cast by the taller edifices and rows of trees that separated the buildings and endless car parks.

Colour-coded signs pointed to a range of different destinations in signposts that resembled explosions. Ambulances screamed in and out, while cars crawled around in the eternal modern trial of attempting to find a parking space.

Saxton had no such problems. The police were miserably regular visitors here, so had spaces set aside, and conveniently at the heart of the site.

They walked fast to Blackbird Ward, where Charl was being treated. 'Blackbird?' Olivia muttered. 'Crow would be more like it.'

She had a point, Ed thought. Nurses, doctors, visitors, no-one was smiling. The correct expression was grimness, often tending to tears. Death was ever-present, lingering everywhere, awaiting his moment, however much the purpose of the place was to keep its customers out of his relentless clutches.

Corridors blurred past as they strode along at police speed, Saxton in the lead. 'She's very fragile, so we've only got a couple of minutes with her,' he said. 'And be gentle.' He turned to Olivia, to emphasise the words. 'That's gentle, okay?'

A wraith of a nurse with an Olympian expression of disapproval signed them into the ward. She walked them down another corridor, narrower and cleaner, to a door at the end. A ridiculously young police officer stood guard outside. He jumped to attention at the sight of Saxton.

'How is she?' the superintendent asked.

'She's supposed to be resting,' the juvenile replied. 'But she calls out to me every couple of minutes, asking for news.'

Saxton nodded, straightened his tunic, and knocked at the door.

If they hadn't known it was Charl lying in the bed, they would never have recognised her. The definition of her face, cheekbones, nose, eyes, was largely gone. Beaten away by the assault of an enraged man who had once solemnly promised to love her.

The swelling was so severe she must have been near blind, with only slits masquerading for eyes. And the colours that daubed her flesh were shades that should never taint a human body.

Ed felt something shift inside him. The guilt and responsibility that had throbbed before now seared like heartburn.

And the knowledge that if Chris should come seeking him out, hunting for revenge, that would not be something to fear. But instead, to welcome.

Beside Ed, Olivia hissed in a breath. Even Saxton, a man who must have seen so many horrors in his policing career, could say nothing. They just stood, because it was all they were able to do.

Charl shifted her head slowly to look at them, the movement an effort of will. And Saxton found some words. Appreciating her pain and distress. Apologising for disturbing her. They meant nothing, but at least they filled the dreadful silence, so choked with remorse.

She listened, waited, and then words emerged from what had once been a mouth. Quiet and distorted with pain, but unmistakeable. Words which had been said to the officer on guard outside, and every visitor, each and every time the door opened.

'Have you found her?'

'No. Not yet.'

Charl's head fell back onto the pillow and those slits of eyes closed.

'But we will,' Saxton continued. 'We will.' And with a new determination, a real power of belief, an apology and a promise, he said again, 'We will find her. And we think you can help us with that. If you feel strong enough?'

Charl didn't move but whispered, 'Anything.'

Ed and Olivia pulled chairs up to the side of the bed so Charl didn't have to raise her voice or move her head. Saxton stood behind them, against the wall, arms folded.

'We need to put out a message that will make Maddy come home,' Ed said quietly. 'You know best what that would be.'

Charl made a strange gurgling noise which might have been an attempt at a chuckle. 'Tell her Hector has come back and he's pining for her. She loved that bloody cat.'

'We can do that. We'll even use a picture of him. No problem at all. But there's something else to think about. What about her future?' Olivia asked with a touching gentleness. 'That's what she's probably thinking about most. What'll happen when she comes back? Where she – you – both of you – are going to live.'

There was a silence, filled only by the noise of Charl's breathing. Finally, she said, 'She's wanted me to leave for ages. Kept on at me, telling me not to take it anymore. Said we should get out and find somewhere else. That anything would be better than what we were going through. And when I asked her where we'd go, she said we'd find something. She was looking up refuges, legal help, all that kind of thing. Bloody amazing that girl is. I sometimes wonder if she's really my daughter. But I wouldn't do it. I wouldn't leave. I couldn't. She got mad at me sometimes. Said if I didn't sort things out, then she would.'

At the side of the little room, Saxton's eyes fell to stare at the floor. As for Ed, he felt it too. The silent stares from the inanimate walls. Unblinking, unrelenting. The looks of accusation, blame, and recrimination.

'It's my fault,' Charl went on. 'I thought he'd change. I really did. When it happened, he'd apologise, we'd make up, and he'd promise it wouldn't happen again. Time after time. He was a good man once. I thought he could be a good man again. I stayed with him for Maddy because I wanted us to be a family. And for myself, I suppose. Because I was frightened of being alone. At my age. With nothing. No job, no home, no qualifications. What choice did I have? That's what I thought anyway. I wasn't brave enough to do the right thing and get out. It was my fault.'

Olivia reached out a hand and took Charl's. 'Don't blame yourself. It's not your fault. If you were guilty of anything, it's only being human. Having faith in people. Giving them a chance. Doubting yourself. Daring to hope. It's nothing to be ashamed of. We all do that. All of us.'

With an effort of will, Charl tilted her head to look more closely at Olivia. And said words which the young woman could not often have heard. 'You're very kind.'

Olivia sighed, deep and long. It was an exhalation of emotion so meaningful that it made both Ed and Saxton study her, wondering what was coming next.

'I'm not kind. I just know. I know all too bloody well. I've been there. Once, when I was younger. I thought I was in love. I thought he was great. So handsome, smart, and so bloody charming. I really fell for him. Right in at the deep end. But he had a dark side. He hid it well, but it didn't take long to come out. He'd go out. Have a drink. And then he'd come back and hit me. I don't know how long I stuck it for. I can hardly remember those days. But whatever, it was too long. Far too long. I got out in the end. And I changed. I became... a different person. I got fit. Got strong. I swore no-one would ever do that to me again. No-one. Ever. And they haven't. And they never will. So don't blame yourself. I've been there. So many of us have been there. You're not alone. Far from it. Very, very far from it.'

For Ed, a new father to this random group he had assembled, it was an effort not to reach out and give Olivia a hug. For all he'd seen in his life, all the emotions he'd been through in the past three days, this moment left him speechless. The explanation beneath the denim armour that Olivia wore.

Charl lay back on her pillow again and took a few seconds to find the strength to continue. 'Maybe we've got something in common then,' she said, reaching out for Olivia's hand. 'Because now I've decided. It makes you think, lying here like this. With your only girl missing. Knowing she's run away because of what you did. Or didn't do.'

'You don't know that...' Olivia began. But Charl cut her off.

'I've decided. I've had enough of being a punch bag. Maddy was right. We're getting out. You can tell her that. Put it in your paper. Say that I'm a fighter, I'm getting better, and I'm going to build a whole new life after this. And say that I need Maddy with me to help me through. It'll be tough, but together we can do it. Say that I love her so much, I miss her, and I need her here with me so we can build a new future together.'

Charl eased back in the bed, her breathing still loud in the small room, but perhaps a little easier. Ed finished writing down what she'd said and he nodded to Saxton. They had what they needed. The sooner the story was published, the better the chances of Maddy seeing it and coming forward. It was time to go.

'I'll do the bit about Maddy not being in any trouble, and that we just need to know where she is,' Saxton said. He made for the door but was interrupted by a grunt from Charl.

'I still blame you,' she managed.

'I'm sorry…' Ed began.

'Not you. Him.'

Charl was sitting up again and pointed a shaky finger at Saxton.

'I'll never forget what you did. He was a good man until that. A good husband and father. And a good cop too. Wasn't he? Go on, admit it. He was, wasn't he? And you screwed all that up. You did it. You bastard.'

For the first time, the superintendent looked less sure of himself. 'Come on now, this isn't the time. We can talk about all that later when you're feeling better.'

They were interrupted by the nurse bustling into the room, and with zeal. 'What's all this fuss? What're you doing, getting my patient all excited? She's here to get better, not be made worse by you. Come on, it's time you left.'

And with all the righteous force of years of medical superiority, Nurse Imperious busily ushered Saxton, Ed and Olivia out of the room.

It was only when they had emerged from the hospital and into the sunlight that Ed said, 'Well then?'

'What?' Saxton asked, heading for the police car and not breaking stride.

'You know what,' Olivia replied.

'That's a private matter.'

'Not if it's anything to do with Maddy disappearing.'

'It isn't. It's an internal police issue.'

'Charl didn't seem to think so.'

'You've got your story. We've got an agreement. So go write it up and get it out there.'

Olivia took the superintendent's arm and, with surprising ease, pulled him to a halt. Saxton tried to resist but it wasn't so simple against a determined Olivia. And there was rarely any other kind.

'If we're working together on trying to get Maddy back, I think we deserve to know.'

'It's not relevant. Now let's get going. I want this story out there.'

'In which case, you'd better answer the question.'

Saxton glared at her, but such looks were as bothersome as summer flies to Olivia. They just bounced right off her armour and she glared right back, entirely unintimidated.

It was Ed who broke the stalemate. 'He's going to come for me, isn't he? Chris, I mean. Charl's not going to press charges against him. Which means he'll be out of the cells soon. And he's going to want revenge for that ambush.'

'I could do without any other complications while we're hunting for Maddy, if you could manage that.'

'But he is, isn't he? He's going to come for me.'

Saxton nodded. 'I'd say that was a fair conclusion.'

'Then I think I've got a right to know what I'm dealing with. Haven't I?'

They had been standing on a pavement by the front of the hospital, in full view of anyone feeling nosey. Which, on planet earth, meant anyone. So Saxton backed into the shade of a sickly looking copse of trees and told his story.

Chris had been a sergeant, and, in fairness to him, apparently a good one. He was identified as a candidate for promotion and was going through the process of becoming an inspector.

One routine Thursday night on patrol, Chris was called to a house on the eastern fringe of Cambridge. The neighbours had reported screams and shouts, along with thudding and crashing, followed by the inevitable sobbing. It was a depressingly familiar call for any cop with more than a few days' experience of life on the beat.

Chris found a modern semi-detached house full of smashed plates, glasses and furniture, and Suzy, a young and slight woman, bleeding and in tears. Zach, her equally young, cheaply tattooed, and far more muscular husband, had calmed a little, but remained full of anger. Chris had, the story went, been cool and professional, to start with at least.

'But being a cop makes you a target,' Saxton said. 'If Zach couldn't fight his wife anymore, the police were the next best thing. You know the type. Too much drink. Too much testosterone. Want to show the world how tough they are. He kept on at Chris. Kept going at him. And maybe Chris was having a bad day, or the guy just got to him. It happens sometimes. But he gave Zach a whack to shut him up. Harder than he meant to, probably.

'Zach goes down, hits his head, and knocks himself out. He was okay in the end. But then Suzy goes mad at Chris. For hitting her guy. Because he's a good man really, it was her fault for provoking him, you know the sort of thing they say. And she videos Zach on the floor, bleeding and out for the count, and does this commentary about what Chris has done. It ends up that she makes the complaint. How ironic is that? The woman he was trying to help. The footage from Chris's body camera confirms her story. So we've got no choice, no matter what the provocation. Cops just can't react like that. We're supposed to be better. We have to put him through a disciplinary. Which means demotion and being told he's got no chance of promotion ever again.'

Saxton shook his head. 'Both Chris and Charl hated me, and the police in general after that. He couldn't leave his job, he didn't have anything else. And maybe he had a point to prove. But he was a bitter and angry man from then on. Which was ironic because what he didn't know is that I did my best to save him, and actually stopped him getting kicked out of the force. But anyway, it was after that that it all started, his domestic issues. And before you ask, yes, we did know about them. Words were had. But Charl would never make a complaint, Chris knows the system, so what can you do? The whole thing was one great big fuck-up.'

'Which culminated in Maddy not being able to take it anymore and running away,' Ed said after a long pause. 'Following our ambush on her dad.'

'I guess we're all in this together then, aren't we?' Saxton replied. 'So you do your bit and try to get her back, will you? This story's been bad enough as it is. Let's try to stop it getting any worse.'

I t was a strange place for a newsroom meeting, but it was about the only choice they had. They didn't want to risk being overheard, which meant no cafés, coffee shops, or bars, and they had to be near to the police station.

In case the story worked and Maddy called in, or was found. Was brought there in a blaze of blue lights, sirens, and relief.

And they were on the spot to capture the moment.

So that Wednesday lunchtime they sat, the staff of the *Last Edition*, in a corner of Parker's Piece, under the canopy of one of the few trees the not-quite-a-park offered. Opposite the police station, always keeping a watchful eye on the comings and goings, and waiting – hoping – for a call.

Under the shaky terms of their shady agreement, Saxton had promised to let Ed know the moment there were any developments. In the hunt for Maddy, or Chris's questioning.

And when he was going to be released from the cells.

A group of young lads put down their sweatshirts and began a game of football, their shouts and laughter carrying easily across the turf.

Florence had brought some sandwiches and water, and shared them around. 'Not a bad spot for a picnic,' she said, making Olivia curl a lip.

She was once again staring at the flat patch of grassy nothingness as though it had offended her.

At least she had some more statistics to distract her. Both the new stories had been posted and were doing well.

'We couldn't have timed it better,' Olivia explained, stretching out her legs into the sunshine. 'Lunchtime always sees a peak in Internet traffic as people take their breaks. There's already huge interest in the story, and we were the right people in the right place at the right time to capitalise.'

Shares, comments and follows had surged to such an extent that Olivia yelped, 'Shit,' and went through some very fast keyboard manoeuvres.

'Dare we ask what that was about?' Mitch said, when the activity had calmed.

'There was so much traffic we were in danger of crashing. Shit, I've never seen that before, apart from with a top-notch cyber-attack. But no worries, I've grabbed us some more capacity and we're fine now.'

With so much going on, it felt a little strange to admire their handiwork, Ed thought. But there was nothing they could do at that moment, except wait. And anyway, there was that motto which had brought them together, and which travelled with them everywhere, even to a working picnic in the park.

Thinking, feeling, writing

A movement over by the police station caught his attention. Ed couldn't be sure, but he thought he saw a figure dip out of sight behind a van. A figure which had been watching this little group sitting on the grass.

He turned his head and watched for a couple more minutes, out of the edge of his eye line, but saw nothing else. So, instead, Ed rejoined the conversation about the stories they had managed to produce so quickly, and which were having such an impact.

Mother's Tearful Plea for Return of Her Missing Girl

The mother of missing 14-year-old Maddy Williams has made a heartrending plea to be reunited with her daughter.

Speaking exclusively to the Last Edition, Charl Williams said, 'I love her so much. I miss her every moment and can't stop thinking about her. Please, Maddy, if you're reading this, get in touch to let me know you're okay. And if anyone knows where she is, please contact the police so you can end this nightmare.'

'Powerful stuff,' Florence said.

'It was hardly difficult,' Olivia replied, but with perhaps the hint of a modest smile. 'All I needed to do was fill the report with Charl's quotes.'

'Some stories are like that,' Ed said. 'It takes a good reporter to know when to keep quiet and let someone speak.'

They had photos of both Maddy and Charl, but not mother and daughter together. That, however, posed little trouble for someone with Olivia's mastery of technology. A quick play with an app and, as if by magic, a lovely picture of the pair appeared.

The rest of the story was filled with more of Charl's words, plus a brief recap about Maddy's disappearance. It concluded with a quote from Saxton.

'I want to emphasise to Maddy that she isn't in trouble. She has my word on that. We just need her to come forward so we can make sure she's safe.'

'How much do we respect this Saxton's word?' Mitch asked, easing himself back on the grass.

'That,' Ed replied, 'is a very good question.'

The story on the search for Maddy followed on from the interview with Charl, and was tagged as an *Eyewitness Despatch*.

'Oh, very good,' Olivia said. 'Very media.'

With the Searchers in the Hunt for Maddy

We came together in hope and fear. Dozens of people from across Cambridge, united only in the basic human instinct of wanting to help.

We hoped to find Maddy. But we never spoke about what we feared.

'That's brilliant,' Ed said. 'Really fine writing. Well done. Florence?'

'It was Mitch,' she said, shifting a little closer to him and reaching out to give him a gentle appreciative touch. 'I added a few bits here and there.'

The man in the hoodie didn't acknowledge the plaudits. He was too busy staring at the police station. His eyes were dark, even in the brightness of the day. And that hood was high up on his shoulders again, moving dangerously close to where it had been when he had first ventured out from the netherworld.

'I owed her that,' Mitch said at last. 'And Charl too. I owed both her and Maddy that.'

'We'll get her back,' Florence told him.

'Will we?'

'Yes. We will. Come on, believe it. We'll get her back.'

A pause, and then, 'I hope you're right.'

Ed knew exactly what Mitch was feeling. He was still going through it himself; had been since he saw Charl only an hour or so earlier. And before too long, Chris would emerge from the police station and the time would come to complete their unfinished business.

In teams led by police officers, we quartered across the cemetery. It was a bitterly ironic place to search, given our unspoken fears. But no-one mentioned that either.

This was no day for small talk. Only for action. All of us doing our best to help in the hunt for one of our own.

Step by step we paced, so focused for anything that might be a clue. Any sign she had been here and that she was still with us. Any hint of hope for us to hold on to.

'Carry on like this, Mitch, and we'll have to put the awards panel on standby,' Ed said. But the man in the hoodie didn't laugh, didn't even smile. The invisible clouds which surrounded him were too thick for any light to get through.

The article went into some pictures and quotes from the searchers. It concluded by mentioning more search parties were being gathered together to scour other parts of the city. And they would keep looking until they found that which they sought.

'What next, then?' Olivia asked.

'We wait,' Ed replied.

'I never got the hang of waiting.'

'Me neither. But I don't think we've got any choice this time.'

Florence turned her face to the sky and let the sun caress the smoothness of her skin. 'I get this feeling we won't be waiting long.'

Bicycles trundled by in their endless procession, flicking lazy shadows across the group. It wasn't a day for cycling fast.

Olivia let out a groan. 'We've got an e-mail from Tyson. It's titled

Pylons' Complaint. He must be pissed. He even apostrophised it. Although, logically, I don't think it should have an apostrophe.'

'I thought that was coming,' Ed said. 'Not the error with the apostrophe. The complaint, I mean. We didn't exactly make him look like a hero. What does it say?'

It took a few seconds for Olivia to reply. And when she did, it was with rare and unexpected laughter.

'He's moaning that he can't go and see a pylon in peace anymore. He says that wherever he goes, there are gangs of other people, all collecting pylon numbers. We've made his hobby too popular, he says.'

'I thought that was what he wanted. You really can't please some people, can you? Is there any news about him finding a special someone to go doing his thing with?'

'He reckons he's got too many women who want to go pyloning with him. And quite a few men too, apparently. Wherever he goes, people want to take photos of him. He says he's become a star and a kind of… you won't believe this.'

'Go on.'

'A sort of anti-hero of an alternative society. That's what people are saying about him, believe it or not. FFS. There are requests for interviews. His recommendations about what pylons to start with if you're taking up the hobby. There's even talk of a book deal. FFS squared! Everyone wants a bit of him, he says.'

'And he's complaining about that?'

'Write back and tell him he's lucky,' Mitch said. 'And if he doesn't start being grateful, we'll come out and do another story on him.'

Ed kept his eyes on the police station. But all was quiet. There was no sign of any excitement or the watcher he thought he had seen earlier. Florence tidied up the sandwich wrappings and took them over to a bin.

'So, what do we do now?' Olivia asked.

'Keep waiting.'

'How long for?'

It really was like having a child sometimes. Except, after her confession to Charl, Ed thought he now understood Olivia much better. 'I don't know,' he said, with all the patience of a father. 'As long as it takes.'

And playing her part in the parent and adolescent performance, Olivia replied, 'Stuff that.'

She got up and jogged over to where the lads were playing football. The remaining three couldn't hear the conversation, but they could see the reaction. The boys were quiet, respectful, and couldn't help themselves edging closer to her.

After a short conversation, Olivia joined one of the teams. It was no surprise to see her quickly jinking her way through a defence, players bouncing off that slight frame in their futile attempts to stop her, and scoring a goal.

Ed was about to clap but his phone rang. It was Saxton.

'Have you found her?'

'No.'

'What's going on then?'

'Something weird's happened.'

'What?'

'You know those cats that went missing? Maddy's and some of her neighbours?'

'It was the first story we did. Of course I know. It's how we met the family and everyone else. What's happened?'

'The cats have come home. All of them, all at the same time. Just like that.'

They headed back to Millhouse Road, and at speed. Or three of the four did. Ed stayed behind, to watch the police station and remain on hand if there should be a hint of Maddy being found.

There was a brief discussion first, but it only took seconds.

'Can we trust this Saxton?' Mitch asked Ed. 'Because the return of the lost cats thing sounds like a classic way of putting us off the scent. Drawing us away from where the real action is.'

'I think we can trust him. Partly anyway. And for now at least.'

'Which isn't exactly a ringing endorsement.'

'So I'll stay here, whatever. Just in case.'

Olivia, as so often, raised the key question. 'Are the cats connected with Maddy disappearing?'

That took a little thought before anyone answered. Then Florence said, 'It's too much of a coincidence not to be, isn't it? And didn't I read in some thriller that coincidences always tell you something's going on?'

'It's weird,' Olivia added, not in the least out of breath after her football match. 'But we know for a fact that Maddy really loved her cat. Hector was her comfort through all she was suffering. And the day after he disappeared, she goes missing.'

'That might've been something to do with her dad being an arsehole and her mum being beaten senseless,' Mitch pointed out.

'Okay, but the logic goes like this: Cat disappears, Maddy vanishes. So if cat reappears…'

'I'd be delighted if it were that simple,' Ed replied. 'The truth is we don't know if there's a connection. But we're not achieving anything with all of us sitting here, waiting. Let's go find out if there might be something in it.'

'Is Maddy's cat definitely back?' Florence asked.

'I didn't have a chance to ask Saxton. He was up to his neck in the search. Let's see the other owners, work out if Maddy's cat is back, and if there might be a connection between the cats and her disappearance.'

'At the very least, we get another story,' Olivia said. 'Agreed?'

Which they all did. Apart from Mitch.

It was only a couple of minutes into the walk to Millhouse Road when Mitch said, 'You two go cat hunting. I'll catch you later.'

'Where are you going?' Florence asked.

'To do some proper work.'

'This could be important,' Olivia said.

'What, taking photos of pussy cats when a young girl's still missing?'

His eyes were blazing in that warning manner. Florence reached out an arm but Mitch shrugged it aside and strode away, pulling his hoodie up over his head.

'That's a bad sign,' she said quietly.

Olivia watched him go, then muttered, 'For fuck's sake.'

'Give him a break. He's suffering.'

'Aren't we all?'

'But we don't all hold ourselves responsible for Maddy disappearing, do we? And if something's happened to her…'

Florence didn't need to finish the sentence. But Olivia wasn't one to tolerate an incomplete equation. 'What?'

'Frankly, I doubt we'd ever see Mitch again. And that's the best we could hope for.'

Ed sat on the grass and watched the police station. On another day, it would be a pleasant way to spend the time. Enjoying the warmth of the sunshine, accompanied by the occasional rustle of the trees. Taking pleasure in the people passing by, strolling or striding, cycling or running. It wasn't so far from the days of being a watcher.

But this was no ordinary day. And every couple of minutes, Ed found himself checking his watch. Then looking at his phone. To make sure it still had a signal. And power.

And then looking back to the police station. For any sign of activity. The smallest hint of a discovery.

A group of people were walking up the road, and some looked familiar. Ed squinted through the sunshine. They were fellow workers from the Falcon Labs, led by none other than Aaron Swift, a highly unlikely general at the head of an improbable army.

'I'd have thought you'd be hot on the trail of a story, not taking it easy,' Swift said with one of his fabulous attempts at humour when he reached Ed.

'We creatives need to recharge occasionally. To make sure the true feelings of life can transmit easily through the ether of our thoughts,' Ed countered. 'To ensure our receptiveness as aerials of the great message, and to ease the beautiful words into graceful flow.'

The angular manager nodded, as if he was fully in tune with the nonsense. 'Of course. I fully understand. It was just my little joke.'

Swift was in shirtsleeves, without a jacket and tie, and looked far from comfortable for it. Quite a crowd followed him and stood watching the conversation. They lingered a little apart, which was probably their way of not wanting to be associated with Swift in public.

Ed couldn't blame them. It was like being released from prison and taken for a walk by your jailer. Steve, the young programmer, gave him a look and rolled his eyes.

'I've awarded everyone a day off,' Swift announced, attempting to puff out a chest which wasn't built for the task. 'Those that can afford to, of course. Some had to stay behind to answer the urgent calls of the business world. But those that could, I invited to join me in assisting the hunt for Maddy. I – we – the bank and I – have given all our companies a rent-free day so they can do their duty to society.'

'That's very inspiring,' Ed managed.

'Indeed so,' Swift replied, ably demonstrating his usual imperviousness to irony. He waited a beat, then added, 'Of course, if you wanted to mention that as part of your next article, I would be happy to provide a quote. As it's you.'

A range of different responses suggested themselves to Ed. But he reminded himself that Swift was his boss, for this stage of life at least. So he got up, took a few photos and dutifully wrote down at least part of what this selfless leader of humankind had to say.

Swift nodded in satisfaction and led his merry band towards the police station. Over his shoulder, without looking back, Steve made a well-known gesture.

If ever it could be doubted that Britain is a nation of cat lovers, Florence and Olivia found proof that would satisfy even one of this city's most pedantic academics.

Elizabeth welcomed them into her cluttered and fussy living room with hugs for each and the exultation, 'He's back! Behold, Regal George.'

The cat was sitting on a chair, utterly indifferent to the follies of the human race, in that classical feline way. George deigned at least to look up at them, albeit briefly. Then he got back on with the far more pressing business of preening his coal-black fur.

'Isn't he gorgeous,' Elizabeth said. 'Oh, my George. My wonderful George.'

Florence and Olivia made the necessary appreciative noises and slowly teased out the story.

Elizabeth had returned home from the hunt for Maddy to get a cup of tea. And there, waiting, was a surprise, a gift from the very heavens; Regal George, sitting on the doorstep, as if he had never been missing.

'My George! My beautiful lovely gorgeous boy. Like a miracle, returned to me!'

Olivia let out a sigh, and Florence gave her a look. They needed to know what had happened and couldn't endanger that with any reaction other than ecstasy at the return of the lost cat. So they took photos and crooned for as long as they needed to, or could stand it.

George was, apparently, in perfectly good health. 'He didn't even want feeding,' Elizabeth said. 'Most unusually for him.'

'Which means, whoever took him looked after him well,' Olivia noted.

'So how do we explain that?' Florence mused aloud.

'Very simple,' Elizabeth replied. 'Whoever the fiend was, they were fattening up poor Regal George for his gorgeous coat. But he outfoxed them, made good his escape, and returned home to me. Oh, brilliant beautiful magnificent George.'

Izzy was out, at school, but Hannah was home. In honour of her military training, she would never have made a banner of her emotions in the way of Elizabeth. But the return of Macavity had still prompted plenty of smiling.

They sat and talked, the demure ginger feline contentedly stretched out on her lap, purring loudly. Just like Regal George, Macavity was in perfect health. He too had clearly been well looked after during his absence.

'What the hell's going on?' Olivia asked.

'My money's on another cat lover who lost their pet and was so cut up about it they had to grab some other cats,' Hannah replied. 'But then they felt guilty and let them go.'

'I know this sounds like a weird question,' Florence said. 'But do you think what happened to the cats has got anything to do with Maddy disappearing?'

Hannah considered the idea as carefully as a general mulling an enemy's tactics. 'None that I can think of. Is Maddy's cat back too?'

'That's what we're going to find out next.'

It was a day of much good news on the feline front. Ben and Vicky's cat, Jones, was also back. Hannah read out a couple of messages from the pair and passed over a picture of them happily cuddling the black and white cat.

They took some photos of Macavity then headed off. On the way to Maddy's street, they tried calling Mitch, but his phone was turned off. Instead, they rang Ed. Nothing was happening at the police station, so they told him about Mitch going off on his own.

'What kind of air did he have about him?'

'Ominous,' Olivia replied.

'Keep an eye out for him. And if you find him, keep him with you. If you can.'

'I can.'

'I'll watch out for him too.'

'Any ideas what he's up to?'

'Yes. But I hope they're wrong.'

'What're you thinking?'

'Let's wait and see what happens.'

'You sound worried.'

'That's because I am.'

Next, it was to Alan's house. They had to knock twice before he answered, and even then it was through a crack in the door.

'Are you okay?' Florence asked the eye peering through the darkness within.

'I'm not feeling well. I think all this excitement has been too much for me.'

Alan's voice was shaky and hoarse. He started coughing in a way which sounded as convincing as a ham actor on a bad night. The crack of the doorway narrowed further.

'Can we come in?' Olivia asked.

'I'd rather you didn't, if you don't mind. I've had an upset stomach and it's not pleasant in here. I really should be getting back to bed…'

'Is Elsa back with you?'

'I'm sorry?'

'Your cat. She disappeared, remember? You were missing her dreadfully.'

'Sorry, yes, apologies. I'm not thinking straight. Yes, she came home. I'm very pleased to see her. Very pleased indeed.'

More affected coughing echoed from within. Alan didn't sound pleased in the slightest and the door moved to within an atom's width of being completely shut.

'Do you know if Hector is back? Maddy's cat?'

If Alan's voice was shaky before, now it was positively trembling. 'No idea. Now please, would you excuse me? I really must get back to bed.'

The policeman was still on guard at the gate to Maddy's house, so Florence and Olivia asked if there was any sign of Hector having returned. Not a hint, according to the smart, upright and efficient young officer.

He had been standing there for hours, he said in a pained tone. And this had been a cat-free zone throughout, he could guarantee that.

There was no suggestion whatsoever of any cat trying to get back into the house, or even lingering hopefully nearby.

To check for themselves, they had a look up and down the street, under cars, up trees, and in neighbouring gardens. There was no hint of Hector anywhere.

'So they're all back, apart from Maddy's cat,' Olivia said. 'What the hell's going on?'

'Maybe there's no link between the cats and her disappearance,' Florence replied.

'But it feels like there is, doesn't it? Don't you get the sense something strange is happening?'

They leant back against a wall and tried to think. But much to her annoyance, even Olivia's supercomputer of a mind came up with no insights into the mystery of the missing, and then quickly reappearing, cats.

'Anyway, that's not the important thing,' Florence said. 'We should be thinking about finding Maddy.'

'How?' Olivia replied.

But to that question, the question, the only answer was another silence.

In Alan's house, the curtains were drawn. But Olivia was sure she saw one, upstairs, flicker with movement, as a watching eye spotted her glance and rapidly retreated.

If Mitch was planning what Ed feared he was planning, he had better be ready. So he shifted position to move closer to the police station.

There was a bus shelter on the street opposite. He sat in that and kept watch, accompanied occasionally by a student or other prospective passenger. There was a good view up and down the road and he took out his phone, played with it, and watched without looking as though he was watching.

It really was just like the old days.

Buses came and went. Cars trundled and bikes clanked. The time shifted ever onwards. The sun edged around in the sky, clouds formed and dispersed, but there was no excitement at the police station and no sign of Mitch.

And then, as is life's way, three things happened at once.

Ed's phone rang. But he ignored it. Because he knew who was calling and why.

A figure had appeared in the doorway of the police station. Even despite the sun casting dark shadows and stark silhouettes, it was a familiar one. And despite years of professionalism and calm, Ed could feel the fight instinct course through his body.

As for the third happening, that was the most significant by far.

The moment the figure in the police station appeared, another did. Only metres away from the doors, from behind a gnarled old brute of a tree. In the perfect position to be shielded from where Ed was sitting.

And in an even more ideal position to stage an ambush on anyone leaving the police station.

This figure was more familiar still. Even from here, through the light of the day, Ed thought he could see that telltale blaze in its eyes.

It was someone Ed had spent a great deal of time with and got to know well over the past three days. Someone he had come to like and respect. The figure of a man Ed had begun to count as a friend.

It was running towards the police station, moving fast. And it was almost there.

A thinker by instinct and conditioning, a tumble of questions span through Ed's mind in that second of realisation.

How had Mitch managed to sneak up on him? Blindside him, and pick the only place he couldn't be seen from – this, an ideal surveillance post? And not just that, but establish a position which gave Mitch a winning advantage in reaching the police station first.

But those questions could wait. Because action was required. Urgently.

For a big man, Mitch was covering the ground fast, and remarkably silently. He was almost upon the figure just outside the doors of the police station, blinking and acclimatising to the sunshine, and dangerously impervious to his presence.

Which meant every second counted, if bad trouble wasn't to become impossible trouble.

Chris stepped out onto the pavement. Free from confinement, into the warmth and air. But if it was a feel good moment, it turned feel bad very fast.

It must have seemed as if Mitch materialised in front of him. A dark presence emerging from the brightness of the day. Turning it cold with menace.

In a gesture of pure symbolism, Mitch slowly pulled back his hood. It was like the reaper revealing himself from under the depths of his cowl. The embodiment of pure nemesis.

For perhaps half a second, no more, the two men stared at each other. As brain cells fired with understandings, strategies, and calculations.

Then, in a nod to primeval ancestry, embracing the dominance of the instinct to survive, both flipped into battle mode.

Chris half crouched, weight well balanced, centre of gravity low, side on, nimble and manoeuvrable, waiting for the attack. He could have stepped back into the police station, safe from the coming storm, but that was never his way.

Particularly not when he had sworn revenge against the man who faced him. The man who, in turn, had sworn vengeance against him.

Mitch could have continued his run, careered into Chris. That might have been the thoughtless way of the out-of-control attacker, overwhelmed by rage. But it wasn't the style of the experienced fighter.

That way, it was too easy for your momentum to be used against you. Too simple to be set off balance, disabled, and potentially destroyed.

His mind remarkably clear and logical as he picked a way across the road, Ed reminded himself to ask Mitch. Another time, when they had a moment to sit down calmly and talk. If that time ever came again.

How did a backroom former scenes of crime officer know so much about the surveillance tricks and fighting tactics of the frontline?

The standoff in a quiet suburban street on this unremarkable Wednesday afternoon, was short. It was no Hollywood denouement this. No old school Western with words exchanged between heroes and villains to establish the righteousness of the moment of destiny.

Mitch shattered this, the falsest of calms, and struck first. A knotted fist and old-fashioned punch, straight for Chris's face.

Which surprised Ed who was now rounding a convoy of cyclists and trying to keep his glasses from falling off, and almost half way across what was feeling like a very wide road. Very wide indeed.

Because it was an obvious move. Which meant Chris saw it coming and swayed easily aside.

And almost smiled. Perhaps with the unexpected thought that this would be much easier than he had feared. Maybe as his fighting mind lit up with a range of attacks of his own to take down this insolent assailant.

And a few beers later in that awful pub, holding court amongst his barfly mates. A new tale to impress them with.

All of which left Mitch free to execute what he had obviously been planning. The punch was a feint. A distraction of misdirection.

Chris had set himself off balance. So Mitch swung his other fist in a mighty roundhouse, a ball of iron connecting squarely with its target. And Chris staggered back against the wall, stunned by the force of the blow, and Mitch was on him again, merciless and relentless.

All this before Ed had even reached the far side of the road. In that strange detached calm he knew so well, he had to admire Mitch's efficiency.

He had Chris by the collars, pinned up against the wall. 'Hello again,' Mitch said, easy as you like, right in his face. 'Remember me?'

'I'll kill you, you bastard,' Chris gasped, blood seeping down his cheek.

'Yeah, that's working well. It's not so easy when your victim's not your wife, is it?'

'Who the fuck do you think you are? This is a police station.'

'All the better for showing the world what you are.'

Years of policing are an excellent instructor in the arts of the street fighter. And Chris, angry, defiant and dirty by making, was far from finished. He'd got some of his breath back and used the energy of the coursing oxygen to launch his knee forwards, aiming for Mitch's groin.

But his opponent was no amateur and very ready for such an old school and obvious move. He blocked the thrust easily. And delivered one of his own.

For learning, for retribution, and for pleasure.

Which left Chris slumped on the pavement. Doubled up in a heap of human wreckage and gasping hard for air.

Ed was there, on the scene at last, albeit far too late to actually achieve anything in the way of a meaningful intervention. The job was done, with speed and dagger efficiency.

Mitch turned, and Ed wondered what he would say. But those searing eyes were radiant with the relish of vengeance, and his only words were, 'Ah, there you are.'

If there's never a cop around when you need one, then, of course, there's always one when you don't.

In this case there were several. A mob, in fact. Which was hardly surprising given the battleground Mitch had chosen. He could scarcely have been more brazen if he'd put a notice in the paper advertising his attack.

A tumble of officers emptied fast out of the police station and, in a semi-circle, converged on Mitch. Chris was still crumpled on the ground, alternately comforting the twin concerns of his face and his groin.

The cops edged forward, surrounding Mitch, a couple with pepper sprays and Tasers drawn. Eyes intent, aware of the danger they were facing. The groans of their fallen comrade loud in their ears.

'Mitch,' Ed warned. But he didn't need to.

'Job done, I'm good,' he said, and held out his wrists for the handcuffs.

Ed watched as his friend was bundled away into the police station, a couple of cops staying behind to look after Chris. It would be quite a while before he could walk easily again, judging by his expression and movements.

Saxton appeared in the doorway, arms folded, an impenetrable look on his face.

'I think we need to have a chat, don't we?' he said to Ed.

This time, it wasn't the honour of the superintendent's office, but an interview room. Ed tried not to take it personally, but given the way Saxton was glowering, he wasn't surprised. The room was in the bowels of the police station, and a template of oppression. It was small, gloomy with a ghastly shades-of-death light, and smelt of damp.

Saxton sat opposite Ed and armed himself with a glare that boasted all the Nordic force of fire and ice. 'Was there something in me saying I'd handle the Chris issue that you found confusing?'

'I saw your point. But it didn't go down well with some of my team.'

'Yes, I noticed that. I could hardly bloody fail to, could I? As he decided to make his point in my front yard.' Saxton's eyes shifted colour as he stared deeper into Ed. 'I don't know if you've forgotten this, but I've got a missing fourteen-year-old girl. You're supposed to be helping me find her. Not making my life harder.'

'It was a rogue operation. I apologise.'

'You've been doing a lot of apologising lately.'

Ed focused on Saxton's beard. It was very fine, beautifully trimmed and shaded with the range of colours of the middle-aged man.

The little things, it was always the little things.

'Maybe I've got a lot to apologise for.' Ed rubbed at his scar, and the prod to Saxton's memory seemed to calm the man.

'Have you got anything which might help with the search for Maddy?'

'Nothing's come into us. Did the stories we ran help?'

'A few *might have seen something* type leads. Plus the usual round of clairvoyants and cranks who can tell us in complete detail what happened to her. But nothing that looks like a breakthrough.'

'So we've still got no real clue where she is?'

'No. And every minute that goes by when she's not found...' Saxton didn't need to finish the sentence. Not in a conversation between two experienced investigators who knew how viciously fast the odds stacked up against them. Not in this crypt of a room, home of deep shadows.

'What next then?' Ed asked.

'We keep looking. It's all we can do. Can you update your story and keep pushing it out there, as you've somehow become the media of choice on this?'

'If you can give us a couple of new lines of quotes. And...'

'What?'

Ed waited, because he knew it wasn't a question which would be well received. 'Is there any way I can have Mitch back?'

But there wasn't the explosion he had expected. None of the shouted *He attacked an officer in front of a police station* type raging.

In fact, Saxton's reaction was odd. He took out a notebook and checked a couple of pages while Ed studied him. It was as though the superintendent was refreshing his mind on something he had prepared earlier, and needed to repeat.

'There's a problem with that, isn't there?' he said, at last. 'I think your friend is heading for prison, and for a long time.'

'I know he attacked a cop. But the guy was off duty. And given what Chris did to Charl, can't you put some pressure on? Persuade him to drop the charges?'

'Not a hope. She still won't complain, so we've got nothing official on him. And he's seriously pissed with your friend. He wants every charge we can think of thrown at him. Plus a few more besides.'

'Come on. There must be something you can–'

'And then there's Mitch's history,' Saxton interrupted. 'His form. For violence. Abusive behaviour. Drunkenness. Disorder. Quite an impressive list of previous convictions. Which a judge will take one look at and...'

When Ed didn't – couldn't – reply, the superintendent went on, 'I see he'd somehow forgotten to mention all that to you.'

The cells were also in the basement and even more inhospitable than the interview room. They smelt of sick, the default aroma for such hotels of last resort. A mad wailing was cutting through the thick steel door of one, punctuated with laments about the death of Princess Diana and John F. Kennedy.

'I'd introduce you, if we had time,' Saxton said. 'That's another Ed. A regular customer of ours. Edward the Confessor, we call him. He has a few drinks, then goes out and bothers the world with ranting nonsense about the dreadful crimes he's committed. You name it, he's done it.'

'That should improve your clear-up rates nicely,' Ed replied. But the superintendent only grunted in reply.

Mitch was in a cell at the other end of the line. Saxton booked Ed in with the custody sergeant, a wizened older officer called Grimmer, and then walked away without a single glance back.

'You're a solicitor, are you, sir?' Grimmer asked in a quiet voice. He eyed Ed's clothes, as far from the suits and predatory smartness of the legal profession as could be.

'New-wave type. You know how it is. We like our clients to feel at ease.'

'Do you now? Any chance you could work your magic on our wailing dervish at the end there?'

'Even the legal profession has its limits,' Ed replied, and was escorted to Mitch's cell.

He found Mitch lain back on a thin blue mattress, staring up at the ceiling. He said nothing, just raised his head and then an eyebrow at Ed's arrival. Grimmer retreated from the cell, leaving the pair to talk.

'I'm not apologising,' Mitch said, hauling himself up to sit on the bed while Ed propped himself against a wall.

'I'm not going to ask you to. Not about that, anyway.'

'How's Chris?'

'He should be able to walk properly again in a few months.'

Mitch smiled. 'That soon? I'm losing my touch.'

'It was your touch I wanted to talk to you about. Amongst other things. How'd you learn those surveillance tricks? And to fight like that?'

'Like what?'

'Like a pro is what.'

'My old days in the police.'

'I thought you were a scenes of crime officer.'

'I was. But you pick up a few things. And I went on some courses.'

It was interesting that Mitch couldn't look him in the eye, Ed thought.

'Some courses. Really? Like a lunch and learn session, here and there. Or an evening class? To study surveillance? And combat? At the local further education college? Run a lot of those courses, do they?'

Mitch still couldn't make eye contact. 'It was to keep me occupied. Take my mind off things. Really interesting they were.'

Ed smiled, couldn't help himself. 'You don't even sound as though you believe that story. Which, as you might have guessed, makes two of us.'

A wail about the killing of Lee Harvey Oswald echoed down the corridor. Mitch tapped a foot on the floor while Ed studied the white-wash of the brick. There were patterns within the patterns, signs of where another coat had been applied, here and there. Judging by the dark stains, probably to hide splatters of blood. Or try to.

'You know what I think?' Ed said at last.

'What?'

'I think you're from the same dark corner that I am. Aren't you?'

The cell door was open, so Ed got up and checked the corridor. No-one was there, no-one lingering and listening. Grimmer was at his post, tapping away at a computer. As if in recognition of the moment, even the Confessor had stopped wailing.

'What were you?' Ed asked Mitch. 'Domestic? Overseas?'

'I don't know what you're talking about.'

But there was a fragility to Mitch, the one Ed had seen from the start, a mere two days earlier. The feel of a man who could stare into a river and wonder how deep the waters might be. Who could swing between throwing a punch and remarkable sensitivity. Between calm and raging anger.

And a man who had seen the inside of a cell too many times before.

'Overseas, I'd say. Distinguished service. At a guess, decommissioned after one near-death experience too many. Post-traumatic stress disorder. And severe. Your very own dark dawns without end. Promises of support, which were never delivered. Isn't that just the same old story? Trying to run away, hence the barge. Finding those dark destructive feelings dog you. Wherever you go, whatever you do. No matter where you run. Fantasising about ending it all. But still with that fight inside which makes it impossible to give up. Desperately searching for another way. Some way out. Some hope in life. Hence you answering my bizarre advert.'

Mitch was still studying the floor, a slow foot tapping out a hollow

226

rhythm. *Tap, tap, tap*. The cell was starting to feel warm and Ed sensed his scar throb.

'Next, trouble with the law, I'd say,' Ed continued. 'That's the way it usually goes. Maybe a bar fight. Some idiot showing how tough they are by picking on the silent guy in the corner, staring into his beer. Maybe someone like Chris, which might just help explain why you were so set on getting him. The idiot thinking they could take you on, not knowing your past. And getting a very nasty surprise.'

Ed waited, but Mitch just kept staring at the floor, that foot still going. *Tap, tap, tap* in the quiet of the cell.

'There's understanding to start with. Maybe a quiet word from your old bosses to help. A ticking off, but nothing much more. Until it happens again. And then again. And now you're being disowned, like so many before you. Because you're in prison, aren't you? Long days and weeks, cooped up staring at a tiny slice of sky through the bars of a cage.'

There was finally a reaction from Mitch. A quiet voice, but full of pain and fear. 'I'm not going back there. Never.' A pause, and then, 'Please, don't let them put me back there. If they try... you know what I'll do.'

Footsteps along the corridor announced the arrival of Grimmer, come to check on his charges. He was greeted with a wail and confession to the murder of Marilyn Monroe from Edward.

To look the part rather more than he did, Ed took out his notebook and a pen. 'Wish everything our other guest said was true,' Grimmer told them from the doorway. 'I'd write a book on it all, and make a fortune. It'd supplement my pension nicely.'

'When're you going to let me out?' Mitch asked.

'When you've seen the magistrate. If he's feeling kind. You've been a naughty boy, haven't you?' Grimmer didn't look concerned in the slightest, and added, 'Even if your victim wasn't exactly the most popular guy around here. But you know what the justice system thinks about attacks on cops.'

They waited for Grimmer to return to his station, whistling his way along the corridor, then continued their conversation.

'Any news on Maddy?' Mitch asked.

'None. And I mean none at all. As far as anyone can tell, she just disappeared. No sightings, no clues, nothing. It's weird.'

'I need to get out of here to help find her.'

'You need to get out of here for a whole lot of reasons.'

'And how're you going to make that happen? Grimmer was right. Attacks on cops… they throw the key away.'

'I have got an idea, but…'

'What?'

Ed took off his glasses and gave them a polish. 'The only way I can think of to get you out of this mess is if Chris decides not to press charges.'

'Great.' Mitch stood up and stretched his arms against the bare walls of the cell. 'And the chances of that being…'

'Not good. Not according to what his boss says. Not knowing him. Unless, that is, we can get some leverage over him.'

The two men stood opposite each other in the small space. As if acknowledging this could be his future for months, perhaps years ahead, Mitch said, 'I'm not going back into prison. You do understand that, don't you?'

'All too well.' Ed tried to find a focus, something to soothe his mind, but it was far from easy in a police cell. They were hardly designed for relaxation therapy. Particularly not when there was so much noise in his head. So many questions buzzing away like summer flies.

'What're the odds?' he said at last.

'Of what?'

'You finding me? A fellow creature of the shadows. The two of us coming together just like that.'

'What're you suggesting?'

'You know exactly what I'm suggesting. You know the game we used to play.'

'You're asking if I'm a plant? Sent to watch you?'

'In other words, a spy. A spy to catch a spy. Well, an ex-spy, anyway.'

Mitch pulled his hoodie up around his neck, and that air of danger was back. 'Given the state of me? The man you found? Hopeless and semi-suicidal? Jagged as a broken window? Who's going to trust me with anything? Work it out for yourself.'

'Acting was part of the old life too.'

'It'd take a hell of an actor to feel the way I do.'

Ed studied him. 'So it's just a coincidence? That we should meet up?'

'Birds of a feather and all that. Maybe we sensed the damage under the surface of each other and it gave us some kind of empathy thing.' Mitch paused, then added, 'Anyway, if you put out an advert asking whether people have lost hope and want to find it again, what sort do you think are going to turn up? You might as well have written *Former Spies Particularly Welcome*.'

Despite himself, and the pressure of the moment, Ed almost managed a smile. 'Fair point.'

From the corridor came another wail and the patient footfall of Grimmer. They could just hear the attempt at soothing words. *We'll take your confession when we get the right people here. Very high up they have to be for what you've done. Yes, it was awful what you did to Princess Diana…*

'Can you last a night in here?' Ed said. 'Without doing something stupid?'

'Like dangling myself from the door with my hoodie tied round my throat?'

'Something like that. Exactly that.'

'Yeah. I can. But…'

'What?'

'More than one night might be different.'

'No pressure, then.'

'You asked. You got it. And we don't lie to each other, do we?'

Ed thought he had better not answer that. Not given their discussion here in this cell, and the rocks below the surface.

'What're you planning?' Mitch asked.

'The direct approach. I can't see any other. You've had your moment with Chris. Now it's time for mine.'

I t had become an uncomfortably familiar sight in this city in the last few hours. Teams of searchers scouring every acre of any kind of space. Each place where a body might conceivably be found.

The time was turning towards the evening, the clear light of a beautiful spring day shifting towards the sunset. But still they searched, and would, until darkness overcame them. Lines of men and women of all ages from across the city and far beyond, guided by police officers. Pacing in step, scanning back and forth, covering grass, thicket and hedge.

There had still been no sightings of Maddy. Not even a lead about where she might be. And as the minutes passed, the searchers exchanged more and more of those kinds of looks.

The light faded a little further, and hope with it.

Ed paused, just for a few seconds, climbed up on a stile and took some photos. The *Last Edition* may still be important in bringing home Maddy, and saving Mitch, although exactly how Ed wasn't quite sure. Not yet, anyway.

The common was busier than it had ever known for an ordinary Wednesday. A police operations van in the corner. Journalists and camera crews alongside. Divers in the river, support boats drifting with them. Searchers along the banks, holding sticks, poking and prodding into weeds and debris. And all across the common, the lines of men and women moving as fast as they could in their race against the oncoming darkness.

He was here, amongst them. It hadn't taken long to find him. In fairness, not in that dreadful pub, drinking and yarning with his fellow barflies. Not wasting time when his daughter was still missing.

But here amongst the searchers.

Ed scanned the common. And there he was. Moving faster than the others, a line, right in the centre, always a step ahead.

Even from here, it was clear he was talking to the rest of the team. Urging them on. Pushing them forwards.

Ed took a second to look to the sky. That wisp of cloud, sailing towards the sun in a crazy whim of glorious self-destruction. A cormorant in a tree, gazing down at the impertinent invasion of its territory. New buds on a branch, tiny ventures of life, a herald of the coming summer.

The little things. It was always the little things.

Almost always, anyway.

Careful not to move too fast or too slow, to be just another public-spirited citizen with no other agenda but being here to help, Ed headed towards Chris.

He might have been intent on the search, but Chris was a cop of many years' standing. By instinct and experience, he knew what was going on around him, and he saw Ed coming.

For the second time that day, the man tensed himself for battle. He kept moving, kept searching, but angled himself, ready for the attack.

None of the others in the line reacted, apart from a couple of nods and polite greetings. Many must have come and gone in the last few hours, joined and departed the groups.

Ed returned the greetings and positioned himself at the end of the line, kept in step, looking back and forth. The ground underfoot was soft, occasionally squelchy, overgrown and uneven with tufts of grass and burrows of earth.

From his station in the middle of the line, Chris watched. Still searching, but always wary. They crossed looks and Ed shifted his head in an unmistakeable invitation. Then spread out his hands to indicate there would be no attack, no fight, no reckoning.

Not here, not in the midst of this search. Some moments were more important than for wasting on mere clashes of human wills.

However, unspokenly, an agreement was reached. Chris talked briefly to his neighbours in the line and made his way to join Ed.

On this patch of common they stepped together, side by side, but such a very long way apart. Neither man looked at the other, and initially, neither spoke. They were too full of speculation and calculation. But time was a luxury they didn't have for a whole range of reasons, so Ed got to the point.

'I can help get Maddy back. But I need your help in return.'

'Bollocks.'

'It's true. I can help get her back. But there's a price. A deal.'

'You want my help? After what you did?' Chris's voice was low and edgy but under control, albeit only just. 'Are you serious?'

'It's not difficult. I don't want to help you, and you don't want to help me. We both get that. But this is for Maddy. Everyone's reading my newswire. I can put out another appeal. Right now. Please help us with one huge effort to find her before night falls.'

'You haven't got her back so far.'

'But now we're at a critical moment. And we've got to keep trying.'

'You're saying you're on my side here?'

'I'm saying we're all on the same side.' Ed paused, then added, 'For now, anyway.'

They paced on, in step, still looking, poking and prodding. But still finding nothing. Just like thousands of others across this city on this fruitless day. No hint, no clue, no sign of what might have happened to Maddy.

From left and right, the lines were converging. The search of the common would soon be completed.

'What do you need?' Chris asked.

'Not much. Just a few quotes. A picture. Of you here, searching. To really give the story impact.'

'A fucking news story? When my daughter's still missing.'

'It's no different to what you're doing here. What we're all doing. Trying everything. Getting as many people looking out for her as possible.'

They stepped on a little further, then Chris said, 'I'm going to kill you fuckers. You and that hoodie wanker mate of yours. I don't forget and I never forgive. You know that, don't you?'

'That must be an exhausting way of life.'

'Don't try to joke your way out of it. I'm going to kill you.'

Ed hardened his voice to match Chris's. 'You're welcome to try. But…'

'What?'

'It's a dangerous trade, trying to kill a killer.'

That, at least, silenced Chris. But as Ed needed the man talking, he went on, 'I could say that we want to kill you too, remember? But we're not like you. Not exactly like you, anyway. Two sides of the same coin, maybe. But we're the side that's not so tarnished. We never forget. But we do forgive. At least a little. When we get what we want and settle our debts.'

'What the fuck does that mean?'

'It means it's your lucky day. We're not going to kill you. We're going to cage you instead.'

'You expect me to believe that? Or be happy about it? Start doing a fucking dance and yelling yippee?'

'No dancing required. I just expect you to listen. To understand. And to do what you're asked. Or what you're told.'

'End of discussion then, isn't it?'

'If our feud's more important to you than finding your daughter, yes.'

They moved a little further apart, skirting a young tree, a sliver of darkness against the sunset. The light was fading fast, as it did at this turning point of the year.

Ed looked to Chris, but the man was focused on the earth and grass, still sweeping back and forth. He gave it a little longer before saying, 'Okay then,' and turned to walk away.

One step. Towards the river, and the divers pulling themselves out of the water. Two steps, towards the city and its welcoming lights. Then three.

But Ed didn't make it to four paces before Chris said, 'Get on with it, then.'

To save time, and because this really wasn't the place for an interview, they agreed on Chris's quotes. Ed recorded them, then said, 'One more thing.'

'Yeah? You surprise me. What?'

'I want you to withdraw your complaint against Mitch.'

Chris snorted. 'Are you fucking kidding? Maybe you missed this, but didn't I mention I was going to kill you two? That wanker attacked me outside a police station. My police station, in fact. In front of my colleagues. He's going to jail. For a long, long time.'

'He attacked you because you beat up your wife. Again. And this time you put her in hospital. A better man might think you deserved that. A better man might think you got off lightly.'

'A better man might keep his nose out of another man's business. Especially given how I told you that you don't know what's going on.'

'I know enough. I know it's something a real man doesn't do, no matter what. And we warned you what would happen if you did.'

'I guess Batman and Superman just discovered the limits of their powers then, didn't they?'

'I could forget about this story appealing for help in finding Maddy.'

Chris nodded towards the journalists clustered around the police van. 'And I could go talk to one of them instead.'

Ed focused on the sky, the firestorm colours of the gathering dusk, then the gentle sound of their footsteps on the earth. 'Okay, that was wrong. We had a deal. I'll stick by it. The story goes out whatever.'

'I thought you might see it that way.' Chris paused, savoured the victory, before adding, 'Are you going to get this story out then? Didn't you say that time was critical?'

'First, let me say this. Mitch is a good man. He's been to prison before. He's much more vulnerable than he looks. He might not last long behind bars.'

'He should have thought about that before he attacked me. You should both have thought about it before you ambushed me and got involved in my business.' Chris nodded to himself in a way which was almost smug. 'That wasn't a smart thing to do. But I don't reckon smart is your specialist subject, is it?'

They were almost back at the police van. Torches were being switched on in the other lines of searchers, small discs of brightness hovering in the gloom. The temperature was falling, a chill creeping across the common, a hint of mist in the air.

'I'll ask you one last time to drop the charges against Mitch,' Ed said. 'The man's served his country and deserves a break.'

'I've served my country too. And I could do with a break in my life as well, believe me. So I'll make this as clear as I can.'

For the first time, Chris turned towards Ed, and there was a surprise waiting in his eyes. They weren't mocking, arrogant, or aloof, but bright and sore, worn out from holding back the emotion of the search.

'My daughter is missing. She's been missing all day. And now it's getting dark. It'll soon be night-time. We both know what that means for the chances of finding her alive. We have no idea where she is, or what's happened to her. Not a clue. Nothing. And it's killing me. You got that? It's fucking killing me. Like a knife in the guts, stabbing right through me.

'As far as I can tell, Maddy ran off after Charl and I had another of our rows. It was the worst we've ever had, actually. It got right out of hand. We fought, really went at it, like we'd never done before. And why was that? Maybe because of you sticking your fucking nose into something that didn't concern you. How'd you feel about that, eh? That this might all be because of you riding valiantly to the rescue when you didn't have a clue what you were getting into.'

Searchers were moving around them, slow figures in the darkening evening, but no-one interrupted. No-one even came close. Any member of the human race could sense this wasn't a moment to intrude upon.

'So I've got no job, no career,' Chris went on, voice low, but still with that killer edge. 'No marriage, no wife. And now no daughter, the one thing I love above all else in this world. Do you understand that? What it means to not know where your girl is, or what's happened to her? Or to be able to do anything to help? When you're her father. The one person who's always supposed to be there for her. To protect her and look after her. Do you know what that feels like?

'So are you clear now on how I feel about you asking me to drop the charges against your mate? Got it, have you? But just in case you haven't, in case you're even stupider than I thought, this is how it goes. I'm going to stand up in court and tell the judge how the fucker helped to ruin my life. How he attacked me and beat me up outside a police station. In front of my colleagues and friends. How people like him – wankers who attack police officers, who are only doing their best to keep our country safe – deserve to be locked up and have the key thrown away. That's how I feel about dropping the charges against your mate. Is that clear enough?'

It was a primeval feeling; that, away in the darkness, just beyond the reach of the campfires, demons lurked. Running free through a land of the night where unimaginable things happened, unseen and unheard, the only evidence found with the revealing light of the morning.

Neither Florence nor Olivia said it. But both felt it.

It was in the way they wrapped their jackets tighter around their bodies. How they stood a little closer together than usual and kept glancing up and down the road.

Even with the streetlights working hard to hold it back, the night lurked all around. The darkness in which a young girl was still missing. And in which the hopes for her diminished and the fears for her grew.

A hope of hope, a journey back to the light had brought them together, these two and these four. And now hope for another was fading with the passing minutes.

They were standing opposite Maddy's house, the young and upright police officer still suffering his sentry duty. Apart from Alan's, next door, it was the only house in the street with no lights showing in the windows.

'What are we doing here?' Olivia asked, yet again.

'I don't know,' Florence replied. 'It just feels like the right place to be somehow.' And then, to distract Olivia, and in truth, herself as well, she added, 'See if any new information's come in.'

'I only looked five minutes ago.'

'Look again. Keep looking. Keep looking until we hear something and we find Maddy. Or...' Florence stopped abruptly, couldn't finish the sentence.

'Or what?'

'Or nothing. Just keep looking.'

The two new stories were making another big splash, not that it meant much to Florence and Olivia. Thousands of shares, hundreds of comments, they were just words, pixels, pulses of information, noughts and ones. For all the e-mails, posts and messages, the outpourings of sympathy and empathy, there was still nothing to suggest where Maddy might be.

Father's Desperate Plea to Help Find Missing Girl

The father of missing Maddy Williams, 14, has appealed to the public to turn out in force to help find her.

Chris Williams, himself with a search party, told the Last Edition, "I'm still sure we can find my girl, safe and well. I've got to keep thinking that. And I know the more people who can come and help in the hunt, the more likely it is we'll find her.

"I'd ask anyone, absolutely anyone who might have some spare time tonight, to please join the search. Look in your sheds and back gardens, look around your local area, look anywhere where there might be a clue about what happened to Maddy.

"And please rack your brains to think if you might have seen her, seen

anything, which could help me to find her. I don't like to say this, but I'm growing desperate, like any father would."

Ed had dictated the words from the common and sent over the photos of Chris amongst the searchers. Olivia had done her work and added Florence's story about the search of the cemetery to make up the latest edition of the newswire.

Searching in Hope and Fear

This was no ordinary assignment, no standard report. It was a mission which left journalism a long way second to the need to join the hunt.

We met up with the searchers, ordinary men and women, as they scoured Millhouse Road Cemetery. Citizens brought together by the call of duty to their neighbours, their fellows, and their community. And we could do nothing to resist becoming part of their work.

'Isn't it a bit flowery?' Olivia asked, in her way.

'A bit feelingy is probably what you mean,' Florence replied. And carried on writing in the way she had begun.

Every pace we took was filled with dread. That each of us might be the one to glimpse the terrible unspeakable sight that would bring the search to an end.

But also, we hoped. That we might find a clue. A note maybe, perhaps a piece of clothing, anything that would lead us to Maddy and see her returned safe.

. . .

'That really is enough,' Olivia said. 'Now get on to some photos and facts, please.'

And that they had done. But for all the comments, all the wailing words, all their hopes, still nothing had emerged which might help them to find Maddy.

Along the road, a group of people were approaching, silhouettes against the streetlights.

'Another search party?' Florence asked. 'Do they know something? Have they found something?'

Both got out their phones, activated the cameras, and waited. But any hope, any excitement, was short-lived. The figures arranged themselves outside Maddy's house, lit some candles, and started to sing. Badly.

'A vigil? A fucking vigil?' Olivia said, even less impressed than usual. 'What the shit use is that?'

'Give them a break. They just want to be doing something.'

'Then some searching would be better than standing here waving a candle. Talk about pointless. FFS.'

It was the first time Florence had heard her friend use the charming abbreviation for a while, and it said something about the pressure they were under. Florence took a series of photos of the vigil anyway, even if half-heartedly. She was about to rejoin Olivia, looking on with contempt that could curdle the air, when something stopped her.

One of the group, wearing an ensemble which was a masterpiece of crochet work, was bending down and fussing over a cat. The creature looked familiar and Florence moved closer. It was tubby and, even in the semi darkness, had that telltale glint of mischief in its eye.

'Hector, it's Hector, bloody Hector,' she called. 'It's Maddy's cat. He's come home.'

Olivia was back beside Florence, and this time she was taking photos, big close-ups of the contented feline. Hector blinked in the light from the phone, but otherwise was as sanguine as ever.

'What does that mean?' Olivia asked. 'Him coming home?'

'No idea. But something weird's going on.'

They eased the cat from the woman's embrace. Hector was purring happily. He looked as healthy as ever, and perhaps even more portly than before.

'He's been well looked after, wherever he got to, just like the others,' Florence said. 'We've got to tell the police he's back. And keep hold of him. He might be evidence.'

Even Olivia, a master of sarcasm, couldn't find the words to describe the ridiculousness of the situation. 'You're telling me this fat-arsed lump of a cat might be evidence? Have we become pet detectives now?'

They carried Hector to the young police officer. In fairness, he listened politely and nodded at the right points. But then, it is a policeman's lot to hear more than his fair share of strange stories.

'I'll tell the inspector when he's free,' the officer said without a hint of irony. 'In case it's important. In the meantime…' He took Hector and ushered him into the silent house.

'What the – bloody hell – is going – on?' Olivia said, as they stood back and stared at the house, tuneless singing still drifting around them.

'It must mean something. That all the cats came back, apart from Hector. And then he reappears.'

'You're telling me it's a sign that Maddy is about to come home?'

'No, but… well, maybe. Hopefully. Who knows?'

'FFS. I mean, FFS squared. Jesus. So, what do we do now?'

But Florence had disappeared into her thoughts, attempting to make sense of the puzzle.

Olivia tried to join her, then realised her heart wasn't in it. She waited as long as her patience would allow, which wasn't long at all, then said,

'I'm going to talk to Alan. Something about what he was like earlier has been bugging me.'

'You think he knows something?'

'No idea. Probably not. He's hardly the finger on the pulse type, is he? But at least it's doing something. And anyway…'

'What?'

'It'll get us away from this bloody awful singing.'

Alan's house was in darkness, a block of dense black framed by silhouettes of trees lurking behind in the cemetery. They knocked twice without an answer. Florence turned to leave, but Olivia said, 'Just a minute.'

She checked around, then skipped over to the window and tried to look inside. But the curtains were tightly drawn, as they were in every window.

'What?' Florence asked.

'Just something.'

'Like what?'

'You know when you…' Olivia searched for an analogy. 'You've almost finished solving an equation, but one of the binomials, or coefficients, doesn't quite fit?'

'Um, no, frankly.'

'Something doesn't feel right, anyway. Like… when you're ill, do you draw all the curtains? Or just in your bedroom?'

Olivia stared at the front door, then checked around again and gave the handle a try. It was securely locked.

'No surprises there,' Florence said. 'He really didn't want us in the house earlier.'

'Yeah, that's what's bothering me.' Olivia put her ear to the door, then swore. 'I can't hear a bloody thing with all that singing. What's in there that he doesn't want us to see?'

'Probably nothing. You know what he's like. Scared of his own shadow. Maybe he's worried Chris is going to come after him. Come on, let's go. We're not doing anything hanging around here.'

'Just give it a minute. They've got to take a break from that alleged singing sometime. For their own sakes.'

'Their own sakes?'

'If they don't, I might knife them.'

Florence and Olivia waited a few minutes, and the singing died down so the vigil could share cups of tea. This being England, a couple of members of the party had brought flasks, not to mention home-made biscuits. They shared the snack with the young and long-faced police officer, which seemed to cheer him up a little.

Olivia placed her ear to the door again. And swore once more, but this time with sufficient venom to make Florence frown.

'You're not going to believe this, but I can hear a cat. Another bloody cat. And it's going crazy.'

She was right. Without the wash of singing, from inside the house they could hear a cat wailing. It was screeching loudly, as if in pain.

Olivia checked around again, then opened the letterbox and looked into the house. And now she swore again, but this time with sufficient force to impress a gang of builders.

'It's Alan. He's lying on the floor. The cat's beside him, wailing. I think I can see blood. He looks like he's dead. Fucking hell!'

A nd so a neighbouring house in this ill-fated street was cordoned off with the familiar police tape. Florence called to the young officer, Bradley, still standing guard outside Maddy's house. His reaction wasn't quite as colourful as Olivia's, but it wasn't far off.

Bradley looked through the letterbox, then broke a window and opened the door. It was the work of a second to confirm Alan was dead, and so another emergency response got underway.

More police were summoned, along with scenes of crime officers. Searches and examinations were in full flow, in this house and its surrounds. Florence and Olivia had been told not to leave the scene as they would need to make statements.

'As witnesses, not suspects,' Bradley reassured them, not entirely reassuringly.

So they watched, took the odd photograph, and passed the time by writing a story, another update to add to their fast-growing portfolio.

A small crowd had gathered around the house, neighbours exchanging gossip. They were certainly getting their share of it in the street.

A little out of breath from his march back from the common, Ed joined Florence and Olivia, and they went through a quick update on what had happened.

'Alan's death, is it connected to Maddy disappearing?' Florence asked.

'Not to mention the mystery of the now-you-see-them now-you-bloody-don't cats,' Olivia added.

'It must be,' Ed replied. 'It's all got to tie in together somehow.'

'But how?' the women asked.

Neither Ed, nor Florence or Olivia had an answer to that, the question of the moment. Instead, he told them about his talk with Chris amidst the search for Maddy.

'There's no way he's going to drop the charges. None at all.'

'Which means Mitch is–'

'In real trouble,' Florence said, before Olivia could continue with words they didn't need to hear. 'So what do we do?'

And neither of the three had an answer to that either. For the third time, Ed looked through the darkness and streetlights, over at the crowd around Alan's house, and thought he saw a man watching him. But each time he looked back, the figure had merged once more into the gloom.

Ed's scar had started to throb again. He rolled his neck and tried to think through everything that had happened in the last three days.

Monday morning, and the crowd at the Falcon Labs seemed like another life. Or yet another life, to be more accurate. How many did a man have to live before the fates decided to give him a break?

Enough of that. It wasn't helpful. And anyway, Ed was jolted from his thoughts by a voice next to his ear. It was Saxton, and the Viking was glowering. It was as though a mortal enemy he had slain in combat had inconsiderately come back to life.

'I think we need to have another chat, don't we? That's yet another chat. I'm getting a little fed up with this.'

There was nowhere private to talk outside, so Saxton led them to a police van. Initially, he just wanted to talk to Ed, but was met with the all-of-us-or-nothing front and had no choice except to relent. A couple of cops were sitting inside the van, sharing cups of tea. But one look from the superintendent prompted them to depart. Fast.

'What the hell's going on?' he asked, sitting on a narrow bench opposite the trio.

'Exactly what we were thinking,' Olivia replied.

'And the answer is?'

'Same as the one you've come up with,' Florence said.

'In short, no idea,' Ed concluded. 'But something is.'

'Yeah, hugely helpful, thank you. Strangely enough, I got that somehow.'

Ed waited, then said, 'It might help us if we knew what happened to Alan. What you've worked out from the scene.'

Saxton gave him a look. 'So you can have another story?'

'No,' Olivia replied with a voice like a whip. 'And don't be so bloody offensive. This isn't about news. It's about finding Maddy. Or trying to. So get your head out of your butt and remember that.'

'How dare you.'

'How dare you,' was the equally fiery reply.

The two exchanged glares, face to face, only inches apart. Saxton may have been a Viking, but Olivia was quite a modern-day warrior too. She was happy to stare him down, in that unblinking way, with those penetrating eyes. And it was the superintendent who broke the look.

'Don't speak to me like that again.'

'Then don't be a dick like that again.'

'If we could just remember what's important here,' Florence intervened. And when it became obvious a reminder was necessary, added, 'Maddy's still missing.'

'No injuries on Alan's body,' Saxton said after a pause. 'Apart from a great big whack on the skull.'

'From an attack?'

247

'From falling over and hitting his head on the floor, it looks like. That's subject to confirmation, but the pathologist's pretty sure.'

'Did he fall?' Florence asked. 'Or was he pushed?'

Saxton nodded. 'That's the question. But there's no sign of a struggle in the house. It's all perfectly neat and tidy. And there's no sign of forced entry either. Apart from what our cop did to get in.'

'Anyone coming and going from the house?'

'No. If there was, the lad on guard outside Maddy's would have seen it. He's young, but he's keen and he doesn't slack.'

'The back door?' Olivia suggested.

'Don't think so. There's no entrance into the garden. Just a big wall between it and the cemetery.'

'So Alan could have died naturally?' Ed said. 'Suffered a heart attack and fallen over, and the knock on the head finished him off.'

'That's a possibility. But, but…' Saxton paused to let the thoughts settle. 'It's one hell of a coincidence he should die right now, in the midst of all this. And anyway, it'll take a lot of tests to know for sure. Which will take time. Time we haven't got.'

There was a clock in the van, the second hand mercilessly unwinding. Quiet, slow and measured, but given their situation, ominously.

Tick, tick, tick.

It was at least twelve hours since Maddy had disappeared. Night was everywhere around. And there was still no sign of her. Not a clue about what had happened to her. Nothing.

Tick, tick, tick.

'Any forensics in the house?' Ed asked.

'Loads of it. Far too much. Probably too much to ever be of any use. Cat and dog hair by the bucket load. Even bloody rabbit fur. And human hair and DNA too. Tonnes of that, as well. Which isn't surprising, given his business. And that owners would come in to proudly inspect their newly groomed pets. Again, it'll take ages to work through all the forensics, if it even helps at all. More time we haven't got.'

Tick, tick, tick.

'How's Mitch?' Florence asked.

'Quiet.'

'Just quiet?'

'Sitting in his cell, staring at the floor. He's being watched. In case he...'

'He'll be okay for tonight,' Ed said. 'He promised me. It's the nights after we have to worry about.'

'I doubt Maddy will even be okay tonight, to be frank,' Saxton replied. 'A fourteen-year-old girl, walking the streets. Or worse. So let's focus on her, shall we? And I've got a question for you lot. Are you involved in her disappearance?'

Tick, tick, tick.

It was a mark of their surprise that, for a few seconds, none of the three could reply. And when the words did come, they were from Olivia, and as forthright as always.

'What the flying fuck are you talking about now?'

'Don't use language like that–'

But Saxton got no further. Trying to stop an Olivia in full force was like trying to stand in the way of a battle tank at full throttle.

'You fucking idiot. Call yourself a superintendent? You're a super halfwit, more like. We're doing our best to help and you ask a question like that. We've been running around, writing stories for you, trying to work out what's going on, trying to get you a clue so you can do your own shitty job, and you say that. You haven't exactly been distinguishing yourself on this, have you? One of your own doing his best to win champion wife beater of the year award, and you twats turn a blind eye. He has another go, turbo style, almost kills her this time, and his daughter's so trau-matised she gets the hell out. You can't even find a clue about what's happened to her, and despite all your efforts, you've still turned up nothing. So don't give us the trying to divert the blame thing. Asshole.'

Saxton gaped. It was about all he could do. It was unlikely many had taken him on at his own axe wielding game, let alone a diminutive young woman, and he was struggling to process it. Which was handy,

Ed reflected, because it gave him a chance to intervene before the battle really got going.

'We're not without blame ourselves,' he said, holding up calming hands. 'So let's wind it down, all of us, and focus on what's most important. Which is finding Maddy, and finding Maddy alone. But for the record, superintendent, we know nothing more than you do. And we're just as committed to getting Maddy back safely.'

Tick, tick, tick.

Saxton blew out a deep breath. He looked tired, his voice was growing hoarse, and maybe, just perhaps, the battle lust was fading. 'You're writing up Alan's death, I take it.'

'We have to,' Ed replied. 'It's hardly a secret.'

'He and Maddy were friends, weren't they?'

'She used to go round there a fair bit, apparently. Even when Chris told her not to, because he thought the guy was a paedophile.'

'Then make it a big splash. And add that Alan left a note addressed to Maddy, but the police won't reveal its contents.'

'Did he leave a note for her?' Florence asked.

'No. But at this stage, I'll try anything that might help her come forward.'

The relative calm of the van was shredded as the door boomed with a mortar barrage of hammering, making them all start. Ed, always more vulnerable than most to anything that sounded like gunfire, felt his heart race into overdrive. It was an effort to stay still and remain calm.

'Uh oh,' Olivia said, stretching to peer out of a window. 'Guess who.'

She got to her feet, ready for the fight, but Saxton said, 'Don't be so damn melodramatic,' and told her to sit down, then opened the door. Outside, looking up at them, blinking in disbelief, was Chris.

'Have you found her? What's going on? What've you got these twats in here for?' And, as an afterthought, he added, 'Sir.'

'Can you control yourself enough to behave?' Saxton asked. 'If you want to hear about the search for your daughter.'

And when Chris nodded, albeit edgily, he was invited into the van.

Ed, Olivia and Florence shuffled up the bench. To give themselves room to react, just in case, and to keep clear of the bogeyman. Chris sat beside Saxton. The superintendent gave him a rapid briefing on what had happened, but Chris's only reaction was to stare at him.

'Nothing? Not a clue? Not a sign of her? No hint where she is?'

'We'll keep searching. All night. We've got everyone out on this. Cops have come back off leave to help. We're all over the city, every-where. We won't give up. I promise you that.'

'But… no sign, none at all. After all this searching. All this time.' Instinctively, they looked to the clock, measuring away the passing seconds.

Tick, tick, tick.

Chris couldn't take his eyes from the clock. He was dishevelled, piti-fully so, covered in mud, with leaves and grass stuck to his coat. There were twigs in his hair and blood was seeping from a gash on his cheek. But he wasn't aware of any of that. Nothing registered. Only his misery.

'Was it that fucker? That Alan? I told you he was a fucking kiddy fiddler. Maybe he had her. Maybe someone else found out and did him in. What if they've got her now? My girl.'

There was a wild look in Chris's eyes, hopeless and despairing. But also ready to fight. To fight Ed, Flo and Olivia, to fight Saxton, to fight the world, if that was what it took.

Ed and Olivia exchanged a look. Both tensed themselves, ready for the attack. But the onslaught didn't come. Chris couldn't even see them. For him, there was no-one in the van. No-one apart from one teenager, whose presence was all around them and everywhere.

'She's dead, isn't she? My little girl. Dead, dead, dead. You're just going to find a corpse. Horribly mutilated. Cut apart and–'

'Hey,' Saxton said, reaching out an arm. 'We're going to find her. We are. Keep believing.'

But Chris was fixated on the clock. Aloof and impervious to the

251

human suffering it compounded with every tiny movement of its hands.

Tick, tick, tick.

Then, without any warning, Chris let out a wail. Ed and Olivia started to get to their feet. This time, surely, to fight off the attack.

But still, it didn't come. Instead, Chris crumpled into himself and sobbed, tormented, gulping breaths and cascades of tears. Saxton wrapped both arms around him and attempted to comfort the wreck of a man.

He nodded to Ed, Florence and Olivia, gestured towards the door, and they got up and climbed out of the van.

Bradley was still on duty outside Maddy's house, and looking as bored as ever. He said good evening to the trio as they lingered outside the van, wondering what to do next.

Ed was about to suggest getting a coffee and having a chat in a café, when Olivia did something strange. Even stranger than her normal strange, to be precise.

First, she stopped dead, as if she had walked into a force field. Then she looked stunned, as if an alien spacecraft, originator of the force field, had just materialised in front of her. But rapidly following that came a look of the most intense, radiant smugness the world may ever have seen. It was as though the rituals of Judgment Day had been completed, and she was the only one deigned worthy of salvation.

Olivia ducked around the van so she was half obscured to Bradley, then said, loudly, 'Of course, Mr Saxton, if it'll help. No trouble at all. We'll get onto it straight away. We appreciate you need every officer you can get on the search.'

She nodded to Bradley and somehow, even on this dark and troubled night, managed to find her best smile. Which, as ever with Olivia and her dealings with the male species, was reciprocated with considerable interest.

'We'll be back in a while,' she told the enchanted young officer. 'Just got to get something for the superintendent first. Do our bit to help.'

Florence and Ed knew better than to say anything, at least until they were around the corner and safe from being overheard.

'Well?' Florence asked.

'Well what?' Olivia replied, with a knowing look, but at least also having the decency to sound a little coy.

'The amateur dramatics about helping Saxton out,' Ed said.

'There's a pet shop on Millhouse Road, isn't there?'

'I think so.'

'Good. We need a cat harness. I've got an idea. A whole lot of ideas, in fact.'

Olivia took the lead, marching so fast along Millhouse Road that the others had to struggle to keep up. They passed restaurants, shops, cafés and bars, striding through the strips of light and interludes of darkness.

Within a couple of minutes, they found the pet shop. Happily, it was also a café and bar, one filled with tanks of serenely swimming fish, and so still open.

The assistant was an older woman with peering eyes and a permanent look of suspicion. As befitted this eccentric corner of a quirky city, she was wearing a tatty old cardigan and Doc Marten boots.

'Never works, you know,' she told Olivia. 'I shouldn't say that, of course. Not if I want to sell the things. It's hardly good business, is it? But they're a waste of time. Cats don't understand discipline. I'm a dog person myself. Labradors, that's me. Daft but loyal. That's the way I like them. Just like men, eh.'

She produced a lecherous chuckle, which was straight out of a 1970s sitcom. Olivia nodded and managed to assemble a patient smile. 'So what've you got?'

'Can't rightly remember. It's been ages since anyone asked for them. Stupid things. They were fashionable for a minute then forgotten. Also like men, eh? But I'll see what I can find.'

The assistant disappeared into a storeroom. The sounds of scraping and thudding emerged, with the addition of some choice swearing.

Florence and Ed looked at Olivia, who shrugged and did her best to smile. 'Just following a hunch.'

Eventually, the assistant emerged, trailing so many cobwebs it looked as though she had been in a fight with a gang of ghosts and daubed with ectoplasm. She held out a handful of cat harnesses.

Olivia chose the longest. It was a shade of bright pink sure to cause a mutiny in any cat with an ounce of self-respect. They paid and left the shop.

They could have got a coffee and sat and recuperated in the pet shop café, or any of the other cafés they passed as they resumed marching along Millhouse Road. But Olivia insisted on walking further.

'Just testing a theory,' she said, and would add no more. Perhaps it was the smugness. It couldn't have been easy to speak through that.

Eventually, they found an Italian coffee shop with tables outside. Being an English spring evening, it was far from warm enough for al fresco dining, but also being England, a few hardy natives were doing so anyway.

'Perfect,' Olivia said, abruptly stopped marching, and sat down.

'Would you mind actually telling us what's going on?' Ed asked, sitting opposite her and cleaning his glasses. They had grown misty with the pace of the walk.

'And getting us a drink to make up for all the messing about,' Florence added.

'Sure. But first, a game.'

'Olivia,' Florence began to protest. 'Maddy's missing, Mitch is still in the cells and…'

But the young woman folded her arms and reinstated her smug look. 'No game, no tell.'

And so they played the game. It was – or might as well have been – called *Count the Passing Cops*.

There were lots of them. In cars, on motorbikes, even some on bicycles, as was the way of this city. Quite a few were on foot, leading parties of volunteers, all keen and full of energy, carrying torches and wearing fluorescent jackets. Even in the increasingly desperate hunt for a missing girl, the diktats of health and safety could not be ignored.

And each and every one that passed was headed out from Millhouse Road. In a diaspora from where all this had begun, out to other areas of the city as yet unsearched.

Olivia watched and nodded. 'Perfect,' she said, as mysterious as the Mona Lisa might have been, had she spoken from her wall.

For Ed and Florence, it was proving to be a frustrating night. Just as the coffees appeared and Olivia was about to tell them what she was thinking, an unexpected arrival materialised out of the darkness. A pair of them, in fact.

With a slightly awkward wave, Swift descended on their table, Steve the programmer following in his slipstream. Without asking whether he could join them, Swift pulled up a chair. Steve had the decency to request to do likewise, and positioned himself next to Olivia, nice and close.

'There you are,' the imperious master of the obvious said. And added, equally obviously, 'I've been looking for you.'

'Great,' Olivia replied, almost without a hint of irony. 'We were just saying, we missed being in the labs. And seeing you.'

Steve grinned but the lofty manager was too preoccupied to notice the not terribly subtle mockery. 'I've got a story for you. For your creative… for your newswire. A big one.'

'We seem to be doing pretty well for stories at the moment,' Ed said.

'Ah, but not like this. No, not like this. Not like this at all.' And when no-one took the bait, he added, 'Wouldn't you like to hear what it is?'

'We'd be honoured,' Florence replied, apparently feeling it was time she joined the irony contest.

Swift nodded proudly. 'I thought you might say that. It's good news, very good news indeed. The bank has been rather pleased with the impact your creative newswire is making. Very pleased, in fact. And also touched by our own efforts at the labs, the search parties I myself organised to help find Marilyn.'

'Madison,' Olivia corrected.

'Yes, indeed. Well, anyway, the bank has been so very pleased by all our efforts that we have decided to put up a reward for information leading to the safe return of Madison. How about that?'

Swift sat back and smiled his way around the table.

It was interesting, Ed thought, that he was no longer obsessed with fiddling with his wedding ring. It was remarkable what a dose of purpose could do for a person. He tried to feel happy for Swift, but largely failed.

After a suitable pause to make her feelings clear, Olivia clapped. Slowly, really slowly. Steve joined in, then Florence and finally Ed. The diners at the other tables started to applaud too. One even began singing happy birthday. It was a soundscape of pure irony.

But Swift, flying high and utterly oblivious to that awful place called Planet Reality, beamed through it all.

'Now then,' he said, when the clapping had stopped. 'No doubt you would wish to interview me. I can spare you a few minutes, I think, before I must rejoin the search for Marilyn. Please go ahead.'

Sometimes, going along with an ordeal is the most painless way to usher it into the past. Ed had learned that early in life, even if it wasn't always easy to put the lesson into practice. In fairness to Swift, fuelled with his mission, he didn't stay long. The interview complete, he headed back out to return to the search for Maddy. Or Marilyn, as Swift might have put it.

Steve followed, but not before he managed a few words to the team. 'You're doing great with all your coverage. You'll bring her home. I know you will.'

And with a lingering look for Olivia, which she held easily, the young programmer also disappeared into the night. The remaining trio ordered some more warming drinks, then returned to their conversation, now happily Swift free.

'So what do we do next?' Florence asked.

'We wait. Just for a while,' Olivia replied.

'What for?'

'For all the cops and searchers to shift away from Maddy's house.'

'What are you planning?' Ed asked, even if he was wondering whether he had an idea.

'I'm not sure you'd believe me if I told you. So let's just give it a try.'

'It's quite a leap of faith, with Maddy missing and us sitting here doing nothing.'

There was only so long Olivia could bear an argument, even with people who might have become her friends. And so, as ever, the breaking strain was breached with all the usual efficiency.

'How smart am I?'

'What?' Florence said. 'What kind of question is that? What kind of person would even ask that?'

'Very smart,' Ed interjected, before another argument could take hold. He'd had more than enough for one night. 'You're very, very smart. We'd be nowhere without you.'

'Then give me a chance. Half an hour here should do it. If my way doesn't work, we can try something else.'

Florence sighed, but said, 'Let's not waste the time then. We need a new story. Let's get writing.'

They were spoiled for choice with news that night. The only dilemma was which story should lead the latest *Last Edition*.

'Expanding the search for Maddy is probably the most important,' Florence said.

'But Alan's death is the biggest hitter,' Olivia pointed out. 'That's the real clickbait.'

'I think we can agree that Swift's reward brings up the rear,' Ed added. 'Although maybe that's not the best way to put it. Anyhow, let's get writing. We don't have much time, and we can decide the order in a while.'

The night was growing colder, but none of the three noticed. Another search party marched past, led by a police officer. Olivia skipped to her feet and took some photos.

'Just what we needed,' she said.

'Remember to kiss. Keep it short and simple with the stories,' Ed told them. 'We've built an audience by being ahead of everyone else on this. Let's keep it that way.'

Once more, they were pleased to find what generations of hacks had discovered, whatever the era. With such strong stories, they were written in just a few minutes.

Comparing headlines, there was only one winner in the contest for the main story. And, given the way she was taking the lead, it was fitting it should be Olivia's.

Death of Neighbour in Maddy Hunt

Police are investigating the sudden death of Alan Skeets, a neighbour of missing Maddy Williams.

A senior police source told the Last Edition it was too early to say whether the death was suspicious, or connected to the hunt for Maddy.

Forensic searches are underway at the house where the body of Mr Skeets was found. A post mortem examination will also be carried out.

Mr Skeets is said, by neighbours, to know the Williams family well, and to have been traumatised by the disappearance of Maddy.

Olivia inserted a couple of photos of police at the house, added a bit of background about Maddy vanishing, then moved on to the next story. It came courtesy of Florence, and was the first to be finished.

Hunt Widens for Missing Maddy

Tonight, police are significantly widening the hunt for Maddy.

Search teams, made up of officers and volunteers, are spreading out across Cambridge.

It follows nothing being found in searches close to her home.

Senior officers still say they have no confirmed sightings of the teenager, and her disappearance remains a mystery.

"The longer she's missing for, the more our concern," one told the Last Edition.

'Great stuff,' Ed told Florence. 'Really good news writing. Ultra sharp and straight to the point.'

Olivia's eyes narrowed. 'And mine wasn't?'

'I was going on to say that applied to both of you.'

If the experience of being a father to his team wasn't bad enough, Ed didn't need the sufferance of being a dad to warring sisters. To distract them, he quickly moved on to his own story. In fairness to

Swift, it was interesting and might just prompt more people to join the search.

Reward Offered in Hunt for Maddy

A large reward has been offered for information leading to the safe return of Maddy.

It's been provided by a well-known bank, which wants to remain anonymous.

The sum is not being disclosed, but sources have told the Last Edition it runs into tens of thousands of pounds.

A senior source at the bank (Ed knew Swift would love that) *said they, "wanted to do anything they could to help bring Maddy home safely."*

Olivia's fingers spun over her keyboard, and within seconds, the latest edition of the *Last Edition* was published.

'Now watch,' she said, clicking to a counter. And numbers started to spin, faster and faster, until they became a blur.

'Thousands of people have registered for any updates,' Olivia explained. 'The moment we post something new, it goes crazy and gets shared everywhere. All around the world. It's amazing.'

'The *Last Edition* is going better than I ever thought possible,' Ed said.

'But at what cost?' Florence observed.

A silence fell between them, reflections in the darkness. It was broken only by the waiter, a young reedy and nervy man, checking if they wanted more drinks.

When he had gone, Florence looked up from the table and quietly said, 'There's something I need to tell you. If we don't find Maddy... if she's... I can't go on with this. I just can't.'

And so came another of those moments. When the world, or at least this tiny corner of it, waits, tense and expectant, wondering what will happen next.

Florence stared away into space, into the darkness, into that unseen land where the search for Maddy went on. Cars passed, the waiter waited, people came and went. But none of the everyday landscape of life had a hope of intruding on this crucible of a meeting place, shared between these three travellers.

Ed looked to Olivia, upright in her denim armour, and waited for the explosion. But it didn't come. Nothing like it. Instead, with that remarkable capacity to surprise, she said quietly, 'I'm not sure I could go on either.'

She hesitated, looked to Florence and said, 'It was hope that brought us together. And if we lose Maddy, and Mitch…'

She didn't need to continue. In his mind, Ed could see the expanse of a graveyard and one new tombstone, mighty and shining above all the others. On it was carved, simply, *Hope*.

Olivia's eyes found Ed, sitting there, cuddling a coffee, for once unable to reply. The old life had its challenges, that was for sure. But none like this.

The recruiters, the trainers, the senior officers, they always told you the same thing. To never get involved.

But you always did. Because you couldn't do anything different. Because you were human.

'It's only been three days,' Olivia continued. 'But shit, the world's changed. My world, I mean.'

'Our world,' Ed replied in a voice as quiet as hers. 'Our world.'

'Before that stupid fucking advert of yours, and you, and Florence and Mitch, I don't know what would have happened to me. What I would have become. Probably still sitting in a lab, staring at a screen, eating crisps and hating everyone and everything else in existence. But you helped me feel… you made me feel… ah, FFS, I don't want to say it.'

Florence shook her head, but kindly. 'I'll say it then. Because it deserves saying. Hope. Sweet damn hope. Bad things happen to me. I don't know why. They just always have. They always do. But you, this, all I did, all we did, it actually made me feel good things can happen as well. I found bloody hope again. And God, it's hard to let go of.'

'Hope,' Ed agreed. 'Hope, bloody hope.'

More silence. More thought. More struggles in the ocean of feeling that was both the blessing and curse of the human race.

'But if there's no Maddy…' Florence went on, 'No Maddy and no Mitch. For everything I've suffered, all the times I've tried to come back and put on a smile again, that would be the end.'

'Yeah, the end,' Olivia agreed. 'The absolute, nowhere else to go, final whistle, end of days' death and cremation of hope, sweet fucking hope. You think the bastard thing's actually real. That it's there, almost within your grasp. And then…'

Ed reached out, gently took Florence's hand, and Olivia's too. Neither woman resisted in the slightest. And maybe, just perhaps, Olivia's grip became a gentle squeeze.

He'd never been the greatest of actors, but Ed tried to find the right voice for what he was about to say. Dignified and sincere, a sombre lament would be ideal, if he could make it happen.

If the wobbles inside didn't betray him. Because this was one hell of a moment, and one great big punt of a gamble.

'So, maybe it's time then? To give up and say goodbye. To each other, and to our old friend…'

Olivia's head snapped to him, whipped around by the force of her anger. 'What the fuck? Jesus, fucking H Christ! FFS! Holy shitting hell. Fuck you. Fuck your whining. Fuck all that.'

'Yeah, fuck that,' Florence agreed with uncommon venom. 'Fuck all that giving in shit. There's still hope.'

'Yeah,' Olivia replied, standing up. 'That there fucking is. Hope, hope, hope. We don't give up that easily. For fuck's sake. I had an idea, remember?'

And then came one of the most bizarre moments in the history of leadership, oratory and authority that the world could ever have seen. Slight but somehow so tall, with such presence, standing upright, shining with anger, defiance and pride, Olivia brandished the pink cat harness and yelled, 'There's still hope. Of course there's still hope. There's always hope. Feel it. Live it, breathe it. Hope, hope, hope! Let it run through you. Love it. Savour it. Rejoice in it. Hope! Come on, follow me! Follow me to find hope!'

Bradley was still on guard, a brooding shadow of disillusionment that was somehow darker than the surrounding night. The young police officer had slumped into himself and was glaring moodily into the distance.

But then, this kind of night wasn't the sort you saw in the recruitment videos. There was no valiant rushing to the aid of defenceless citizens, no helicopters cutting through the sky, sirens wailing in the heroic pursuit of the lawless.

It was just standing there, in the cold, in front of an empty house that no-one wanted anything much to do with anyway. As was so often the case, the side of the mouth whispers about what had unfolded there had already taken hold.

Which meant the young man's reaction to the approach of Olivia was no great surprise. A moping silhouette became a smart and upright beacon of the law, readying a warm smile and a cheery greeting.

Unusually for her, Olivia could feel the breathlessness inside. On the whole, it was good to know she was human, after all. But there were times when it wasn't such a blessing.

She kept her walk steady and let slip no hint of what she was doing.

Which was scanning around, checking for more cops, search parties, or anyone who might get in the way of what she was planning.

But there was no-one and nothing. The street was deserted. Apart from her and Bradley, and Florence and Ed, waiting, hidden around the corner.

Exactly as they had witnessed, the search for Maddy had shifted to other areas of the city. It was just another quiet suburban evening; whatever currents might flow beneath the surface.

Everything was in place for the plan to do its thing; save Maddy and free Mitch from the cells. That was the theory, anyway. But there were quite a few obstacles to surmount first, before they reached the glorious ending of the script running through Olivia's mind.

She cleared her throat and gripped a little tighter at the cat harness, totem of her intent, however ridiculous. Ed's words of just a few minutes earlier, when she'd explained her thinking, wouldn't leave her mind.

'If this works, it'll be the most bizarre way to solve a problem that history's ever seen.'

'No worse than putting an advert in a paper in an attempt to find hope again,' she had replied.

And they had almost laughed. Almost, but not quite. Not that night.

'Evening,' Olivia said, and the greeting was returned, as expected. 'How're you doing?'

'Not so bad, thank you,' Bradley replied. 'Yourself?'

'Not so bad either.'

Olivia forced herself to concentrate. Small talk had never been her thing, and certainly not when there was so much else going on in her mind. But it was important, she knew, not to rush on in and stir up suspicions.

'Anything happening with the search?' Olivia asked, propping herself up against the wall as casually as she could.

'Still no sign of Maddy, sad to say.'

'Not even a hint of where she might be? It is strange, isn't it?'

'You're not trying to get information out of me, are you?'

'Wouldn't dream of it. I just keep wondering what's happened to her, the poor girl, and wanted to know.'

Bradley smiled and straightened his tunic. 'Because you'd have to pin me down and force me to talk, if you wanted information.'

Olivia took a second to compute. FFS. This, she suspected, was called flirting. FFS squared. Why was it always this way? But men were men, and apparently she had to play her part.

'That doesn't sound so bad to me,' she heard herself say. 'But...'

'What?'

'I've got a little job to do first. A favour for Mr Saxton.'

At the invoking of a senior officer's name, Bradley stiffened. 'Which is?'

'You wouldn't believe it.'

'You wouldn't believe the things I've already seen in this job which you, um, wouldn't believe,' the young officer replied, not terribly eloquently. But then Olivia had that ruffling effect on the male species. 'So this favour is?'

She held out the harness. 'I've got to take Hector the cat out. For a bit of exercise. And to do his business. Mr Saxton wants all the officers he's got out searching for Maddy, so I volunteered to help.'

Bradley studied Olivia, doing her best to nonchalantly prop up the wall and smile her way through what felt like a choking smog of bullshit.

'Maybe I'd better check with Mr Saxton,' he said.

'Sure,' Olivia replied, wondering what to do next. 'But do you mind being quick? He's so busy with the search. And you know what cats are like. The mess they can make.'

As if a sign from the heavens that Olivia's crazy plan might just have a hope of success, they were interrupted by a loud feline wail from the house. It was followed by the unmistakeable sound of claws scratching on the door.

'Make that very quick,' Olivia said.

'I think I can deal with this myself,' Bradley replied, turning towards the house. 'If I open the door, you catch the cat.'

Given their decades of companionship with the human race, it's probably for the better that cats can't talk. Who knows what judgment they would pass? But Hector hardly needed words. His look of contempt when Olivia laced the bright pink harness around him was quite enough.

Initially, Hector had refused to move, no matter the amount of gentle tugging or cooed persuasion. He had just glared feline disdain in that lofty way which cats have. Maybe he was worried about his street cred amongst his peers.

Eventually, Olivia apologised to Bradley and picked up Hector. She explained she would take him to the cemetery for his exercise, as it was the closest patch of green space, and be back in a few minutes.

'See you soon,' the officer called with a smile and a wave. 'I'll be waiting.'

'Look forward to that.'

Ed and Florence were still safely hidden in the shadows of a parked jeep.

'All okay?' Florence asked, rubbing Hector's ears, which did nothing to stop his struggling.

'Yep. But we don't have long.'

'So let's go,' Ed said. And together, they walked into the cemetery.

A low moon was rising in the southern sky, frosting the land with its haunting light. Gravestones shone like pale lanterns amidst the bushes and overgrowth. At the centre, through the trees, the old mausoleum cast an angular silhouette. The cemetery was quiet, not even the rustle of a nocturnal creature scared by the unexpected visitors to this sacred domain.

At the stone arch, portal to their destination, Ed, Florence and Olivia stood together and watched. Not expecting to see anything, hardly even convinced of what they were doing. But they waited anyway, just in case.

Hector had stopped struggling and grown content at being cuddled, even if he did keep biting at the harness. But he was also a weight, so Olivia passed him to Ed, which only made him twitch again. And still they waited, and watched.

After a few minutes, Florence said, 'Nothing's happening here. Everyone's searching other places. So, what's the plan?'

'We need to get a move on,' Ed said. 'Before Bradley starts to wonder what's happened to the cat. And Olivia, of course.'

'There are two ways of doing this,' she replied. 'But given Maddy is going to be scared, maybe really terrified, and quite probably traumatised, the simplest is best.'

As the carrier of the cat, they agreed Ed would stay at the arch. He would wait five minutes for Olivia and Florence to reach the entrances in the other corners of the cemetery. And then, when they had triangulated their hunting ground, they would act.

In case anyone happened to pass by, Ed retreated into the hideout of some bushes. Hector looked around, but seemed to have resigned himself to being carried and closed his eyes.

'Stay with me, cat,' Ed told him. 'We're going to need you in a minute. If this ridiculous plan has any chance of working.'

It was interesting how long five minutes could take to pass. In the days of the old life, Ed was used to waiting, usually for hours and hours, and often for nothing. He had tricks to deal with it. But he was out of practice and had no desire to get back into it.

He thought about Mitch, still in the cells, and wondered how the man was doing.

The man? Didn't he mean his friend? Or did Ed still have to keep a distance, as he had with the whole of the human race for so long? Particularly given what Mitch would start contemplating if he spent more than just tonight in the cells.

As his ears became attuned to the quiet of the cemetery, Ed heard sounds. Rustling in the overgrowth, perhaps a marker of the night-time patrol of some creature of its territory. The whispers of the tallest trees as the sky stirred with a faint breath of wind.

And still the moon rose, beaming out its luminescence. Behind their walls, lights were on in most of the houses bordering the cemetery. But those of Maddy's family, and Alan's, side by side, were in darkness.

Five minutes. Ed checked that Hector's harness was firm around the cat's body. This wasn't the time to go losing him. The culmination of this hunt had been farcical enough as it was. He lowered Hector to the ground and the cat stood, looking around, perhaps bristling a little as he analysed his surroundings.

Hector sniffed at the grass on the edge of the mud-worn track. Then some shrubs. And finally, the tomcat moved. Silently, along the path, heading deeper into the cemetery, tail held aloft like a standard of battle.

Trying to move just as quietly, and ensure there was plenty of slack on the harness, Ed followed.

Regardless of beliefs and superstitions, a cemetery at night can hardly fail to recall the past and murmur of the future that awaits us all. Ed found himself remembering family and friends who had fallen on the way; some easily, others after such dreadful struggles. And that one day when he himself had expected nothing other than his own marker in a plot of land similar to the one he trod across now.

In the old life, they had staged some ridiculous operations to secure their ends. But nothing as strange as this. Pacing silently across a cemetery at night, being led around by a tomcat on a pink harness. If only his peers of the days of old could see him now.

Or perhaps not.

It could easily have been wishful thinking. But Hector seemed to have picked up a trail. Slowly, patiently, in that predatory way of the instinctive hunter, he was following a route along the path and into the heart of the cemetery.

Ed squinted through the darkness. He couldn't see them, not in the starkness of the silver and black landscape, but he thought he could sense small movements. Nothing more than dark flickers against the backdrop of the night.

Florence and Olivia were easing their way forward, converging on the same place.

If this worked, maybe he would go back to his old employers and tell them how they had been going wrong for so many years. Forget sniffer dogs. It's sniffer cats you need.

Hector stopped and wound his way through a bush. Then started to rub his face against a branch, purring loudly enough to be heard across the cemetery.

'What've you found?' Ed whispered. 'You're not seriously telling me this might be working, are you?'

A cat indulging himself is not a creature to be rushed, so Ed waited, even if the impatience was biting hard. He stared up at the sky and the stud of light of a planet rising alongside the moon. A wisp of cloud passing by, as if hosting a sightseeing trip for mysterious celestial beings. Serenity was all around, everywhere, apart from within himself.

The little things. It was always the little things.

Onwards Hector moved at last. Still towards the centre of the cemetery. Ahead, and from his side, Ed sensed more movement and thought he could see Olivia through a run of young trees.

It was clear they were heading towards the old mausoleum. Once a noble resting place, now rundown and boarded up. Surrounded by ramshackle trees and overgrowth, and covered in the obligatory foul-mouthed graffiti.

Another movement. This time from the opposite side. Florence, peering around a tree. Ed gave her a quick wave, indicated not to speak, and they carried on, approaching the mausoleum in a pincer movement.

But then came a problem. The trees and bushes which had been their friends fell away. It was open ground towards the denseness of the once-grand building, the occasional angle of its walls and roof showing through the surrounding foliage.

If they approached any closer, they would surely alert anyone hiding there. If, that was – if – anyone was. And the harness wasn't long enough to allow Hector the leeway to make his own approach.

Ed looked to Florence, who shrugged. There was no other choice, not now. Not when they could be so close, and Ed let the cat off its leash.

Instead of running, celebrating his new-found freedom, Hector continue to pad, soft and careful, sniffing every step of the way. Together, in the wizened hideout of an aged tree, Ed and Florence watched with unblinking eyes. Both were breathing hard, trying to control the iron tension building within, but with no chance of succeeding.

Ed felt Florence's hand find his and offer a quick, reassuring squeeze. And he squeezed right back.

Hector had sniffed his way around a lopsided gravestone and disappeared into the bushes. Still they waited, counting off the seconds, wondering what would happen.

In the cacophony of the silence, straining their senses, it was difficult to be sure. But Ed thought he heard the cat let out a miaow, followed by the gentlest hint of a human voice.

The sound of a young girl.

Olivia must have heard it too. As if detonated by the noise, on the other side of the mausoleum, running feet crashed through bushes. Quickly, other feet joined them, also moving fast, sounding panicked, blundering past trees and branches, half tripping, almost stumbling, but carrying on.

Florence and Ed both tensed, crouched, ready for an attack, ready for anything.

And from the overgrowth burst the girl, running hard and wild, straight towards them. Ed reached out an arm, caught her, and pulled the struggling body to his chest.

Florence was with him in an instant, cuddling, soothing, whispering love, kindness and reassurance. And from the darkness, Olivia emerged, cat in her arms, and for once, just this once, her moment in life, she was smiling broadly.

If the mausoleum was designed to be a peaceful and homely resting place, or a soothing base camp to ready a soul for the journey to the afterlife, time and fate had robbed it of any such dignity.

The graffiti on the outside had grown unchecked to become a technicolour gallery of outpourings; everything from straightforward ranting abuse to social commentary. And all accompanied by plenty of pictures that, even given the curious tastes of modern art probably would not have impressed a trendy critic.

The fine stone carvings that once dominated this sombre chamber had been rendered nothing more than chips and blocks. A pile of bottles decorated one corner, along with evidence of attempts to start a fire. Rags of clothing were strewn across the floor, mixed with plastic, cardboard and packaging. The skeleton of a bike was propped up against a wall, and the smell of decay was heavy in the damp air.

The whole space was hollow and cold, and as inhospitable as you could wish for. In other words, the worst place for what they had to do.

Ed had wanted to get Maddy away somewhere. To a room that was homely, warm and comfortable. Where she could wash, eat and drink. Where they could reassure her she was safe, and talk about what had happened. Find a way to keep her out of trouble; with the police, the law, her parents, all those who had searched for her. In short, just about everyone.

But there was no chance of that. Not with the whole of the city, all of the country in fact, obsessed with the hunt for Maddy. And time so very limited.

A plan was forming, which was every bit as crazy as those which had gone before. But Ed found that thought curiously reassuring. If there was a time in life for mad plans, this was surely it. They had developed a useful habit of working.

But if his idea was to have any chance of success, they would have to move fast. Very fast.

Which meant talking to Maddy there, doing all they needed to do, and quickly. When it was really no time for rushing the girl at all, and certainly no place.

Not given how she was sitting, more slumped in truth, against the wall of the mausoleum. Arms wrapped around her knees, head bowed. Florence was beside her, an arm laced around her shoulders, talking away, quiet and gentle. Trying to calm Maddy, reassure her, draw her out of herself.

Trying to find out what had happened. If it had been as Olivia had imagined.

Ed paced back and forth across the ramshackle space of the mausoleum and waited for Florence to work her soothing magic. She was cuddled in close to Maddy, stroking her hair, talking to her about everything and nothing.

What a beautiful cat Hector was. How strange life could be. When she was young, and bullied for being kind. The time she went to Jamaica to find her roots, and hated it, found it far too hot and couldn't wait to get back to Leicester.

'Much better curry in Leicester,' she said, making Maddy look up and smile, however briefly.

Olivia returned from her mission to restore Hector to Bradley, and deflect his fumbling attempts at flirting. She exchanged a look with Ed. Olivia was never one for patience, but she had a point. It was nearly time to start talking.

But they waited a little longer. Just a little. Because it was a fine balance. Needing Maddy to open up, but risking her shutting down. And she was looking around more often. Seeing both Ed and Olivia, and nodding to them. She had guts this girl, and more even than anyone might have believed, given what she had done.

She was grimy, face shaded with the ghosts of mud trails and scratches, even after Florence had done her best to wipe away some of the dirt. Maddy's eyes were strangely bright, far too much so, as if her mind was burning away, trying to make sense of the past day. And her hands gripped tight at her coat, balling up the material, pushing and squeezing, trying to release the stress and fear within her.

But she was here, and safe. While across the city, thousands of people still searched for her.

And the night was passing by.

Slowly, Ed and Olivia walked over and sat down beside Maddy and Florence.

'Are you up to talking?' Florence asked her. 'I'm sorry we don't have more time, but we've got a few things to straighten out.'

There was no reply, just a nod.

'You can trust us, you know,' Florence went on. 'We're here to help.'

Another nod. Then, quietly, with a voice full of dread, 'How's Mum?'

'Doing well. You'll be able to see her soon.'

'Promise?'

'Yes.'

Maddy turned to Ed and pointed a shaky finger. 'But you promised to make things better with Dad. To stop him hitting Mum. And he...'

Her words faded into the quiet air and Florence cuddled her tighter. Ed let out a long breath. He was being judged by a fourteen-year-old girl. Fairly and accurately. As they had thought from the start, Maddy was much older than her years.

'I got that wrong, I know,' Ed said. 'And I'm sorry. But I'm going to make it right. We're going to sort everything out. I promise you that. We're going to get you back with Mum, and make everything right.'

Maddy stared at him, just stared, those eyes even brighter. 'How can you? How can you make everything right when I killed him? When I killed Alan?'

Olivia might have been maddeningly clever, but, to her credit, she wasn't one for crowing. She didn't even acknowledge the looks Ed and Florence gave her, and instead said, 'We know what happened. Or think we do, anyway. That's how we found you. But why don't you take it from the beginning?'

'That's how stories generally work best,' Florence added, with one of her smiles.

'Like you do in the *Last Edition*?' Maddy replied. 'I read you all the time when I was at Alan's. You always seemed to know what was going on.'

'I'm not sure about that,' Ed said. 'But we tried.'

'You nearly got me to come out. Give myself up. With that story you did with Mum.'

'That was the idea.'

'That's what I thought.'

'And why you didn't come out?'

Maddy nodded, modest enough not to flaunt her outthinking of those who were much older. 'I'd like to be a writer. When I'm older. When I get out of prison.'

'You're not going to prison,' Olivia said with all her formidable spirit. 'No way. Okay? We'll make sure of that.'

'And of course you can be a writer. In fact, I'd recommend it. Thinking, feeling, writing, it's always the way. Maybe you can write something for us,' Ed added. 'But let's get your story straight first.'

Florence cuddled Maddy a little tighter, to help her tell the tale. The words started slowly and quietly, making them strain to hear.

'I wanted to help Mum. I wanted her to get away. I said she should. But she always said Dad was a good man really, and he didn't mean what he did, hitting her like that. She said he'd had a bad time at work, but it would get better. And she always asked where we would go if we did get out.'

'You tried to help her with that, didn't you?' Olivia asked, perching herself on a pile of tumbledown stone next to Maddy. 'You looked at shelters and refuges.'

'I didn't really want us to go away. I just wanted Dad to get a shock so he'd stop hitting Mum. I thought maybe if he saw we were serious about getting out, he'd stop it. Or maybe we'd go away for a few days, then come back and it would all be better.'

'But Mum wouldn't go, would she?' Florence asked.

'No.'

'And that was when you made your plan?' Olivia added. 'To get Alan to help you.'

'I was only going to disappear for a day or two. That was what we said. Enough to make Dad think and make things better.'

'That was why the cats disappeared? You wanted Hector to keep you company. But if only he disappeared, it might look suspicious, like you'd taken him to someone's house.'

Maddy nodded. 'So we took in lots of cats. It was really easy. Most of them knew me or Alan anyway, and hung around here. We just gave them some food and they came into Alan's house.'

'That's cats,' Florence observed.

Olivia went on, 'And when… what happened to Alan, you let the cats go? Apart from Hector.' Another nod. 'What did Alan say when you asked him to help you? Was he okay to do it?'

At hearing the name, Maddy flinched, and Florence gave her another long hug. 'He said it was a crazy idea. That he shouldn't have anything to do with it.'

'But you didn't give up, did you?' Olivia asked. 'You persuaded him.'

'I thought he'd never go for it. But it wasn't that hard. Alan was weird. It was like he knew he shouldn't do it, but he kind of wanted to.'

The three adults exchanged glances, then Ed said, 'And when Dad hit Mum again, that was what made up your mind. And Alan's, maybe? You went to his house and he let you in.'

'Just for a day or two, he said.'

Ed and Florence nodded. Olivia had been right. That was why there was no CCTV, no witnesses who had seen Maddy being abducted, or running away. Her flight had been no further than next door. And it would explain why Alan was so agitated, not wanting them in his house, feigning illness and closing all the curtains.

They were approaching the most difficult part of the conversation. Florence knew that, and did her best to ease the way.

'It must have been strange, watching all those people outside, looking for you.'

'I didn't look outside much. I didn't want to. I just looked online to see what was happening.'

'And what happened with Alan?' Olivia asked, as softly as such a question could be raised.

Maddy looked down and shuddered, prompting another tender cuddle from Florence. 'He was really weird. Kept saying I had to go and give myself up to the police. But also that he was really pleased to have me with him, and wanted to help me.' Maddy hesitated, then added, 'He kept looking at me in this funny way. It frightened me. It was like he…'

'I think we can probably imagine,' Ed interrupted. 'And what happened to Alan? Be honest. You can trust us. We're going to help you. I promise you that.'

Another pause. Maddy slid her feet back and forth on the stone floor of the mausoleum. Outside, faint in the distance, an owl hooted.

'He said he was worried about me. That he wanted to cuddle me, to make me feel better. He had this weird look on his face. I said I didn't want a cuddle, but he said it would do me good, and he tried to grab me. I pushed out at him and he kind of slipped and hit his head on the floor. He made these horrible noises, and that was it. He was just dead.'

The tears were flowing, glistening tracks in the grime of Maddy's face. 'I killed him, didn't I? And I ran away. It's all my fault. What's going to happen to me? Will I have to go to prison? I don't want to go to prison.'

Olivia slid over and joined Florence in cuddling Maddy. She was sobbing, her body shaking, grabbing hard at her knees, tucking into a ball, trying to hide within herself.

Ed stood up and paced over to the doorway. Outside, the night was quiet and still, the moon high in the sky. The time was moving towards ten o'clock. They had an hour at most.

From some bushes came a rustling noise, and a young fox emerged, eyes shining in the moonlight.

'Hello, my friend,' Ed said. 'What've you come to tell me? That it's time for some cunning? I think I probably got that, but thanks for the reminder.'

The creature stared at Ed, calm and unafraid, perhaps a little bemused at the appearance of this intruder in its territory. The fox seemed to nod to itself before trotting off across the cemetery, brush of a tail hovering effortlessly in the silver air.

The little things. It was always the little things.

'I think we can make sure you don't go to prison,' Ed said, walking back over to the trio cuddled together on the stone floor of the mausoleum. 'Actually, I think there's a way this can work out for all of us. But you're going to have to help us, so we can help each other.'

38

He was there again, holding court amongst the barflies. Of course he was. It was what he did.

Even with his daughter still missing, as far as he knew anyway. Even with his wife still in hospital.

In fairness to Chris, the search had been called off for the night. He had done his utmost, amongst so many others. And perhaps he just needed comfort. Who didn't, sometimes? Familiar surroundings, people he thought of as his friends, however unreal the associations.

On his walk there, Ed had seen police cars returning to their stations. They were somehow driving aimlessly, with none of the vigour and determination of earlier. Faces in the windscreens blank.

The people he passed, in their little groups, were the same. Where they had set out with energy and hope, they were returning deflated. No longer striding and chattering, but wandering and silent.

Still no sign of her, the searchers were saying. Not a hint, not a clue. What could possibly have happened to Maddy? Who had taken her? Where had she gone?

We've tried to hold reality at bay. But now we're starting to expect the worst.

If only they knew.

Maddy was perfectly safe, sat with Olivia and Florence, as fine a pair of guardians as anyone could wish for. Still hiding in the cemetery, waiting for his return. And she had deceived them all with her plan; her, a fourteen-year-old girl.

No wonder Maddy and Olivia had discovered a bond.

Florence had found a takeaway and bought them much needed coffee and food to share. The chips and pizza, with a faint nod to the healthy uplands of salad, weren't exactly five-star cuisine. But they had instilled new life into Maddy.

She had thought about what they were suggesting, and quickly agreed. Yes, she understood it was a lifelong pact. If the truth ever emerged, she could find herself in prison. And they, the three who were trying to help her, would serve months or years of time inside the hopeless brick walls too.

But if they all told the same story, both now and forever, there might just be a happy ending waiting somewhere over the hill, the culmination of this long and very winding road.

There had been one more surprise before Ed set off for the Glorious Empire. Florence followed him out from the mausoleum, and asked, 'Is there any word about Mitch?'

Always softly spoken, forever gentle, endlessly fearful of hurt, as had been her lot so often in life, this time Florence's voice was different. There was a vulnerability in her words Ed hadn't heard before.

It was above and beyond the norm; as though she had found something which she had sought for many years and was trying to control the terror of it being stolen away. As everything else she had ever loved had been taken from this tender woman who had done nothing whatsoever to deserve such spiteful treatment from the fates.

'Don't worry too much about him,' Ed replied, then saw her expression and added, 'Or try not to, anyway. He promised me he'll be okay for tonight. He's a man of his word. And tonight is all we're going to need.'

'Thank you. Just, please…'

'Yes?'

'Make this work. Somehow. For me, Mitch, Olivia, Maddy, you, Charl...'

'For all of us, you mean.'

'Yes. For all of us. For...'

'For?'

'For hope.'

Hope. Hope, bloody hope. It was always hope. The hope that had brought them together, bound them together, and would deliver them through this together.

Or so Ed hoped, anyway.

Florence held his look, the two of them standing, wrapped in moonlight. She quickly kissed Ed on the cheek and ducked back into the mausoleum.

The pub went quiet when Ed walked in. Drinkers stopped talking, every head turning to stare at him. It was like an old-fashioned Western, and would have been comical if it hadn't been for his mission.

Propped up at the bar, half drunk he may have been, blood shot eyes in the dim light, Chris's hand nonetheless moved for a bottle.

'There's no need for that,' Ed said. 'I just want a chat.' And when Chris only gripped his makeshift weapon harder, Ed added, 'It's about Maddy. I might be able to help.'

'You didn't do so well last time with that fucking paper of yours.'

'I'm not so sure about that. Maybe it has helped. Maybe I've got something to tell you.' Ed held up his phone. 'A message, in fact.'

And there Ed stood, in the heart of enemy territory. Calm and in control. Facing them down; not in the way they were used to, with bluster, threats and anger, but with certainty and assurance.

The other drinkers were looking at Chris.

'Twat him,' one tattooed ape grunted. 'Go on.'

'Don't be a dick,' his shell-suited friend replied, and told Chris,

'You'd better hear what he's got to say.' There was a pause, then he added, 'Twat him after that.'

The barman, a real sweat-ball slug of a man with peering eyes said, gruffly, 'Sit in the corner over there. Where we can keep an eye on you. You'll be okay.'

'I'll be okay whatever,' Chris replied, finding a reserve of his standard bravado. 'Come on, then. Five minutes.'

'That's all I'll need,' Ed replied. 'And all you'll need.'

The corner was the darkest of the dingy, a real cave in the far reaches of the pub. Furthest from the clicking balls of the pool table, the cinema screen TVs, and the desperation hidden in drink. Given how busy the Empire never was, such a far corner could hardly have been in demand. But the table was sticky nonetheless, and the chairs threadbare.

The extra-terrestrial barman eyed them regularly, as did the locals, doing their best to puff out their chests, parade their tattoos, and put on their tough-guy looks. But largely it was the usual show of cockerels without hens, and Ed and Chris were left alone to talk.

They sat across a corner of the table, to any casual observer, old friends meeting for a drink. All very standard, until that was, a second glance. And the alertness, the readiness in both, always prepared for an attack.

Just like the old days, Ed thought. Did the bloody past never leave you?

'How're you doing?' he asked, after the ritual period of suspicion and silence.

'How'd you fucking think?'

Maybe it wasn't the time for small talk to ease his way into what Ed had to say. 'Still no word of Maddy?'

'Do you think I'd be here if there was?'

Ed let the hiatus run, waited for his moment, then said, 'I know where she is.'

The punch landed, and Chris didn't even bother trying to disguise it. 'You what?'

'I've just seen her. She's safe. She's fine.'

'Fuck off.'

'But if you want her back, there's something I need first.'

'You what? What the hell are you talking about?' His voice was rising, and drinkers were looking over.

'I'd suggest you're a little quieter,' Ed said. 'If you want to know where your daughter is. If you want to get to see her. And soon.'

'You don't know where she is. You're shitting me. Trying it on. We have fuckers like you all the time, calling 999 and getting off on pretending you know something. You sick bastard.'

Chris took a swig from his bottle. His voice was slurred and his breath stale with beer.

'That appeal you did, when we were on the common. It worked,' Ed said. 'We got some information about where Maddy was. An anonymous e-mail, just like that. We didn't tell the police because we didn't believe it, and didn't want to waste their time. Like you said. They have plenty enough of that. So we checked it out ourselves. And would you believe it, we found her.'

'Lying twat. I don't believe you.'

'I thought you might say that. So I've brought you proof.'

Ed slowly took out his phone. He was aware of eyes across the pub watching him, even more closely now. The two guys at the pool table were gripping their cues a little too eagerly.

'When I show you this, I don't want you to react,' he went on. 'Do you understand? If you do anything, that's it. The deal's off and I walk out of here. Even if I have to go through your mates to do it. I can and I will. You know that. But most importantly, you'll never see me, or your daughter, again.'

Chris hissed but nodded, and Ed found the videos. This wasn't exactly his specialist subject, and he made sure to choose the right one of the pair. The recording was only brief, just a few seconds.

But it showed Maddy, waving dutifully at the camera and producing a fleeting, unconvincing smile. She looked tired and dirty, but very much alive. The time and date on the recording told Chris it had been filmed only a few minutes earlier.

'What the fuck…?' Chris began, but Ed interrupted.

'I said no reaction. None. Or this ends here. You got that?'

Chris glared at him, eyes tight, stained teeth bared in a primeval fashion. 'Where is she? Where is she, you bastard?'

'Safe and well, and not so far away. You can get to see her soon. Very soon, in fact. That is, if we can agree on what we're going to do.'

'I could just beat it out of you, where she is. Give you a good kicking.'

'I'm sure you'd love to try. But it didn't work so well the last time, did it?'

'Or I could arrest you and seize that recording.'

'It's set to delete the moment I hit the button. Which I will. Right after I've hit you. And put you down. Which I also will. Quite happily. Then I deny everything, you've got no evidence of this ridiculous story of mine, and you never get to see your daughter again. Never… ever.'

Another silence. Slow and watchful movements continued around the pub. Life there, such as it was, went on. But there was no doubting the centre of attention, however much the rest of the cast might be trying to pretend otherwise.

Eventually, Chris said, 'What's this deal then? What do you want?'

'I want my friend back. That's all. I want Mitch released from the cells. And for that, you drop the charges against him. That's all I want. Drop the charges and you can have your daughter back.'

All around, the eyes were still on them, even more intense. Chris was quiet for a few more seconds, sitting still, apart from one finger tapping on the table.

Then he lifted his head and said, 'I don't think so. I know you. You're a soft twat. You think you're a hero. God's gift to the fucking world, you and your mates, that's what you reckon. Moral crusaders, showing us all how life should be done, or so you reckon. But you're just a bunch of no-good dickless losers. You'd never hurt her. Maddy's going to be just fine. If I say no to your shit arse of a deal, you'll turn her in anyway, and that's it. Your pal goes to jail, I get my girl back, everyone's happy. Apart from you, that is. So that's my deal. Call it a counter offer, okay? Wanker.'

Chris sat back, folded his arms and smirked. Around them, the pub relaxed. Drinkers lifted their glasses once more, pool balls rolled again.

The battle was won. Normal service resumed.

'Clever old you. What a smart boy. You've got me there,' Ed replied, before hardening his voice. 'Or you would have, I suppose. Yes, you would have… if that wasn't exactly what I was expecting an idiot like you to say. And if it wasn't for this other video I've got.'

39

Across the road from the entrance to the cemetery, they waited.
Ed, Florence and Olivia, hiding in the darkness along a convenient, if smelly, alley, and all as nervous as they were pretending not
to be.

It was Florence's idea, to complement Olivia about the videos, and a
good one. *A real team effort this whole odyssey had been*, Ed thought. He
couldn't have assembled a finer group if he'd carried out days of interviews, rather than whimsically putting a random advert in a newspaper
and following his feelings.

Fortunately, in this city of intellects and opulence, it didn't take long
for the perfect couple to walk past. They had doubtless been to a college
dinner, or the theatre for some avant-garde student performance which
would be quickly, and happily, forgotten.

They were older, both upright, elegant, and dressed in fine evening
coats. Maybe retired fellows of an ancient college, fresh from a night
reliving old times. But they were not so old as to be unwilling to take up
the mantle they were about to be offered.

They were talking in the clear and educated voices which were the
familiar accents of this city. And most importantly, they were as trust-

worthy and honourable a pair as anyone who needed impeccable witnesses could wish for. A couple of Cambridge's very finest.

Perfect.

Ed, Florence and Olivia ran out into the road in front of them, putting on a fine show of being breathless and excited. As might have been expected, the couple stopped in an instant.

'It's okay, it's okay,' Olivia said, before the pair could start handing over their valuables and pleading for their lives. 'We think we know where Maddy is.'

'I'm sorry?' the woman replied, impressively polite, even in the face of such strangeness.

'The missing girl,' Florence helped out. 'We're from the online paper, the *Last Edition*. We've had a tip off.'

'Ah,' the man said, managing to make the single syllable last for several seconds. 'We have indeed been reading you. A fine addition to the plurality of the local media, I must say. Very fresh and innovative, if sometimes a tad too tabloid for my taste. Indeed, we were considering inviting you to the university to give a lecture on your work.'

'That'd be an honour, but we're in a rush,' Ed said. 'Maddy, this missing girl…'

'A tip off?' the woman asked. 'How exciting. We did join the hunt for her, didn't we, Winston? Earlier on, that is. We couldn't help tonight as we had tickets for the opera. I'm Felicity, by the way.'

Despite the absurdity of the moment, they all shook hands, as the regulations of Englishness dictate.

'We've got a tip she might be in the cemetery,' Olivia said. 'In the mausoleum. Is there any chance you can come help us? In case she is there and we have to carry her, or some of us need to stay with her while the others call the police?'

There were no more hesitations. They set off together towards the cemetery, Felicity and Winston leading the way.

It didn't take long for the mausoleum to become another emergency services circus. The police descended in their droves, along with ambulances and many of the volunteers who had been out searching for Maddy.

The area was lit bright with arc lights, cordoned off, and Ed, Florence, and Olivia sat in a police van with tea and coffee to await questioning. Winston and Felicity had already been spoken to, and had given exactly the accounts that were required.

Winston, who it turned out was a professor of early mathematical language, even offered his opinion that the *Last Edition* team should be honoured for their work, bless him. They were heroes for diligently publicising the hunt for Maddy, and her eventual discovery, in his view.

Perfect.

Maddy herself was taken to hospital for the obligatory check ups. And so Olivia, Florence, and Ed sat together on a narrow wooden bench in the back of the police van and waited. To be interviewed, yes, but first to see Saxton, who was on his way.

The wizened old sergeant who told them produced a certain look, which suggested an interesting conversation lay ahead.

The team used the waiting time wisely. Between them, with their new-found skills, it took only a few minutes to write up the story and publish it. Olivia even snuck open the doors of the van to take some photos of the scene.

Missing Maddy Found Safe and Well

'That's the best headline we've ever written,' Florence said, and no-one disagreed.

. . .

Fourteen-year-old Maddy Williams, who had been missing amid serious concerns for her safety, has been found, the Last Edition can reveal.

Her disappearance led to huge hunts for the teenager, with hundreds of members of the public turning out to help, and emotional appeals from her parents.

But tonight, she was found bound and gagged, but otherwise unharmed, in the mausoleum at Millhouse Road Cemetery.

The discovery followed a tip off to the Last Edition, and we were on the scene to witness Maddy being found.

Olivia added the photos, including one of Maddy being led away by police officers, and published. Together, they watched the news spread around the world, as had become the familiar way for their stories.

'Maybe we should write an eyewitness despatch about what it felt like to find her,' Olivia said.

'Later,' Ed replied. 'That can be a follow-up, if we've got the energy left. Let's get through our chat with Saxton first.'

The superintendent decreed it was just Ed he wanted to talk to, for now anyway, and would tolerate no arguments. Even Olivia's forceful efforts made no headway. Saxton led Ed into the mausoleum for their conversation, and in a slow and deliberate manner. Ed would have smiled, if he hadn't known how closely he was being watched.

He couldn't blame Saxton. He'd used the same trick plenty of times himself. Take a suspect back to a scene and scrutinise their reactions for any clues about what had happened there.

So Ed remembered his acting classes, one of the more ridiculous elements of his training all those years ago. He thought he pulled off a good job of looking fascinated at what was unfolding around him, yet entirely innocent.

Forensic investigations of that area complete, Saxton led him to the very spot where Maddy had been found, which Ed reacted to not in the slightest. And there they talked, as scenes of crime officers came and went around them, white suits bright in the arc lights.

Ed explained about the anonymous, and conveniently untraceable, e-mail which had come in to the *Last Edition*, leading them to Maddy.

'You didn't think to call us?' Saxton asked. He was clearly trying to restrain his Viking instincts, keep calm and reasonable. But that chest was out, as ready for battle as a battering ram, and his beard bristling in a warlike way.

'We didn't believe it. We thought it was just another time waster.'

'But you checked it out anyway?'

'It would have been negligent not to. We just did what any good citizens would. Left you to your more important work, trying to find Maddy, while we checked on the one-in-a-million chance there was anything in it. And what a good job we did.'

'What a happy piece of fortune,' Saxton replied with a swing of his well-honed sarcasm axe.

'I'm sorry?' Ed replied.

'You seem to have been blessed with a great deal of good fortune. All sorts of strange things have been happening lately, none apparently in any way connected with you.'

'Life can be strange.' Ed tried a smile, but it didn't really work. After all those years and all those experiences, his face wasn't much up to it anymore. 'Don't you think so?'

'With you about, certainly.'

They waited while a woman carried a couple of evidence bags past. Ed did his best not to try to see what was in them.

'So, this story of yours,' Saxton continued.

'You mean what happened.'

'This story… you came running in here after you got the e-mail.'

'As witnessed by the fine upstanding Felicity and Winston.'

'Yes, very convenient. And you found Maddy here. Tied up and blindfolded, but otherwise unhurt.'

'Felicity and Winston found her, to be accurate. They went first.'

'And you helped to untie her and take the blindfold off. Which is no doubt why we'll find your DNA on the rope and the blindfold.'

'Inevitably. Naturally I wanted to preserve the integrity of the scene, to help your investigation. But protection of life always comes first, eh?'

'This is not a job interview,' Saxton said.

'I wasn't applying,' Ed replied, cleaning his glasses to give himself something to do with his hands.

'I'm very glad to hear it. But as I was saying, according to your story…'

'What happened, you mean. As witnessed by two impeccable members of the community.'

'According to your story, while you were saving Maddy, you saw a movement at the back of the mausoleum. Which you assumed was the abductor.'

'That would be my guess.'

'And you gave chase. But the man, or woman – this person unknown – had vanished.'

'It was quite dark. They had a head start. I'm not as young as I was. And the cemetery is full of places to hide.'

'And you can't describe this person at all?'

'I so wish I could,' Ed replied, remembering his session in sincerity, and imagining he was talking to his grandmother. 'But it was just a fleeting glimpse. No detail at all.'

Saxton nodded in a knowing manner. 'What a coincidence.'

'In what way?'

'Maddy can't describe her abductor at all either. When she was taken, she says she felt arms around her from behind, then something over her mouth, and passed out. This person, he or she, didn't speak. Maddy couldn't even tell if it was a man or woman. On the couple of occasions she wasn't blindfolded, Maddy says the unknown abductor always wore all black and a mask. All she can say is they were average height and build.'

'Not very helpful, that.'

'To say the least.' Saxton studied the air in front of him and nodded to himself again. 'And then there's the death of Alan.'

'Have you found something?' Ed asked, this time imagining the beautiful sun-blessed beach he planned to head for if he ever got out of there.

'No. Not a bloody thing. We still can't even tell if it was an accident or not.'

'It's probably just a tragic accident, then. Not connected with Maddy's abduction at all, in which case.'

'Another coincidence then?'

'It looks like it.'

'And nothing whatsoever to do with the mystery faceless and descriptionless abductor who took Maddy and managed to evade you at the cemetery, leaving no trace at all in their wake?'

'It doesn't seem so.'

'And do you know something else? It's funny that we can't find any trace of the abductor on Maddy, or in the mausoleum here, either.'

'We know they were very careful, don't we? They must have planned it all well to get away with it, so far, at least.'

Saxton must have been nearing the breaking strain of his tolerance. He let out a snort. 'And I suppose all the cats going missing isn't anything to do with anything, either?'

Ed remembered his training once more. Body language was critical, they had been taught. He saw a sun lounger waiting on that beautiful beach; warm, comfortable and relaxing. He shook his head. 'I don't see how it can be.'

'And then there's Chris.'

'What about him?'

'You don't know?'

With all the innocence of a host of angels, Ed asked, 'Don't know what?'

This time Saxton turned away. And when he looked back, Ed couldn't tell if there were the beginnings of a smile forming on his face, or a blood-curdling war cry.

'He's withdrawn his complaint against your friend Mitch. Wants no further action to be taken. Says it was all just a big misunderstanding. Only two old friends larking about, apparently.'

'I'm glad to hear that,' Ed replied, as neutrally as ever.

'And not connected with anything else that's gone on in the slightest?'

'Again, I just don't see how it could be. Do you?'

Saxton studied Ed. 'I have some ideas. But maybe it's better not to go into them.' He paused, then added, 'I imagine it's a waste of time talking to your two friends. They're going to tell me exactly the same story, aren't they?'

'Of course. Because it's the truth.'

'And Maddy too?'

'I expect so. The truth is the truth is the truth, eh?'

'Hmmm.'

Saxton nodded, something he'd been doing a lot in this conversation. Perhaps it was his coping mechanism.

'What a shit story,' he pronounced at last. 'I've heard some utter crap in my time, but this is an award winner.'

Ed let the silence run, then asked, 'Is that all you need from me, superintendent? If so, I'd like to get home. It's been quite a day.'

Saxton gave him a look. Then in a strange voice, said, 'Just a minute,' paced away from Ed and made a call on his phone.

Outside the mausoleum, blue lights were still colouring the darkness. A small group of cops was staring over at him, chattering away, but Ed ignored them. Saxton hadn't asked for Ed's phone, or Florence's, or Olivia's, which was odd. The video was still there, safely copied on all three in case they should need it. Heavily protected and encrypted, of course.

Although, as things stood, it was looking as though they wouldn't need their special short film. For now, anyway. There was still a long way to go if this story was to have the happy ending they had planned.

Ed yawned and stamped his feet. They were getting cold, just as they used to in the winter stakeouts of the old days. Everyone has a weakness, one of the instructors had said. If yours is just your feet, you're doing pretty well.

Saxton was taking a long time on his call and looked like he was working hard not to glance over. What was he up to? Ed passed the time by thinking of Mitch and seeing him walk free from the police station. Then Tommy, and how he would have a whole fresh lettuce all to himself tomorrow. The tortoise would love that, in his slow and primeval way.

Eventually, Saxton strode back over. With new energy and purpose.

Which meant trouble.

'How's Mitch?' Ed asked, to forestall him. 'Have you released him yet?'

'Well, well,' Saxton replied, looking much happier than he had all evening. 'Yet another coincidence.'

'Meaning?'

'Mitch would like to see you.'

It was something in the way Saxton spoke. For the first time, the smooth passage of the great plan hit some grit.

'Good,' Ed replied. 'Of course. That'd be great.'

'But here's the strange part. Mitch has got someone with him who'd also like to have a chat with you. And they want to do it right now, and guess where? In the cells. Nice and quietly, apparently, in a place where you can't be overheard.'

40

The police station was just the police station, albeit alive with light for that time of night. The walk down to the cells was just the walk along corridors, down, and into the heart of the building. Saxton was just Saxton.

But something was different. Something was wrong.

Two sizeable police officers walked behind Ed and Saxton. Blocking any hope of escape. And, presumably, not for the superintendent.

A coincidence, maybe. But Ed had the same view as Saxton of coincidences.

Particularly that night. With all that had happened.

And may yet be still to come.

Ed had that feeling he'd been told about. The one he'd been fortunate enough never to suffer himself, but which was a legend of fear amongst the ghosts of the old life.

Whether it was in Northern Ireland, Russia, Iraq or so many other places where lives were fragile in their secret world. The walk along the corridor to that room. The waiting men. The ambush. The chair with the straps. The shiny sinister instruments. The water.

At the bars which marked the entrance to the cells, Saxton stopped. Ed waited to see what he would do. The two cops also stopped, a little further back along the corridor. Still watchful, without looking that way. Still barring any hope of escape.

Face to face, a little apart in the narrow corridor, Saxton said, 'I now apparently have to forget that you came down here.'

'I wouldn't hold that against you.'

'I wish I could forget. But it's not that simple. You know, don't you?'

'I have a suspicion.'

'Are you going to be okay?'

'It depends what they've come here for.'

Saxton nodded, and in front of Ed, with nothing changing, the man transformed. The Viking warrior was gone and a husband and father took their place.

'Whatever happened tonight, or in the last few days, you got Maddy back. I appreciate that. Thank you.'

They shook hands. Saxton opened the metal gate, and Ed walked through.

The door was open and he could hear conversation coming from Mitch's cell. Two voices, even if Ed couldn't make out the words. Neither sounded tense, nor angry. He hesitated for a second, then walked on.

The cellblock was deserted. There was no sign of the custody sergeant at the desk at the end of the corridor. All the other cells Ed passed were empty.

He paused again, then paced on. To the doorway of Mitch's cell.

Sitting either end of the thin ledge of a bed, were Mitch and Steve, the young programmer. They were chatting away like old friends. Both were stretched out and relaxed.

Not quite what Ed had anticipated. And in the doorway of the cell he lingered. Wondering what would happen. Half expecting others to appear from nowhere, ready to pin him down and tie him up. But nothing happened. Nothing at all. The two men ignored him and kept talking.

About a football match at the weekend. A bet that Liverpool would win. Just a few pounds. A gentle wager, the sort old friends make all the time.

Ed waited, cleaned his glasses, then let out a polite cough.

'Come in, come in,' Mitch said, as if welcoming an old friend to a house party.

And when Ed hesitated and checked behind him, Steve added, 'Please, come on, there's nothing to be worried about. Not now, anyway. But we do need to have a chat.'

It might have been the years of inbred mistrust, it could just have been the strangeness of the moment. But Ed remained in the doorway for the conversation.

It was irrational, he knew. There was nowhere to run to, but it felt more comfortable. Even if it seemed like running wouldn't be required.

Mitch had realised Ed wasn't moving. He stood up and shook hands. 'Well done. On getting through all this. And thank you. For being a friend and never giving up on me. Despite my best efforts to make you do so.'

'That's okay,' Ed replied slowly, trying to work out exactly what was going on.

'You've already met him in one guise,' Mitch continued. 'But now you'd better meet him properly. This is...'

'Steve,' the young man sitting on the bed interrupted. 'Steve will do.'

'This whole operation has been Steve's baby,' Mitch said.

'Has it?' Ed replied, as levelly as he could. 'Which might explain the looks I remember passing between you two back in the labs. The way you played a couple of situations when the *Last Edition* could have been in trouble. This has been a set-up, hasn't it?'

'Don't be angry,' Mitch went on. 'We've been on your side. Really, we have. Even if we could hardly say so. And things could have turned out a lot worse.'

'A whole lot worse,' Steve agreed.

Ed leaned against the door of the cell and tried to focus. It was difficult to take in what Steve and Mitch were telling him. He concentrated on the riveting of the door. It was geometric and elegant, in a way he doubted anyone had ever appreciated before.

The little things. It was always the little things.

'There was a big fight over you, and right up at the highest level,' Steve said, stretching out on the bed, arms laced behind his head. 'It was classic stuff. You know the sort of thing. You remember the lectures. And the reality. Hawks versus doves.'

'We knew how you'd done your bit in your day,' Mitch said. 'The service you'd given. Your courage and the missions you'd carried out. How much you'd suffered.'

Ed felt his fingers lift to his scar, as they always did at the memory, as if to soothe the reminder of that day. One day amongst so many days.

'We knew you were struggling,' Steve went on. 'The darkness of the dawns, isn't that what you call it? Very poetic, very nice. We might even adopt that for standard service speak. We could do with softening our image a bit. Anyway, the point is, we knew you were suffering. What we didn't know was how it would come out.'

'How you would come out, more importantly,' Mitch added.

'It's tough to say this, but some of the bosses wanted to make sure there wasn't a problem with you.'

'You knew so much. Some of the operations you'd been on. The secrets you were a part of. If you'd started talking...'

'So some were saying we couldn't risk you going rogue, and we had to make certain there was no chance of that happening. If you know what we mean.'

'I know exactly what you mean,' Ed replied, checking over his shoulder again.

'But others – us included – said you deserved a chance. You're still held in high esteem in the service, with the things you did. So we came to a compromise.'

Ed managed not to say anything. Compromise wasn't a word that was often heard in his old life. Unless it was a compromise between a bullet and a blade.

'We decided to watch you,' Mitch said. 'There was the usual fuss about resources, so we even cut a deal on that. I'm on sabbatical. It's been quite fun, to be honest. A welcome change.'

Those eyes were bright again, but not blazing. Maybe Mitch saved that for when he wanted to be intimidating. Ed wondered whether Mitch could control them, have them on some kind of inner dimmer switch. Was that humanly possible?

He would have to ask. If he got out of there safely. If they were still talking. If they ever wanted to talk again.

'I've been overseeing the operation, but also helping out with the actual on-the-ground work in my spare time,' Steve said. 'Which has been damn refreshing as well, to be honest. It's so good to get out from behind a desk occasionally. And back to an old and happy haunt.'

'You were recruited here too?'

'Who wasn't? You can take the spy out of Cambridge, but...'

'Were any others involved?' Ed asked, and the pair understood the point of the question immediately.

'If you mean Florence and Olivia, no. They're completely innocent, have no idea what's been going on. They're just themselves. But you may have had a hint of other people watching you.'

'I thought I'd seen a few shadows in the night.'

Steve smiled, and it looked genuine. 'I'm not surprised. You always were good at this game. That's partly why we thought we owed you a chance.'

'So you just watched what I was up to, with the advert in the paper, and let it run?'

'It was a little more complicated than that. We had to set some wheels in motion, and fast.'

'Like me and my barge,' Mitch said. 'We needed an insider, of course.'

'Of course.'

'And my position at the Falcon Labs,' Steve added.

'Which is why you invested money in the *Last Edition*? To make sure we kept going, for a while at least.'

'Spot on. We thought you deserved a chance to see where your crazy idea would lead.'

'And what about our intervention with Chris? I wondered why Mitch was so effective in grabbing and holding him. Not to mention how he managed to blindside me when he sneaked up on the police station and attacked Chris.'

Steve and Mitch exchanged a look. 'We had words about that,' the young man said. 'Both your initial intervention with Chris, and Mitch's highly unauthorised follow-up. But, to be frank, who's on the side of a wife-beating cop?'

'And when Maddy disappeared? You must have been worried then.'

'The law of unintended consequences in its pomp. Yes, we were worried. But again, we decided to let you run. You were trying to do the right thing.' Steve lowered his voice, as if Saxton might be lingering outside somewhere, listening. 'Frankly, we had more faith in you than the local police to get it sorted and get her back.'

'And we were right,' Mitch added. 'I'm happy to say.'

'That was Olivia,' Ed replied. 'She should come and join you. She'd be a natural.'

Steve smiled again. 'The thought had occurred to me.'

'Along with some other thoughts about Olivia,' Mitch noted, with an arch of the eyebrow.

Steve rolled up his sleeves. The barcode tattoo had gone. Ed wasn't surprised. Those who lived in the shadow world didn't care for distinguishing features, and certainly not those that were self-inflicted.

'So, what now?' Ed asked.

'You've passed, and with flying colours,' Steve, or whatever his name was, replied, getting up from the bed. 'So I'd better be getting back to square it all with the suits. Then it's onto some other work. There's always plenty to be done, as you know. Back behind a desk, sadly. So it goes.'

'You're just going to leave the story about how Maddy was found as it is? Our story, I mean.'

'Why not? What's to be gained by raking up a whole lot of the truth?'

Ed wondered if he should say something, but decided to stay quiet. He might be a journalist now, a news editor even, and so committed to the truth, in theory at least. But every career had its limits.

'The only thing I'm concerned about is Chris,' Ed said. 'I think we've got him boxed in for now. And if he behaves, as he's promised to, there's even hope he might be a passable human being, and father to Maddy. That's what he says he wants. But just in case...'

Ed took out his phone and showed the video to Steve and Mitch. Maddy describing in detail how her father had beaten her mother. The injuries he had inflicted. The dreadful screams. The blood, the shattered house. How many times he had launched the vicious unprovoked drunken attacks. How they had finally prompted her to run away, endangering her own life and leading to a huge search.

Maddy's tearful face, in full close up, dirty and wretched, filled the screen. Ed paired the phones, copied the video over to Mitch and said, 'As a backup. Olivia and Florence also have copies. So if there's one hint of trouble from Chris, and we're somehow unable to release it... you know what to do.'

Steve nodded. 'Nice moves. I don't suppose you fancy coming back? To the old life?'

Ed didn't answer. He didn't have to.

Mitch produced a heavy bunch of keys and the three men walked out of the cell. It felt like that whole level of the police station was deserted, no doubt on the orders of the mysterious Steve. At the metal gate, they stopped and shook hands.

'It's been a pleasure working with you,' Steve told Ed.

'With?'

'In the orbit of, then.'

'So, is that it?' he asked.

'It is for me. I'm glad to say I'll be reporting that you've shown your-self to be both reliable and dependable, and so public spirited that you could be considered a model citizen.'

But Mitch put a hand on Ed's arm. 'That's not quite it from me, though. There's one other thing we need to talk about.'

If this was to be their final newsroom meeting, it was the perfect place. So much so that Ed was a little annoyed he hadn't thought of it himself.

The sun was proudly soaring into the sky to announce the arrival of another blessing of a spring day.

The common was bathed in its gentle warmth, and the Cam, never a river to trouble itself with rapidly flowing waters, was even more languid than usual.

They sat on the deck of Mitch's barge, in a little square, watched the world go by, sipped at teas and coffees, and talked. Originally, the plan had been to meet at the Labs. But Florence had been the first to reach the building, only to find a scrum of journalists, photographers and camera crews surrounding it.

'I nearly walked right on in,' she told them, in her touchingly modest way. 'I never thought they might be waiting for us. Until Swift arrived, and they mobbed him, asking where we were.'

That caused plenty of laughter, and quite a debate. Whether the angular manager's new-found love of the media would mean he enjoyed the moment, or was irritated at the disruption to the labs' orderly business.

Florence had called the others, picked up some croissants, and suggested they meet at Mitch's barge instead. It was nearby, more private than a café, and a beautiful place to talk. Strangely homely, in fact.

At that stage, Ed hadn't fully realised the implications of what Florence said. In fairness, he was a little preoccupied after the previous night.

Olivia and Florence had been waiting when he and Mitch walked out the police station. The women had been questioned and told the same stories. Maddy had stuck to her version of events, as agreed by a modern-day version of a blood oath. Everyone had regurgitated the script as required.

A hunt was underway for the mysterious figure who had kidnapped Maddy. But, as Saxton had put it, 'So far, we've narrowed the pool of suspects down to seventy-five per cent of the population.'

There was so much to talk about, but all four were also exhausted. So they headed home for the night to get some rest, however forlorn a hope that might have been.

Ed checked around, in his usual way, when he got back to the mobile home park. But this time, he was content there were no watchers. It was a strange feeling, a sort of light-headedness, and it took a while, staring up at the moon and stars, to realise why.

It was as though part of the past had left him.

Tommy was carrying out another expedition around the lounge at his usual stately pace. Ed found him some lettuce and smiled, as the contemporary dinosaur paused his explorations and instead set about a steady, and impressively loud, chomping.

Ed lay back on the sofa, and found, yet again, that the noise of a tortoise dining was a curiously comforting one. He never expected to sleep, but quickly did, and rested easily through the night, only to be woken by another perfect dawn.

They tried a little small talk, the staff of the *Last Edition*. How is everyone, how did you sleep? But Olivia, never one for such unproductive pleasantries, only managed to tolerate a few seconds of it.

'Can we get on with it?' she asked. Then remembered all the progress she'd made journeying into the brave new world of humanity, and added, 'Please.'

'Where do we start?' Ed asked.

'That's for you to answer,' Mitch replied. And when the only reply was a thoughtful silence, added, 'It depends on how much of the past you want to talk about.'

In the old life it was ingrained in everything they did, that talking freely was forbidden. Drunk, emotional, in love, raging with anger, whichever and no matter what, the cover story was the only story. With practice, and given time, a lie could become the truth.

Only yesterday, Ed would have struggled to feel any differently. But today, sitting in the sunshine, amongst people he could at last call friends, the world had changed.

He told them a little of his history, the edited highlights. The tap on the shoulder, here in this city, genesis of so many secret lives. The training, then the first nervous faltering missions. The chases, the fights, the near-death experiences. The rising through the ranks. The secrets, the endless secrets, some so shocking as to be unbelievable. The bodies of comrades. The far too many funerals, secret services hidden within this most secret of services.

And the last few days. A brief recap. Emphasising the points which would become important as Mitch told his story.

If he chose to tell it. That was a matter for him. Depending on which future he had chosen.

Ed waited, watching a cormorant drying its wings in the sunshine. The dark rainbows of the bird's compact feathers. The lethal cut of its beak.

Beauty and death, side by side, as so very often in life.

The little things. It was always the little things.

'My turn, then,' Mitch said after a while, and told his own story. Of his life in the shadows, but without the detail Ed had given them. Of the respect in the service for how Ed had served, but also the concerns about what he could reveal. The operation to watch him, and its conclusion.

If anyone was going to pass judgment on what they had just heard, it would be Olivia. And she didn't disappoint.

'FFS,' she said. 'You're telling me this whole thing has been a set-up?'

'Of course not,' Florence pointed out in her soothing way. 'No-one could have known what would happen, and how things would turn out. Ed did what he thought was right in putting the advert in the paper. We applied to join. There was no agenda in any of that. Apart from Mitch's, when he made sure he got in... somehow.'

'We thought my cover story would appeal,' he replied. 'It was carefully put together. And we tilted the odds even further my way by making sure I met up with Ed before everyone else did. Plus, of course, I had the psychological insights to write my hundred words in a way which would appeal to him.'

'What about your own troubles with your past?' Olivia asked. 'And your writing? You couldn't have made that *No Man Left Behind* report sound so real, surely? And that stuff about your criminal record?'

'A bit of the criminal record was true, some made up,' Mitch replied. 'I did have a wobble. Similar to Ed's. Most people in the service do. It's hardly surprising, is it? The things we know and see.'

'Did it surprise you? All that coming out? And getting so involved with Ed and the rest of us?'

Mitch stared out at the slow river, tracing the blaze of the sunshine. Those eyes were bright again, but in a very different way to any Ed had seen before. 'A lot of things have surprised me in the past few days,'

Mitch replied at last. 'And bizarrely, given my life, they've been pleasant surprises.'

He got up and threw the remains of his coffee into the river, prompting a flurry of excitement from a gang of ducks. Mitch wasn't wearing that familiar hoodie. Just a T-shirt. Plain, simple and new. Maybe because of the warmth of the morning, or perhaps for a deeper reason.

'Aren't you always told to never get involved?' Florence asked.

'That didn't work so well,' Mitch replied, smiling at her in a meaningful way.

'It never does,' Ed added. 'You hear it all the time, but it never works. Ultimately, we're all human. We all have faults and feelings. Don't we?'

For a reason no-one wanted to voice, at that point their eyes found Olivia. But she just shook her head, muttered, 'FFS,' and shrunk a little further into her denim armour.

Another barge chugged by, gliding slowly along the river. In silence they watched its passage, a dog on the deck staring out, like a shaggy figurehead.

'So, what now?' Ed asked, looking at Mitch and Florence, sitting a little closer side by side than mere friends might.

But before either could speak, phone in hand, perhaps seeking a distraction, Olivia said, 'The stats for the latest edition are going crazy. It's that eyewitness report about finding Maddy that's done it.'

While they waited for Ed and Mitch to emerge from the police station the previous night, Florence and Olivia had written the story. They'd added a line, which Olivia had used her charm to glean from a police officer, about Maddy being taken to visit Charl. Mum was feeling much better and due to be released from hospital today.

'That's a first,' Florence said. 'A good news story making such a splash. Long may it continue.'

'What happens with Chris?' Olivia asked, and couldn't help adding, 'The fuckwit arsehole.'

Ed replied, 'Kept at arm's length to start with, but then allowed to see Maddy and Charl, and depending on how he behaves... who knows?'

'Let's hope your video does the trick,' Florence replied.

Instinctively, each of the four checked their phones, reassured in the knowledge that Maddy's words were safely stored in their electronic minds.

'So then,' Ed said, making a point of looking at Florence and Mitch, and smiling. 'What next? Is there something you want to tell us, by any chance?'

But what could have been a beautiful moment was put on hold by Olivia asking Ed, 'Haven't you got something to tell us first?'

They were all looking at him, these three friends. They all knew, as friends did. They all remembered what he had said. But they hadn't asked, because they also knew how to wait for the right moment.

Which, Ed supposed, was now. Here, in the warming sunshine on this beautiful river, in this peaceful, ancient city. Where his journey into the secret world had begun.

He wondered if he could remember that day being similar to this. Sunshine, warmth and hope.

A lifetime and more away from the day of the explosion. The greatest trauma amongst a catalogue of horrors.

'Any guesses?' he asked.

'You tell us,' Florence replied. 'In your own words, in your own time.'

'This is your moment,' Mitch added. 'You found hope for us. And for you we found...'

'What I said. What was in this for me is a friend of hope. Maybe her best friend. One who walks hand in hand with her, and is just as mesmerising.'

'Did you find her?' Olivia said.

310

'Let me put it this way,' Ed replied. 'My scar doesn't seem to be throbbing, itching, or bothering me anymore.'

And so the four of them sat in comfortable and companionable silence, and watched the river flow. Until Olivia – it was always going to be Olivia, of course – said, 'Mitch, Flo, about what Ed was asking earlier?'

'What?' Mitch replied. 'What'd you mean?'

'You know exactly what I mean.'

'We all know exactly what you mean,' Ed added. 'And we're very happy about it. So we'd like to hear about it.'

Mitch and Florence looked to each other, and then, in the classic way of so many couples over the years, both spoke at the same time. Which, this being England, prompted apologies, and an insistence that the other did the talking.

Eventually, Olivia said, 'I'll bloody say it, then. It's not hard, is it? Jesus, you might as well have it printed on a couple of T-shirts. You're in love and you're going off together.'

It wasn't exactly Shakespeare. But it was Olivia. And maybe that was right for this moment.

Mitch and Florence looked at each other, before Florence said simply, 'Yes.'

'That's wonderful,' Ed replied, and then waited, waited, waited, and eventually prompted, 'Isn't it, Olivia?'

'Yeah. Of course. Great. Well done.'

To try to rescue the beauty of the occasion, Ed asked, 'What's your plan?'

'You won't believe this,' Mitch said, 'But I think I've fallen in love with my cover story as well as Florence. You might call it a double delight.'

The barge, which had been hastily purchased and moored in exactly the right place, had become an unexpected refuge for Mitch. The home he didn't know he was looking for.

'I thought it was just another base camp to start with,' he said. 'But the first night I stayed here, I really slept well. Maybe the first time I've slept properly in years. I think it was the lapping of the water. The gentle rocking, like being in a cradle. Maybe the occasional sound of a bird in the darkness. It was like being a kid again. I felt safe, warm and at home. I didn't realise how much I'd missed that feeling.'

Florence spent some time aboard too and said she had felt the same. 'There's something about being on a river. So that's what we're going to do. Spend the summer on the barge and see how things go.'

Mitch explained he had extended his sabbatical. He had enough savings to buy the barge, and sufficient goodwill amongst his superiors to accept his choice.

'We're heading upstream to start with,' he said. 'Then maybe over to the Midlands, or out to the fens.'

'Part of the fun is not actually knowing where we're going yet,' Florence added. 'We'll just set off and see what happens. A real journey of adventure.'

'When are you leaving?' Olivia asked.

One more look between the couple, and Mitch said, 'Right away. Before something else happens. We think it's for the best. You do understand, don't you?'

Ed and Olivia managed smiles and nods, but couldn't find any words to say.

They stood together on the riverbank and watched the barge chug an unhurried way under the old bridge. Ed waved, and after the benefit of a nudge, Olivia did likewise. Flo and Mitch waved back, blurred unreal movements in the brilliance of the sunshine, and the boat disappeared into the darkness.

For a moment Ed and Olivia waited, not knowing quite what to do. The memories of the group hug they had shared, and the hidden tears replaying in their minds. The promises of keeping in touch, which somehow they knew would not be honoured.

Times end. Worlds change. That's life. So it goes.

Ed sighed and gave his glasses a thoughtful polish. 'I guess that's it, then.'

'What's it?'

'It's it. That's it. All over. Done and dusted. No more *Last Edition*, no more stories, no more us. The end.'

Olivia gave him one of her looks. 'Like fuck it is.'

She squared up, as consistent as ever, this redoubtable woman; always ready for a fight, be it with friend or foe. Bring it on. Bring them on. Bring anyone on.

'Don't give me the *that's it then* shit. Look what we've done. All that we've achieved. The *Last Edition's* become a worldwide success. FFS! Thousands of people are waiting to see what we do next. We've gone from nothing to a big hit in a few days. And that's only part of it. What about us, eh? What would we do without it? What about you? What about me, more to the point?'

An Olivia in full flow wasn't a phenomenon to waste time and energy arguing with. 'Walk with me, then,' was all Ed could reply, to give himself a moment to think, and slowly they set off along the riverbank. Past other barges in their heritage colours, through the smudges of drifting wood smoke, the light and shade of the playing willows.

On the common, two young boys were kicking a ball back and forth, yelling in delight. One fell over, started to cry, and the other picked him up, gave him a hug, and the game resumed.

The little things. It was always the little things. Bless them.

'So, first off, there's the paper,' Olivia continued.

'The newswire.'

'The whatever.'

'And then there's us. You. Me. Florence. Mitch. Our legacy. What we set out to find. Remember your ad? That stupid dickweed advert? And what it all led to. What we found together. Remember that?'

Oh, yes. That. That which had brought them all together in their search. That which they thought they had lost. But which, it turned out, had only been hiding, waiting for the right moment.

That. Such a beautiful beguiling creature. That.

They had travelled far, all four of them, these last few days. Not miles across this flat land, but inside themselves, where the most important journeys always unfold.

And Olivia demonstrated it with a change of gear so sudden, it left Ed blinking.

'I believe in you,' she said, that usual edge gone in an instant. 'We all did. We all do. You took us somewhere we thought we'd never go. That's a precious gift, to be able to do that. You shouldn't waste it. There are so many others whose lives you could change.'

They walked on in silence. Sometimes in life, there were simply no words to say. A pair of magnificent herons watched them pass from the lofty perch of a budding tree.

'So, what do you suggest?' Ed asked when he'd recovered from Olivia's unexpected bombardment of roses. 'We're down fifty per cent in our staffing. The media's camped out around our office. And we've got no stories to work on.'

'The media will go. They've got the attention span of retarded goldfish. There'll be other stories. Shit, if we've learnt anything, we've learnt that. And there're lots more people who'll want to work with us. Look at all applications that've come in. And you've still got the list of people who came along on Monday.'

'Set up another Armpit Posse, you mean?'

'Christ, you remember me saying that?'

'I was hardly going to forget.'

'I didn't mean… I only meant… I was a bit different then…' Olivia muttered in a rare display of humility.

'Don't worry. I quite liked it. It kind of summed us up, I thought. But this time around, maybe we should start afresh.'

'Oh God, not another ad like the last one.'

'A bit different, perhaps. Maybe this time I'll say we know the way back to hope and can help guide you there.'

'Shit squared. Jesus, man. Are you serious? We'll be mobbed.'

They continued walking along the river, perhaps a little closer together now. The two boys had finished their game and were walking back home, hand in hand.

'One thing, first,' Ed said. 'Before we get to all that other stuff.'

'What? What now?'

'What now is we're going to be like normal people. For once. And we're going to have a day off.'

Olivia stopped walking, as abruptly as if she had collided with the wall of the alien concept. 'A day off? Like... not doing anything, you mean?'

'Something like that.'

'How does that work?'

'I don't know. I've never really tried. But apparently it does. And it's supposed to be quite pleasant. So, let's go and find out, shall we?'

'Yeah, okay, but...'

'But what?'

'I've got this feeling something might happen.'

'Why doesn't that surprise me? Doesn't it always with us? In which case...'

Olivia stopped again. 'What?'

'You pick the way. Choose a direction.'

'Are you for real?'

'Sometimes. Mostly. Maybe. I think.'

'Is it important?'

'I get this feeling it might be. Don't you?'

The young woman in the denim armour stood upright on the common and slowly turned around. Working her way through the flatness of this most unbroken of flatlands. Towards the magnificent spires of the ancient churches and colleges, whispering trees, the rows of houses, riverboats, and the perfect skies.

In the distance, back towards the city, a smear of smoke was rising, darkening and fattening as they watched. Sirens were being drawn towards it, a whole pack of them, wailing hard in their urgency.

'That way,' Olivia said.

'Are you sure?'

'When aren't I sure?'

Ed should have known better than to ask. 'Silly of me, apologies. Okay, let me rephrase the question. Why that way?'

But Olivia had already begun to stride towards the omen growing in the sky. Over her shoulder, she called, 'Because when was a quiet life ever any fun?'

ACKNOWLEDGMENTS

Betsy, Fred, Tara, Morgen, and all the gang at Bloodhound for their bonhomie and brilliance.

.

Printed in Great
Britain
by Amazon